THE
DARK HALF

Praise for the #1 *New York Times*
bestseller from

STEPHEN KING

"A chiller . . . few writers are better than Stephen
King at giving readers what they want."
—*The New York Times Book Review*

"Evil . . . moves at high speed, [a] white-knuckle
read . . . terror comes often enough to lower [your]
body temperature."
—*Chicago Tribune*

"Vivid . . . King reasserts his mastery of the modern
horror story."
—*Detroit Free Press*

"A solid horrorfest shocker . . . chilling . . . hooks
the reader by the collar and shoves [you] into the
front seat for a fast spin. Hold on tight!"
—*Boston Herald*

STEPHEN KING

THE DARK HALF

A NOVEL

G

GALLERY BOOKS

New York London Toronto Sydney New Delhi

Gallery Books
An Imprint of Simon & Schuster, Inc.
1230 Avenue of the Americas
New York, NY 10020

Grateful acknowledgment is made for permission to reprint an excerpt from "John Wesley Harding" by Bob Dylan. Copyright © Dwarf Music, 1968. All rights reserved. International copyright secured. Reprinted by permission.

First Gallery Books trade paperback edition February 2016

GALLERY BOOKS and colophon are registered trademarks of Simon & Schuster, Inc.

For information about special discounts for bulk purchases, please contact Simon & Schuster Special Sales at 1-866-506-1949 or business@simonandschuster.com.

The Simon & Schuster Speakers Bureau can bring authors to your live event. For more information or to book an event, contact the Simon & Schuster Speakers Bureau at 1-866-248-3049 or visit our website at www.simonspeakers.com.

Manufactured in the United States of America

10 9 8 7 6 5 4 3 2 1

Library of Congress Cataloging-in-Publication Data is available.

ISBN 978-1-5011-4419-6
ISBN 978-1-5011-4114-0 (ebook)

This book is for Shirley Sonderegger,
who helps me mind my business,
and for her husband, Peter.

AUTHOR'S NOTE

I'm indebted to the late Richard Bachman for his help and inspiration. This novel could not have been written without him.

S.K.

THE
DARK HALF

THE
DARK HALF

PROLOGUE

"Cut him," Machine said. "Cut him while I stand here and watch. I want to see the blood flow. Don't make me tell you twice."

—*Machine's Way*
by George Stark

People's lives—their real lives, as opposed to their simple physical existences—begin at different times. The real life of Thad Beaumont, a young boy who was born and raised in the Ridgeway section of Bergenfield, New Jersey, began in 1960. Two things happened to him that year. The first shaped his life; the second almost ended it. That was the year Thad Beaumont was eleven.

In January he submitted a short story to a writing contest sponsored by *American Teen* magazine. In June, he received a letter from the magazine's editors telling him that he had been awarded an Honorable Mention in the contest's Fiction category. The letter went on to say that the judges would have awarded him Second Prize had his application not revealed that he was still two years away from becoming a bona fide "American Teen." Still, the editors said, his story, "Outside Marty's House," was an extraordinarily mature work, and he was to be congratulated.

Two weeks later, a Certificate of Merit arrived from *American Teen*. It came registered mail, insured. The certificate had his name on it in letters so convolutedly Old English that he could barely read them, and a gold seal at the bottom, embossed with the *American Teen* logo—the silhouettes of a crewcut boy and a pony-tailed girl jitterbugging.

His mother swept Thad, a quiet, earnest boy who could never seem to hold onto things and often tripped over his own large feet, into her arms and smothered him with kisses.

His father was unimpressed.

"If it was so goddam good, why didn't they give him some money?" he grunted from the depths of his easy-chair.

"Glen—"

"Never mind. Maybe Ernest Hemingway there could run me in a beer when you get done maulin him."

His mother said no more . . . but she had the original letter and the certificate which followed it framed, paying for the job out of her pin-money, and hung it in his room, over the bed. When relatives or other visitors came, she took them in to see it. Thad, she told her company, was going to be a great writer someday. She had always felt he was destined for greatness, and here was the first proof. This embarrassed Thad, but he loved his mother far too much to say so.

Embarrassed or not, Thad decided his mother was at least partly right. He didn't know if he had it in him to be *a great* writer or not, but he was going to be *some* kind of a writer no matter what. Why not? He was good at it. More important, he got off on doing it. When the words came right, he got off on it in a big way. And they wouldn't always be able to withhold the money from him on a technicality. He wouldn't be eleven forever.

The second important thing to happen to him in 1960 began in August. That was when he began to have headaches. They weren't bad at first, but by the time school let in again in early

September, the mild, lurking pains in his temples and behind his forehead had progressed to sick and monstrous marathons of agony. He could do nothing when these headaches held him in their grip but lie in his darkened room, waiting to die. By the end of September, he hoped he *would* die. And by the middle of October, the pain had progressed to the point where he began to fear he would not.

The onset of these terrible headaches was usually marked by a phantom sound which only he could hear—it sounded like the distant cheeping of a thousand small birds. Sometimes he fancied he could almost see these birds, which he thought were sparrows, clustering on telephone lines and rooftops by the dozens, the way they did in the spring and the fall.

His mother took him to see Dr. Seward.

Dr. Seward peeked into his eyes with an ophthalmoscope, and shook his head. Then, drawing the curtains closed and turning off the overhead light, he instructed Thad to look at a white space of wall in the examination room. Using a flashlight, he flicked a bright circle of light on and off rapidly while Thad looked at it.

"Does that make you feel funny, son?"

Thad shook his head.

"You don't feel woozy? Like you might faint?"

Thad shook his head again.

"Do you smell anything? Like rotten fruit or burning rags?"

"No."

"What about your birds? Did you hear them while you were looking at the flashing light?"

"No," Thad said, mystified.

• • •

"It's nerves," his father said later, when Thad had been dismissed to the outer waiting room. "The goddam kid's a bundle of nerves."

"I think it's migraine," Dr. Seward told them. "Unusual in one so young, but not unheard of. And he seems very . . . intense."

"He is," Shayla Beaumont said, not without some approval.

"Well, there may be a cure someday. For now, I'm afraid he'll just have to suffer through them."

"Yeah, and us with him," Glen Beaumont said.

But it was not nerves, and it was not migraine, and it was not over.

Four days before Halloween, Shayla Beaumont heard one of the kids with whom Thad waited for the schoolbus each morning begin to holler. She looked out the kitchen window and saw her son lying in the driveway, convulsing. His lunchbox lay beside him, its freight of fruit and sandwiches spilled onto the driveway's hot-top surface. She ran out, shooed the other children away, and then just stood over him helplessly, afraid to touch him.

If the big yellow bus with Mr. Reed at the wheel had pulled up any later, Thad might have died right there at the foot of the driveway. But Mr. Reed had been a medic in Korea. He was able to get the boy's head back and open an airway before Thad choked to death on his own tongue. He was taken to Bergenfield County Hospital by ambulance and a doctor named Hugh Pritchard just happened to be in the E.R., drinking coffee and swapping golf-lies with a friend, when the boy was wheeled in. And Hugh Pritchard also just happened to be the best neurologist in the State of New Jersey.

Pritchard ordered the X-rays and read them. He showed them to the Beaumonts, asking them to look with particular care at a vague shadow he had circled with a yellow wax pencil.

"This," he said. "What's this?"

"How the hell should we know?" Glen Beaumont asked. "You're the goddam doctor."

"Right," Pritchard said dryly.

"The wife said it looked like he pitched a fit," Glen said.

Dr. Pritchard said, "If you mean he had a seizure, yes, he did. If you mean he had an *epileptic* seizure, I'm pretty sure he didn't. A seizure as serious as your son's would surely have been *grand mal,* and Thad showed no reaction whatever to the Litton Light Test. In fact, if Thad had *grand mal* epilepsy, you wouldn't need a doctor to point the fact out to you. He'd be doing the Watusi on the living room rug every time the picture on your TV set decided to roll."

"Then what is it?" Shayla asked timidly.

Pritchard turned back to the X-ray mounted on the front of the light-box. "What is *that?*" he responded, and tapped the circled area again. "The sudden onset of headaches coupled with any lack of previous seizures suggests to me that your son has a brain tumor, probably still small and hopefully benign."

Glen Beaumont stared at the doctor stonily while his wife stood beside him and wept into her handkerchief. She wept without making a sound. This silent weeping was the result of years of spousal training. Glen's fists were fast and hurtful and almost never left marks, and after twelve years of silent sorrow, she probably could not have cried out loud even if she had wanted to.

"Does all this mean you want to cut his brains?" Glen asked with his usual tact and delicacy.

"I wouldn't put it quite that way, Mr. Beaumont, but I believe exploratory surgery is called for, yes." And he thought: *If there really is a God, and if He really made us in His Own image, I don't like to think about why there are so damned many men like this one walking around with the fates of so many others in their hands.*

Glen was silent for several long moments, his head down, his brow furrowed in thought. At last he raised his head and asked the question which troubled him most of all.

"Tell me the truth, Doc—how much is all this gonna cost?"

The assisting O.R. nurse saw it first.

Her scream was shrill and shocking in the operating room, where the only sounds for the last fifteen minutes had been Dr. Pritchard's murmured commands, the hiss of the bulky life-support machinery, and the brief, high whine of the Negli saw.

She stumbled backward, struck a rolling Ross tray on which almost two dozen instruments had been neatly laid out, and knocked it over. It struck the tiled floor with an echoing clang which was followed by a number of smaller tinkling sounds.

"Hilary!" the head nurse shouted. Her voice was full of shock and surprise. She forgot herself so far as to actually take half a step toward the fleeing woman in her flapping green-gown.

Dr. Albertson, who was assisting, kicked the head nurse briefly in the calf with one of his slippered feet. "Remember where you are, please."

"Yes, Doctor." She turned back at once, not even looking toward the O.R. door as it banged open and Hilary exited stage left, still screaming like a runaway fire engine.

"Get the hardware in the sterilizer," Albertson said. "Right away. Chop-chop."

"Yes, Doctor."

She began to gather up the instruments, breathing hard, clearly flustered but under control.

Dr. Pritchard seemed to have noticed none of this. He was looking with rapt attention into the window which had been carved in Thad Beaumont's skull.

"Incredible," he murmured. "Just incredible. This is really one for the books. If I weren't seeing it with my own eyes—"

The hiss of the sterilizer seemed to wake him up, and he looked at Dr. Albertson.

"I want suction," he said sharply. He glanced at the nurse. "And what the fuck are *you* doing? The Sunday *Times* crossword? Get your ass over here with those!"

She came, carrying the instruments in a fresh pan.

"Give me suction, Lester," Pritchard said to Albertson. "Right now. Then I'm going to show you something you never saw outside of a county fair freak-show."

Albertson wheeled over the suction-pump, ignoring the head nurse, who leaped back out of his way, balancing the instruments deftly as she did so.

Pritchard was looking at the anesthesiologist.

"Give me good B.P., my friend. Good B.P. is all I ask."

"He's one-oh-five over sixty-eight, Doctor. Steady as a rock."

"Well, his mother says we've got the next William Shakespeare laid out here, so keep it that way. Suck on him, Lester—don't tickle him with the goddam thing!"

Albertson applied suction, clearing the blood. The monitoring equipment beeped steadily, monotonously, comfortingly, in the background. Then it was his own breath he was sucking in. He felt as if someone had punched him high up in the belly.

"Oh my God. Oh Jesus. Jesus Christ." He recoiled for a moment . . . then leaned in close. Above his mask and behind his horn-rimmed spectacles, his eyes were wide with sudden glinting curiosity. "What is it?"

"I think you see what it is," Pritchard said. "It's just that it takes a second to get used to. I've read about it but never expected to actually see it."

Thad Beaumont's brain was the color of a conch shell's outer edge—a medium gray with just the slightest tinge of rose.

Protruding from the smooth surface of the dura was a single blind and malformed human eye. The brain was pulsing slightly. The eye pulsed with it. It looked as if it were trying to wink at them. It was this—the look of the wink—which had driven the assisting nurse from the O.R.

"Jesus God, what is it?" Albertson asked again.

"It's nothing," Pritchard said. "Once it might have been part of a living, breathing human being. Now it's nothing. Except trouble, that is. And this happens to be trouble we can handle."

Dr. Loring, the anesthesiologist, said: "Permission to look, Dr. Pritchard?"

"He still steady?"

"Yes."

"Come on, then. It's one to tell your grandchildren about. But be quick."

While Loring had his look, Pritchard turned to Albertson. "I want the Negli," he said. "I'm going to open him a little wider. Then we probe. I don't know if I can get all of it, but I'm going to get all of it I can."

Les Albertson, now acting as head O.R. nurse, slapped the freshly sterilized probe into Pritchard's gloved hand when Pritchard called for it. Pritchard—who was now humming the *Bonanza* theme-song under his breath—worked the wound quickly and almost effortlessly, referring to the dental-type mirror mounted on the end of the probe only occasionally. He worked chiefly by sense of touch alone. Albertson would later say he had never witnessed such a thrilling piece of seat-of-the-pants surgery in his entire life.

In addition to the eye, they found part of a nostril, three fingernails, and two teeth. One of the teeth had a small cavity in it. The eye went on pulsing and trying to wink right up to the second when Pritchard used the needle-scalpel to first puncture and then excise it. The entire operation, from initial probe to final excision, took only twenty-seven minutes. Five chunks of flesh plopped wetly into the stainless-steel pan on the Ross tray beside Thad's shaven head.

"I think we're clear," Pritchard said at last. "All the foreign tissue seemed to be connected by rudimentary ganglia. Even if there *are* other chunks,

I think the chances are good that we've killed them."

"But . . . how can that be, if the kid's still alive? I mean, it's all a part of *him,* isn't it?" Loring asked, bewildered.

Pritchard pointed toward the tray. "We find an eye, some teeth, and a bunch of fingernails in this kid's head and you think it was a part of him? Did you see any of his nails missing? Want to check?"

"But even cancer is just a part of the patient's own—"

"This wasn't cancer," Pritchard told him patiently. His hands went about their own work as he talked. "In a great many deliveries where the mother gives birth to a single child, that child actually started existence as a twin, my friend. It may run as high as two in every ten. What happens to the other fetus? The stronger absorbs the weaker."

"Absorbs it? Do you mean it *eats* it?" Loring asked. He looked a little green. "Are we talking about *in utero* cannibalism here?"

"Call it whatever you like; it happens fairly often. If they ever develop the sonargram device they keep talking about at the med conferences, we may actually get to find out *how* often. But no matter how frequently or infrequently it happens, what we saw today is much more rare. Part of this boy's twin went unabsorbed. It happened to end up in his prefrontal lobe. It could just as easily have wound up in his intestines, his spleen, his spinal cord, anywhere. Usually the only doctors who see something like this are pathologists—it turns up in autopsies, and I've never heard of one where the foreign tissue was the cause of death."

"Well, what happened here?" Albertson asked.

"Something set this mass of tissue, which was probably submicroscopic in size a year ago, going again. The growth clock of the absorbed twin, which should have run down forever at least a month before Mrs. Beaumont gave birth, somehow got wound up again . . . and the damned thing actually started to run. There is no mystery about what happened; the intracranial pressure alone was enough to cause the kid's headaches and the convulsion that got him here."

"Yes," Loring said softly, "but *why* did it happen?"

Pritchard shook his head. "If I'm still practicing anything more demanding than my golf-stroke thirty years from now, you can ask me then. I might have an answer. All I know now is that I have located and excised a very specialized, very rare sort of tumor. *A benign* tumor. And, barring complications, I believe that's all the parents need to know. The kid's father would make Piltdown Man look like one of the Quiz Kids. I can't see explaining to him that I gave his eleven-year-old son an abortion. Les, let's close him up."

And, as an afterthought, he added pleasantly to the O.R. nurse:

"I want that silly cunt who ran out of here fired. Make a note, please."

"Yes, Doctor."

Thad Beaumont left the hospital nine days after his surgery. The left side of his body was distressingly weak for nearly six months afterward, and occasionally, when he was very tired, he saw odd, not-quite-random patterns of flashing lights before his eyes.

His mother had bought him an old Remington 32 typewriter as a get-well present, and these flashes of light happened most frequently when he was hunched over it in the hour before bedtime, struggling with the right way to say something or trying to figure out what should happen next in the story he was writing. Eventually these passed, too.

That eerie, phantom chirruping sound—the sound of squadrons of sparrows on the wing—did not recur at all following the operation.

He continued to write, gaining confidence and polishing his emerging style, and he sold his first story—to *American Teen*—six years after his real life began. After that, he just never looked back.

So far as his parents or Thad himself ever knew, a small benign tumor had been removed from the prefrontal lobe of his brain in the autumn of his eleventh year. When he thought about it at all (which he did less and less frequently as the years passed), he thought only that he had been extremely lucky to survive.

Many patients who underwent brain surgery in those primitive days did not.

I

FOOL'S STUFFING

Machine straightened the paper-clips slowly and carefully with his long, strong fingers. "Hold his head. Jack," he said to the man behind Halstead. "Hold it tightly, please."

Halstead saw what Machine meant to do and began to scream as Jack Rangely pressed his big hands against the sides of his head, holding it steady. The screams rang and echoed in the abandoned warehouse. The vast empty space acted as a natural amplifier. Halstead sounded like an opera singer warming up on opening night.

"I'm back," Machine said. Halstead squeezed his eyes shut, but it did no good. The small steel rod slid effortlessly through the left lid and punctured the eyeball beneath with a faint popping sound. Sticky, gelatinous fluid began to seep out. "I'm back from the dead and you don't seem glad to see me at all, you ungrateful son of a bitch."

—Riding to Babylon
by George Stark

One

PEOPLE WILL TALK

1

The May 23rd issue of *People* magazine was pretty typical.

The cover was graced by that week's Dead Celebrity, a rock and roll star who had hanged himself in a jail cell after being taken into custody for possession of cocaine and assorted satellite drugs. Inside was the usual smorgasbord: nine unsolved sex murders in the desolate western half of Nebraska; a health-food guru who had been busted for kiddie porn; a Maryland housewife who had grown a squash that looked a bit like a bust of Jesus Christ—if you looked at it with your eyes half-closed in a dim room, that was; a game paraplegic girl training for the Big Apple Bike-A-Thon; a Hollywood divorce; a New York society marriage; a wrestler recovering from a heart attack; a comedian fighting a palimony suit.

There was also a story about a Utah entrepreneur who was marketing a hot new doll called Yo Mamma! Yo Mamma! supposedly looked like "everyone's favorite (?) mother-in-law." She had a built-in tape recorder which spat out bits of dialogue such as "Dinner was never cold at *my* house when he was growing up, dear" and "Your *brother* never acts like I'm dog-breath when I come to spend a couple of weeks." The real howler was that, instead of pulling a string in the back of Yo Mamma! to get her to talk, you *kicked* the fucking thing as hard as you could. "Yo Mamma! is well-padded, guaranteed not to break, and also guaranteed not to chip walls and furniture," said its proud inventor, Mr. Gaspard Wilmot (who, the piece mentioned in passing, had once been indicted for income tax evasion—charges dropped).

And on page thirty-three of this amusing and informative issue of America's premier amusing and informative magazine, was a page headed with a typical *People* cut-line: punchy, pithy, and pungent. BIO, it said.

"People," Thad Beaumont told his wife Liz as they sat side by side at the kitchen table, reading the article together for the second time, "likes to get right to the point. BIO. If you don't want a BIO, move on to IN TROUBLE and read about the girls who are getting greased deep in the heart of Nebraska."

"That's not that funny, when you really think about it," Liz Beaumont said, and then spoiled it by snorting a giggle into one curled fist.

"Not ha-ha, but certainly peculiar," Thad said, and began to leaf through the article again. He rubbed absently at the small white scar high on his forehead as he did so.

Like most *People* BIOs, it was the one piece in the magazine where more space was allotted to words than to pictures.

"Are you sorry you did it?" Liz asked. She had an ear cocked for the twins, but so far they were being absolutely great, sleeping like lambs.

"First of all," Thad said, "*I* didn't do it. *We* did

it. Both for one and one for both, remember?" He tapped a picture on the second page of the article which showed his wife holding a pan of brownies out to Thad, who was sitting at his typewriter with a sheet rolled under the platen. It was impossible to tell what, if anything, was written on the paper. That was probably just as well, since it had to be gobbledegook. Writing had always been hard work for him, and it wasn't the sort of thing he could do with an audience—particularly if one member of the audience happened to be a photographer for *People* magazine. It had come a lot easier for George, but for Thad Beaumont it was goddam hard. Liz didn't come near when he was trying—and sometimes actually succeeding—in doing it. She didn't bring him *telegrams,* let alone brownies.

"Yes, but—"

"Second of all . . ."

He looked at the picture of Liz with the brownies and him looking up at her. They were both grinning. These grins looked fairly peculiar on the faces of people who, although pleasant, were careful doling out even such common things as smiles. He remembered back to the time he had spent as an Appalachian Trail Guide in Maine, New Hampshire, and Vermont. He'd had a pet raccoon in those dim days, name of John Wesley Harding. Not that he'd made any attempt to domesticate John; the coon had just sort of fallen in with him. He liked his nip on cold evenings, too, did old J.W., and sometimes, when he got more than a single bite from the bottle, he would grin like that.

"Second of all what?"

Second of all, there's something funny about a one-time National Book Award nominee and his wife grinning at each other like a couple of drunk raccoons, he thought, and could hold onto his laughter no longer: it bellowed out of him.

"Thad, you'll wake the twins!"

He tried, without much success, to muffle the gusts.

"Second of all, we look like a pair of idiots and I don't mind a bit," he said, and hugged her tight and kissed the hollow of her throat.

In the other room, first William and then Wendy started to cry.

Liz tried to look at him reproachfully, but could not. It was too good to hear him laugh. Good, maybe, because he didn't do enough of it. The sound of his laughter had an alien, exotic charm for her. Thad Beaumont had never been a laughing man.

"My fault," he said. "I'll get them."

He began to get up, bumped the table, and almost knocked it over. He was a gentle man, but strangely clumsy; that part of the boy he had been still lived in him.

Liz caught the pitcher of flowers she had set out as a centerpiece just before it could slide over the edge and shatter on the floor.

"Honestly, Thad!" she said, but then she began to laugh, too.

He sat down again for a moment. He didn't take her hand, exactly, but caressed it gently between both of his. "Listen, babe, do *you* mind?"

"No," she said. She thought briefly of saying *It makes me uneasy, though. Not because we look mildly foolish but because . . . well, I don't know the because. It just makes me a little uneasy, that's all.*

Thought of it but didn't say it. It was just too good to hear him laugh. She caught one of his hands and gave it a brief squeeze. "No," she said. "I don't mind. I think it's fun. And if the publicity helps *The Golden Dog* when you finally decide to get serious about finishing the damned thing, so much the better."

She got up, pressing him back down by the shoulders when he tried to join her.

"You can get them next time," she said. "I want you to sit right there until your subconscious urge to destroy my pitcher finally passes."

"Okay," he said, and smiled. "I love you, Liz."

"I love you, too." She went to get the twins, and Thad Beaumont began to leaf through his BIO again.

Unlike most *People* articles, the Thaddeus Beaumont BIO began not with a full-page photograph but with one which was less than a quarter-page. It caught the eye regardless, because some layout man with an eye for the unusual had bordered the picture, which showed Thad and Liz in a graveyard, in black. The lines of type below stood out in almost brutal contrast.

In the photograph, Thad had a spade and Liz had a pick. Set off to one side was a wheelbarrow with more cemetery implements in it. On the grave itself, several bouquets of flowers had been arranged, but the gravestone itself was still perfectly readable.

GEORGE STARK

1975–1988

Not a Very Nice Guy

In almost jagged contrast to the place and the apparent act (a recently completed interment of what, from the dates, should have been a boy barely in his teens), these two bogus sextons were shaking their free hands across the freshly placed sods—and laughing cheerily.

It was a posed job, of course. All of the photos accompanying the article—burying the body, exhibiting the brownies, and the one of Thad wandering lonely as a cloud down a deserted Ludlow woods road, presumably "getting ideas"—were posed. It was funny. Liz had been buying *People* at the supermarket for the last five years or so, and they both made fun of it, but they both took their turn leafing through it at supper, or possibly in the john if there wasn't a good book handy. Thad had mused from time to time on the magazine's success, wondering if it was its devotion to the celebrity sideshow that made it so weirdly interesting, or just the way it was set up, with all those big black-and-white photographs, and the boldface text, consisting mostly of simple declarative sentences. But it had never crossed his mind to wonder if the pictures were staged.

The photographer had been a woman named Phyllis Myers. She informed Thad and Liz that she had taken a number of photographs of teddy bears in child-sized coffins, all of the teddies dressed in children's clothes. She hoped to sell these as a book to a major New York publisher. It was not until late on the second day of the photo-and-interview session that Thad realized the woman was sounding him out about writing the text. *Death and Teddy Bears,* she said, would be "the final, perfect comment on the American way of death, don't you think so, Thad?"

He supposed that, in light of her rather macabre interests, it wasn't all that surprising that the Myers woman had commissioned George Stark's tombstone and brought it with her from New York. It was *papier-mâché.*

"You don't mind shaking hands in front of this, do you?" she had asked them with a smile that was at the same time wheedling and complacent. "It'll make a *wonderful* shot."

Liz had looked at Thad, questioning and a little horrified. Then they both had looked at the fake tombstone which had come from New York City (year-round home of *People* magazine) to Castle Rock, Maine (summer home of Thad and Liz Beaumont), with a mixture of amazement and bemused wonder. It was the inscription to which Thad's eye kept returning:

Not a Very Nice Guy

Stripped to its essentials, the story *People* wanted to tell the breathless celebrity-watchers of America was pretty simple. Thad Beaumont was a well-regarded writer whose first novel, *The Sudden Dancers,* had been nominated for the National Book Award in 1972. This sort of thing swung some weight with literary critics, but the breathless celebrity-watchers of America didn't care a dime about Thad Beaumont, who had only published one other novel under his own name since. The man many of them *did* care about wasn't a real man at all. Thad had written one huge best-seller and three extremely successful follow-up novels under another name. The name, of course, was George Stark.

Jerry Harkavay, who was the Associated Press's entire Waterville staff, had been the first to break the George Stark story wide after Thad's agent, Rick Cowley, gave it to Louise Booker at *Publishers Weekly* with Thad's approval. Neither Harkavay nor Booker had got the whole story—for one thing, Thad was adamant about not giving that smarmy little prick Frederick Clawson so much as a mention—but it was still good enough to rate a wider circulation than either the AP wire service or the book-publishing industry's trade magazine could give. Clawson, Thad had told Liz and Rick, was not the story—he was just the asshole who was forcing them to go public with the story.

In the course of that first interview, Jerry had asked him what sort of a fellow George Stark was. "George," Thad had replied, "wasn't a very nice guy." The quote had run at the top of Jerry's piece, and it had given the Myers woman the inspiration to actually commission a fake tombstone with that line on it. Weird world. Weird, weird world.

All of a sudden, Thad burst out laughing again.

2

There were two lines of white type on the black field below the picture of Thad and Liz in one of Castle Rock's finer boneyards.

THE DEAR DEPARTED WAS EXTREMELY CLOSE TO THESE TWO PEOPLE, read the first.

SO WHY ARE THEY LAUGHING? read the second.

"Because the world is one *strange* fucking place," Thad Beaumont said, and snorted into one cupped hand.

Liz Beaumont wasn't the only one who felt vaguely uneasy about this odd little burst of publicity. He felt a little uneasy himself. All the same, he found it difficult to stop laughing. He'd quit for a few seconds and then a fresh spate of guffaws would burst out of him as his eye caught on that line—Not a Very Nice Guy—again. Trying to quit was like trying to plug the holes in a poorly constructed earthen dam; as soon as you got one leak stopped up, you saw a new one someplace else.

Thad suspected there was something not quite right about such helpless laughter—it was a form of hysteria. He knew that humor rarely if ever had anything to do with such fits. In fact, the cause was apt to be something quite the opposite of funny.

Something to be afraid of, maybe.

You're afraid of a goddam article in People *magazine? Is that what you're thinking? Dumb. Afraid of being embarrassed, of having your colleagues in the English Department look at those pictures and think you've lost the poor cracked handful of marbles you had?*

No. He had nothing to fear from his colleagues, not even the ones who had been there since dinosaurs walked the earth. He finally had tenure, and also enough money to face life as—flourish of trumpets, please!—a full-time writer if he so desired (he wasn't sure he did; he didn't care much for the bureaucratic and administrative aspects of university life, but the teaching part was just fine). Also no because he had passed beyond caring much about what his colleagues thought of him some years ago. He cared about what his *friends* thought, yes, and in some cases his friends, Liz's friends, and the friends they had in common happened to be colleagues, but he thought those people were also apt to think it was sort of a hoot.

If there was anything to be afraid of, it was—

Stop it, his mind ordered in the dry, stern tone that had a way of causing even the most obstreperous of his undergrad English students to fall pale and silent. *Stop this foolishness right now.*

No good. Effective as that voice might be when he used it on his students, it wielded no power over Thad himself.

He looked down again at that picture and this time his eye paid no attention to the faces of his wife and himself, mugging cheekily at each other like a couple of kids performing an initiation stunt.

GEORGE STARK
1975–1988
Not a Very Nice Guy

That was what made him uneasy.

That tombstone. That name. Those dates. Most of all that sour epitaph, which made him bellow laughter but was not, for some reason, one bit funny *underneath* the laughter.

That name.

That epitaph.

"Doesn't matter," Thad muttered. "Motherfucker's dead now."

But the uneasiness remained.

When Liz came back in with a freshly changed and dressed twin curled in each arm, Thad was bent over the story again.

"Did I murder him?"

Thaddeus Beaumont, once hailed as America's most promising novelist and a National

Book Award nominee for *The Sudden Dancers* in 1972, repeats the question thoughtfully. He looks slightly bemused. "Murder," he says again, softly, as if the word had never occurred to him . . . even though murder was almost all his "dark half," as Beaumont calls George Stark, *did* think about.

From the wide-mouthed mason jar beside his old-fashioned Remington 32 typewriter, he draws a Berol Black Beauty pencil (all Stark would write with, according to Beaumont) and begins to gnaw lightly on it. From the look of the dozen or so other pencils in the mason jar, the gnawing is a habit.

"No," he says at last, dropping the pencil back into the jar. "I didn't murder him." He looks up and smiles. Beaumont is thirty-nine, but when he smiles in that open way, he might be mistaken for one of his own undergrads. "George died of natural causes."

Beaumont says George Stark was his wife's idea. Elizabeth Stephens Beaumont, a cool and lovely blonde, refuses to take sole credit. "All I did," she says, "was suggest he write a novel under another name and see what happened to it. Thad was suffering from serious writer's block, and he needed a jump-start. And really"—she laughs—"George Stark was there all along. I'd seen signs of him in some of the unfinished stuff that Thad did from time to time. It was just a case of getting him to come out of the closet."

According to many of his contemporaries, Beaumont's problems went a little further than writer's block. At least two well-known writers (who refused to be quoted directly) say that they were worried about Beaumont's sanity during that crucial period between the first book and the second. One says he believes Beaumont may have attempted suicide following the publication of *The Sudden Dancers,* which earned more critical acclaim than royalties.

Asked if he ever considered suicide, Beaumont only shakes his head and says, "That's a stupid idea. The real problem wasn't popular acceptance; it was writer's block. And dead writers have a terminal case of that."

Meanwhile, Liz Beaumont kept "lobbying"—Beaumont's word—for the idea of a pseudonym. "She said I could kick up my heels for once, if I wanted to. Write any damn thing I pleased without *The New York Times Book Review* looking over my shoulder the whole time I wrote it. She said I could write a Western, a mystery, a science fiction story. Or I could write a crime novel."

Thad Beaumont grins.

"I think she put that one last on purpose. She knew I'd been fooling around with an idea for a crime novel, although I couldn't seem to get a handle on it.

"The idea of a pseudonym had this funny *draw* for me. It felt *free,* somehow—like a secret escape hatch, if you see what I mean.

"But there was something else, too. Something that's very hard to explain."

Beaumont stretches a hand out toward the neatly sharpened Berols in the mason jar, then withdraws it. He looks off toward the

window-wall at the back of his study, which
gives on a spring spectacular of greening trees.

"Thinking about writing under a pseudonym was like thinking about being invisible," he finally says almost hesitantly. "The
more I played with the idea, the more I felt
that I would be . . . well . . . reinventing
myself."

His hand steals out and this time succeeds
in filching one of the pencils from the mason
jar while his mind is otherwise engaged.

Thad turned the page and then looked up at
the twins in their double high chair. Boy-girl
twins were always fraternal . . . or brother-and-
sisteral, if you didn't want to be a male chauvinist
pig about it. Wendy and William were, however,
about as identical as you could get without *being*
identical.

William grinned at Thad around his bottle.

Wendy also grinned at him around *her* bottle, but she was sporting an accessory her brother
didn't have—one single tooth near the front,
which had come up with absolutely no teething
pain, simply breaking through the surface of the
gum as silently as a submarine's periscope sliding
through the surface of the ocean.

Wendy took one chubby hand from her plastic
bottle. Opened it, showing the clean pink palm.
Closed it. Opened it. A Wendy-wave.

Without looking at her, William removed one
of *his* hands from *his* bottle, opened it, closed it,
opened it. A William-wave.

Thad solemnly raised one of his own hands from
the table, opened it, closed it, opened it.

The twins grinned around their bottles.

He looked down at the magazine again. Ah, *People,* he thought—where would we be, what would we do, without you? This is American star-time, folks.

The writer had dragged out all the soiled linen there was to drag out, of course—most notably the four-year-long bad patch after *The Sudden Dancers* had failed to win the NBA—but that was to be expected, and he found himself not much bothered by the display. For one thing, it wasn't all that dirty, and for another, he had always felt it was easier to live with the truth than with a lie. In the long run, at least.

Which of course raised the question of whether or not *People* magazine and "the long run" had anything at all in common.

Oh well. Too late now.

The name of the guy who had written the piece was Mike—he remembered that much, but Mike what? Unless you were an earl tattling on royalty or a movie star tattling on other movie stars, when you wrote for *People* your byline came at the end of the piece. Thad had to leaf through four pages (two of them full-page ads) to find the name. Mike Donaldson. He and Mike had sat up late, just shooting the shit, and when Thad had asked the man if anyone would really care that he had written a few books under another name, Donaldson said something which had made Thad laugh hard. "Surveys show that most *People* readers have extremely narrow noses. That makes them hard to pick, so they pick as many other people's as they can. They'll want to know all about your friend George."

"He's no friend of mine," Thad had responded, still laughing.

Now he asked Liz, who had gone to the stove, "You got it together, babe? You need some help?"

"I'm fine," she said. "Just cooking up some goo for the kiddos. You haven't got enough of yourself yet?"

"Not yet," Thad said shamelessly, and went back to the article.

> "The hardest part was actually coming up with the name," Beaumont continues, nipping lightly at the pencil. "But it was important. I *knew* it could work. I knew it could break the writer's block I was struggling with . . . if I had an identity. The *right* identity, one that was separate from mine."
>
> How did he choose George Stark?
>
> "Well, there's a crime writer named Donald E. Westlake," Beaumont explains. "And under his real name, Westlake uses the crime novel to write these very funny social comedies about American life and American mores.
>
> "But from the early sixties until the mid-seventies or so, he wrote a series of novels under the name of Richard Stark, and those books are very different. They're about a man named Parker who is a professional thief. He has no past, no future, and in the best books, no interests other than robbery.
>
> "Anyway, for reasons you'd have to ask Westlake about, he eventually stopped writing novels about Parker, but I never forgot something Westlake said after the pen name

was blown. He said *he* wrote books on sunny days and Stark took over on the rainy ones. I liked that, because those were rainy days for me, between 1973 and early 1975.

"In the best of those books, Parker is really more like a killer robot than a man. The robber robbed is a pretty consistent theme in them. And Parker goes through the bad guys—the *other* bad guys, I mean—*exactly like* a robot that's been programmed with one single goal. 'I want my money,' he says, and that's just about *all* he says. 'I want my money, I want my money.' Does that remind you of anyone?"

The interviewer nods. Beaumont is describing Alexis Machine, the main character of the first and last George Stark novels.

"If *Machine's Way* had finished up the way it started out, I would have shoved it in a drawer forever," Beaumont says. "Publishing it would have been plagiarism. But about a quarter of the way through, it found its own rhythm, and everything just clicked into place."

The interviewer asks if Beaumont is saying that, after he had spent awhile working on the book, George Stark woke up and started to talk.

"Yes," Beaumont says. "That's close enough."

Thad looked up, almost laughing again in spite of himself. The twins saw him smiling and grinned back around the pureed peas Liz was feeding them. What he had actually said, as he remembered, was: *"Christ,* that's melodramatic! You make it sound like the part of *Frankenstein* where the lightning finally strikes the rod on the highest castle battlement and juices up the monster!"

"I'm not going to be able to finish feeding them if you don't stop that," Liz remarked. She had a very small dot of pureed peas on the tip of her nose, and Thad felt an absurd urge to kiss it off.

"Stop what?"

"You grin, *they* grin. You can't feed a grinning baby, Thad."

"Sorry," he said humbly, and winked at the twins. Their identical green-rimmed smiles widened for a moment.

Then he lowered his eyes and went on reading.

"I started *Machine's Way* on the night in 1975 I thought up the name, but there *was* one other thing. I rolled a sheet of paper into my typewriter when I got ready to start . . . and then I rolled it right back out again. I've typed all my books, but George Stark apparently didn't hold with typewriters."

The grin flashes out briefly again.

"Maybe because they didn't have typing classes in any of the stone hotels where he did time."

Beaumont is referring to George Stark's "jacket bio," which says the author is thirty-nine and has done time in three different prisons on charges of arson, assault with a deadly weapon, and assault with intent to kill. The jacket bio is only part of the story, however; Beaumont also produces an author-sheet from Darwin Press, which details his alter-ego's history in the painstaking detail which only a good novelist could create out of whole cloth. From his birth in Manchester, New Hampshire, to his final residence in Oxford, Mississippi, everything is there except for George Stark's interment six weeks ago at Homeland Cemetery in Castle Rock, Maine.

"I found an old notebook in one of my desk drawers, and I used these." He points toward the mason jar of pencils, and seems mildly surprised to find he's holding one of them in the hand he uses to point. "I started writing, and the next thing I knew, Liz was telling me it was midnight and asking if I was ever going to come to bed."

Liz Beaumont has her own memory of that night. She says, "I woke up at 11:45 and saw he wasn't in bed and I thought, 'Well, he's writing.' But I didn't hear the typewriter, and I got a little scared."

Her face suggests it might have been more than just a little.

"When I came downstairs and saw him scribbling in that notebook, you could have knocked me over with a feather." She laughs. "His nose was almost touching the paper."

The interviewer asks her if she was relieved.

In soft, measured tones, Liz Beaumont says: "*Very* relieved."

"I flipped back through the notebook and saw I'd written sixteen pages without a single scratch-out," Beaumont says, "and I'd turned three-quarters of a brand-new pencil into shavings in the sharpener." He looks at the jar with an expression which might be either melancholy or veiled humor. "I guess I ought to toss those pencils out now that George is dead. I don't use them myself. I tried. It just doesn't work. Me, I can't work without a typewriter. My hand gets tired and stupid.

"George's never did."

He glances up and drops a cryptic little wink.

"Hon?" He looked up at his wife, who was concentrating on getting the last of William's peas into him. The kid appeared to be wearing quite a lot of them on his bib.

"What?"

"Look over here for a sec."

She did.

Thad winked.

"Was that cryptic?"

"No, dear."

"I didn't think it was."

The rest of the story is another ironic chapter in the larger history of what Thad Beaumont calls "the freak people call the novel."

Machine's Way was published in June of 1976 by the smallish Darwin Press (Beaumont's "real" self has been published by Dutton) and became that year's surprise success, going to number one on best-seller lists coast to coast. It was also made into a smash-hit movie.

"For a long time I waited for someone to discover I was George and George was me," Beaumont says. "The copyright was registered in the name of George Stark, but my agent knew, and his wife—she's his ex-wife

now, but still a full partner in the business—
and, of course, the top execs and the comptroller at Darwin Press knew. He *had* to know,
because George could write novels in longhand, but he had this little problem endors-
ing checks. And of course, the IRS had to
know. So Liz and I spent about a year and a
half waiting for somebody to blow the gaff. It
didn't happen. I think it was just dumb luck,
and all it proves is that, when you think someone has just *got* to blab, they all hold their
tongues."

And went on holding them for the next ten
years, while the elusive Mr. Stark, a far more
prolific writer than his other half, published
another three novels. None of them ever
repeated the blazing success of *Machine's Way,*
but all of them cut a swath up the best-seller
lists.

After a long, thoughtful pause, Beaumont
begins to talk about the reasons why he finally
decided to call off the profitable charade. "You
have to remember that George Stark was only
a paper man, after all. I enjoyed him for a long
time . . . and hell, the guy was making money.
I called it my f—— you money. Just knowing
I could quit teaching if I wanted to and go on
paying off the mortgage had a tremendously
liberating effect on me.

"But I wanted to write my own books
again, and Stark was running out of things
to say. It was as simple as that. I knew it, Liz
knew it, my agent knew it. . . . I think that
even George's editor at Darwin Press knew
it. But if I'd kept the secret, the temptation

to write another George Stark novel would eventually have been too much for me. I'm as vulnerable to the siren-song of money as anyone else. The solution seemed to be to drive a stake through his heart once and for all.

"In other words, to go public. Which is what I did. What I'm doing right now, as a matter of fact."

Thad looked up from the article with a little smile. All at once his amazement at *People's* staged photographs seemed itself a little sanctimonious, a little posed. Because magazine photographers weren't the only ones who sometimes arranged things so they'd have the look readers wanted and expected. He supposed most interview subjects did it, too, to a greater or lesser degree. But he guessed he might have been a little better at arranging things than some; he was, after all, a novelist . . . and a novelist was simply a fellow who got paid to tell lies. The bigger the lies, the better the pay.

Stark was running out of things to say. It was as simple as that.

How direct.

How winning.

How utterly full of shit.

"Honey?"

"Hmmm?"

She was trying to wipe Wendy clean. Wendy was not keen on the idea. She kept twisting her small face away, babbling indignantly, and Liz kept chasing it with the washcloth. Thad thought his wife would catch her eventually, although he supposed there was always a chance she would tire first.

It looked like Wendy thought that was a possibility, too.

"Were we wrong to lie about Clawson's part in all this?"

"We didn't lie, Thad. We just kept his name out of it."

"And he was a nerd, right?"

"No, dear."

"He wasn't?"

"No," Liz said serenely. She was now beginning to clean William's face. "He was a dirty little Creepazoid."

Thad snorted. "A Creepazoid?"

"That's right. A Creepazoid."

"I think that's the first time I ever heard that particular term."

"I saw it on a videotape box last week when I was down at the corner store looking for something to rent. A horror picture called *The Creepazoids*. And I thought, 'Marvelous. Someone made a movie about Frederick Clawson and his family. I'll have to tell Thad.' But I forgot until just now."

"So you're really okay on that part of it?"

"Really very much okay," she said. She pointed the hand holding the washcloth first at Thad and then at the open magazine on the table. "Thad, you got your pound of flesh out of this. *People* got *their* pound of flesh out of this. And Frederick Clawson got jack shit . . . which was just what he deserved."

"Thanks," he said.

She shrugged. "Sure. You bleed too much sometimes, Thad."

"Is that the trouble?"

"Yes—*all* the trouble . . . William, honestly! Thad, if you'd help me just a little—"

Thad closed the magazine and carried Will into the twins' bedroom behind Liz, who had Wendy. The chubby baby was warm and pleasantly heavy, his arms slung casually around Thad's neck as he goggled at everything with his usual interest. Liz laid Wendy down on one changing table; Thad laid Will down on the other. They swapped dry diapers for soggy ones, Liz moving a little faster than Thad.

"Well," Thad said, "we've been in *People* magazine, and that's the end of that. Right?"

"Yes," she said, and smiled. Something in that smile did not ring quite true to Thad, but he remembered his own weird laughing fit and decided to leave it be. Sometimes he was just not very sure about things—it was a kind of mental analogue to his physical clumsiness—and then he picked away at Liz. She rarely snapped at him about it, but sometimes he could see a tiredness creep into her eyes when he went on too long. What had she said? *You bleed too much sometimes, Thad.*

He pinned Will's diapers closed, keeping a forearm on the wriggling but cheerful baby's stomach while he worked so Will wouldn't roll off the table and kill himself, as he seemed determined to do.

"Bugguyrah!" Will cried.

"Yeah," Thad agreed.

"Divvit!" Wendy yelled.

Thad nodded. "That makes sense, too."

"It's good to have him dead," Liz said suddenly.

Thad looked up. He considered for a moment, then nodded. There was no need to specify who *he* was; they both knew. "Yeah."

"I didn't like him much."

That's a hell of a thing to say about your husband, he

almost replied, then didn't. It wasn't odd, because
she wasn't talking about him. George Stark's meth-
ods of writing hadn't been the only essential difference between the two of them.

"I didn't, either," he said. "What's for supper?"

Two

BREAKING UP HOUSEKEEPING

1

That night Thad had a nightmare. He woke from it near tears and trembling like a puppy caught out in a thunderstorm. He was with George Stark in the dream, only George was a real estate agent instead of a writer, and he was always standing just behind Thad, so he was only a voice and a shadow.

2

The Darwin Press author-sheet—which Thad had written just before starting *Oxford Blues,* the second George Stark opus—stated that Stark drove "a 1967 GMC pick-up truck held together by prayer and primer paint." In the dream, however, they had been riding in a dead-black Toronado, and Thad knew he had gotten the pick-up truck part wrong. *This* was what Stark drove. This jet-propelled hearse.

The Toronado was jacked in the back and didn't look like a realtor's car at all. What it looked like was something a third-echelon mobster might drive around in. Thad looked over his shoulder at it as they walked toward the house Stark was for some reason showing him. He thought he would see Stark, and an icicle of sharp fear slid into his heart. But now Stark was standing just behind his other shoulder (although Thad had no idea how he could have gotten there so fast and so soundlessly), and all he could see was the car, a steel tarantula gleaming in the sunlight. There was a sticker on the high-rise rear bumper. HIGH-TONED SON OF A BITCH, it read. The words were flanked left and right by a skull and cross-bones.

The house Stark had driven him to was *his* house—not the winter home in Ludlow, not too far from the University, but the summer place in Castle Rock. The north bay of Castle Lake opened out behind the house, and Thad could hear the faint sound of waves lapping against the shore. There was a FOR SALE sign on the small patch of lawn beyond the driveway.

Nice house, isn't it? Stark almost whispered from behind his shoulder. His voice was rough yet caressing, like the lick of a tomcat's tongue.

It's *my* house, Thad answered.

You're quite wrong. The owner of this one is dead. He killed his wife and children and then himself. He pulled the plug. Just wham and jerk and bye-bye. He had that streak in him. You didn't have to look hard to see it, either. You might say it was pretty stark.

Is that supposed to be funny? he intended to ask—it seemed very important to show Stark he wasn't frightened of him. The *reason* it was important was that he was utterly terrified. But before he could frame the words, a large hand which appeared to have no lines on it at all (although it was hard to tell for sure because the way the fingers were folded cast a tangled shadow over the palm) was reaching over his shoulder and dangling a bunch of keys in his face.

No—not dangling. If it had just been that, he might have spoken anyway, might even have brushed the keys away in order to show how little he feared this fearsome man who insisted on standing behind him. But the hand was bringing the keys *toward* his face. Thad had to grab them to keep them from crashing into his nose.

He put one of them into the lock on the front door, a smooth oak expanse broken only by the knob and a brass knocker that looked like a small bird. The key turned easily, and that was strange, since it wasn't a housekey at all but a typewriter key on the end of a long steel rod. All the other keys on the ring appeared to be skeleton keys, the kind burglars carry.

He grasped the knob and turned it. As he did, the iron-bound wood of the door shrivelled and shrank in on itself with a series of explosions as loud as firecrackers. Light showed through the new cracks between the boards. Dust puffed out. There was a brittle snap and one of the decorative pieces of ironmongery fell off the door and thumped on the doorstep at Thad's feet.

He stepped inside.

He didn't want to; he wanted to stand on the stoop and argue with Stark. More! *Remonstrate* with him, ask him why in God's name he was doing this, because going inside the house was even more frightening than Stark himself. But this was a dream, a bad one, and it seemed to him that the essence of bad dreams was lack of control. It was like being on a roller-coaster that might at any second crest an incline and plunge you down into a brick wall where you would die as messily as a bug slapped with a fly-swatter.

The familiar hallway had been rendered unfamiliar, almost hostile, by no more than the absence of the faded turkey-colored rug-runner which Liz kept threatening to replace . . . and while this seemed a small thing during the dream itself, it was what he kept returning to later, perhaps because it was authentically horrifying—horrifying outside the context of the dream. How secure could any life be if the subtraction of something as minor as a hallway rug-runner could cause such strong feelings of disconnection, disorientation, sadness, and dread?

He didn't like the echo his footfalls made on the hardwood floor, and not just because they made the house sound as if the villain standing behind him had told the truth—that it was untenanted, full of the still ache of absence. He didn't like the sound because his own footsteps sounded lost and dreadfully unhappy to him.

He wanted to turn and leave, but he couldn't do that. Because Stark was behind him, and somehow he knew that Stark was now holding Alexis Machine's pearl-handled straight-razor, the one his mistress had used at the end of *Machine's Way* to carve up the bastard's face.

If he turned around, George Stark would do a little whittling of his own.

Empty of people the house might be, but except for the rugs (the wall-to-wall salmon-colored carpet in the living room was also gone), all the furnishings were still there. A vase of flowers stood on the little deal table at the end of the hall, where you could either go straight ahead into the living room with its high cathedral ceiling and window-wall facing the lake, or turn right into the kitchen. Thad touched the vase and it exploded into shards and a cloud of acrid-smelling ceramic powder. Stagnant water poured out, and the half-dozen garden roses which had been blooming there were dead and gray-black before they landed in the puddle of smelly water on the table. He touched the table itself. The wood gave a dry, parched crack and the table split in two, seeming to swoon rather than fall to the bare wood floor in two separate pieces.

What have you done to my house? he cried to the man behind him . . . but without turning. He didn't *need* to turn in order to verify the presence of the straight-razor, which, before Nonie Griffiths had used it on Machine, leaving his cheeks hanging in red and white flaps and one eye dangling from its socket, Machine himself had employed to flay the noses of his "business rivals."

Nothing, Stark said, and Thad didn't have to see him in order to verify the smile he heard in the man's voice. *You* are doing it, old hoss.

Then they were in the kitchen.

Thad touched the stove and it split in two with a dull noise like the clanging of a great bell clotted with dirt. The heating coils popped upward and askew, funny spiral hats blown cocked in a gale. A noxious stench eddied out of the dark hole in the stove's middle, and, peering in, he saw a turkey. It was putrescent and noisome. Black fluid filled with unnameable gobbets of flesh oozed from the cavity in the bird.

Down here we call that fool's stuffing, Stark remarked from behind him.

What do you mean? Thad asked. *Where* do you mean, down here?

Endsville, Stark said calmly. This is the place where all rail service terminates, Thad.

He added something else, but Thad missed it. Liz's purse was on the floor, and Thad stumbled over it. When he grasped the kitchen table to keep himself from falling, the table fell into splinters and sawdust on the linoleum. A bright nail spun into one corner with a tiny metallic chittering noise.

Stop this right now! Thad cried. I want to wake up! I *hate* to break things!

You always *were* the clumsy one, old hoss, Stark said. He spoke as if Thad had had a great many siblings, all of them as graceful as gazelles.

I don't *have* to be, Thad informed him in an anxious voice that teetered on the edge of a whine. I don't *have* to be clumsy. I don't *have* to break things. When I'm careful, everything is fine.

Yes—too bad you stopped being careful, Stark said in that same smiling I-am-just-remarking-on-how-things-are voice. And they were in the back hall.

Here was Liz, sitting splay-legged in the corner by the door to the woodshed, one loafer off, one loafer on. She was wearing nylon stockings, and Thad could see a run in one of them. Her head was down, her slightly coarse honey-blonde hair obscuring her face. He didn't *want* to see her face. As he hadn't needed to see either the razor or Stark's razor grin to know that both were there, so he didn't need to see Liz's face to know she was not sleeping or unconscious but dead.

Turn on the lights, you'll be able to see better, Stark said in that same smiling I-am-just-passing-the-time-of-day-with-you-my-friend voice. His hand appeared over Thad's shoulder, pointing to the lights Thad himself had installed back here. They were electric, of course, but looked quite authentic: two hurricane lamps mounted on a wooden spindle and controlled by a dimmer switch on the wall.

I don't want to see!

He was trying to sound hard and sure of himself, but this was starting to get to him. He could hear a hitching, uneven quality to his voice which meant he was getting ready to blubber. And what he said seemed to make no difference anyway, because he reached for the circular rheostat on the wall. When he touched it, blue painless electric fire squirted out between his fingers, so thick it was more like jelly than light. The rheostat's round ivory-colored knob turned black, blew off the wall, and zizzed across the room like a miniature flying saucer. It broke the small window on the other side and disappeared into a day which had taken on a weird green cast of light, like weathered copper.

The electric hurricane lamps glowed supernaturally bright and the spindle began to turn, winding up the chain from which the fixture depended and sending shadows flying across the room in a lunatic carousel dance. First one and then the other of the lamp-chimneys shattered, showering Thad with glass.

Without thinking he leaped forward and grabbed his sprawled wife, wanting to get her out from under before the chain could snap and drop the heavy wooden spindle on her. This impulse was so strong it overrode everything, including his sure knowledge that it didn't matter, she was dead, Stark could have uprooted the Empire State Building and dropped it on her and it wouldn't have mattered. Not to her, anyway. Not anymore.

As he slid his arms under hers and locked his hands between her shoulder-blades, her body shifted forward and her head lolled back. The skin of her face was cracking like the surface of a Ming vase. Her glazed eyes suddenly exploded. Noxious green jelly, sickeningly *warm,* spurted up into his face. Her mouth gaped ajar and her teeth flew out in a white storm. He could feel their small smooth hardnesses peppering his checks and brow. Half-clotted blood jetted from between her pitted gums. Her tongue rolled out of her mouth and fell off, plummeting into the lap of her skirt like a bloody chunk of snake.

Thad began to shriek—in the dream and not for real, thank God, or he would have frightened Liz very badly.

I'm not done with you, cock-knocker, George Stark said softly from behind him. His voice was no longer smiling. His voice was as cold as Castle Lake in November. Remember that. You don't want to fuck with me, because when you fuck with me . . .

3

Thad woke with a jerk, his face wet, his pillow, which he had clutched convulsively against his face, also wet. The moisture might have been sweat or it might have been tears.

". . . you're fucking with the best," he finished

into the pillow, and then lay there, knees pulled up to his chest, shuddering convulsively.

"Thad?" Liz muttered thickly from somewhere in the thickets of her own dream. "Twins okay?"

"Okay," he managed. "I . . . nothing. Go back to sleep."

"Yeah, everything's . . ." She said something else, but he caught it no more than he had caught whatever Stark had said after telling Thad that the house in Castle Rock was Endsville . . . the place where all rail service terminates.

Thad lay inside his own sweaty outline on the sheet, slowly releasing his pillow. He rubbed his face with his bare arm, and waited for the dream to let go of him, waited for the shakes to let go of him. They did, but with surprising slowness. At least he had managed not to wake Liz.

He stared thoughtlessly into the darkness, not trying to make sense of the dream, only wanting it to go *away,* and some endless time later Wendy awoke in the next room and began to cry to be changed. William of course awoke moments later, deciding *he* needed to be changed (although when Thad took off his diapers he found them quite dry).

Liz woke at once and sleepwalked into the nursery. Thad went with her, considerably more awake and grateful for once that the twins needed servicing in the middle of the night. The middle of *this* night, anyway. He changed William while Liz changed Wendy, neither of them speaking much, and when they went back to bed, Thad was grateful to find himself drifting toward sleep again. He'd had an idea that he was probably through sleeping for the night. And when he had first awakened with the image of Liz's explosive decomposition still fresh behind his eyes, he had thought he would never sleep again.

It'll be gone in the morning, the way dreams always are.

This was his last waking thought of the night, but when he woke the next morning he remembered the dream in all its details (although the lost and lonely echo of his footfalls in the bare corridor was the only one which retained its full emotional color), and it did not fade as days went by, the way dreams usually do.

That was one of the rare ones he kept with him, as real as a memory. The key that was a typewriter key, the lineless palm, and the dry, almost uninflected voice of George Stark, telling him from behind his shoulder that he wasn't done with him, and that when you fucked with this high-toned son of a bitch, you were fucking with the best.

Three

GRAVEYARD BLUES

1

The head of Castle Rock's three-man groundskeeping crew was named Steven Holt, so of course everyone in The Rock called him Digger. It is a nickname thousands of public groundskeepers in thousands of small New England towns hold in common. Like most of them, Holt was responsible for a fairly large amount of work, given the size of his crew. The town had two Little League fields that needed tending, one near the railroad trestle between Castle Rock and Harlow, the other in Castle View; there was a town common which had to be seeded in the spring, mown in the summer, and raked clear of leaves in the fall (not to mention the trees that needed pruning and sometimes cutting, and the upkeep of the bandstand and the seats around it); there were the town parks, one on Castle Stream near the old sawmill, the other out by Castle Falls, where love-children beyond numbering had been conceived since time out of mind.

He could have been in charge of all this and remained plain old Steve Holt until his dying day. But Castle Rock also had three graveyards, and his crew was also in charge of these. Planting the customers was the least of the work involved in cemetery maintenance. There was planting, raking, and re-sodding. There was litter patrol. You had to get rid of the old flowers and faded flags after the holidays—Memorial Day left the biggest pile of crap to clear up, but July Fourth, Mother's Day, and Father's Day were also busy. You also had to clean off the occasional disrespectful comments kids scrawled on tombs and grave-markers.

All that didn't matter to the town, of course. It was the planting of the customers which earned fellows like Holt their nickname. His mother had christened him Steven, but Digger Holt he was, Digger Holt he had been since he took the job in 1964, and Digger Holt he would be until his dying day, even if he took another job in the meanwhile—which, at the age of sixty-one, he was hardly likely to do.

At seven in the morning on the Wednesday which was the first of June, a fine bright pre-summer day, Digger pulled his truck up to Homeland Cemetery and got out to open the iron gates. There was a lock on them, but it was used only twice a year—on graduation night at the high school and Halloween. Once the gates were open, he drove slowly up the central lane.

This morning was strictly reconnaissance. There was a clipboard beside him on which he would note the areas of the cemetery which needed work between now and Father's Day. After finishing with Homeland, he would go on to Grace Cemetery across town, and then out to the Stackpole bone-yard at the intersection of Stackpole Road and Town Road #3. This afternoon he and his crew would start whatever work needed to be done. It shouldn't be too bad; the heavy work had been done in late April, which Digger thought of as spring cleaning time.

During those two weeks he and Dave Phillips and Deke Bradford, who was the head of the town Public Works Department, had put in ten-hour days, as they did each spring, clearing blocked culverts, re-sodding places where the spring run-off had torn the old ground-cover away, righting tombstones and monuments which had been toppled by ground-heaves. In spring there were a thousand chores, great and small, and Digger would go home barely able to keep his eyes open long enough to cook himself a little dinner and have a can of beer before tumbling into bed. Spring cleaning always ended on the same day: the one on which he felt that his constant backache was going to drive him completely out of his mind.

June spruce-up wasn't anywhere near as bad, but it was important. Come late June the summer people would start arriving in their accustomed droves, and with them would come old residents (and their children) who had moved away to warmer or more profitable parts of the country but who still held property in town. These were the people Digger regarded as the real ass-aches, the ones who would raise the roof if one blade was off the old water-wheel down at the sawmill or if Uncle Reginald's gravestone had tumbled over on its inscription.

Well, winter's coming, he thought. It was what he used to comfort himself with in all seasons, including this one, when winter seemed as distant as a dream.

Homeland was the biggest and prettiest of the town boneyards. Its central lane was almost as wide as a regular road, and it was crossed by four narrower lanes, little more than wheel-tracks with neatly mown grass growing up between them. Digger drove up the central avenue through Homeland, crossed the first and second intersections, reached the third . . . and slammed on the brakes.

"Oh piss in the shithouse!" he exclaimed, turning off the pick-up's engine and getting out. He walked down the lane toward a ragged hole in the grass some fifty feet down and to the right of the crosslane. Brown clumps and piles of dirt lay around the hole like shrapnel around a grenade explosion. "Gawdam kids!"

He stood by the hole, big callused hands planted on the hips of his faded green work-pants. This was a mess. On more than one occasion he and his co-workers had had to clean up after a bunch of kids who had either talked or drunk themselves into a little midnight grave-digging—it was usually an initiation stunt or just a handful of teenage dimbulbs, randy with the moonlight and kicking up their heels. To Digger Holt's knowledge, none of them had actually dug up a coffin or, God forbid, disinterred one of the paying customers—no matter how drunk these happy assholes happened to be, they usually didn't do more than dig a hole two or three feet deep before getting tired of the game and leaving off. And, although digging holes in one of the local boneatoriums was in bad taste (unless you happened to be a fellow like Digger, who was paid and duly empowered to plant the customers, that was), the mess wasn't too bad. Usually.

This, however, wasn't a case of usually.

The hole had no definition; it was just a blob. It surely didn't look like a *grave,* with neatly squared corners and a rectangular shape. It was deeper than the drunks and high-school kids usually managed, but its depth was not uniform; it tapered to a kind of cone, and when Digger realized what the hole *did* look like he felt a nasty chill race up his spine.

It looked the way a grave would look if someone had been buried before he was dead, come to, and dug his way out of the ground with nothing but his bare hands.

"Oh, cut it out," he muttered. "Fucking prank. Fucking *kids.*"

Had to be. There was no coffin down there and no tumbled headstone up here, and that made perfect sense because there was no *body* buried here. He didn't have to go back to the toolshed, where a detailed map of the graveyard was tacked up on the wall, to know *that.* This was part of the six-plot segment owned by the town's First Select-man, Danforth "Buster" Keeton. And the only plots actually occupied by customers held the bodies of Buster's father and uncle. They were off to the right, their headstones standing straight and unmolested.

Digger remembered this particular plot well for another reason. This was where those New York people had set up their fake gravestone when they were doing their story on Thad Beaumont. Beaumont and his wife had a summer home here in town, on Castle Lake. Dave Phillips caretook their place, and Digger himself had helped Dave tarring the driveway last fall, before the leaves fell and things got busy again. Then this spring, Beau-mont had asked *him* in kind of an embarrassed way if some photographer could set up a fake tombstone in the cemetery for what he called "a trick shot."

"If it's not okay, just say so," Beaumont had told him, sounding more embarrassed than ever. "It's really not a big deal."

"You go right ahead," Digger had answered kindly. "*People* magazine, did you say?"

Thad nodded.

"Well, say! That's something, isn't it? Somebody from town in *People* magazine! I'll have to get that issue for sure!"

"I'm not sure *I* will," Beaumont said. "Thanks, Mr. Holt."

Digger liked Beaumont, even if he was a writer. Digger had only gone as far as the eighth grade himself—and had to try twice before he could get through that one—and it wasn't everybody in town called him "Mister."

"Darn magazine folk'd prob'ly like to take your pitcher stark naked with your old hog-leg stuck up a Great Dane's poop-chute if they could get it that way, wouldn't they?"

Beaumont went off into a rare gale of laughter. "Yeah, that's just what they *would* like, I think," he had said, and clapped Digger on the shoulder.

The photographer had turned out to be a woman of the sort Digger called A High-Class Cunt from the City. The city in this case was, of course, New York. She walked as if she had a spindle up her box and another one tucked up her butt and both of them turning just as brisk as you please. She'd gotten a station wagon from one of the car-rental places at the Portland Jetport, and it was stuffed so full of photo equipment it was a wonder there was room for her and her assistant inside. If the car got *too* full and it came to a choice between getting rid of her assistant or some of that photo equipment, Digger reckoned there would be one pansy from the Big Apple trying to hitch him a ride back to the airport.

The Beaumonts, who followed in their own car and parked it behind the station wagon, had looked both embarrassed and amused. Since they seemed to be with the High-Class Cunt from the City of their own free will, Digger guessed that amusement still held the upper hand with them. Still, he had leaned in to make sure, ignoring the High-Class Cunt's snooty look. "Everything fine, Mr. B.?" he had asked.

"Christ, no, but I guess it'll do," he had replied, and dropped Digger a wink. Digger dropped him one right back.

Once he had it clear in his mind that the Beaumonts intended to go through with the thing, Digger had settled back to watch—he had as much appreciation for a free show as the next man. The woman had a big fake gravestone tucked in amidst the rest of her travelling goods, the old-fashioned kind that was round on top. It looked more like the ones Charles Addams drew in his cartoons than any of the real ones Digger had set up just lately. She fussed around it, getting her assistant to set it up again and again. Digger had stepped in once to ask if he could help, but she just said no thank you in her snotty New York way, so Digger had retreated again.

Finally she had it the way she wanted it, and got the assistant to work dicking around with the lights. That used up another half-hour or so. And all the time Mr. Beaumont had stood there and watched, sometimes rubbing the small white scar on his forehead in that odd, characteristic way he had. His eyes fascinated Digger.

Man's takin his own photographs, he thought. *Probably better than hers, and apt to last a lot longer, to boot.*

*He's storin her up to put in a book someday and she don't
even know it.*

At last the woman had been ready to take a few
pictures. She had the Beaumonts shake hands over
that gravestone a dozen times if she had them do
it once, and it was pretty gawdam raw that day,
too. Ordered them around just like she did that
squeaky, mincing assistant of hers. Between her
braying New York voice and the repeated orders
to do it over again because the light wasn't right or
their faces weren't right or maybe her own damned
asshole wasn't right, Digger had kept expecting
Mr. Beaumont—not exactly the longest-tempered
of men according to the gossip he'd heard—to
explode all over her. But Mr. Beaumont—and his
wife, too—seemed more amused than pissed off,
and they just kept on doing what the High-Class
Cunt from the City told them to do, even though
it had been right nippy that day. Digger believed
that, if it had been *him, he* would have gotten a
dight pissed off at the lady after awhile. Like in
about fifteen seconds.

And it was here, right where this stupid gawdam hole was, that they had planted that fake
grave-marker. Why, if he needed any further proof,
there were still round marks in the sod, marks
which had been left by that High-Class Cunt's
heels. She had been from New York, all right;
only a New York woman would show up in high
heels at the end of slop season and then goose-step
around a cemetery in them, taking pitchers. If that
wasn't—

His thoughts broke off, and that feeling of coldness reasserted itself in his flesh again. He had been
looking at the fading tattoos left by the photogra-

pher's high heels, and as he looked at *those* marks, his eye happened on other, fresher marks.

2

Tracks? Were those *tracks?*

'Course they ain't, it's just that the doofus who dug this hole flang some of the dirt further than he did the rest of it. That's all it is.

Except that wasn't all, and Digger Holt *knew* it wasn't. Before he could even get to the first blotch of dirt on the green grass, he saw the deep impression of a shoe in the pile of dirt closest to the hole.

So there's footprints, so what? Did you think whoever done this just sorta floated around with a shovel in his hand like Casper the Friendly Ghost?

There are people in the world who are quite good at lying to themselves, but Digger Holt wasn't one of them. That nervous, scoffing voice in his mind could not change what his eyes saw. He had tracked and hunted wild things all his life, and this sign was just too easy to read. He wished to Christ it wasn't.

Here in this pile of dirt close to the grave was not only a footprint, but a circular depression almost the size of a dinner dish. This dimple was to the left of the footprint. And on either side of the circular print and the footmark, but farther back, were grooves in the dirt that were clearly the marks of fingers, fingers which had slipped a little before catching hold.

He looked beyond the first footprint and saw another. Beyond that, on the grass, was half of a third, formed when some of the dirt on the shoe which stepped there fell off in a clump. It had fallen off, but remained moist enough to hold the impression . . . and that's what the three or four others which had originally caught his eye had done. If he hadn't come so cussed early in the morning, while the grass was still wet, the sun would have dried the earth and it would have fallen apart in loose little crumbles that meant nothing.

He wished he *had* come later, that he had gone out to Grace Cemetery first, as he had set out to do when he left home.

But he hadn't, and that was all.

The fragments of footprints petered out less than twelve feet from the

(*grave*)

hole in the ground. Digger suspected the dewy grass farther on might still hold impressions, though, and he supposed he would check on that, although he didn't much want to. For the time being, however, he re-directed his gaze to the clearest marks, the ones in the little pile of dirt close to the hole.

Grooves which had been drawn by fingers; a round impression slightly ahead of them; a footprint beside the round mark. What story did that configuration tell?

Digger hardly had to ask himself before the answer dropped into his mind like the secret woid on that old Groucho Marx show, *You Bet Your Life.* He saw it as clearly as if he had been here when it happened, and that was precisely why he didn't want any more to do with this at all. Gawdam creepy was what it was.

Because look: here's a man standing in a new-dug hole in the ground.

Yes, but how'd he get down there?

Yes, but did he make the hole, or did someone else do it?

Yes, but how come the little roots look twisted and frayed and torn, as if the sods were pulled apart with bare hands instead of sheared cleanly apart with a spade?

Never mind the buts. Never mind them at all. It was better, maybe, not to think of them. Just stick with the man standing in the hole, a hole that is a little too deep to just jump out of. So what does he do? He puts his palms in the closest pile of dirt and *boosts* himself out. No particular trick to do that, if it was a full-grown man, that was, and not a kid. Digger looked at the few clear and complete tracks he could see and thought, *If it was a kid, he had awful damn big feet. Those have got to be size twelves, at least.*

Hands out. Boost the body up. During the boost, the hands slip a little bit in the loose dirt, so you dig in with your fingers, leaving those short grooves. Then you're out, and you balance your weight on one knee, creating that round depression. You put one foot down next to the knee you're balanced on, shift your weight from the knee to the foot, get up, and walk away. Simple as knitting kitten-britches.

So some guy dug himself out of his grave and just walked away, is that it? Maybe got a little hungry down there and decided to hit Nan's Luncheonette for a cheeseburger and a beer?

"Gawdammit, it ain't a *grave*, it's a friggin *hole* in the ground!" he said aloud, and then jumped a little as a sparrow scolded him.

Yes, nothing but a hole in the ground—hadn't

he said so himself? But how come he couldn't see any marks of the sort he associated with spade-work? How come there was just that one set of foot-prints going away from the hole and none around it, none pointing toward it, the way there would be if a fellow had been digging and stepping in his own dirt every now and then, as fellows digging holes tended to do?

It occurred to him to wonder just what he was going to do about all this, and Digger was gaw-damned if he knew. He supposed that, technically, a crime had been committed, but you couldn't accuse the criminal of grave-robbing—not when the plot which had been dug over didn't contain a body. The worst you could call it was vandal-ism, and if there was more to be made of it than that, Digger Holt wasn't sure he was the one who wanted to do the making.

Best, maybe, to just fill the hole back in, replace what flaps of sod he could find whole, get enough fresh sod to finish the job, then forget the whole thing.

After all, he told himself for the third time, *it ain't as if anyone was really buried there.*

In the eye of his memory, that rainy spring day glimmered momentarily. My, that gravestone had looked real! When you saw that willowy assistant carrying it around, you knew it was make-believe, but when they had it set up, with those fake flowers in front of it and all, you'd have sworn it was real, and that there was really somebody—

His arms were crawling with hard little knots of flesh.

"You just quit on it, now," he told himself harshly, and when the sparrow scolded again, Digger welcomed its unlovely but perfectly real and perfectly ordinary sound. "You go on and yell, Mother," he said, and walked over to the last fragment of footprint.

Beyond it, as he had more or less suspected, he could see other prints smashed into the grass. They were widely spaced. Looking at them, Digger didn't think the fellow had been running, but he sure hadn't been wasting any time. Forty yards farther along, he found his eye could mark the fellow's progress in another way: a large basket of flowers had been kicked over. Although he couldn't see any prints that far away, the basket would have been right in the path of the prints he *could* see. Man could have gone around that basket, but he hadn't chosen to do so. Instead, he had simply kicked it aside and kept on going.

Men who did things like that were not, in Digger Holt's opinion, the sort of men you wanted to fuck around with unless you had a damned good reason.

Moving diagonally across the cemetery, he had been, as if on his way to the low wall between the boneyard and the main road. Moving like a man who had places to go and things to do.

Although Digger was not much better at imagining things than he was at fooling himself (the two things, after all, have a way of going hand in hand), Digger saw this man for a moment, literally *saw* him: a big fellow with big feet, striding through this silent suburb of the dead in the darkness, moving confidently and steadily on his big feet, booting the basket of flowers out of his way without even breaking stride when he came to it. He was not afraid, either—not *this* man. Because if there were things here which were still lively, as some people believed, *they* would be afraid of *him*. Moving, walking, *striding,* and God befriend the man or woman who got in his way.

The bird scolded.

Digger jumped.

"Forget it, Chummy," he told himself once more. "Just fill the friggin thing in and never mind thinkin about it!"

Fill it in he did, and forget it he intended to, but late that afternoon Deke Bradford found him out at the Stackpole Road burying ground and told him the news about Homer Gamache, who had been found late that morning less than a mile up from Homeland on Route 35. The whole town had been agog with rumors and speculation most of the day.

Then, reluctantly, Digger Holt went to talk to Sheriff Pangborn. He didn't know if the hole and the tracks had anything to do with the murder of Homer Gamache, but he thought he'd best tell what he knew and let those who were paid for it do the sorting out.

Four

DEATH IN A
SMALL TOWN

1

Castle Rock has been, at least in recent years, an unlucky town.

As if to prove that old saw about lightning and how often it strikes in the same place isn't always right, a number of bad things had happened in Castle Rock over the last eight or ten years—things bad enough to make the national news. George Bannerman was the local Sheriff when those things occurred, but Big George, as he had been affectionately called, would not have to deal with Homer Gamache, because Big George was dead. He had survived the first bad thing, a series of rape-strangulations committed by one of his own officers, but two years later he had been killed by a rabid dog out on Town Road #3—not just killed, either, but almost literally torn apart. Both of these cases had been extremely strange, but the world was a strange place. And a hard one. And, sometimes, an unlucky one.

The new Sheriff (he had been in office going on eight years, but Alan Pangborn had decided he was going to be "the new Sheriff" at least until the year 2000—always assuming, he told his wife, that he went on running and being elected that long) hadn't been in Castle Rock then; until 1980 he had been in charge of highway enforcement in a small-going-on-medium-sized city in upstate New York, not far from Syracuse.

Looking at Homer Gamache's battered body, lying in a ditch beside Route 35, he wished he was still there. It looked like not all of the town's bad luck had died with Big George Bannerman after all.

Oh, quit it—you don't wish you were anyplace else on God's green earth. Don't say you do, or bad luck will really come down and take a ride on your shoulder. This has been a damned good place for Annie and the boys, and it's been a damned good place for you, too. So why don't you just get off it?

Good advice. Your head, Pangborn had discovered, was *always* giving your nerves good advice they couldn't take. They said *Yessir, now that you mention it, that's just as true as it can be.* And then they went right on jumping and sizzling.

Still, he had been due for something like this, hadn't he? During his tour of duty as Sheriff he had scraped the remains of almost forty people off the town roads, broken up fights beyond counting, and been faced with maybe a hundred cases of spouse and child abuse—and those were just the ones reported. But things have a way of evening out; for a town that had sported its very own mass killer not so long ago, he had had an unusually sweet ride when it came to murder. Just four, and only one of the perps had run—Joe Rodway, after he blew his wife's brains out. Having had some acquaintance of the lady, Pangborn was almost sorry when he got a telex from the police in Kingston, Rhode Island, saying they had Rodway in custody.

One of the others had been vehicular manslaughter, the remaining two plain cases of second-degree, one with a knife and one with bare knuckles—the latter a case of spouse abuse that had simply gone too far, having only one odd wrinkle to distinguish it: the wife had beaten the husband to death while he was dead drunk, giving back one final apocalyptic tit for almost twenty years of tat. The woman's last set of bruises had still been a good, healthy yellow when she was booked. Pangborn hadn't been a bit sorry when the judge let her off with six months in Women's Correctional followed by six years' probation. Judge Pender had probably done that only because it would have been impolitic to give the lady what she really deserved, which was a medal.

Small-town murder in real life, he had found, rarely bore any likeness to the small-town murders in Agatha Christie novels, where seven people all took a turn at stabbing wicked old Colonel Storping-Goiter at his country house in Puddleby-on-the-Marsh during a moody winter storm. In real life, Pangborn knew, you almost always arrived to find the perp still standing there, looking down at the mess and wondering what the fuck he'd done; how it had all jittered out of control with such lethal speed. Even if the perp had strolled off, he usually hadn't gone far and there were two or three eyewitnesses who could tell you exactly what had happened, who had done it, and where he had gone. The answer to the last question was usually the nearest bar. As a rule, small-town murder in real life was simple, brutal, and stupid.

As a rule.

But rules are made to be broken. Lightning sometimes *does* strike twice in the same place, and from time to time murders that happen in small towns are not immediately solvable . . . murders like this one.

Pangborn could have waited.

2

Officer Norris Ridgewick came back from his cruiser, which was parked behind Pangborn's. Calls from the two police-band radios crackled out in the warm late-spring air.

"Is Ray coming?" Pangborn asked. Ray was Ray Van Allen, Castle County's medical examiner and coroner.

"Yep," Norris said.

"What about Homer's wife? Anybody tell her about this yet?"

Pangborn waved flies away from Homer's upturned face as he spoke. There was not much left but the beaky, jutting nose. If not for the prosthetic left arm and the gold teeth which had once been in Gamache's mouth and now lay in splinters on his wattled neck and the front of his shirt, Pangborn doubted if his own mother would have known him.

Norris Ridgewick, who bore a passing resemblance to Deputy Barney Fife on the old *Andy Griffith Show,* scuffled his feet and looked down at his shoes as if they had suddenly become very interesting to him. "Well . . . John's on patrol up in the View, and Andy Clutterbuck's in Auburn, at district court—"

Pangborn sighed and stood up. Gamache was— had been—sixty-seven years old. He'd lived with his wife in a small, neat house by the old railroad depot less than two miles from here. Their children were grown and gone away. It was Mrs. Gamache who had called the Sheriff's office early this morning, not crying but close, saying she'd wakened at seven to find that Homer, who sometimes slept in one of the kids' old rooms because she snored, hadn't come home at all last night. He had left for his league bowling at seven the previous evening, just like always, and should have been home by midnight, twelve-thirty at the latest, but the beds were all empty and his truck wasn't in the dooryard or the garage.

Sheila Brigham, the day dispatcher, had relayed the initial call to Sheriff Pangborn, and he had used the pay phone at Sonny Jackett's Sunoco station, where he had been gassing up, to call Mrs. Gamache back.

She had given him what he needed on the truck—Chevrolet pick-up, 1971, white with maroon primer-paint on the rust-spots and a gun-rack in the cab, Maine license number 96529Q. He'd put it out on the radio to his officers in the field (only three of them, with Clut testifying up in Auburn) and told Mrs. Gamache he would get back to her just as soon as he had something. He hadn't been particularly worried. Gamache liked his beer, especially on his league bowling night, but he wasn't completely foolish. If he'd had too much to feel safe driving, he would have slept on the couch in one of his bowling buddies' living rooms.

There was one question, though. If Homer had decided to stay at the home of a teammate, why hadn't he called his wife and told her so? Didn't he know she'd worry? Well, it was late, and maybe he didn't want to disturb her. That was one possibility. A better one, Pangborn thought, was that he *had* called and she had been fast asleep in bed, a closed door between her and the one telephone in the house. And you had to add in the probability that she was snoring like a Jimmy-Pete doing seventy on the turnpike.

Pangborn had said goodbye to the distraught woman and hung up, thinking her husband would show by eleven o'clock this morning at the latest, shamefaced and more than a little hung-over. Ellen would give the old rip the sandpaper side of her tongue when he did. Pangborn would thus make it a point to commend Homer—quietly—for having the sense not to drive the thirty miles between South Paris and Castle Rock while under the influence.

About an hour after Ellen Gamache's call, it had occurred to him that something wasn't right about his first analysis of the situation. If Gamache had slept over at a bowling buddy's house, it seemed to Alan that it must have been the first time he ever did so. Otherwise, his wife would have thought of it herself and at least waited awhile longer before calling the Sheriff's office. And then it struck Alan that Homer Gamache was a little bit old to be changing his ways. If he had slept over someplace last night, he *should* have done it before, but his wife's call suggested he hadn't. If he had gotten shitfaced at the lanes before and then driven home that way, he probably would have done it again last night . . . but hadn't.

So the old dog learned a new trick after all, he thought. *It happens. Or maybe he just drank more than usual. Hell, he might even have drunk about the same amount as always and gotten drunker than usual. They say it does catch up with a person.*

He had tried to forget Homer Gamache, at least

for the time being. He had yea paperwork on his
desk, and sitting there, rolling a pencil back and
forth and thinking about that old geezer out someplace in his pick-up truck, that old geezer with
white hair buzzed flat in a crewcut and a mechan-
ical arm on account of he'd lost the real one at a
place called Pusan in an undeclared war which
had happened when most of the current crop of
Viet Nam vets were still shitting yellow in their
didies . . . well, none of that was moving the paper
on his desk, and it wasn't finding Gamache, either.

All the same, he had been walking over to Sheila
Brigham's little cubbyhole, meaning to ask her to
raise Norris Ridgewick so he could find out if *Norris*
had found anything out, when Norris himself had
called in. What Norris had to report deepened Alan's
trickle of unease to a cold and steady stream. It ran
through his guts and made him feel lightly numb.

He scoffed at those people who talked about
telepathy and precognition on the call-in radio pro-
grams, scoffed in the way people do when hint and
hunch have become so much a part of their lives
that they barely recognize them when they are
using them. But if asked what he believed about
Homer Gamache *at that moment,* Alan would have
replied: *When Norris called in . . . well, that's when I
started knowing the old man was hurt bad or dead. Probably choice number two.*

3

Norris had happened to stop at the Arsenault place
on Route 35 about a mile south of Homeland
Cemetery. He hadn't even been thinking about

Homer Gamache, although the Arsenault farm and Homer's place were less than three miles apart, and if Homer had taken the logical route home from South Paris the night before, he would have passed the Arsenaults'. It didn't seem likely to Norris that any of the Arsenaults would have seen Homer the night before, because if they had, Homer would have arrived home safe and sound ten minutes or so later.

Norris had only stopped at the Arsenault farm because they kept the best roadside produce stand in the three towns. He was one of those rare bachelors who like to cook, and he had developed a terrific hankering for fresh sugarpeas. He had wanted to find out when the Arsenaults would have some for sale. As an afterthought, he'd asked Dolly Arsenault if she had happened to see Homer Gamache's truck the night before.

"Now you know," Mrs. Arsenault had said, "it's funny you should mention that, because I *did*. Late last night. No . . . now that I think about it, it was early this morning, because Johnny Carson was still on, but getting toward the end. I was going to have another bowl of ice cream and watch a little of that David Letterman show and then go to bed. I don't sleep so well these days, and that man on the other side of the road put my nerves up."

"What man was that, Mrs. Arsenault?" Norris asked, suddenly interested.

"I don't know—just some man. I didn't like his looks. Couldn't even hardly see him and I didn't like his looks, how's that? Sounds bad, I know, but that Juniper Hill mental asylum isn't all that far away, and when you see a man alone on a country road at almost one in the morning, it's enough to make anyone nervous, even if he *is* wearing a suit."

"What kind of suit was he wear—" Norris began, but it was useless. Mrs. Arsenault was a fine old country talker, and she simply rolled over Norris Ridgewick with a kind of relentless grandiosity. He decided to wait her out and glean what he could along the way. He took his notebook out of his pocket.

"In a way," she went on, "the suit almost made me *more* nervous. It didn't seem *right* for a man to be wearing a suit at that hour, if you see what I mean. Probably you don't, probably you think I'm just a silly old woman, and probably I *am* just a silly old woman, but for a minute or two before Homer come along, I had an idea that man was maybe going to come to the house, and I got up to make sure the door was locked. He looked over this way, you know, I saw him do that. I imagine he looked because he could probably see the window was still lighted even though it was late. Probably could see *me,* too, because the curtains are only sheers. I couldn't really see his face—no moon out last night and I don't believe they'll *ever* get streetlights out this far, let alone cable TV, like they have in town— but I could see him turn his head. Then he *did* start to cross the road—at least I *think* that was what he was doing, or was thinking about doing, if you see what I mean—and I thought he would come and knock on the door and say his car was broke down and could he use the phone, and I was wondering what I should say if he did *that,* or even if I should answer the door. I suppose I am a silly old woman, because I got thinking about that *Alfred Hitchcock Presents* show where there was a crazyman who could just about charm the birdies down from the trees, only he'd used an axe to chop somebody all up, you know, and he put the pieces in the trunk of his car, and they only caught him because one of his taillights was out, or something like that—but the other side of it was—"

"Mrs. Arsenault, I wonder if I could ask—"

"—was that I didn't want to be like the Philistine or Saracen or Gomorran or whoever it was that passed by on the other side of the road," Mrs. Arsenault continued. "You know, in the story of the Good Samaritan. So I was in a little bit of a tither about it. But I said to myself—"

By then Norris had forgotten all about sugarpeas. He was finally able to bring Mrs. Arsenault to a stop by telling her that the man she had seen might figure in what he called "an ongoing investigation." He got her to back up to the beginning and tell him everything she had seen, leaving out *Alfred Hitchcock Presents* and the story of the Good Samaritan as well, if possible.

The story as he related it over the radio to Sheriff Alan Pangborn was this: She had been watching *The Tonight Show* alone, her husband and the boys asleep in bed. Her chair was by the window which looked out on Route 35. The shade was up. Around twelve-thirty or twelve-forty, she had looked up and had seen a man standing on the far side of the road . . . which was to say, the Homeland Cemetery side.

Had the man walked from that direction, or the other?

Mrs. Arsenault couldn't say for sure. She had an idea he *might* have come from the direction of Homeland, which would have meant he was heading away from town, but she couldn't say for sure what gave her that impression, because she had looked out the window once and only seen the road, then looked out again before getting up to get her ice cream and he was there. Just standing there and looking toward the lighted window—toward *her,* presumably. She thought he was going to cross the road or had started to cross the road (probably just stood there, Alan thought; the rest was nothing but the woman's nerves talking), when lights showed on the crest of the hill. When the man in the suit saw the approaching lights, he had cocked his thumb in the timeless, stateless gesture of the hitchhiker.

"It was Homer's truck, all right, and Homer at the wheel," Mrs. Arsenault told Norris Ridgewick. "At first I thought he'd just go on by, like any normal person who sees a hitchhiker in the middle of the night, but then his taillights flashed on and that man ran up to the passenger side of the cab and got in."

Mrs. Arsenault, who was forty-six and looked twenty years older, shook her white head.

"Homer must have been lit to pick up a hitchhiker that late," she told Norris. "Lit or simple-minded, and I've known Homer almost thirty-five years. He ain't simple."

She paused for thought.

"Well . . . not *very.*"

Norris tried to get a few more details from Mrs. Arsenault on the suit the man had been wearing, but had no luck. He thought it really was sort of a pity that the streetlamps ended at the Homeland Cemetery grounds, but small towns like The Rock had only so much money to do with.

It had been a suit, she was sure of that, not a

sport-coat or a man's jacket, and it hadn't been black, but that left quite a spectrum of colors to choose from. Mrs. Arsenault didn't think the hitch-hiker's suit had been pure white, but all she was willing to swear to was that it hadn't been black.

"I'm not actually asking you to *swear*, Mrs. A.," Norris said.

"When a body's speaking with an officer of the law on official business," Mrs. A. replied, folding her hands primly into the arms of her sweater, "it comes to the same thing."

So what she knew boiled down to this: she had seen Homer Gamache pick up a hitchhiker at about quarter to one in the morning. Nothing to call in the FBI about, you would have said. It only got ominous when you added in the fact that Homer had picked up his passenger three miles or less from his own dooryard . . . but hadn't arrived home.

Mrs. Arsenault was right about the suit, too. Seeing a hitchhiker this far out in the boonies in the middle of the night was odd enough—by quarter of one, any ordinary drifter would have laid up in a deserted barn or some farmer's shed—but when you added in the fact that he had also been wearing a suit and a tie ("Some dark color," Mrs. A. said, "just don't ask me to swear *what* dark color, because I can't, and I won't"), it got less comfort-able all the time.

"What do you want me to do next?" Norris had asked over the radio once his report was complete.

"Stay where you are," Alan said. "Swap *Alfred Hitchcock Presents* stories with Mrs. A. until I get there. I always used to like those myself."

But before he had gone half a mile, the location of the meeting between himself and his officer had been changed from the Arsenault place to a spot about a mile west of there. A boy named Frank Gavineaux, walking home from a little early fishing down at Strimmer's Brook, had seen a pair of legs protruding from the high weeds on the south side of Route 35. He ran home and told his mother. She had called the Sheriff's Office. Sheila Brigham relayed the message to Alan Pangborn and Norris Ridgewick. Sheila maintained protocol and mentioned no names on the air—too many little pitchers with big Cobras and Bearcats were always listening in on the police bands—but Alan could tell by the upset tone of Sheila's voice that even she had a good idea who those legs belonged to.

About the only good thing which had happened all morning was that Norris had finished emptying his stomach before Alan got there, and had maintained enough wit to throw up on the north side of the road, away from the body and any evidence there might be around it.

"What now?" Norris asked, interrupting the run of his thoughts.

Alan sighed heavily and quit waving the flies away from Homer's remains. It was a losing battle. "Now I get to go down the road and tell Ellen Gamache the widow-maker paid a visit early this morning. You stay here with the body. Try to keep the flies off him."

"Gee, Sheriff, why? There's an awful lot of em. And he's—"

"Dead, yeah, I can see that. I don't *know* why. Because it just seems like the right thing to do, I guess. We can't put his fucking arm back on, but at least we can keep the flies from shitting on what's left of his nose."

"Okay," Norris said humbly. "Okay, Sheriff."

"Norris, do you think you could call me 'Alan' if you really worked on it? If you practiced?"

"Sure, Sheriff, I guess so."

Alan grunted and turned for one last look at the area of the ditch that would, in all probability, be cordoned off with bright yellow CRIME SCENE DO NOT CROSS tapes attached to surveyor's poles when he got back. The county coroner would be here. Henry Payton from the Oxford State Police Barracks would be here. The photographer and the technicians from the Attorney General's Capital Crimes Division probably wouldn't be—unless there happened to be a couple of them in the area already on another case—but they would arrive shortly after. By one in the afternoon, the State Police's rolling lab would be here, too, complete with hot and cold running forensics experts and a guy whose job it was to mix up plaster and take moulage casts of the tire-prints Norris had either been smart enough or lucky enough not to run over with the wheels of his own cruiser (Alan opted, rather reluctantly, for lucky).

And what would it all come to? Why, just this. A half-drunk old man had stopped to do a favor for a stranger. (*Hop on up here, boy,* Alan could hear him saying, *I ain't going only a couple of miles, but I'll get you a little further on your way),* and the stranger had responded by beating the old man to death and then stealing his truck.

He guessed the man in the business suit had asked Homer to pull over—the most likely pretext would have been to say he needed to take a leak— and once the truck was stopped, he'd clipped the old man, dragged him out, and—

Ah, but that was when it got bad. So very god-dam bad.

Alan looked down into the ditch one final time, to where Norris Ridgewick squatted by the bloody piece of meat that had been a man, patiently waving the flies away from what had been Homer's face with his citation clipboard, and felt his stomach turn over again.

He was just an old man, you son of a whore—an old man who was half in the bag and only had one honest arm to boot, an old man whose one little pleasure left was his bowling league night. So why didn't you just clip him that one good one in the cab of his truck and then leave him be? It was a warm night, and even if it'd been a little chilly, he most likely would have been okay. I'd bet my watch we're going to find a whole lot of antifreeze in his system. And the truck's license plate number goes out on the wire either way. So why this? Man, I hope I get a chance to ask you.

But did the reason matter? It sure didn't to Homer Gamache. Not anymore. Nothing was ever going to matter to Homer again. Because after clipping him that first one, the hitchhiker had pulled him out of the cab and dragged him into the ditch, probably hauling him by the armpits. Alan didn't need the boys from Capital Crimes to read the marks left by the heels of Gamache's shoes. Along the way, the hitcher had discovered Homer's disability. And at the bottom of the trench, he had wrenched the old man's prosthetic arm from his body and bludgeoned him to death with it.

Five

96529Q

"Hold it, hold it," Connecticut State Trooper Warren Hamilton said in a loud voice, although he was the only one in the cruiser. It was the evening of June 2nd, some thirty-five hours after the discovery of Homer Gamache's body in a Maine town Trooper Hamilton had never heard of.

He was in the lot of the Westport 1-95 McDonald's (southbound). He made it a habit to swing into the lots of the food-and-gas stops when he was cruising the Interstate; if you crawled up the last row of the parking spots at night with your lights off, you sometimes made some good busts. Better than good. Awesome. When he sensed he might have come upon such an opportunity, he very often talked to himself. These soliloquies often started with *Hold it, hold it,* then progressed to something like *Let's check this sucker out* or *Ask Mamma if she believes this.* Trooper Hamilton was very big on asking Mamma if she believed this when he was on the scent of something juicy.

"What have we got here?" he murmured this time, and reversed the cruiser. Past a Camaro. Past a Toyota which looked like a slowly aging horseturd in the beaten copper glare of the arc-sodium lights. And . . . ta-DA! An old GMC pick-up truck that looked orange in the glare, which meant it was—or had been—white or light gray.

He popped his spotlight and trained it on the license plate. License plates, in Trooper Hamilton's humble opinion, were getting better. One by one, the states were putting little pictures on them. This made them easier to identify at night, when varying light conditions transformed actual colors into all sorts of fictional hues. And the worst light of all for plate ID were these goddam orange hi-intensity lamps. He didn't know if they foiled rapes and muggings as they were designed to do, but he was positive they had caused hardworking cops such as himself to bugger plate IDs on stolen cars and fugitive vehicles without number.

The little pictures went a long way toward fixing that. A Statue of Liberty was a Statue of Liberty in both bright sunlight and the steady glare of these copper-orange bastards. And no matter what the color, Lady Liberty meant New York.

Same as that fucked-up crawdaddy he had the spot trained on right now meant Maine. You didn't have to strain your eyes for VACATION-LAND anymore, or try to figure out if what looked pink or orange or electric blue was really white. You just looked for the fucked-up crawdaddy. It was really a lobster, Hamilton knew that, but a fucked-up crawdaddy by any other name was still a fucked-up crawdaddy, and he would have gobbled shit right out of a pig's ass before he put one of those fucking crawdads in *his* mouth, but he was mighty glad they were there, all the same.

Especially when he had a want on a crawdaddy license plate, as he did tonight.

"Ask Mamma if she believes *this*," he murmured, and put the cruiser in Park. He took his clipboard from the magnetized strip which held it to the center of the dash just above the driveshaft hump, flipped past the blank citation form all cops kept as a shield over the hot-sheet (no need for the general public to be gawking at the license plate numbers the cops were particularly interested in while the cop to whom the sheet belonged was grabbing a hamburger or taking an express dump at a handy filling station), and ran his thumbnail down the list.

And here it was. 96529Q; State of Maine; home of the fucked-up crawdaddies.

Trooper Hamilton's initial pass had shown him no one was in the cab of the truck. There was a rifle-rack, but it was empty. It was possible—not likely, but possible—that there might be someone in the *bed* of the truck. It was even possible that the someone in the bed of the truck might have the rifle which belonged in the rack. More likely, the driver was either long gone or grabbing a burger inside. All the same . . .

"Old cops, *bold* cops, but no *old* bold cops," Trooper Hamilton said in a low voice. He snapped off the spot and slowly cruised on down the line of cars. He paused twice more, snapping the spot on both times, although he didn't even bother to look at the cars he was lighting up. There was always the possibility that Mr. 96529Q had seen Hamilton spotlighting the stolen truck while on his way back from the restaurant *cum* dumpatorium, and if he saw the trooper car had passed on up the line and was checking other cars, he might not take off.

"Safe is safe, sorry is sorry, and that's all I know, by the great by-Gorry!" Trooper Hamilton exclaimed. This was another of his favorites, not quite up there with asking Mamma if she believed this, but close.

He pulled into a slot where he could observe the pick-up. He called his base, which was less than four miles up the road, and told them he had found the GMC pick-up Maine wanted in a murder case. He requested back-up units and was told they would arrive shortly.

Hamilton observed no one approaching the pick-up, and decided it would not be over-bold to approach the vehicle with caution. In fact, he would look like a wimp if he was still sitting here in the dark, one row over, when the other units arrived.

He got out of his cruiser, thumbing the strap off his gun but not unholstering it. He had unholstered his piece only twice while on duty, and fired it not at all. Nor did he want to do either one now. He approached the pick-up at an angle that allowed him to observe both the truck—especially the *bed* of the truck—and the approach from Mickey D's. He paused as a man and woman walked from the restaurant to a Ford sedan three rows closer to the restaurant, then moved on when they got in their car and headed for the exit.

Keeping his right hand on the butt of his service revolver, Hamilton dropped his left hand to his hip. Service belts, in Hamilton's humble opinion, were *also* getting better. He had, both as man and boy, been a huge fan of Batman, a.k.a. the Caped Crusader—he suspected, in fact, that the Batman was one of the reasons he had become a cop (this was a little factoid he hadn't bothered to put on his application). His favorite Batman accessory had not been the Batpole or the Batarang, not even the Batmobile itself, but the Caped Crusader's utility belt. That wonderful item of apparel was like a good gift-shop: It had a little something for all occasions, be it a rope, a pair of night-vision goggles, or a few capsules of stun-gas. His service belt was nowhere near as good, but on the left side there *were* three loops holding three very useful items. One was a battery-powered cylinder marketed under the name Down, Hound! When you pressed the red button on top, Down, Hound! emitted an ultrasonic whistle that turned even raging pit-bulls into bowls of limp spaghetti. Next to it was a pressure-can of Mace (the Connecticut State Police version of Batman's stun-gas), and next to the Mace was a four-cell flashlight.

Hamilton pulled the flashlight from its loop, turned it on, then slid his left hand up to partially hood the beam. He did this without once removing his right hand from the butt of his revolver. Old cops; bold cops; no *old* bold cops.

He ran the beam along the bed of the pick-up truck. There was a scrap of tarpaulin in there, but nothing else. The truck-bed was as empty as the cab.

Hamilton had remained a prudent distance away from the GMC with the crawdaddy plates all the while—this was so ingrained he hadn't even thought about it. Now he bent and shone the flashlight *beneath* the truck, the last place where someone who meant him harm might be lurking. Unlikely, but when he finally kicked off, he didn't want the minister to begin his eulogy by saying, "Dear friends, we are here today to mourn the unlikely passing of Trooper Warren Hamilton." That would be *très* tacky.

He swept the beam quickly left to right under the truck and observed nothing but a rusty muffler which was going to drop off in the near future—

not, from the look of the holes in it, that the driver would notice much difference when it did.

"I think we're alone, dear," Trooper Hamilton said. He examined the area surrounding the truck one final time, paying particular attention to the approach from the restaurant. He observed no one observing *him,* and so stepped up to the passenger window of the cab and shone his light inside.

"Holy shit," Hamilton murmured. "Ask Mamma if she believes *this* happy crappy." He was suddenly very glad for the orange lamps which sent their glare across the parking lot and into the cab, because they turned what he knew was maroon to a color which was almost black, making the blood look more like ink. "He drove it like that? Jesus Christ, all the way from Maine he *drove* it like that? Ask Mamma—"

He tipped his flashlight downward. The seat and the floor of the GMC was a sty. He saw beer cans, soft-drink cans, empty or near-empty potato chip and pork rind bags, boxes which had contained Big Macs and Whoppers. A wad of what looked like bubble-gum was squashed onto the metal dashboard above the hole where there had once been a radio. There were a number of unfiltered cigarette butts in the ashtray.

Most of all, there was blood.

There were streaks and blotches of blood on the seat. Blood was grimed into the steering wheel. There was a dried splatter of blood on the horn-ring, almost entirely obscuring the Chevrolet symbol embossed there. There was blood on the driver's inside doorhandle and blood on the mirror—that spot was a small circle that wanted to be an oval, and Hamilton thought that Mr. 96529Q might have left an almost perfect thumbprint in his victim's blood when he adjusted his rearview. There was also a large splatter of gore on one of the Big Mac boxes. That one looked like there might be some hair stuck in it.

"What did he tell the drive-up girl?" Hamilton muttered. "He cut himself shaving?"

There was a scraping noise behind him. Hamilton whirled, feeling too slow, feeling all too sure that he had, despite his routine precautions, been too bold to ever get old, because there was nothing routine about this, no *sir,* the guy had gotten behind him and soon there would be more blood in the cab of the old Chevrolet pick-up, *his* blood, because a guy who would drive a portable abattoir like this from Maine almost to the New York State line was a psycho, the sort of guy who would kill a State Trooper with no more thought than he'd take to buy a quart of milk.

Hamilton drew his revolver for the third time in his career, thumbed the hammer back, and almost triggered a shot (or two, or three) into nothing but darkness; he was wired to the max. But there was no one there.

He lowered the gun by slow degrees, blood thumping in his temples.

A little gust of wind puffed the night. The scraping noise came again. On the pavement he saw a Filet-O-Fish box—from this very McDonald's, no doubt, how clever you are, Holmes, do not mention it, Watson, it was really elementary—skitter five or six feet at the whim of the breeze and then come to rest again.

Hamilton let out a long, shaky breath and carefully dropped the hammer on his revolver. "Almost embarrassed yourself, there, Holmes," he said in a voice that was not at all steady. "Almost stuck yourself with a CR-14." A CR-14 was a "shot(s) fired" form.

He thought about holstering his gun again, now that it was clear there was nothing to shoot but an empty fish sandwich box, and then decided he would just hold onto it until he saw the other units arriving. It felt good in his hand. Comforting. Because it wasn't just the blood, or the fact that the man some Maine cop wanted for murder had driven four hundred miles or so in that mess. There was a stench around the truck which was in a way like the stench around the spot in some country road where a car has hit and crushed a skunk. He didn't know if the arriving officers would pick it up or if it was just for him, and he didn't much care. It wasn't a smell of blood, or rotten food, or B.O. It was, he thought, just the smell of *bad.* Something very, very bad. Bad enough so that he didn't want to holster his revolver even though he was almost positive that the owner of that smell was gone, probably hours ago—he heard none of the ticking noises which came from an engine that was still warm. It didn't matter. It didn't change what he knew: for awhile the truck had been the den of some terrible animal, and he wasn't going to take the slightest risk that the animal might return and find him unprepared. And Mamma could make book on that.

He stood there, gun in hand, hairs on the back of his neck prickling, and it seemed a very long time before the back-up units finally came.

Six

DEATH IN THE BIG CITY

Dodie Eberhart was pissed off, and when Dodie Eberhart was pissed off, there was one broad in the nation's capital you didn't want to fuck with. She climbed the stairs of the L Street apartment building with the stolidity (and nearly the bulk) of a rhino crossing an open stretch of grassland. Her navy-blue dress stretched and relaxed over a bosom which was rather too large to simply be called ample. Her meaty arms swung like pendulums.

A good many years ago, this woman had been one of Washington's most stunning call-girls. In those days her height—six-foot-three—as well as her good looks had made her more than just a naughty bit of fluff; she was so sought after that a night with her was almost as good as a trophy in a sporting gentleman's den, and if one were to carefully review the photographs of various Washington *fêtes* and *soirées* taken during the second Johnson administration and the first Nixon administration, one might spot Dodie Eberhart in many of them, usually on the arm of a man whose name appeared frequently in weighty political articles and essays. Her height alone made her hard to miss.

Dodie was a whore with the heart of a bank-teller and the soul of an acquisitive cockroach. Two of her regular johns, one a Democratic Senator and the other a Republican Representative with a good deal of seniority, had provided her with enough cash to retire from the business. They had not exactly done this of their own volition. Dodie was aware that the risk of disease was not exactly decreasing (and highly placed government officials are as vulnerable to AIDS and various lesser—but still troubling—venereal diseases as the commoners). Her age wasn't decreasing, either. Nor did she completely trust these gentlemen to leave her something in their wills, as both had promised to do. I'm sorry, she'd told them, but I don't believe in Santa Claus or the Tooth Fairy anymore either, you see. Little Dodie is all on her own.

Little Dodie purchased three apartment houses with the money. Years passed. The one hundred and seventy pounds which had brought strong men to their knees (usually in front of her as she stood nude before them) had now become two hundred and eighty. Investments which had done well in the mid-seventies had soured in the eighties, when it seemed everyone else in the country with money in the stock market was getting well. She'd had two excellent brokers on her short list right up until the end of the active phase of her career; there were times she wished she'd held onto them when she retired.

One apartment house had gone in '84; the second in '86, following a disastrous IRS audit. She had held onto this one on L Street as grimly as a losing player in a cutthroat game of Monopoly, convinced that it was in a neighborhood which was about to Happen. But it hadn't Happened yet, and she didn't think it would Happen for another year or two . . . if then. When it did, she meant to pack her bags and move to Aruba. In the meantime, the landlady who had once been the capital city's most sought-after fuck would just have to hang on.

Which she always had.

Which she intended to keep on doing.

And God help anyone who got in her way.

Like Frederick "Mr. Bigshot" Clawson, for instance.

She reached the second-floor landing. Guns n' Roses was bellowing out of the Shulmans' apartment.

"TURN THAT FUCKING RECORD-PLAYER DOWN!" she yelled at the top of her lungs . . . and when Dodie Eberhart raised her voice to its maximum decibel level, windows cracked, the eardrums of small childen ruptured, and dogs fell dead.

The music went from a scream to a whisper at once. She could sense the Shulmans quivering against each other like a pair of scared puppies in a thunderstorm and praying it was not them the Wicked Witch of L Street had come to see. They were afraid of her. That was not an unwise way to feel. Shulman was a corporate lawyer with a high-powered firm, but he was still two ulcers away from being high-powered enough to give Dodie pause. If he should cross her at this stage of his young life, she would wear his guts for garters, and he knew it, and that was very satisfactory.

When the bottom dropped out of both your bank accounts and your investment portfolio, you had to take your satisfactions where you found them.

Dodie turned the corner without breaking stride and started up the stairs to the third floor, where Frederick "Mr. Bigshot" Clawson lived in solitary splendor. She walked with that same even rhino-crossing-the-veldt stride, head up, not in the least out of breath in spite of her poundage, the staircase shaking the tiniest bit in spite of its solidity.

She was looking forward to this.

Clawson wasn't even on a low rung of a corporate-law ladder. As of now, he wasn't on the ladder at all. Like all the law students she had ever met (mostly as tenants; she had certainly never fucked any in what she now thought of as her "other life"), he was composed chiefly of high aspirations and low funds, both of them floating on a generous cushion of bullshit. Dodie did not, as a rule, confuse any of these elements. Falling for a law student's line of bull was, in her mind, as bad as turning a trick for free. Once you started in with behavior like that, you might as well hang up your jock.

Figuratively speaking, of course.

Yet Frederick "Mr. Bigshot" Clawson had partially breached her defenses. He had been late with the rent four times in a row and she had allowed this because he had convinced her that in his case the tired old scripture was really the truth (or might come to be): he *did* have money coming in.

He could not have done this to her if he had claimed Sidney Sheldon was really Robert Ludlum, or Victoria Holt was really Rosemary Rogers, because she didn't give a shit about those people or their billions of write-alikes. She was into crime novels, and if they were real gutbucket crime novels, so much the better. She supposed there were plenty of people out there who went for the romantic slop and the spy shit, if the *Post* Sunday bestseller list was any indication, but she had been reading Elmore Leonard for years before he hit the lists, and she had also formed strong attachments for Jim Thompson, David Goodis, Horace McCoy, Charles Willeford, and the rest of those guys. If you wanted it short and sweet, Dodie Eberhart liked novels where men robbed banks, shot each other, and demonstrated how much they loved their women mostly by beating the shit out of them.

George Stark, in her opinion, was—or had been—the best of them. She had been a dedicated fan from *Machine's Way* and *Oxford Blues* right up to *Riding to Babylon,* which looked to be the last of them.

The bigshot in the third-floor apartment had been surrounded by notes and Stark novels the first time she came to dun him about the rent (only three days overdue that time, but of course if you gave them an inch they took a mile), and after she had taken care of her business and he had promised to deliver a check to her by noon the following day, she asked him if the collected works of George Stark were now required reading for a career before the bar.

"No," Clawson had said with a bright, cheerful, and utterly predatory smile, "but they might just *finance* one."

It was the smile more than anything else which had hooked her and caused her to pay out line in his case where she had snubbed it brutally tight in all others. She had seen that smile many times before in her own mirror. She had believed then that such a smile could not be faked, and, just for the record, she still believed it. Clawson really *had* had the goods on Thaddeus Beaumont; his mistake had been believing so confidently that Beaumont would go along with the plans of a Mr. Bigshot like

Frederick Clawson. And it had been her mistake, too.

She had read one of the two Beaumont novels—*Purple Haze*—following Clawson's explanation of what he had discovered, and thought it an exquisitely stupid book. In spite of the correspondence and photocopies Mr. Bigshot had shown her, she would have found it difficult or impossible to believe both writers were the same man. Except . . . about three-quarters of the way through it, at a point where she had been about ready to throw the boring piece of shit across the room and forget the whole thing, there was a scene in which a farmer shot a horse. The horse had two broken legs and needed to be shot, but the thing was, old Farmer John had *enjoyed* it. Had, in fact, put the barrel of the gun against the horse's head and then jerked himself off, squeezing the trigger at the moment of climax.

It was, she thought, as if Beaumont had stepped out to get a cup of coffee when he got to that part . . . and George Stark had stepped in and written the scene, like a literary Rumpelstiltskin. Certainly it was the only gold in that particular pile of hay.

Well, none of it mattered now. All it proved was that no one was immune to bullshit forever. The bigshot had taken her for a ride, but at least it had been a *short* ride. And it was now over.

Dodie Eberhart reached the third-floor landing, her hand already curling into the sort of tight fist she made when the time had come not for polite knocking but hammering, and then she saw hammering would not be necessary. The bigshot's door was standing ajar.

"Jesus wept!" Dodie muttered, her lip curling.

This wasn't a junkie neighborhood, but when it came to ripping off some idiot's apartment, the junkies were more than willing to cross boundary lines. The guy was even stupider than she had thought.

She rapped on the door with her knuckles and it swung open. "Clawson!" she called in a voice which promised doom and damnation.

There was no answer. Looking up the short corridor, she could see the shades in the living room were drawn and the overhead light was burning. A radio was playing softly.

"Clawson, I want to talk to you!"

She started up the short corridor . . . and stopped. One of the sofa cushions was on the floor.

That was all. No sign that the place had been trashed by a hungry junkie, but her instincts were still sharp, and her wind was up in a moment. She smelled something. It was very faint, but it was there. A little like food which had spoiled but not yet rotted. That wasn't it, but it was as close as she could come. Had she smelled it before? She thought she had.

And there was another smell, although she didn't think it was her nose which was making her aware of it. She knew that one right away. She and Trooper Hamilton from Connecticut would have agreed at once on what it was: the smell of bad.

She stood just outside the living room, looking at the tumbled cushion, listening to the radio. What the climb up three flights of stairs hadn't been able to do that one innocent cushion had— her heart was beating rapidly under her massive left breast, and her breath was coming shallowly through her mouth. Something was not right here.

Very much not right. The question was whether or not she would become a part of it if she hung around.

Common sense told her to go, go while she still had a chance, and common sense was very strong. Curiosity told her to stay and peek . . . and it was stronger.

She edged her head around the entrance to the living room and looked first to her right, where there was a fake fireplace, two windows giving a view on L Street, and not much else. She looked to the left and her head suddenly stopped moving. It actually seemed to lock in position. Her eyes widened.

That locked stare lasted no more than three seconds, but it seemed much longer to her. And she saw everything, down to the smallest detail; her mind made its own photograph of what it was seeing, as clear and sharp as those the crime photographer would soon take.

She saw the two bottles of Amstel beer on the coffee-table, one empty and the other half-full, with a collar of foam still inside the bottle-neck. She saw the ashtray with CHICAGOLAND! written on its curving surface. She saw two cigarette butts, unfiltered, squashed into the center of the tray's pristine whiteness, although the bigshot didn't smoke—not cigarettes, at least. She saw the small plastic box which had once been full of push-pins lying on its side between the bottles and the ashtray. Most of the push-pins, which the bigshot used to tack things to his kitchen bulletin board, were scattered across the glass surface of the coffee-table. She saw a few had come to rest on an open copy of *People* magazine, the one featuring the Thad Beaumont/George Stark story. She could see Mr. and Mrs. Beaumont shaking hands across Stark's gravestone, although from here they were upside down. It was the story that, according to Frederick Clawson, would never be printed. It was going to make him a moderately wealthy man instead. He had been wrong about that. In fact, it seemed he had been wrong about everything.

She could see Frederick Clawson, who had gone from Mr. Bigshot to no shot at all, sitting in one of his two living-room chairs. He had been tied in. He was naked, his clothes thrown into a snarly ball under the coffee-table. She saw the bloody hole at his groin. His testicles were still where they belonged; his penis had been stuffed into his mouth. There was plenty of room, because the murderer had also cut out Mr. Bigshot's tongue. It was tacked to the wall. The push-pin had been driven into its pink meat so deeply that she could only see a grinning crescent of bright yellow which was the push-pin's top, and her mind relentlessly photographed this, too. Blood had drizzled down the wallpaper below it, making a wavery fan-shape.

The killer had employed another push-pin, this one with a bright green head, to nail the second page of the *People* magazine article to the ex-bigshot's bare chest. She could not see Liz Beaumont's face—it was obscured by Clawson's blood—but she could see the woman's hand, holding out the pan of brownies for Thad's smiling inspection. She remembered that picture in particular had irked Clawson. *What a put-up job!* he had exclaimed. *She hates to cook—she said so in an interview just after Beaumont published his first novel.*

Finger-written in blood above the severed tongue tacked to the wall were these five words:

THE SPARROWS ARE FLYING AGAIN.

Jesus Christ, some distant part of her mind thought. *It's just like a George Stark novel . . . like something Alexis Machine would do.*

From behind her came a soft bumping sound.

Dodie Eberhart screamed and whirled. Machine came at her with his terrible straight-razor, its steely glitter now sleeved with Frederick Clawson's blood. His face was the twisted mask of scars which was all Nonie Griffiths had left after she carved him up at the end of *Machine's Way,* and—

And there was no one there at all.

The door had swung shut, that was all, the way doors sometimes do.

Is that so? the distant part of her mind asked . . . except it was closer now, raising its voice, urgent with fright. *It was standing partway open with no problem at all when you came up the stairs. Not wide open, but enough so you could tell it wasn't shut.*

Now her eyes went back to the beer-bottles on the coffee-table. One empty. One half-full, with a ring of foam still on the inside of the neck.

The killer had been behind the door when she came in. If she had turned her head she would almost surely have seen him . . . and now she would be dead, too.

And while she had been standing here, mesmerized by the colorful remains of Frederick "Mr. Bigshot" Clawson, he had simply gone out, closing the door behind him.

The strength flowed out of her legs and she

slipped to her knees with a weird kind of grace, looking like a girl about to take communion. Her mind ran frantically over the same thought, like a gerbil on an exercise wheel: *Oh I shouldn't have screamed, he'll come back, oh I shouldn't have screamed, he'll come back, oh I shouldn't have screamed—*

And then she heard him, the measured thud of his big feet on the hall carpet. Later she became convinced that the goddam Shulmans had turned up their stereo again, and she had mistaken the steady thump of the bass for footsteps, but at that moment she was convinced it was Alexis Machine and he was returning . . . a man so dedicated and so murderous that not even death would stop him.

For the first time in her life, Dodie Eberhart fainted.

She came to less than three minutes later. Her legs would still not support her, so she crawled back down the short apartment hallway to the door with her hair hanging in her face. She thought of opening the door and looking out, but could not bring herself to do it. She turned the thumblock instead, then shot the bolt and clicked the police-bar into its steel foot. Those things done, she sat against the door, gasping, the world a gray blur. She was vaguely aware that she had locked herself in with a mutilated corpse, but that wasn't so bad. It wasn't bad at all, when you considered the alternatives.

Little by little her strength came back and she was able to get to her feet. She slipped around the corner at the end of the hall and then into the kitchen, where the phone was. She kept her eyes averted from what remained of Mr. Bigshot, although it was an empty exercise; she would see that mind-photograph in all its hideous clarity for a long time to come.

She called the police and when they came she wouldn't let them in until one of them slid his ID under the door.

"What's your wife's name?" she asked the cop whose laminated badge identified him as Charles F. Toomey, Jr. Her voice was high and quivery, utterly unlike her usual one. Close friends (had she had any) would not have recognized it.

"Stephanie, ma'am," the voice on the other side of the door replied patiently.

"I can call your station-house and check that, you know!" she nearly shrieked.

"I know you can, Mrs. Eberhart," the voice responded, "but you'd feel safer quicker if you just let us in, don't you think?"

And because she still recognized the Voice of Cop as easily as she had recognized the Smell of Bad, she unlocked the door and let Toomey and his partner in. Once they were, Dodie did something else she had never done before: she went into hysterics.

Seven

POLICE BUSINESS

1

Thad was upstairs in his study, writing, when the police came.

Liz was reading a book in the living room while William and Wendy goofed with each other in the oversized playpen they shared. She went to the door, looking out through one of the narrow ornamental windows which flanked it before opening it. This was a habit she had gotten into since what was jokingly called Thad's "debut" in *People* magazine. Visitors—vague acquaintances for the most part, with a generous mixture of curious town residents and even a few total strangers (these latter unanimously Stark fans) thrown in for good measure—had taken to dropping by. Thad called it the "see-the-living-crocodiles syndrome" and said it would peter out in another week or two. Liz hoped he was right. In the meantime, she worried that one of the new callers might be a mad crocodile-hunter of the sort who had killed John Lennon, and peeked through the side window first. She didn't know if she would recognize a *bona fide* madman if she saw one, but she could at least keep Thad's train of thought from derailing during the two hours each morning he spent writing. After that he went to the door himself, usually throwing her a guilty little-boy look to which she didn't know how to respond.

The three men on the front doorstep this Saturday morning were not fans of either Beaumont or Stark, she guessed, and not madmen either . . . unless some of the current crop had taken to driving State Police cruisers. She opened the door, feeling the uneasy twinge even the most blameless people must feel when the police show up without being called. She supposed if she'd had children old enough to be out whooping and hollering this rainy Saturday morning, she would already be wondering if they were okay.

"Yes?"

"Are you Mrs. Elizabeth Beaumont?" one of them asked.

"Yes, I am. May I help you?"

"Is your husband home, Mrs. Beaumont?" a second asked. These two were wearing identical gray rain-slickers and State Police hats.

No, that's the ghost of Ernest Hemingway you hear clacking away upstairs, she thought of saying, and of course didn't. First came the has-anybody-had-an-accident fright, then the phantom guilt which made you want to come out with something harsh or sarcastic, something which said, no matter what the actual words: *Go away. You are not wanted here. We have done nothing wrong. Go and find someone who has.*

"May I ask why you'd like to see him?"

The third policeman was Alan Pangborn. "Police business, Mrs. Beaumont," he said. "May we speak with him, please?"

2

Thad Beaumont did not keep anything resembling an organized journal, but he did sometimes write about the events in his own life which interested, amused, or frightened him. He kept these accounts in a bound ledger, and his wife did not care much for them. They gave her the creeps, in fact, although she had never told Thad so. Most were strangely passionless, almost as if a part of him was standing aside and reporting on his life with its own divorced and almost disinterested eye. Following the visit of the police on the morning of June 4th, he wrote a long entry with a strong and unusual subcurrent of emotion running through it.

"I understand Kafka's *The Trial* and Orwell's *1984* a little better now [Thad wrote]. To read them as political novels and no more is a serious mistake. I suppose the depression I went through after finishing *Dancers* and discovering there was nothing waiting behind it—except for Liz's miscarriage, that is—still counts as the most wrenching emotional experience of our married life, but what happened today *seems* worse. I tell myself it's because the experience is still fresh, but I suspect it's a lot more than that. I suppose if my time in the darkness and the loss of those first twins are wounds which have healed, leaving only scars to mark the places where they were, then this new wound will also heal . . . but I don't believe time will ever gloss it over completely. It will also leave its scar, one which is shorter but deeper—like the fading tattoo of a sudden knife-slash.

"I'm sure the police behaved according to their oaths (if they still take them, and I guess they do).

Yet there was then and still is now a feeling that I was in danger of being pulled into some faceless bureaucratic machine, not men but a *machine* which would go methodically on about its business until it had chewed me to rags . . . because chewing people to rags is the machine's business. The sound of my screams would neither hurry nor delay that machine's chewing action.

"I could tell Liz was nervous when she came upstairs and told me the police wanted to see me about something but wouldn't tell her what it was. She said one of them was Alan Pangborn, the Castle County Sheriff. I may have met him once or twice before, but I only really recognized him because his picture is in the Castle Rock *Call* from time to time.

"I was curious, and grateful for a break from the typewriter, where my people have been insisting on doing things I don't want them to do for the last week. If I thought anything, I suppose I thought it might have something to do with Frederick Clawson, or some bit of fallout from the *People* article.

"I don't know if I can get the tone of the meeting which followed right or not. I don't know if it even matters, only that it seems important to try. They were standing in the hall near the foot of the stairs, three large men (it's no wonder people call them bulls) dripping a little water onto the carpet.

" 'Are you Thaddeus Beaumont?' one of them— it was Sheriff Pangborn—asked, and that's when the emotional change I want to describe (or at least indicate) began to happen. Puzzlement joined the curiosity and pleasure at being released, however briefly, from the typewriter. And a little worry. My full name, but no 'Mister.' Like a judge addressing a defendant upon whom he is about to pass sentence.

" 'Yes, that's right,' I said, 'and you're Sheriff Pangborn. I know, because we've got a place on Castle Lake.' Then I put out my hand, that old automatic gesture of the well-trained American male.

"He just looked at it, and an expression came over his face—it was as if he'd opened the door of his refrigerator and discovered the fish he'd bought for supper had spoiled. 'I have no intention of shaking your hand,' he said, 'so you might as well put it back down again and save us both some embarrassment.' It was a hell of a strange thing to say, a downright *rude* thing to say, but that didn't bother me as much as the way he said it. It was as if he thought I was out of my mind.

"And just like that, I was terrified. Even now I find it difficult to believe how rapidly, how goddam *rapidly*, my emotions lensed through the spectrum from ordinary curiosity and some pleasure at the break in an accustomed routine to naked fear. In that instant I knew they weren't here just to talk to me about something but because they believed I had *done* something, and in that first moment of horror—'I have no intention of shaking your hand'—I was sure that *I had.*

"*That's* what I need to express. In the moment of dead silence that followed Pangborn's refusal to shake my hand, I thought, in fact, that I had done *everything* . . . and would be powerless not to confess my guilt."

3

Thad lowered his hand slowly. From the corner of his eye he could see Liz with her hands clasped into a tight white ball between her breasts, and suddenly he wanted to be furious at this cop, who had been invited freely into his home and had then refused to shake his hand. This cop whose salary was paid, at least in some small part, by the taxes the Beaumonts paid on their house in Castle Rock. This cop who had frightened Liz. This cop who had frightened *him.*

"Very well," Thad said evenly. "If you won't shake hands with me, then perhaps you'll tell me why you're here."

Unlike the State cops, Alan Pangborn was wearing not a rainslicker but a waterproof jacket which came only to his waist. He reached into his back pocket, brought out a card, and began to read from it. It took Thad a moment to realize he was hearing a variation of the *Miranda* warning.

"As you said, my name is Alan Pangborn, Mr. Beaumont. I am the Sheriff of Castle County, Maine. I'm here because I have to question you in connection with a capital crime. I will ask you these questions at the Orono State Police Barracks. You have the right to remain silent—"

"Oh dear Jesus, please, what *is* this?" Liz asked, and layered on top of that Thad heard himself saying, "Wait a minute, wait just a damn minute." He intended to *roar* this, but even with his brain telling his lungs to turn the volume up to a full lecture-hall-quieting bellow, the best he could manage was a mild objection that Pangborn overrode easily.

"—and you have the right to legal counsel. If you cannot afford legal counsel, such will be provided for you."

He replaced the card in his back pocket.

"Thad?" Liz was crowding against him like a small child frightened by thunder. Her huge puzzled eyes stared at Pangborn. Every so often they flicked to the State Troopers, who looked big enough to play defense on a pro football team, but mostly they remained on Pangborn.

"I'm not going anywhere with you," Thad said. His voice was shaking, jigging up and down, changing registers like the voice of a young adolescent. He was still trying to be furious. "I don't believe you can compel me to do that."

One of the Troopers cleared his throat. "The alternative," he said, "is for us to go back and get a warrant for your arrest, Mr. Beaumont. On the basis of information in our possession, that would be very easy."

The Trooper glanced at Pangborn.

"It might be fair to add that Sheriff Pangborn wanted us to bring one with us. He argued very strongly for it, and I guess he would have gotten his way if you weren't . . . something of a public figure."

Pangborn looked disgusted, possibly by this fact, possibly because the Trooper was informing Thad of the fact, most likely both.

The Trooper saw the look, shuffled his wet shoes as if a trifle embarrassed, but pushed on anyway. "With the situation being what it is, I have no problem with you knowing that." He looked questioningly at his partner, who nodded. Pangborn just went on looking disgusted. And angry. *He looks,* Thad thought, *as if he'd like to rip me open with his fingernails and wrap my guts around my head.*

"That *sounds* very professional," Thad said. He was relieved to find he was getting at least some of his wind back and his voice was settling down.

He wanted to be angry because anger would allay the fear, but he could still manage no more than bewilderment. He felt sucker-punched. "What it ignores is the fact that I don't have the slightest idea what this goddam situation *is.*"

"If we believed that to be the case, we wouldn't be here, Mr. Beaumont," Pangborn said. The expression of loathing on his face finally turned the trick: Thad was suddenly infuriated.

"I don't care what you think!" Thad said. "I told you that I know who you are, Sheriff Pangborn. My wife and I have owned a summer house in Castle Rock since 1973—long before you ever heard of the place. I don't know what you're doing here, a hundred and sixty-odd miles from your territory, or why you're looking at me like I was a splat of bird-shit on a new car, but I can tell you I'm not going anywhere with you until I find out. If it's going to take an arrest warrant, you go on and get one. But I want you to know that if you do, you're going to be up to your neck in a kettle of boiling shit and I'll be the one underneath stoking the fire. Because I haven't done anything. This is fucking outrageous. Just . . . fucking . . . *outrageous!"*

Now his voice had reached full volume, and both the Troopers looked a little abashed. Pangborn did not. He went on staring at Thad in that unsettling way.

In the other room, one of the twins began to cry.

"Oh Jesus," Liz moaned, "what *is* this? Tell us!"

"Go take care of the kids, babe," Thad said, not unlocking his gaze from Pangborn's.

"But—"

"Please," he said, and then both babies were crying. "This will be all right."

She gave him a final trembling look, her eyes saying *Do you promise?* and then went into the living room.

"We want to question you in connection with the murder of Homer Gamache," the second Trooper said.

Thad broke his hard stare at Pangborn and turned to the Trooper. *"Who?"*

"Homer Gamache," Pangborn repeated. "Are you going to tell us the name means nothing to you, Mr. Beaumont?"

"Of course I'm not," Thad said, astonished. "Homer takes our trash to the dump when we're in town. Makes some small repairs around the house. He lost an arm in Korea. They gave him the Silver Star—"

"Bronze," Pangborn said stonily.

"Homer's dead? Who killed him?"

The Troopers now looked at each other, surprised. After grief, astonishment may be the most difficult human emotion to fake effectively.

The first Trooper replied in a curiously gentle voice: "We have every reason to believe *you* did, Mr. Beaumont. That's why we're here."

4

Thad looked at him with utter blankness for a moment and then laughed. "Jesus. Jesus Christ. This is crazy."

"Do you want to get a coat, Mr. Beaumont?" the other Trooper asked. "Raining pretty hard out there."

"I'm not going anywhere with you," he repeated

absently, entirely missing Pangborn's sudden expression of exasperation. Thad was thinking.

"I'm afraid you are," Pangborn said, "one way or the other."

"It'll have to be the other, then," he said, and then came out of himself. "When did this happen?"

"Mr. Beaumont," Pangborn said, speaking slowly and enunciating carefully—it was as if he were speaking to a four-year-old, and not a terribly bright one at that. "We're not here to give *you* information."

Liz came back into the doorway with the babies. All color had drained from her face; her forehead shone like a lamp. "This is crazy," she said, looking from Pangborn to the Troopers and then back to Pangborn again. "Crazy. Don't you *know* that?"

"Listen," Thad said, walking over to Liz and putting an arm around her, "I didn't kill Homer, Sheriff Pangborn, but I understand now why you're so pissed. Come on upstairs to my office. Let's sit down and see if we can't figure this out—"

"I want you to get your coat," Pangborn said. He glanced at Liz. "Forgive my French, but I've had about all the bullshit I can put up with for a rainy Saturday morning. We have you cold."

Thad looked at the older of the two State Troopers. "Can you talk some sense to this man? Tell him that he can avoid a whole lot of embarrassment and trouble just by telling me when Homer was killed?" And, as an afterthought: "And where. If it was in The Rock, and I can't imagine what Homer would be doing up here . . . well, I haven't been out of Ludlow, except to go to the University, in the last two and a half months." He looked at Liz, who nodded.

The Trooper thought it over, and then said: "Excuse us a moment."

The three of them went back down the hallway, the Troopers almost appearing to lead Pangborn. They went out the front door. As soon as it was shut, Liz burst into a spate of confused questions. Thad knew her well enough to suspect her terror would have come out as anger—fury, even—at the cops, if not for the news of Homer Gamache's death. As things were, she was on the edge of tears.

"It's going to be all right," he said, and kissed her on the cheek. As an afterthought, he also bussed William and Wendy, who were beginning to look decidedly troubled. "I think the State Troopers already know I'm telling the truth. Pangborn . . . well, he knew Homer. You did, too. He's just pissed as hell." *And from the look and sound of him, he must have what seems like unshakable evidence tying me to the murder,* he thought but did not add.

He walked down the hall and peered out the narrow side window as Liz had done. If not for the situation, what he saw would have been funny. The three of them were standing on the stoop, almost but not quite out of the rain, having a conference. Thad could get the sound of their voices, but not the sense. He thought they looked like ballplayers conferring on the mound during a late-inning rally by the other team. Both State cops were talking to Pangborn, who was shaking his head and replying heatedly.

Thad went back down the hall.

"What are they doing?" Liz asked.

"I don't know," Thad said, "but I think the State cops are trying to talk Pangborn into telling me why he's so sure I killed Homer Gamache. Or at least *some* of the why."

"Poor Homer," she muttered. "This is like a bad dream."

He took William from her and told her again not to worry.

5

The policemen came in about two minutes later. Pangborn's face was a thundercloud. Thad surmised the two State cops had told him what Pangborn himself already knew but didn't want to admit: the writer was exhibiting none of the tics and twitches they associated with guilt.

"All right," Pangborn said. He was trying to avoid surliness, Thad thought, and doing a pretty good job. Not quite succeeding, but doing a pretty good job all the same, considering he was in the presence of his number-one suspect in the murder of a one-armed old man. "These gentlemen would like me to ask you at least one question here, Mr. Beaumont, and so I will. Can you account for your whereabouts during the time-period from eleven p.m. on May thirty-first until four a.m. on June first?"

The Beaumonts exchanged a glance. Thad felt a great weight around his heart loosen. It did not quite fall off, not yet, but he felt as if all the catches holding that weight had been unbuckled. Now all it would take was one good push.

"Was it?" he murmured to his wife. He thought it was, but it seemed just a little too good to be true.

"I'm sure it was," Liz responded. "The thirty-first, did you say?" She was looking at Pangborn with radiant hope.

Pangborn looked back suspiciously. "Yes, ma'am. But I'm afraid your unsubstantiated word won't be—"

She was ignoring him, counting backward on her fingers. Suddenly she grinned like a schoolgirl. "Tuesday! Tuesday *was* the thirty-first!" she cried to her husband. "It *was!* Thank God!"

Pangborn looked puzzled and more suspicious than ever. The Troopers looked at each other and then looked back at Liz. "You want to let us in on it, Mrs. Beaumont?" one asked.

"We had a party here the night of Tuesday the thirty-first!" she replied, and flashed Pangborn a look of triumph and vicious dislike. "We had a *houseful!* Didn't we, Thad?"

"We sure did."

"In a case like this, a good alibi itself is cause for suspicion," Pangborn said, but he looked off-balance.

"Oh, you silly, arrogant man!" Liz exclaimed. Bright color now flamed in her cheeks. Fear was passing; fury was arriving. She looked at the Troopers. "If my husband doesn't have an alibi for this murder you say he committed, you take him to the police station! If he does, *this* man says it probably means he did it anyway! What are you, afraid of a little honest work? Why are you *here?*"

"Quit now, Liz," Thad said quietly. "They've got good reasons for being here. If Sheriff Pangborn were on a wild-goose chase or running on hunch, I believe he would come alone."

Pangborn gave him a sour look, then sighed. "Tell us about this party, Mr. Beaumont."

"It was for Tom Carroll," Thad said. "Tom has been in the University English Department for nineteen years, and he's been chairman for the last five. He retired on May twenty-seventh, when the academic year officially ended. He's always been a great favorite in the Department, known to most of us old war-horses as Gonzo Tom because of his great liking for Hunter Thompson's essays. So we decided to throw a retirement party for him and his wife."

"What time did this party end?"

Thad grinned. "Well, it was over before four in the morning, but it ran late. When you put a bunch of English teachers together with an almost unlimited supply of booze, you could burn down a weekend. Guests started arriving around eight, and . . . who was last, honey?"

"Rawlie DeLesseps and that awful woman from the History Department he's been going out with since Jesus was a baby," she said. "The one who goes around blaring: 'Just call me Billie, everyone does.' "

"Right," Thad said. He was grinning now. "The Wicked Witch of the East."

Pangborn's eyes were sending a clear you're-lying-and-we-both-know-it message. "And what time did these friends leave?"

Thad shuddered a little. "Friends? Rawlie, yes. That woman, most definitely not."

"Two o'clock," Liz said.

Thad nodded. "It had to have been at least two when we saw them out. Damn near *poured* them out. As I indicated, it will be a snowy day in hell before I'm inducted into the Wilhemina Burks Fan Club, but I would have insisted they stay over if he'd had more than three miles to drive, or if it had been earlier. No one on the roads at that hour on a Tuesday night—Wednesday morning, sorry—anyhow. Except maybe a few deer raiding the gardens." He shut his mouth abruptly. In his relief he was close to babbling.

There was a moment's silence. The two Troopers were now looking at the floor. Pangborn had an expression on his face Thad could not read—he didn't believe he had ever seen it before. Not chagrin, although chagrin was a part of it.

What in the fuck is going on here?

"Well, that's very convenient, Mr. Beaumont," Pangborn said at last, "but it's a long way from rock-solid. We've got the word of you and your wife—or guesstimate—as to when you saw this last couple out. If they were as blasted as you seem to think, *they'll* hardly be able to corroborate what you've said. And if this DeLesseps fellow really is a friend, he might say . . . well, who knows?"

All the same, Alan Pangborn was losing steam. Thad saw it and believed—no, *knew*—the State Troopers did, too. Yet the man wasn't ready to let it go. The fear Thad had felt initially and the anger which had followed it were changing to fascination and curiosity. He thought he had never seen puzzlement and certainty so equally at war. The fact of the party—and he must accept as fact something which could so easily be checked—had shaken him . . . but not convinced him. Nor, he saw, were the Troopers entirely convinced. The only difference was that the Troopers weren't so hot under the collar. They hadn't known Homer Gamache personally, and so they didn't have any personal stake in this. Alan Pangborn had, and did.

I knew him, too, Thad thought. *So maybe I have a stake in it, too. Apart from my hide, that is.*

"Look," he said patiently, keeping his gaze locked with Pangborn's and trying not to return hostility in kind, "let's get real, as my students like to say. You asked if we could effectively prove our whereabouts—"

"*Your* whereabouts, Mr. Beaumont," Pangborn said.

"Okay, *my* whereabouts. Five pretty difficult hours. Hours when most people are in bed. Thanks to nothing more than blind luck, we—*I*, if you prefer—can cover at least three of those five hours. Maybe Rawlie and his odious lady friend left at two, maybe they left at one-thirty or two-fifteen. Whenever it was, it was *late.* They'll corroborate *that,* and the Burks woman wouldn't lie me an alibi even if Rawlie would. I think if Billie Burks saw me washed up drowning on the beach, she'd throw a bucket of water on me."

Liz gave him an odd, grimacing little smile as she took William, who was beginning to squirm, from him. At first he didn't understand that smile, and then it came to him. It was that phrase, of course—*lie me an alibi.* It was a phrase which Alexis Machine, arch-villain of the George Stark novels, sometimes used. It *was* odd, in a way; he could not remember ever using a Stark-ism in conversation before. On the other hand, he had never been accused of murder before, either, and murder was a George Stark kind of situation.

"Even supposing we're off by an hour and the last guests left at one," he continued, "and *further* supposing I jumped into my car the minute—the *second*—they were gone over the hill, and then drove like a mad bastard for Castle Rock, it would be four-thirty or five o'clock in the morning before I could possibly get there. No turnpike going west, you know."

One of the Troopers began: "And the Arsenault woman said it was about quarter of one when she saw——"

"We don't need to go into that right now," Alan interrupted quickly.

Liz made a rude, exasperated sound, and Wendy goggled at her comically. In the crook of her other arm, William stopped squirming, suddenly engrossed in the wonderfulness of his own twiddling fingers. To Thad she said. "There were still lots of people here at one, Thad. *Lots* of them."

Then she rounded on Alan Pangborn—*really* rounded on him this time.

"What is *wrong* with you, Sheriff? Why are you so bullheadedly determined to lay this off on my husband? Are you a stupid man? A lazy man? A *bad* man? You don't look like any of those things, but your behavior makes me wonder. It makes me wonder very much. Perhaps it was a lottery. Was that it? Did you draw his name out of a fucking *hat?*"

Alan recoiled slightly, clearly surprised—and discomfited—by her ferocity. "Mrs. Beaumont——"

"I have the advantage, I'm afraid, Sheriff," Thad said. "You *think* I killed Homer Gamache——"

"Mr. Beaumont, you have not been charged with——"

"No. But you think it, don't you?"

Color, solid and bricklike, not embarrassment, Thad thought, but frustration, had been slowly climbing into Pangborn's cheeks like color in a thermometer. "Yes, sir," he said. "I *do* think it. In spite of the things you and your wife have said."

This reply filled Thad with wonder. What, in God's name, could have happened to make this man (who, as Liz had said, did not look at all stupid) so sure? So goddamned *sure?*

Thad felt a shiver go up his spine . . . and then a peculiar thing happened. A phantom sound filled his mind—not his head but his *mind*—for a moment. It was a sound which imparted an aching sense of *déjà vu,* for it had been almost thirty years since he had last heard it. It was the ghostly sound of hundreds, perhaps thousands, of small birds.

He put a hand up to his head and touched the small scar there, and the shiver came again, stronger this time, twisting through his flesh like wire. *Lie me an alibi, George,* he thought. *I'm in a bit of a tight here, so lie me an alibi.*

"Thad?" Liz asked. "Are you all right?"

"Hmmm?" He looked around at her.

"You're pale."

"I'm fine," he said, and he was. The sound was gone. If it had really been there at all.

He turned back to Pangborn.

"As I said, Sheriff, I have a certain advantage in this matter. You think I killed Homer. I, however, *know* I didn't. Except in books, I've never killed anyone."

"Mr. Beaumont—"

"I understand your outrage. He was a nice old man with an overbearing wife, a funky sense of humor, and only one arm. I'm outraged, too. I'll do anything I can to help, but you'll have to drop this secret police stuff and tell me why you're here—

what in the world led you to me in the first place. I'm bewildered."

Alan looked at him for a very long time and then said: "Every instinct in my body says you are telling the truth."

"Thank God," Liz said. "The man sees sense."

"If it turns out you are," Alan said, looking only at Thad, "I will personally find the person in A.S.R. and I. who screwed up this ID and pull his skin off."

"What's A.S. and whatever?" Liz asked.

"Armed Services Records and Identification," one of the Troopers said. "Washington."

"I've never known them to screw up before," Alan went on in the same slow tone. "They say there's a first time for everything, but . . . if they *haven't* screwed up and if this party of yours checks out, I'm going to be pretty damned bewildered myself."

"Can't you tell us what this is all about?" Thad asked.

Alan sighed. "We've come this far; why not? In all truth, the last guests to leave your party don't matter that much anyway. If you were here at midnight, if there are witnesses who can swear you were—"

"Twenty-five at least," Liz said.

"—then you're off the hook. Putting together the eyewitness account of the lady the Trooper mentioned and the Medical Examiner's post-mortem, we can be almost positive Homer was killed between one and three a.m. on June first. He was bludgeoned to death with his own prosthetic arm."

"Dear Jesus," Liz muttered. "And you thought Thad—"

"Homer's truck was found two nights ago in the parking lot of a rest stop on I-95 in Connecticut, close to the New York border." Alan paused. "There were fingerprints all over it, Mr. Beaumont. Most were Homer's, but a good many belonged to the perpetrator. Several of the perp's were excellent. One was almost moulage-cast in a wad of gum the guy took out of his mouth and then stuck on the dashboard with his thumb. It hardened there. The best one of all, though, was on the rearview mirror. It was every bit as good as a print made in a police station. Only the one on the mirror was rolled in blood instead of ink."

"Then why *Thad?*" Liz was demanding indignantly. "Party or no party, how could you think that *Thad—*"

Alan looked at her and said, "When the people at A.S.R. and I. fed the prints into their graphics computer, your husband's service record came back. Your husband's *prints* came back, to be exact."

For a moment Thad and Liz could only look at each other, stunned to silence. Then Liz said: "It was a mistake, then. Surely the people who check these things *do* make mistakes from time to time."

"Yes, but they're rarely mistakes of this magnitude. There are gray areas in print identification, sure. Laymen who grow up watching shows like *Kojak* and *Barnaby Jones* get the idea that fingerprinting is an exact science, and it isn't. But computerization has taken a lot of the grays out of print comparisons, and this case yielded prints which were extraordinarily good. When I say they were your husband's prints, Mrs. Beaumont, I mean what I say. I've seen the computer sheets, and I've seen the overlays. The match is not just close."

Now he turned back to Thad and stared at him with his flinty blue eyes.

"The match is *exact*."

Liz stared at him with her mouth open, and in her arms first William and then Wendy began to cry.

Eight

PANGBORN PAYS A VISIT

1

When the doorbell rang again at quarter past seven that evening, it was Liz again who went to answer it because she was done getting William ready for bed and Thad was still hard at work on Wendy. The books all said parenting was a learned skill which had nothing to do with the sex of the parent, but Liz had her doubts. Thad pulled his weight, was in fact scrupulous about doing his share, but he was *slow.* He could whip out to the store and back on a Sunday afternoon in the time it took her to work her way over to the last aisle, but when it came to getting the twins ready for bed, well . . .

William was bathed, freshly diapered, zippered into his green sleep-suit, and sitting in the playpen while Thad was still laboring over Wendy's diapers (and he hadn't gotten all the soap out of her hair, she saw, but considering the day they'd put in, she believed she'd get it herself with a washcloth later on and say nothing).

Liz walked through the living room to the front door and looked out the side window. She saw Sheriff Pangborn standing outside. He was alone this time, but that didn't do much to alleviate her distress.

She turned her head and called across the living room and into the downstairs bathroom *cum* baby service station, "He's back!" Her voice carried a clearly discernible note of alarm.

There was a long pause and then Thad came into the doorway on the far side of the parlor. He was barefoot, wearing jeans and a white t-shirt. "Who?" he said in an odd, slow voice.

"Pangborn," she said. "Thad, are you okay?" Wendy was in his arms, wearing her diaper but nothing else, and she had her hands all over his face . . . but the little Liz could see of him just didn't look right.

"I'm fine. Let him in. I'll get this one in her suit." And before Liz could say anything else, he was abruptly gone.

Alan Pangborn, meanwhile, was still standing patiently on the stoop. He had seen Liz look out and hadn't rung again. He had the air of a man who wished he had worn a hat so he could hold it in his hands, perhaps even wring it a little.

Slowly, and with no welcoming smile at all, she took the chain off and let him in.

2

Wendy was wiggly and full of fun, which made her hard to handle. Thad managed to get her feet into the sleep-suit, then her arms, and was finally able to pop her hands out of the cuffs. She immediately reached up with one of them and honked his nose briskly. He recoiled instead of laughing as he usually did, and Wendy looked up at him from the changing-table in mild puzzlement. He reached for the zipper which ran up the suit from the left leg to the throat, then stopped and held his hands out in front of him. They were shaking. It was a tiny tremble, but it was there.

What the hell are you scared about? Or do you have the guilts again?

No; not the guilts. He almost wished it was. The fact was, he'd just had another scare in a day which had been too full of them.

First had come the police, with their odd accusation and their even odder certainty. Then that strange, haunted, cheeping sound. He hadn't known what it was, not for sure, although it had been familiar.

After supper it had come again.

He had gone up to his study to proof what he had done on the new book, *The Golden Dog,* that day. And suddenly, as he was bending over the sheaf of manuscript to make a minor correction, the sound filled his head. Thousands of birds, all cheeping and twittering at once, and this time an image came with the sound.

Sparrows.

Thousands and thousands of them, lined up along roofpeaks and jostling for place along the telephone wires, the way they did in the early spring, while the last snows of March were still lying on the ground in dirty little granulated piles.

Oh the headache is coming, he thought with dismay, and the voice in which that thought spoke— the voice of a frightened boy—was what tipped familiarity over into memory. Terror leaped up his throat then and seemed to clutch at the sides of his head with freezing hands.

Is it the tumor? Has it come back? Is it malignant this time?

The phantom sound—the voices of the birds—grew suddenly louder, almost deafening. It was joined by a thin, tenebrous flutter of wings. Now he could see them taking off, all of them at once; thousands of small birds darkening a white spring sky.

"Gonna hook back north, hoss," he heard himself say in a low, guttural voice, a voice which was not his own.

Then, suddenly, the sight and sound of the birds was gone. It was 1988, not 1960, and he was in his study. He was a grown man with a wife, two kids, and a Remington typewriter.

He had drawn a long, gasping breath. There had been no ensuing headache. Not then, not now. He felt fine. Except . . .

Except when he looked down at the sheaf of manuscript again, he saw that he had written something there. It was slashed across the lines of neat type in large capital letters.

THE SPARROWS ARE FLYING AGAIN, he had written.

He had discarded the Scripto pen and used one of the Berol Black Beauties to write it, although he had no memory of trading one for the other. He didn't even use the pencils anymore. The Berols belonged to a dead age . . . a dark age. He tossed the pencil he had used back into the jar and then bundled the whole thing into one of the drawers. The hand he used to do this was not quite steady.

Then Liz had called him to help get the twins ready for bed, and he had gone down to help her.

He had wanted to tell her what had happened, but found that simple terror—terror that the childhood tumor had recurred, terror that this time it would be malignant—had sealed his lips. He might have told her just the same . . . but then the doorbell had rung, Liz had gone to answer it, and she had said exactly the wrong thing in exactly the wrong tone.

He's back! Liz had cried in perfectly understandable irritation and dismay, and terror had swept through him like a cold, clear gust of wind. Terror, and one word: *Stark.* In the one second before reality reasserted itself, he was positive that was who she meant. George Stark. The sparrows were flying and Stark had returned. He was dead, dead and publicly buried, he had never really existed in the first place, but that didn't matter; real or not, he was back just the same.

Quit it, he told himself. *You're not a jumpy man, and there's no need to let this bizarre situation make you into one. The sound you heard—the sound of the birds— is a simple psychological phenomenon called "persistence of memory." It's brought on by stress and pressure. So just get yourself under control.*

But some of the terror lingered. The sound of the birds had caused not only *déjà vu,* that sense of having experienced something before, but *presque vu* as well.

Presque vu: a sense of experiencing something which has not happened yet but will. Not precognition, exactly, but misplaced memory.

Misplaced bullshit, that's what you mean.

He held his hands out and looked fixedly at them. The trembling became infinitesimal, then stopped altogether. When he was sure he wasn't going to pinch Wendy's bath-pink skin into the zipper of her sleep-suit, he pulled it up, carried her into the living room, popped her into the playpen with her brother, then went out to the hall, where Liz was standing with Alan Pangborn. Except for the fact that Pangborn was alone this time, it could have been this morning all over again.

Now this is a legitimate time and place for a little vu *of one kind or another,* he thought, but there was nothing funny in it. That other feeling was still too much with him . . . and the sound of the sparrows. "What can I do for you, Sheriff?" he asked, not smiling.

Ah! Something else that wasn't the same. Pangborn had a six-pack in one hand. Now he held it up. "I wondered if we could all have a cold one," he said, "and talk this over."

3

Liz and Alan Pangborn both had a beer; Thad drank a Pepsi from the fridge. As they talked, they watched the twins play with each other in their oddly solemn way.

"I have no business being here," Alan said. "I'm socializing with a man who is now a suspect in not just one murder but two."

"Two!" Liz cried.

"I'll get to it. In fact, I'll get to everything. I guess I'm going to spill it all. For one thing, I'm sure your husband has an alibi for this second murder, as well. The State cops are, too. They're quietly running around in circles."

"Who's been killed?" Thad asked.

"A young man named Frederick Clawson, in Washington, D.C." He watched as Liz jerked in her chair, spilling a little beer over the back of her hand. "I see you know the name, Mrs. Beaumont," he added without noticeable irony.

"What's going on?" she asked in a strengthless whisper.

"I don't have the slightest idea what's going on. I'm going crazy trying to figure it out. I'm not here to arrest you or even to hassle you, Mr. Beaumont, although I'll be goddamned if I can understand how someone else can have committed these two crimes. I'm here to ask for your help."

"Why don't you call me Thad?"

Alan shifted uncomfortably in his seat. "I think I'd be more comfortable with Mr. Beaumont, for the time being."

Thad nodded. "Just as you like. So Clawson's dead." He looked down meditatively for a moment, then up at Alan again. "Were my fingerprints all over the scene of this crime, as well?"

"Yes—and in more ways than one. *People* magazine did a write-up on you recently, didn't they, Mr. Beaumont?"

"Two weeks ago," Thad agreed.

"The article was found in Clawson's apartment. One page appears to have been used as a symbol in what looks like a highly ritualized murder."

"Christ," Liz said. She sounded both tired and horrified.

"Are you willing to tell me who he is to you?" Alan asked.

Thad nodded. "There's no reason not to. Did you happen to read that article, Sheriff?"

"My wife brings the magazine home from the

supermarket," he said, "but I better tell you the truth—I only looked at the pictures. I intend to go back and read the text as soon as I can."

"You didn't miss much—but Frederick Clawson is the reason that article happened. You see—"

Alan held up a hand. "We'll get to him, but let's go back to Homer Gamache first. We've rechecked with A.S.R. and I. The prints on Gamache's truck—and in Clawson's apartment, too, although none of them are as perfect as the bubble-gum print and the mirror print—do seem to match yours exactly. Which means if you didn't do it, we have two people with exactly the same prints, and *that* one belongs in the *Guinness Book of World Records.*"

He looked at William and Wendy, who were trying to play pat-a-cake in their playpen. They seemed to be mostly endangering each other's eyesight. "Are they identical?" he asked.

"No," Liz said. "They *do* look alike, but they're brother and sister. And brother-sister twins are never identical."

Alan nodded. "Not even identical twins have identical prints," he said. He paused for a moment and then added in a casual voice which Thad believed was completely counterfeit: *"You* don't happen to have a twin brother, do you, Mr. Beaumont?"

Thad shook his head slowly. "No," he said. "I don't have any siblings at all, and my folks are dead. William and Wendy are my only living blood relatives." He smiled at the children, then looked back at Pangborn. "Liz had a miscarriage back in 1974," he said. "Those . . . those first ones . . . were also twins, I understand, although I don't suppose there's any way of telling if they would have been identical—not when the miscarriage comes in the third month. And if there is, who would want to know?"

Alan shrugged, looking a little embarrassed.

"She was shopping at Filene's. In Boston. Someone pushed her. She fell all the way down an escalator, cut one arm pretty badly—if a security cop hadn't been there to put a tourniquet right on it, it would have been touch and go for her, too—and she lost the twins."

"Is this in the *People* article?" Alan asked.

Liz smiled humorlessly and shook her head. "We reserved the right to edit our lives when we agreed to do the story, Sheriff Pangborn. We didn't tell Mike Donaldson, the man who came to do the interview, of course, but that's what we did."

"Was the push deliberate?"

"No way to tell," Liz said. Her eyes settled on William and Wendy . . . brooded upon them. "If it was an accidental bump, it was a damned hard one, though. I went flying—didn't touch the escalator at all until I was almost halfway down. All the same, I've tried to convince myself that's what it was. It's easier to get along with. The idea that someone would push a woman down a steep escalator just to see what happened . . . that's an idea guaranteed to keep you awake nights."

Alan nodded.

"The doctors we saw told us Liz would probably never have another child," Thad said. "When she got pregnant with William and Wendy, they told us she'd probably never carry them all the way to term. But she sailed through it. And, after ten years, I've finally gotten to work on a new book under my own name. It'll be my third. So you see, it's been good for both of us."

"The other name you wrote under was George Stark."

Thad nodded. "But that's over now. It started being over when Liz got into her eighth month, still safe and sound. I decided if I was going to be a father again, I ought to start being myself again, as well."

4

There was a kind of beat in the conversation then— not quite a pause. Then Thad said, "Confess, Sheriff Pangborn."

Alan raised his eyebrows. "Beg your pardon?"

A smile touched the corners of Thad's mouth. "I won't say you had the scenario all worked out, but I bet you at least had the broad strokes. If I had an identical twin brother, maybe *he* hosted our party. That way I could have been in Castle Rock, murdering Homer Gamache and putting my fingerprints all over his truck. But it couldn't stop there, could it? My twin sleeps with my wife and keeps my appointments while I drive Homer's truck to that rest stop in Connecticut, steal another car there, drive to New York, ditch the hot car, then take a train or a plane to Washington, D.C. Once I'm there, I waste Clawson and hurry back to Ludlow, pack my twin off to wherever he was, and he and I both take up the threads of our lives again. Or all three of us, if you assume Liz here was part of the deception."

Liz stared at him for a moment, and then began

to laugh. She did not laugh long, but she laughed hard while she did. There was nothing forced about it, but it was grudging laughter, all the same—an expression of humor from a woman who has been surprised into it.

Alan was looking at Thad with frank and open surprise. The twins laughed at their mother for a moment—or perhaps with her—and then resumed rolling a large yellow ball slowly back and forth in the playpen.

"Thad, that's *horrible*," Liz said when she had gained control of herself.

"Maybe it is," he said. "If so, I'm sorry."

"It's . . . pretty involved," Alan said.

Thad grinned at him. "You're not a fan of the late George Stark, I take it."

"Frankly, no. But I have a deputy, Norris Ridgewick, who is. He had to explain to me what all the hoop-de-doo was about."

"Well, Stark messed with some of the conventions of the mystery story. Never anything so Agatha Christie as the scenario I just suggested, but that doesn't mean I can't think that way if I put my mind to it. Come on, Sheriff—had the thought crossed your mind, or not? If not, I really *do* owe my wife an apology."

Alan was silent for a moment, smiling a little and clearly thinking a lot. At last he said, "Maybe I *was* thinking along those lines. Not seriously, and not just that way, but you don't have to apologize to your good lady. Since this morning I've found myself willing to consider even the most outrageous possibilities."

"Given the situation."

"Given the situation, yes."

Smiling himself, Thad said: "I was born in Bergenfield, New Jersey, Sheriff. There's no need to take my word when you can check the records for any twin brothers I may have, you know, forgotten."

Alan shook his head and drank some more of his beer. "It was a wild idea, and I feel a little like a horse's ass, but that's not completely new. I've felt that way since this morning, when you sprang that party on us. We ran down the names, by the way. They check out."

"Of course they do," Liz said with a touch of asperity.

"And since you don't have a twin brother anyway, it pretty well closes the subject."

"Suppose for a second," Thad said, "just for the sake of argument, that it *did* happen the way I suggested. It would make a hell of a yarn . . . up to a point."

"What point is that?" Alan asked.

"The fingerprints. Why would I go to all the trouble of setting up an alibi *here* with a fellow who looked just like me . . . then bugger it all by leaving fingerprints at the scenes of the murders?"

Liz said, "I bet you really *will* check the birth records, won't you, Sheriff?"

Alan said stolidly: "The basis of police procedure is beat it until it's dead. But I already know what I'll find if I do." He hesitated, then added, "It wasn't just the party. You came across as a man who was speaking the truth, Mr. Beaumont. I've had some experience telling the difference. So far as I've been able to tell in my time as a police officer, there are very few good liars in the world. They may show up from time to time in those mystery novels you were talking about, but in real life they're pretty rare."

"So why the fingerprints at all?" Thad asked. "That's what interests me. Is it just an amateur with my prints you're looking for? I doubt it. Has it crossed your mind that the very *quality* of the prints is suspect? You spoke of gray areas. I know a little bit about prints as a result of the research I did for the Stark novels, but I'm really quite lazy when it comes to that end of the job—it's so much easier just to sit there in front of the typewriter and make up lies. But don't there have to be a certain number of points of comparison before fingerprints can even be entered into evidence?"

"In Maine it's six," Alan said. "Six perfect compares have to be present for a fingerprint to be admitted as evidence."

"And isn't it true that in most cases fingerprints are only half-prints, or quarter-prints, or just smudgy blurs with a few loops and whorls in them?"

"Yeah. In real life, criminals hardly ever go to jail on the basis of fingerprint evidence."

"Yet here you have one on the rearview mirror which you described as being as good as any print rolled in a police station, and another all but molded in a wad of gum. Somehow that's the one that really gets me. It's as if the fingerprints were put there for you to find."

"It's crossed our minds." In fact, it had done a good deal more. It was one of the most aggravating aspects of the case. The Clawson murder looked like a classic gang-land hit on a blabbermouth: tongue cut out, penis in the victim's mouth, lots of blood, lots of pain, yet no one in the building had heard a goddam thing. But if it had been a professional job, how come Beaumont's prints were all over the place? Could anything which looked so much like a frame not *be* a frame? Not unless someone had come up with a brand-new gimmick. In the meantime, the old maxim still held good with Alan Pangborn: if it walks like a duck, quacks like a duck, and swims like a duck, it's probably a duck.

"Can fingerprints be planted?" Thad asked.

"Do you read minds as well as write books, Mr. Beaumont?"

"Read minds, write books, but honey, I don't do windows."

Alan had a mouthful of beer, and laughter so surprised him that he almost sprayed it over the carpet. He managed to swallow, although some went down his windpipe and he began to cough. Liz got up and whammed him briskly on the back several times. It was perhaps an odd thing to do, but it did not strike her as odd; life with two small babies had conditioned her. William and Wendy stared from the playpen, the yellow ball stopped dead and forgotten between them. William began to laugh. Wendy took her cue from him.

For some reason, this made Alan laugh harder.

Thad joined in. And, still pounding on his back, Liz also began to laugh.

"I'm okay," Alan said, still coughing and laughing. "Really."

Liz whacked him one final time. Beer splurted up the neck of Alan's bottle like a geyser letting off steam and splatted onto the crotch of his pants.

"S'okay," Thad said. "Diapers we got."

Then they were laughing all over again, and at

some time between the moment when Alan Pangborn started coughing and the one when he finally
managed to stop laughing, the three of them had
become at least temporary friends.

5

"So far as I know or have been able to find out, fingerprints can't be planted," Alan said, picking
up the thread of conversation some time later—
by now they were on their second round, and the
embarrassing stain on the crotch of his pants was
beginning to dry. The twins had fallen asleep in
the playpen, and Liz had left the room to go to the
bathroom. "Of course, we're still checking, because
up until this morning we had no reason to suspect
anything like that might even have been tried in
this case. I know it *has* been tried; a few years ago
a kidnapper took imprints of his prisoner's finger-
pads before killing him, turned them into . . . dies,
I suppose you'd call them . . . and stamped them
into very thin plastic. He put the plastic finger-
tips over the pads of his own fingers, and attempted
to leave the prints all over his victim's mountain
cabin, so the police would think the whole kidnap-
ping was a hoax and the guy was free."

"It didn't work?"

"The cops got some lovely prints," Alan said.
"The perp's. The natural oils on the guy's fingers
flattened the counterfeit fingerprints, and because
the plastic was thin and naturally receptive to even
the most delicate shapes, it rose up again in the
guy's own prints."

"Maybe a different material—"

"Sure, maybe. This happened in the mid-fifties, and I imagine a hundred new kinds of polymer plastic have been invented since then. It could be. All we can say for now is that no one in forensics or criminology has ever heard of it being done, and I think that's the way it'll stay."

Liz came back into the room and sat down, curling her feet under her like a cat and pulling her skirt over her calves. Thad admired the gesture, which seemed to him somehow timeless and eternally graceful.

"Meantime, there are other considerations here, Thad."

Thad and Liz exchanged a flicker of a glance at Alan's use of the first name, so swift Alan missed it. He had drawn a battered notebook from his hip pocket and was looking at one of the pages.

"Do you smoke?" he asked, looking up.

"No."

"He quit seven years ago," Liz said. "It was very hard for him, but he stuck with it."

"There are critics who say the world would be a better place if I'd just pick a spot and die in it, but I choose to spite them," Thad said. "Why?"

"You did smoke, though."

"Yes."

"Pall Malls?"

Thad had been raising his can of soda. It stopped six inches shy of his mouth. "How did you know that?"

"Your blood-type is A-negative?"

"I'm beginning to understand why you came primed to arrest me this morning," Thad said. "If I hadn't been so well alibied, I'd be in jail right now, wouldn't I?"

"Good guess."

"You could have gotten his blood-type from his R.O.T.C. records," Liz said. "I assume that's where his fingerprints came from in the first place."

"But not that I smoked Pall Mall cigarettes for fifteen years," Thad said. "So far as I know, stuff like that's not part of the records the army keeps."

"This is stuff that's come in since this morning," Alan told them. "The ashtray in Homer Gamache's pick-up was full of Pall Mall cigarette butts. The old man only smoked an occasional pipe. There were a couple of Pall Mall butts in an ashtray in Frederick Clawson's apartment, as well. He didn't smoke at all, except maybe for a joint now and then. That's according to his landlady. We got our perp's blood-type from the spittle on the butts. The serologist's report also gave us a lot of other information. Better than fingerprints."

Thad was no longer smiling. "I don't understand this. I don't understand this at all."

"There's one thing which doesn't match," Pangborn said, "Blonde hairs. We found half a dozen in Homer's truck, and we found another on the back of the chair the killer used in Clawson's living room. Your hair is black. Somehow I don't think you're wearing a rug."

"No—Thad's not, but maybe the killer was," Liz said bleakly.

"Maybe," Alan agreed. "If so, it was made of human hair. And why bother changing the color of your hair if you're going to leave fingerprints and cigarette butts everywhere? Either the guy is very dumb or he was deliberately trying to implicate you. The blonde hair doesn't fit either way."

"Maybe he just didn't want to be recognized,"

Liz said. "Remember, Thad was in *People* magazine barely two weeks ago. Coast to coast."

"Yeah, that's a possibility. Although if this guy also *looks* like your husband, Mrs. Beaumont—"

"Liz."

"Okay, Liz. If he looks like your husband, he'd look like Thad Beaumont with blonde hair, wouldn't he?"

Liz looked fixedly at Thad for a moment and then began to giggle.

"What's so funny?" Thad asked.

"I'm trying to imagine you blonde," she said, still giggling. "I think you'd look like a very depraved David Bowie."

"Is that funny?" Thad asked Alan. "*I* don't think that's funny."

"Well. . ." Alan said, smiling.

"Never mind. The guy could have been wearing sunglasses and deelie-boppers as well as a blonde wig, for all we know."

"Not if the killer was the same guy Mrs. Arsenault saw getting into Homer's truck at quarter of one in the morning of June first," Alan said.

Thad leaned forward. *"Did* he look like me?" he asked.

"She couldn't tell much except that he was wearing a suit. For what it's worth, I had one of my men, Norris Ridgewick, show her your picture today. She said she didn't *think* it was you, although she couldn't say for sure. She said she thought the man who got into Homer's truck was bigger." He added dryly: "That's one lady who believes in erring on the side of caution."

"She could tell a size difference from a picture?" Liz asked doubtfully.

"She's seen Thad around town, summers," Alan said. "And she *did* say she couldn't be sure."

Liz nodded. "Of course she knows him. Both of us, for that matter. We buy fresh stuff at their vegetable stand all the time. Dumb. Sorry."

"Nothing to apologize for," Alan said. He finished his beer and checked his crotch. Dry. Good. There was a light stain there, probably not anything anyone but his wife would notice. "Anyhow, that brings me to the last point . . . or aspect . . . or whatever the hell you want to call it. I doubt if it's even a part of this, but it never hurts to check. What's your shoe-size, Mr. Beaumont?"

Thad glanced at Liz, who shrugged. "I've got pretty small paws for a guy who goes six-one, I guess. I take a size ten, although half a size either way is—"

"The prints reported to us were probably bigger than that," Alan said. "I don't think the prints are a part of it, anyway, and even if they are, footprints can be faked. Stick some newspaper in the toes of shoes two or even three sizes too big for you and you're set."

"What footprints are these?" Thad asked.

"Doesn't matter," Alan said, shaking his head. "We don't even have photos. I think we've got almost everything on the table that belongs there, Thad. Your fingerprints, your blood-type, your brand of cigarettes—"

"He doesn't—" Liz began.

Alan held up a placatory hand. "*Old* brand of cigarettes. I suppose I could be crazy for letting you in on all this—there's a part of me that says I am, anyway—but as long as we've gone this far, there's no sense ignoring the forest while we look at a few trees. You're tied in other ways, as well. Castle Rock is your legal residence as well as Ludlow, being as how you pay taxes in both places. Homer Gamache was more than just an acquaintance; he did . . . would odd jobs be correct?"

"Yes," Liz said. "He retired from full-time caretaking the year we bought the house—Dave Phillips and Charlie Fortin take turns doing that now—but he liked to keep his hand in."

"If we assume that the hitchhiker Mrs. Arsenault observed killed Homer—and that's the assumption we're going on—a question arises. Did the hitchhiker kill him because Homer was the first person to come along who was stupid enough—or drunk enough—to pick him up, or did he kill him because he was Homer Gamache, acquaintance of Thad Beaumont?"

"How could he know Homer *would* come along?" Liz asked.

"Because it was Homer's bowling night, and Homer is—was—a creature of habit. He was like an old horse, Liz; he always went back to the barn by the same route."

"Your first assumption," Thad said, "was that Homer didn't stop because he was drunk but because he recognized the hitchhiker. A stranger who wanted to kill Homer wouldn't have tried the hitchhiking ploy at all. He would have figured it for a long shot, if not a totally lost cause."

"Yes."

"Thad," Liz said in a voice which would not quite remain steady. "The police thought he stopped because he saw it was Thad . . . didn't they?"

"Yes," Thad said. He reached across and took her hand. "They thought only someone like me—

someone who knew him—would even try it that way. I suppose even the suit fits in. What else does the well-dressed writer wear when he's planning on doing murder in the country at one o'clock in the morning? The good tweed, of course . . . the one with the brown suede patches on the elbows of the jacket. All the British mysteries insist it's absolutely *de rigueur.*"

He looked at Alan.

"It's pretty goddamned odd, isn't it? The whole thing."

Alan nodded. "It's as odd as a cod. Mrs. Arsenault thought he'd started to cross the road or was at least on the verge of it when Homer came poking along in his pick-up. But the fact that you also knew this Clawson fellow in D.C. makes it seem more and more likely that Homer was killed because of who he was, not just because he was drunk enough to stop. So let's talk about Frederick Clawson, Thad. Tell me about him."

Thad and Liz exchanged a glance.

"I think," Thad said, "that my wife might do the job more quickly and concisely than I could. She'll also swear less, I think."

"Are you sure you want me to do it?" Liz asked him.

Thad nodded. Liz began to speak, slowly at first, then picking up speed. Thad interrupted once or twice near the start, then settled back, content to listen. For the next half-hour, he hardly spoke. Alan Pangborn took out his notebook and jotted in it, but after a few initial questions, he did not interrupt much, either.

Nine

THE INVASION
OF THE CREEPAZOID

1

"I call him a Creepazoid," Liz began. "I'm sorry that he's dead . . . but that's what he was, just the same. I don't know if genuine Creepazoids are born or made, but they rise to their own slimy station in life either way, so I guess it doesn't matter. Frederick Clawson's happened to be Washington, D.C. He went to the biggest legal snake-pit on earth to study for the bar.

"Thad, the kiddos are stirring—will you give them their night-bottles? And I'd like another beer, please."

He got her the beer and then went out into the kitchen to warm the bottles. He wedged the kitchen door open so he could hear better . . . and slammed his kneecap in the process. This was something he had done so many times before that he barely noticed it.

The sparrows are flying again, he thought, and rubbed at the scar on his forehead as he first filled a saucepan with warm water, then put it on the stove. *Now if I only knew what the fuck that means.*

"We eventually got most of this story from Clawson himself," Liz went on, "but his perspective was naturally a little skewed—Thad likes to say all of us are the heroes of our own lives, and according to Clawson he was more of a Boswell than a Creepazoid . . . but we were able to put together a more balanced version by adding stuff we got from the people at Darwin Press, which published the novels Thad wrote under Stark's name, and the stuff Rick Cowley passed along."

"Who is Rick Cowley?" Alan asked.

"The literary agent who handled Thad under both names."

"And what did Clawson—your Creepazoid—want?"

"Money," Liz said dryly.

In the kitchen, Thad took the two night-bottles (only half full to help cut down on those inconvenient changes in the middle of the night) from the fridge and popped them in the pan of water. What Liz had said was right . . . but it was also wrong. Clawson had wanted a great deal more than money.

Liz might have read his mind.

"Not that money was *all* he wanted. I'm not even sure that was the main thing. He also wanted to be known as the man who exposed George Stark's real identity."

"Sort of like being the one who finally manages to unmask The Incredible Spider-Man?"

"Exactly."

Thad put a finger in the saucepan to test the water, then leaned back against the stove with his arms crossed, listening. He realized that he wanted a cigarette—for the first time in years he wanted a cigarette again.

Thad shivered.

2

"Clawson was in too many right places at too many right times," Liz said. "Not only was he a law student, he was a part-time bookstore clerk. Not only was he a bookstore clerk, he was an avid fan of George Stark's. And he may have been the only George Stark fan in the country who had also read Thad Beaumont's two novels."

In the kitchen, Thad grinned—not without some sourness—and tested the water in the saucepan again.

"I think he wanted to create some sort of grand drama out of his suspicions," Liz went on. "As things turned out, he had to work his fanny off to rise above the pedestrian. Once he had decided Stark was really Beaumont and vice-versa, he called Darwin Press."

"Stark's book publisher."

"Right. He got to Ellie Golden, the woman who edited the Stark novels. He asked the question straight out—please tell me if George Stark is really Thaddeus Beaumont. Ellie said the idea was ridiculous. Clawson then asked about the author photo on the back of the Stark novels. He said he wanted the address of the man in the picture. Ellie told him she couldn't give out the addresses of the publishing company's authors.

"Clawson said, 'I don't want *Stark's* address, I want the address of the man in the picture. The man *posing* as Stark.' Ellie told him he was being ridiculous—that the man in the author photo *was* George Stark."

"Previous to this, the publisher never came out

and said it was just a pen name?" Alan asked. He sounded genuinely curious. "They took the position that he was a real man all along?"

"Oh yes—Thad insisted."

Yes, he thought, taking the bottles out of the saucepan and testing the milk against the inside of his wrist. *Thad insisted. In retrospect, Thad doesn't know just why he insisted, does not in fact have the slightest idea, but Thad did indeed insist.*

He took the bottles back into the living room, avoiding a collision with the kitchen table on the way. He gave a bottle to each twin. They hoisted them solemnly, sleepily, and began to suck. Thad sat down again. He listened to Liz and told himself that the thought of a cigarette was the furthest thing from his mind.

"Anyway," Liz said, "Clawson wanted to ask more questions—he had a whole truckload of them, I guess—but Ellie wouldn't play. She told him to call Rick Cowley and then hung up on him. Clawson then called Rick's office and got Miriam. She's Rick's ex-wife. Also his partner in the agency. The arrangement's a little odd, but they get along very well.

"Clawson asked her the same thing—if George Stark was really Thad Beaumont. According to Miriam, she told him yes. Also that she was Dolley Madison. 'I've divorced James,' she said, 'Thad is divorcing Liz, and we two shall marry in the spring!' And hung up. She then rushed into Rick's office and told him some guy in Washington, D.C., was prying around the edges of Thad's secret identity. After that, Clawson's calls to Cowley Associates netted him nothing but quick hang-ups."

Liz took a long swallow of her beer.

"He didn't give up, though. I've decided that real Creepazoids never do. He just decided that pretty-please wasn't going to work."

"And he didn't call Thad?" Alan asked.

"No, not once."

"You have an unlisted number, I suppose."

Thad made one of his few direct contributions to the story. "We're not listed in the public directories, Alan, but the phone here in Ludlow *is* listed in the Faculty Directory. It has to be. I'm a teacher, and I have advisees."

"But the guy never went directly to the horse's mouth," Alan marvelled.

"He got in touch later on . . . by letter," Liz said. "But that's getting ahead of things. Should I go on?"

"Please," Alan said. "It's a fascinating story in its own right."

"Well," Liz said, "it took our Creepazoid just three weeks and probably less than five hundred dollars to ferret out what he was positive about all along—that Thad and George Stark were the same man.

"He started with *Literary Market Place,* which publishing types just call *LMP.* It's a digest of names, addresses, and business phone numbers for just about everyone in the field—writers, editors, publishers, agents. Using that and the 'People' column in *Publishers Weekly,* he managed to isolate half a dozen Darwin Press employees who left the company between the summer of 1986 and the summer of 1987.

"One of them had the information and was willing to spill it. Ellie Golden's pretty sure the culprit was the girl who was the chief comptroller's secretary for eight months in '85 and '86. Ellie called her a slut from Vassar with bad nasal habits."

Alan laughed.

"Thad believes that's who it was, too," Liz went on, "because the smoking gun turned out to be photostats of royalty statements for George Stark. They came from the office of Roland Burrets."

"The Darwin Press chief comptroller," Thad said. He was watching the twins while he listened. They were lying on their backs now, sleep-suited feet pressed chummily together, bottles pointed toward the ceiling. Their eyes were glassy and distant. Soon, he knew, they would fall asleep for the night . . . and when they did, they would do it together. *They do everything together,* Thad thought. *The babies are sleepy and the sparrows are flying.*

He touched the scar again.

"Thad's name wasn't on the photostats," Liz said. "Royalty statements sometimes lead to checks, but they're not checks themselves, so it didn't *have* to appear there. You follow that, don't you?"

Alan nodded.

"But the address still told him most of what he needed to know. It was Mr. George Stark, P.O. Box 1642, Brewer, Maine 04412. That's a long way from Mississippi, where Stark was supposed to live. A look at a Maine map would have told him that the town immediately south of Brewer is Ludlow, and he knew what well-regarded if not exactly famous writer lived there. Thaddeus Beaumont. What a coincidence.

"Neither Thad nor I ever saw him in person, but *he* saw *Thad.* He knew when Darwin Press mailed out its quarterly royalty checks from the photostats he had already received. Most royalty checks go to the author's agent first. Then the agent issues a new one, which reflects the original amount minus his commission. But in Stark's case, the comptroller mailed the checks directly to the Brewer post office box."

"What about the agent's commission?" Alan asked.

"Clipped off the total amount at Darwin Press and sent to Rick by separate check," Liz said. "That would have been another clear signal to Clawson that George Stark wasn't what he claimed to be . . . only by then, Clawson didn't need any more clues. He wanted hard proof. And set out to get it.

"When it was time for the royalty check to be issued, Clawson flew up here. He stayed at the Holiday Inn nights; he spent his days 'staking out' the Brewer post office. That's exactly how he put it in the letter Thad got later on. It was a stakeout. All very *film noir.* It was a pretty cut-rate investigation, though. If 'Stark' hadn't shown up to collect his check on the fourth day of his stay, Clawson would have had to fold his tent and steal back into the night. But I don't think it would have ended there. When a genuine Creepazoid gets his teeth in you, he doesn't let go until he's bitten out a big chunk."

"Or until you knock his teeth out," Thad grunted. He saw Alan turn in his direction, eyebrows raised, and grimaced. Bad choice of words. Someone had apparently done just that to Liz's Creepazoid . . . or something even worse.

"It's a moot question, anyway," Liz resumed, and Alan turned back to her. "It didn't take that long. On the third day, while he was sitting on a park bench across from the post office, he saw Thad's Suburban pull into one of the ten-minute parking slots near the post office."

Liz took another swallow of beer and wiped foam off her upper lip. When her hand came away, she was smiling.

"Now here's the part I like," she said. "It's just *d-d-delicious,* as the gay fellow in *Brideshead Revisited* used to say. Clawson had a camera. This little tiny camera, the sort you can cup in the palm of your hand. When you're ready to take your shot, you just spread your fingers a little to let the lens peek through, and bingo! There you are."

She giggled a little, shaking her head at the image.

"He said in his letter he got it from some catalogue that sells spy gear—telephone bugs, goo you swab on envelopes to turn them transparent for ten or fifteen minutes, self-destructing briefcases, stuff like that. Secret Agent X-9 Clawson, reporting for duty. I bet he would have gotten a hollow tooth filled with cyanide if it was legal to sell them. He was heavily into the image.

"Anyhow, he got half a dozen fairly passable photos. Not arty stuff, but you could see who the subject was and what he was doing. There was a shot of Thad approaching the post office boxes in the lobby, a shot of Thad putting his key into box 1642, and one of him removing an envelope."

"He sent you copies of these?" Alan asked. She had said he wanted money, and Alan guessed the lady knew what she was talking about. The setup did more than smell of blackmail; it reeked of it.

"Oh yes. And an enlargement of the last one. You can read part of the return address—the letters DARW, and you can clearly make out the Darwin Press colophon above it."

"X-9 strikes again," Alan said.

"Yes. X-9 strikes again. He got the photos developed, and then he flew back to Washington. We got his letter, with the photos included, only a few days later. The letter was really marvelous. He skated up to the edge of threat, but never once over the edge."

"He *was* a law student," Thad said.

"Yes," Liz agreed. "He knew just how far he could go, apparently. Thad can get you the letter, but I can paraphrase. He started by saying how much he admired both halves of what he called Thad's 'divided mind.' He recounted what he'd found out and how he'd done it. Then he went on to his real business. He was very careful about showing us the hook, but the hook was there. He said he was an aspiring writer himself, but he didn't have much time to write—his law studies were demanding, but that was only part of it. The real problem, he said, was that he had to work in a bookstore to help pay his tuition and other bills. He said he would like to show Thad some of his work, and if Thad thought it showed promise, perhaps he might feel moved to put together an assistance package to help him along the way."

"An assistance package," Alan said, bemused. "Is *that* what they're calling it these days?"

Thad threw back his head and laughed.

"That's what Clawson called it, anyway. I think I can quote the last bit by heart. 'I know this must seem a very forward request to you on first reading,' he said, 'but I am sure that if you studied my work, you would quickly understand that such an arrangement might hold advantages for both of us.'

"Thad and I raved about it for awhile, then

we laughed about it, then I think we raved some more."

"Yeah," Thad said. "I don't know about the laughing, but we sure did do a lot of raving."

"Finally we got down to just plain talking. We talked almost until midnight. We both recognized Clawson's letter and his photographs for what they were, and once Thad got over being angry—"

"I'm *still* not over being angry," Thad interjected, "and the guy's dead."

"Well, once the yelling died down, Thad was almost relieved. He'd wanted to jettison Stark for quite awhile, and he'd already gotten to work on a long, serious book of his own. Which he's still doing. It's called *The Golden Dog.* I've read the first two hundred pages, and it's lovely. Much better than the last couple of things he churned out as George Stark. So Thad decided—"

"*We* decided," Thad said.

"Okay, *we* decided that Clawson was a blessing in disguise, a way to hurry along what was already coming. Thad's only fear was that Rick Cowley wouldn't like the idea much, because George Stark was earning more for the agency than Thad, by far. But he was a real honey about it. In fact, he said it might just generate some publicity that would help in a number of areas: Stark's backlist, Thad's own backlist—"

"All two books of it," Thad put in with a smile.

"—and the new book, when it finally comes out."

"Pardon me—what's a backlist?" Alan asked.

Grinning now, Thad said: "The old books they no longer put in the fancy dump-bins at the front of the chain bookstores."

"So you went public."

"Yes," Liz said. "First to the AP here in Maine and to *Publishers Weekly,* but the story popped up on the national wire—Stark was a best-selling writer, after all, and the fact that he never really existed at all made for interesting filler on the back pages. And then *People* magazine got in touch.

"We got one more squealing, angry letter from Frederick Clawson, telling us how mean and nasty and thankless we were. He seemed to think we had no right to take him out of things the way we had, because he had done all the work and all Thad had done was to write a few books. After that he signed off."

"And now he's signed off for good," Thad said.

"No," Alan said. "Someone signed off for him . . . and that's a big difference."

Another silence fell among them. It was short . . . but very, very heavy.

3

Alan thought for several minutes. Thad and Liz let him. At last he looked up and said, "Okay. Why? Why would anyone resort to murder over this? Especially after the secret had already come out?"

Thad shook his head. "If it has to do with me, or the books I wrote as George Stark, I don't know who *or* why."

"And over a pen name?" Alan asked in a musing voice. "I mean—no offense intended, Thad, but it wasn't exactly a classified document or a big military secret."

"No offense taken," Thad said. "In fact, I couldn't agree more."

"Stark had a lot of fans," Liz said. "Some of them were angry that Thad wasn't going to write any more novels as Stark. *People* got some letters after the article, and Thad's gotten a bunch. One lady went so far as to suggest that Alexis Machine should come out of retirement and cook Thad's goose."

"Who's Alexis Machine?" Alan had produced the notebook again.

Thad grinned. "Soft, soft, my good Inspector. Machine's just a character in two of the novels George wrote. The first and the last."

"A fiction by a fiction," Alan said, putting the notebook back. "Great."

Thad, meanwhile, looked mildly startled. "A fiction by a fiction," he said. "That's not bad. Not bad at all."

"My point was this," Liz said. "Maybe Clawson had a friend—always assuming Creepazoids *have* friends—who was a rabid Stark fan. Maybe he knew Clawson was really responsible for blowing the story wide open, and got so mad because there wouldn't be any more Stark novels that he . . ."

She sighed, looked down at her beer-bottle for a moment, then raised her head again.

"That's actually pretty lame, isn't it?"

"I'm afraid so," Alan said kindly, then looked at Thad. "You ought to be down on your knees thanking God for your alibi now, even if you weren't before. You do realize this makes you look even tastier as a suspect, don't you?"

"I suppose in a way it does," Thad agreed. "Thaddeus Beaumont has written two books hardly anybody has read. The second, published eleven years ago, didn't even review very well. The infinitesimal advances he got didn't earn out; it'll be a wonder if he can even get published again, with the business being what it is. Stark, on the other hand, makes money by the fistful. They're *discreet* fistfuls, but the books still earn four times what I make teaching each year. This guy Clawson comes along, with his carefully worded blackmail threat. I refuse to cave in, but my only option is to go public with the story myself. Not long after, Clawson is killed. It looks like a great motive, but it's really not. Killing a would-be blackmailer after you've already told the secret yourself would be dumb."

"Yes . . . but there's always revenge."

"I suppose—until you look at the rest of it. What Liz told you is perfectly true. Stark was just about ready for the scrap-heap, anyway. There might have been one more book, but *only* one. And one of the reasons Rick Cowley was such a honey, as Liz put it, was because he knew it. And he was right about the publicity. The *People* article, silly as it was, has done wonders for sales. Rick tells me *Riding to Babylon* has a shot at going back on the bestseller list, and sales are up on all Stark novels. Dutton's even planning to bring *The Sudden Dancers* and *Purple Haze* back into print. You look at it that way, Clawson did me a favor."

"So where does that leave us?" Alan asked.

"I'll be damned if I know," Thad replied.

Into the silence that followed, Liz said in a soft voice: "It's a crocodile-hunter. I was thinking about them just this morning. It's a crocodile-hunter, and he's just as crazy as a loon."

"Crocodile-hunter?" Alan turned to her.

Liz explained about Thad's see-the-living-crocodiles syndrome. "It *could* have been a crazy fan," she said. "It's not *that* lame, not when you think about the fellow who shot John Lennon and the one who tried to kill Ronald Reagan to impress Jodie Foster. They *are* out there. And if Clawson could find out about Thad, someone else could have found out about Clawson."

"But why would a guy like that try to implicate me, if he loves my stuff so much?" Thad asked.

"Because he *doesn't!*" Liz said vehemently. "*Stark's* the man the crocodile-hunter loves. He probably hates you almost as much as he hates—hated—Clawson. You said you weren't sorry Stark was dead. That could be reason enough right there."

"I still don't buy it," Alan said. "The finger-prints—"

"You say prints have never been copied or planted, Alan, but since they were in both places, there *must* be a way. It's the only thing that fits."

Thad heard himself say, "No, you're wrong, Liz. If there *is* such a guy, he doesn't just *love* Stark." He looked down at his arms and saw they were covered with goosebumps.

"No?" Alan asked.

Thad looked up at them both.

"Have you thought that the man who killed Homer Gamache and Frederick Clawson might think he *is* George Stark?"

4

On the steps, Alan said: "I'll keep you in touch, Thad." In one hand he held photocopies—made on the machine in Thad's office—of Frederick Clawson's two letters. Thad thought privately that Alan's willingness to accept photocopies—at least for the present—rather than insisting on taking the originals into evidence was the clearest sign of all that he had given over most of his suspicions.

"And be back to arrest me if you find the loophole in my alibi?" Thad asked, smiling.

"I don't think that's going to happen. The only thing I'd ask is that you keep *me* in touch, as well."

"If something comes up, you mean?"

"Yes. That's what I mean."

"I'm sorry we couldn't be more helpful," Liz told him.

Alan grinned. "You've helped me a lot. I couldn't decide whether to hang on another day, which would mean another night in a cinderblock Ramada Inn room, or drive back to Castle Rock. Thanks to what you've told me, I'm opting for the drive. Starting now. It'll be good to get back. Just lately my wife Annie's been a little under the weather."

"Nothing serious, I hope," Liz said.

"Migraine," Alan said briefly. He started down the walk, then turned back. "There *is* one other thing."

Thad rolled his eyes at Liz. "Here it comes," he said. "It's the old Columbo crumpled-raincoat zinger."

"Nothing like that," Alan said, "but the Washington P.D. is holding back one piece of physical evidence in the Clawson killing. It's common practice; helps to weed out the crazies who like to confess to crimes they didn't commit. Something was written on the wall of Clawson's apartment." Alan paused and then added, almost apologetically: "It was written in the victim's blood. If I tell you what it was, will you give me your word you'll keep it under your hats?"

They nodded.

"The phrase was 'The sparrows are flying again.' Does that mean anything to either of you?"

"No," Liz said.

"No," Thad said in a neutral voice after a momentary hesitation.

Alan's gaze stayed on Thad's face for a moment. "You are quite sure?"

"Quite sure."

Alan sighed. "I doubted if it would, but it seemed like a shot worth taking. There are so many other weird connections, I thought there just might be one more. Goodnight, Thad. Liz. Remember to get in touch if anything occurs."

"We will," Liz said.

"Count on it," Thad agreed.

A moment later they were both inside again, with the door closed against Alan Pangborn—and the dark through which he would make his long trip home.

Ten

LATER THAT NIGHT

1

They carried the sleeping twins upstairs, then began to get ready for bed themselves. Thad undressed to his shorts and undershirt—his form of pajamas—and went into the bathroom. He was brushing his teeth when the shakes hit. He dropped the toothbrush, spat a mouthful of white foam into the basin, and then lurched over to the toilet on legs with no more feeling in them than a pair of wooden stilts.

He retched once—a miserable dry sound—but nothing came up. His stomach began to settle again . . . at least on a trial basis.

When he turned around, Liz was standing in the doorway, wearing a blue nylon nightie that stopped several inches north of the knee. She was looking at him levelly.

"You're keeping secrets, Thad. That's no good. It never was."

He sighed harshly and held his hands out in front of him with the fingers splayed. They were still trembling. "How long have you known?"

"There's been something off-beat about you ever since the Sheriff came back tonight. And when he asked that last question . . . about the thing written on Clawson's wall . . . you might as well have had a neon sign on your forehead."

"Pangborn didn't see any neon."

"Sheriff Pangborn doesn't know you as well as I do . . . but if you didn't see him do a double-take there at the end, you weren't looking. Even *he* saw *something* wasn't quite kosher. It was the way he looked at you."

Her mouth drew down slightly. It emphasized the old lines in her face, the ones he had first seen after the accident in Boston and the miscarriage, the ones which had deepened as she watched him struggle harder and harder to bring water from a well which seemed to have gone dry.

It was around then that his drinking had begun to waver out of control. All these things—Liz's accident, the miscarriage, the critical and financial failure of *Purple Haze* following the wild success of *Machine's Way* under the Stark name, the sudden binge drinking—had combined to bring on a deep depressive state. He had recognized it as a selfish, inward-turning frame of mind, but recognition hadn't helped. Finally he had washed a handful of sleeping pills down his throat with half a bottle of Jack Daniel's. It had been an unenthusiastic suicide attempt . . . but a suicide attempt it had been. All of these things had taken place in a period of three years. It had seemed much longer at the time. At the time it had seemed forever.

And of course, little or none of it had made it into the pages of *People* magazine.

Now he saw Liz looking at him the way she had looked at him then. He hated it. The worry was bad; the mistrust was worse. He thought outright hate would have been easier to bear than that odd, wary look.

"I hate it when you lie to me," she said simply.

"I didn't lie, Liz! For God's sake!"

"Sometimes people lie just by being quiet."

"I was going to tell you anyway," he said. "I was only trying to find my way to it."

But was that true? Was it really? He didn't know. It was weird shit, crazy shit, but that wasn't the reason he might have lied by silence. He had felt the urge to be silent the way a man who has observed blood in his stool or felt a lump in his groin might feel the urge to be silent. Silence in such cases is irrational . . . but fear is also irrational.

And there was something else: he was a writer, an imaginer. He had never met one—including himself—who had more than the vaguest idea of why he or she did *anything.* He sometimes believed that the compulsion to make fiction was no more than a bulwark against confusion, maybe even insanity. It was a desperate imposition of order by people able to find that precious stuff only in their minds . . . never in their hearts.

Inside him a voice whispered for the first time: *Who* are *you when you write, Thad? Who are you* then?

And for that voice he had no answer.

"Well?" Liz asked. Her tone was sharp, teetering on the edge of anger.

He looked up out of his own thoughts, startled. "Pardon?"

"Have you found your way to it? Whatever *it* may be?"

"Look," he said, "I don't understand why you sound so *pissed,* Liz!"

"Because I'm *scared!"* she cried angrily . . . but he saw tears in the corners of her eyes now. "Because you held out on the Sheriff, and I still wonder if you won't hold out on *me!* If I hadn't seen that expression on your face . . ."

"Oh?" Now he began to feel angry himself. "And what expression *was* it? What did it look like to you?"

"You looked guilty," she snapped. "You looked the way you used to look when you were telling people you'd stopped drinking and you hadn't. When——" She stopped then. He did not know what she saw in his face—wasn't sure he *wanted* to know—but it wiped away her anger. A stricken look replaced it. "I'm sorry. That wasn't fair."

"Why not?" he said dully. "It was true. For awhile."

He went back into the bathroom and used the mouthwash to rinse away the last of the toothpaste. It was non-alcoholic mouthwash. Like the cough medicine. And the ersatz vanilla in the kitchen cupboard. He had not taken a drink since completing the last Stark novel.

Her hand touched his shoulder lightly. "Thad . . . we're being angry. That hurts us both, and it won't help whatever is wrong. You said there might be a man out there—a psychotic—who thinks he *is* George Stark. He's killed two people we know. One of them was partly responsible for blowing the Stark pseudonym. It must have occurred to you that you could be high on that man's enemies list. But in spite of that, you held something back. What was that phrase?"

"The sparrows are flying again," Thad said. He looked at his face in the harsh white light thrown by the fluorescents over the bathroom mirror. Same old face. A little shadowy under the eyes, maybe, but it was still the same old face. He was glad. It was no movie star's mug, but it was his.

"Yes. That meant something to you. What was it?"

He turned off the bathroom light and put his arm over her shoulders. They walked to the bed and lay down on it.

"When I was eleven years old," he said, "I had an operation. It was to remove a small tumor from the frontal lobe—I *think* it was the frontal lobe—of my brain. You knew about that."

"Yes?" She was looking at him, puzzled.

"I told you I had bad headaches before that tumor was diagnosed, right?"

"Right."

He began to stroke her thigh absently. She had lovely long legs, and the nightie was really very short.

"What about the sounds?"

"Sounds?" She looked puzzled.

"I didn't think so . . . but you see, it never seemed very important. All that happened such a long time ago. People with brain tumors often have headaches, sometimes they have seizures, and sometimes they have both. Quite often these symptoms have their own symptoms. They're called sensory precursors. The most common ones are smells—pencil shavings, freshly cut onions, mouldy fruit. My sensory precursor was auditory. It was birds."

He looked at her levelly, their noses almost touching. He could feel a stray strand of her hair tickling against his forehead.

"Sparrows, to be exact."

He sat up, not wanting to look at her expression of sudden shock. He took her hand.

"Come on."

"Thad . . . where?"

"The study," he said. "I want to show you something."

2

Thad's study was dominated by a huge oak desk. It was neither fashionably antique nor fashionably modern. It was just an extremely large, extremely serviceable hunk of wood. It stood like a dinosaur under three hanging glass globes; the combined light they threw upon the work-surface was just short of fierce. Very little of the desk's surface was visible. Manuscripts, piles of correspondence, books, and galley-proofs which had been sent to him were stacked everywhere and anywhere. On the white wall beyond the desk was a poster depicting Thad's favorite structure in the whole world: the Flatiron Building in New York. Its improbable wedge shape never failed to delight him.

Beside the typewriter was the manuscript of his new novel, *The Golden Dog.* On top of the typewriter was that day's output. Six pages. It was his usual number . . . when he was working as himself, that was. As Stark he usually did eight, and sometimes ten.

"This is what I was fooling with before Pangborn showed up," he said, picking up the little stack of pages on top of the typewriter and handing them to her. "Then the sound came—the sound of the sparrows. For the second time today, only this time it was much more intense. You see what's written across that top sheet?"

She looked for a long time, and he could see only

her hair and the top of her head. When she looked back at him, all the color had dropped out of her face. Her lips were pressed together in a narrow gray line.

"It's the same," she whispered. *"It's the very same.* Oh, Thad, what *is* this? What—"

She swayed and he moved forward, afraid for a moment she was actually going to faint. He grasped her shoulders, his foot tangled in the X-shaped foot of his office chair, and he almost spilled them both onto his desk.

"Are you all right?"

"No," she said in a thin voice. "Are you?"

"Not exactly," he said. "I'm sorry. Same old clumsy Beaumont. As a knight in shining armor, I make a hell of a good doorstop."

"You wrote this *before* Pangborn ever showed up," she said. She seemed to find this impossible to fully grasp. *"Before."*

"That's right."

"What does it *mean?"* She was looking at him with frantic intensity, the pupils of her eyes large and dark in spite of the bright light.

"I don't know," he said. "I thought you might have an idea."

She shook her head and put the pages back on his desk. Then she rubbed her hand against the short nylon skirt of her nightie, as if she had touched something nasty. Thad didn't believe she was aware of what she was doing, and he didn't tell her.

"Now do you understand why I held it back?" he asked.

"Yes . . . I think so."

"What would he have said? Our practical Sheriff from Maine's smallest county, who puts his faith in computer print-outs from A.S.R. and I. and eye-witness testimony? Our Sheriff who found it more plausible that I might be hiding a twin brother than that someone has somehow discovered how to duplicate fingerprints? What would he have said to *this?*"

"I . . . I don't know." She was struggling to bring herself back, to haul herself out of the shock-wave. He had seen her do it before, but that did not lessen his admiration for her. "I don't know what he would have said, Thad."

"Me either. I think at the very worst, he might assume some foreknowledge of the crime. It's probably more likely he'd believe I ran up here and wrote that after he left tonight."

"Why would you do a thing like that? *Why?*"

"I think insanity would be the first assumption," Thad said dryly. "I think a cop like Pangborn would be a lot more likely to believe insanity than to accept an occurrence which seems to have no explanation outside the paranormal. But if you think I'm wrong to hold this back until I have a chance to make something of it myself—and I might be—say so. We can call the Castle Rock Sheriff's Office and leave a message for him."

She shook her head. "I don't know. I've heard—on some talk-show or other, I guess—about psychic links . . ."

"Do you believe in them?"

"I never had any reason to think much about the idea one way or the other," she said. "Now I guess I do." She reached over and picked up the sheet with the words scrawled on it. "You wrote it with one of George's pencils," she said.

"It was the closest thing to hand, that's all," he

said testily. He thought briefly of the Scripto pen and then shut it out of his mind. "And they aren't *George's* pencils and never were. They're mine. I'm getting goddam tired of referring to him as a separate person. It's lost any marginal cuteness it might once have had."

"Yet you used one of his phrases today, too—'lie me an alibi.' I never heard you use it before, outside of a book. Was that just coincidence?"

He started to tell her that it was, of *course* it was, and stopped. It *probably* was, but in light of what he had written on that sheet of paper, how could he know for sure?

"I don't know."

"Were you in a trance, Thad? Were you in a trance when you wrote this?"

Slowly, reluctantly, he replied: "Yes. I think I was."

"Is this all that happened? Or was there more?"

"I can't remember," he said, and then added even more reluctantly: "I think I might have said something, but I really can't remember."

She looked at him for a long time and said, "Let's go to bed."

"Do you think we'll sleep, Liz?"

She laughed forlornly.

3

But twenty minutes later he was actually drifting away when Liz's voice brought him back. "You have to go to the doctor," she said. "On Monday."

"There are no headaches this time," he protested. "Just the bird-sounds. And that *weird* thing

I wrote." He paused, then added hopefully: "You don't suppose it could just be a coincidence?"

"I don't know what it is," Liz said, "but I've got to tell you, Thad, coincidence is *very* low on my list."

For some reason this struck them both as funny and they lay in bed, giggling as softly as they could, so as not to wake the babies, and holding each other. It was all right between them again, anyway—there was not much Thad felt he could be sure of just now, but that was one thing. It was all right. The storm had passed. The sorry old bones had been buried again, at least for the time being.

"I'll make the appointment," she said when their giggles had dried up.

"No," he said. "I'll do it."

"And you won't indulge in any creative forgetting?"

"No. I'll do it first thing Monday. Honest John."

"All right, then." She sighed. "It'll be a goddam miracle if I get any sleep." But five minutes later she was breathing softly and regularly, and not five minutes after that, Thad was asleep himself.

4

And dreamed the dream again.

It was the same (or seemed so, anyway) right up until the very end: Stark took him through the deserted house, always remaining behind him, telling Thad he was mistaken when Thad insisted in a trembling, distraught voice that this was his own house. You are quite wrong, Stark said from behind his right shoulder (or was it the left? and did it

matter?). The owner of this house, he told Thad
again, was dead. The owner of this house was in
that fabled place where all rail service terminated,
that place which everyone down here (wherever
that was) called Endsville. Everything the same.
Until they got to the back hall, where Liz was no
longer alone. Frederick Clawson had joined her. He
was naked except for an absurd leather coat. And he
was just as dead as Liz.

From over his shoulder, Stark said reflectively:
"Down here, that's what happens to squealers.
They get turned into fool's stuffing. Now *he's* taken
care of. I'm going to take care of all of them, one by
one. Just make sure I don't have to take care of *you.*
The sparrows are flying again, Thad—remember
that. The sparrows are flying."

And then, outside the house, Thad *heard* them:
not just thousands of them but millions, perhaps
billions, and the day turned dark as the gigantic
flock of birds first began to cross the sun and then
blotted it out entirely.

"I can't see!" he screamed, and from behind him
George Stark whispered: "They're flying again, old
hoss. Don't forget. *And don't get in my way.*"

He woke up, trembling and cold all over, and
this time sleep was a long time coming. He lay
in the dark, thinking how absurd it was, the idea
the dream had brought with it—perhaps it had
the first time, too, but it had been so much clearer
this time. How totally absurd. The fact that he
had always visualized Stark and Alexis Machine
as looking alike (and why not, since in a very real
sense both had been born at the same time, with
Machine's Way), both tall and broad-shouldered—
men who looked not as if they had grown but as if

they had somehow been built out of solid blocks of material—and both blonde . . . that fact didn't change the absurdity. Pen names did not come to life and murder people. He would tell Liz at breakfast, and they would laugh over it . . . well, maybe they wouldn't actually *laugh,* considering the circumstances, but they would share a rueful grin.

I will call it my William Wilson complex, he thought, drifting back into sleep again. But when the morning came, the dream did not seem worth talking about—not on top of everything else. So he didn't . . . but as the day passed, he found his mind returning to it again and again, considering it like a dark jewel.

Eleven

ENDSVILLE

1

Early Monday morning, before Liz could bug him about it, he made an appointment with Dr. Hume. The removal of the tumor in 1960 was a part of his medical records. He told Hume that he had recently had two recurrences of the bird-sounds which had presaged his headaches during the months leading up to the diagnosis and the excision. Dr. Hume wanted to know if the headaches themselves had returned. Thad told him they had not.

He said nothing about the trance state, or what he had written while in that state, or what had been found written on the apartment wall of a murder victim in Washington, D.C. It already seemed as distant as last night's dream. In fact, he found himself trying to pooh-pooh the whole thing.

Dr. Hume, however, took it seriously. Very seriously. He ordered Thad to go to the Eastern Maine Medical Center that afternoon. He wanted both a cranial X-ray series and a computerized axial tomography . . . a CAT-scan.

Thad went. He sat for the pictures and then put his head inside a machine which looked like an industrial clothes-dryer. It clashed and ratcheted for fifteen minutes, and then he was released from captivity . . . for the time being, anyway. He telephoned Liz, told her they could expect results around the end of the week, and said he was going up to his office at the University for a little while.

"Have you thought any more about calling Sheriff Pangborn?" she asked.

"Let's wait for the test results," he said. "Once we see what we've got, maybe we can decide."

2

He was in his office, clearing a semester's worth of deadwood out of his desk and off his shelves, when the birds began to cry inside his head again. There were a few isolated twitters, these were joined by others, and they quickly became a deafening chorus.

White sky—he saw a white sky broken by the silhouettes of houses and telephone poles. And everywhere there were sparrows. They lined every roof, crowded every pole, waiting only for the command of the group mind. Then they would explode skyward with a sound like thousands of sheets flapping in a brisk wind.

Thad staggered blindly toward his desk, groped for his chair, found it, collapsed into it.

Sparrows.

Sparrows and the white sky of late spring.

The sound filled his head, a jumbled cacophony, and when he drew a sheet of paper toward him and began to write, he was not aware of what he was doing. His head lolled back on his neck; his eyes stared sightlessly at the ceiling. The pen flew back and forth and up and down, seeming to do so of its own accord.

In his head, all the birds took wing in a dark cloud that blotted out the white sky of March in the Ridgeway section of Bergenfield, New Jersey.

3

He came back to himself less than five minutes after the first isolated cries had begun to sound in his mind. He was sweating heavily and his left wrist throbbed, but there was no headache. He looked down, saw the paper on his desk—it was the back of an order-form for complimentary American Lit textbooks—and stared stupidly at what was written there.

SIS
SIS
CATS FOOLS NOW SISSY FLYING AGAIN
PHONE MIR FOREVER FOOLS
ENDSVILLE SIS
TERMINATE
SIS THE CATS PHONE SISSY
THE CUTS RAZOR SIS DOWN
SPARROWS MIR SIS RAZOR HERE
AND FOREVER MIR SIS RAZOR SIS
SISSY NOW AND FOREVER
MIR CATS STUFF SISSY SPARROW

"It means nothing," he whispered. He was rubbing his temples with the tips of his fingers, waiting for the headache to start, or for the scrawled words on the paper to connect and make some sense.

He did not want either of those things to happen . . . and neither of them did. The words were
just words, repeated over and over. Some were obviously culled from his dream of Stark; the others
were so much unconnected gibberish.

And his head felt just fine.

I'm not going to tell Liz this time, he thought.
*Be damned if I will And not just because I'm scared,
either . . . although I am. It's perfectly simple—not all
secrets are bad secrets. Some are good secrets. Some are necessary secrets. And this one is both of those.*

He didn't know if that was really true or not,
but he discovered something which was tremendously liberating: he didn't care. He was very tired
of thinking and thinking and still not knowing.
He was also tired of being frightened, like a man
who has entered a cave on a lark and now begins to
suspect he is lost.

Stop thinking about it, then. That's the solution.

He suspected that *was* true. He did not know if
he could do it or not . . . but he intended to give
it the old college try. Very slowly he reached out,
took the order-form in both hands, and began to
tear it into strips. The stew of squirming words
written on it began to disappear. He turned the
strips lengthwise, tore them across again, and
tossed the pieces in the wastebasket, where they
rested like confetti on top of all the other crap he
had dumped in there. He sat staring at the pieces
for almost two minutes, half-expecting them to
fly back together and then return to his desk, like
the images in a reel of movie-film which is run
backward.

At last he picked up the wastebasket and took
it down the hall to a stainless-steel panel set into

the wall next to the elevator. The sign beneath read INCINERATOR.

He opened the panel and dumped his trash down the black chute.

"There," he said into the odd summer silence of the English-Math building. "All gone."

Down here we call that fool's stuffing.

"Up here we call it horseshit," he muttered, and walked back down to his office with the empty wastebasket in his hand.

It was gone. Down the chute into oblivion. And until his test results came back from the hospital— or until there was another blackout, or trance, or fugue, or whatever the hell it was—he intended to say nothing. Nothing at all. More than likely the words written on that sheet of paper had been wholly grown in his own mind, like the dream of Stark and the empty house, and had nothing at all to do with either the murder of Homer Gamache or that of Frederick Clawson.

Down here in Endsville, where all rail service terminates.

"It means nothing at all," Thad said, in a flat, emphatic voice . . . but when he left the University that day, he was almost fleeing.

Twelve

SIS

She knew something was wrong when she went to slide her key into the big Kreig lock on her apartment door and instead of slipping into the slot with its familiar and reassuring series of clicks, it pushed the door open instead. There was no moment of thinking how stupid she had been, going off to work and leaving her apartment door unlocked behind her, gee, Miriam, why not just hang a note on the door that says HELLO ROBBERS, I KEEP EXTRA CASH IN THE WOK ON THE TOP KITCHEN SHELF?

There was no moment like that because once you'd been in New York six months, maybe even four, you didn't forget. Maybe you only locked up when you were going away on vacation if you lived in the sticks, and maybe you forgot to lock up once in awhile when you went to work if you lived in a small city like Fargo, North Dakota, or Ames, Iowa, but after you'd been in the maggoty old Big Apple for awhile, you locked up even if you were just taking a cup of sugar to a neighbor down the hall. Forgetting to lock up would be like exhaling a breath and just forgetting to take the next one. The city was full of museums and galleries, but the city was also full of junkies and psychos, and you didn't take chances. Not unless you had been born stupid, and Miriam had not been born that way. A little silly, maybe, but not stupid.

So she knew something was wrong, and while the thieves Miriam was sure had broken into her apartment had probably left three or four hours ago, taking everything there was even a remote chance of hocking (not to mention the eighty or ninety dollars in the wok . . . and maybe the wok itself, now that she thought of it; after all, was it not a hockable wok?), they *could* still be in there. It was the assumption you made, anyway, just as boys who have received their first real guns are taught, before they are taught anything else, to assume the gun is always loaded, that even when you take it out of the box in which it came from the factory, the gun is loaded.

She began to step away from the door. She did this almost at once, even before the door had stopped its short inward swing, but it was already too late. A hand came out of the darkness, shooting through the two-inch gap between door and jamb like a bullet. It clamped over her hand. Her keys dropped to the hall carpet.

Miriam Cowley opened her mouth to scream. The big blonde man had been standing just inside the door, waiting patiently for just over four hours now, not drinking coffee, not smoking cigarettes. He wanted a cigarette, and would have one as soon as this was over, but before, the smell might have alerted her—New Yorkers were like very small animals cowering in the underbrush, senses attuned for danger even when they thought they were having a good time.

He had her right wrist in his right hand before she could even think. Now he put the palm of his left hand against the door, bracing it, and yanked the woman forward just as hard as he could. The door looked like wood, but it was of course metal, as were all good apartment doors in the maggoty old Big Apple. The side of her face struck its edge with a thud. Two of her teeth broke off at the gum-line and cut her mouth. Her lips, which had tight-ened, relaxed in shock and blood spilled over the lower one. Droplets spattered on the door. Her cheekbone snapped like a twig.

She sagged, semi-conscious. The blonde man released her. She collapsed to the hall carpet. This had to be very quick. According to New York folk-lore, no one in the maggoty old Big Apple gave a shit what went down, as long as it didn't go down on *them*. According to the folklore, a psycho could stab a woman twenty or forty times outside of a twenty-chair barber-shop at high noon on Sev-enth Avenue and no one would say a thing except maybe *Could you trim it a little higher over the ears* or *I think I'll skip the cologne this time, Joe.* The blonde man knew the folklore was false. For small, hunted animals, curiosity is a part of the survival package. Protect your own skin, yes, that was the name of the game, but an incurious animal was apt to be a dead animal very soon. Therefore, speed was of the essence.

He opened the door, seized Miriam by the hair, and yanked her inside.

A bare moment later he heard the snick of a deadbolt being released down the hall, followed by the click of an opening door. He didn't have to look out to see the face which would now be peering out of another apartment, a little hairless rabbit face, nose almost twitching.

"You didn't break it, Miriam, did you?" he asked in a loud voice. He changed to a higher register, not quite falsetto, cupped both hands about two inches from his mouth to create a sound baffle, and became the woman. "I don't think so. Can you help me pick it up?" Removed his hands. Reverted to his normal tone of voice.

"Sure. Just a sec."

He closed the door and looked out through the peephole. It was a fish-eye lens, giving a distorted wide-angle view of the corridor, and in it he saw exactly what he had expected to see: a white face peering around the edge of a door on the other side of the hall, peering like a rabbit looking out of its hole.

The face retreated.

The door shut.

It did not *slam* shut; it simply *swung* shut. Silly Miriam had dropped something. The man with her—maybe a boyfriend, maybe her ex—was helping her pick it up. Nothing to worry about. All does and baby rabbits, as you were.

Miriam was moaning, starting to come to.

The blonde man reached into his pocket, brought out the straight-razor, and shook it open. The blade gleamed in the dim glow of the only light he'd left on, a table lamp in the living room.

Her eyes opened. She looked up at him, seeing his face upside down as he leaned over her. Her mouth was smeared red, as if she had been eating strawberries.

He showed her the straight-razor. Her eyes, which had been dazed and cloudy, came alert and opened wide. Her wet red mouth opened.

"Make a sound and I'll cut you, sis," he said, and her mouth closed.

He wound a hand in her hair again and pulled

her into the living room. Her skirt whispered on the polished wood floor. Her butt caught a throw-rug and it snow-plowed beneath her. She moaned in pain.

"Don't do that," he said. "I told you."

They were in the living room. It was small but pleasant. Cozy. French Impressionist prints on the walls. A framed poster which advertised *Cats:* NOW AND FOREVER, it said. Dried flowers. A small sectional sofa, upholstered in some nubby wheat-colored fabric. A bookcase. In the bookcase he could see both of Beaumont's books on one shelf and all four of Stark's on another. Beaumont's were on a higher shelf. That was wrong, but he had to assume this bitch just didn't know any better.

He let go of her hair. "Sit on the couch, sis. That end." He pointed at the end of the couch next to the little end-table where the phone and the message recorder sat.

"Please," she whispered, making no move to get up. Her mouth and cheek were beginning to swell up now, and the word came out mushy: *Preesh.* "Anything. Everything. Money's in the wok." *Moneesh inna wok.*

"Sit on the couch. That end." This time he pointed the razor at her face with one hand while he pointed at the couch with the other.

She scrambled onto the couch and cringed as far into the cushions as they would allow, her dark eyes very wide. She swiped at her mouth with her hand and looked unbelievingly at the blood on her palm for a moment before looking back at him.

"What do you want?" *Wha ooo you wan?* It was like listening to someone talk through a mouthful of food.

"I want you to make a phone call, sissy. That's all." He picked up the telephone and used the hand holding the straight-razor long enough to thumb the ANNOUNCE button on the phone answering machine. Then he held the telephone handset out to her. It was one of the old-fashioned ones that sit in a cradle looking like a slightly melted dumbbell. Much heavier than the handset of a Princess phone. He knew it, and saw from the subtle tightening of her body when he gave it to her that she knew it, too. An edge of a smile showed on the blonde man's lips. It didn't show anyplace else; just on his lips. There was no summer in that smile.

"You're thinking you could brain me with that thing, aren't you, sis?" he asked her. "Let me tell you something—that's not a happy thought. And you know what happens to people who lose their happy thoughts, don't you?" When she didn't answer, he said, "They fall out of the sky. It's true. I saw it in a cartoon once. So you hold that telephone receiver in your lap and concentrate on getting your happy thoughts back."

She stared at him, all eyes. Blood ran slowly down her chin. A drop fell off and landed on the bodice of her dress. Never get that out, sis, the blonde man thought. They say you can get it out if you rinse the spot fast in cold water, but it isn't so. They have machines. Spectroscopes. Gas chromatographs. Ultraviolet. Lady Macbeth was right.

"If that bad thought comes back, I'll see it in your eyes, sis. They're such big, dark eyes. You wouldn't want one of those big dark eyes running down your cheek, would you?"

She shook her head so fast and hard her hair flew in a storm around her face. And all the time she was shaking her head, those beautiful dark eyes never left his face, and the blonde man felt a stirring along his leg. Sir, do you have a folding ruler in your pocket or are you just happy to see me?

This time the smile touched his eyes as well as his mouth, and he thought she relaxed just the tiniest bit.

"I want you to lean forward and dial Thad Beaumont's number."

She only gazed at him, her eyes bright and lustrous with shock.

"Beaumont," he said patiently. "The writer. Do it, sis. Time fleets ever onward like the winged feet of Mercury."

"My book," she said. Her mouth was now too swollen to close comfortably and it was getting harder to understand her. *Eye ook,* it sounded like.

"Eye ook?" he asked. "Is that anything like a skyhook? I don't know what you're talking about. Make sense, sissy."

Carefully, painfully, enunciating: "My book. *Book.* My address book. I don't remember his number."

The straight-razor slipped through the air toward her. It seemed to make a sound like a human whisper. That was probably just imagination, but both of them heard it, nevertheless. She shrank back even further into the wheat-colored cushions, swollen lips pulling into a grimace. He turned the razor so the blade caught the low, mellow light of the table lamp. He tipped it, let the light run along it like water, then looked at her as if they would both be crazy not to admire such a lovely thing.

"Don't shit me, sis." Now there was a soft Southern slur to his words. "That's one thing you never want to do, not when you're dealing with a fella like me. Now dial his motherfucking number." She might not have *Beaumont's* number committed to memory, not all that much business to do there, but she would have *Stark's.* In the book biz, Stark was your basic movin unit, and it just so happened the phone number was the same for both men.

Tears began to spill out of her eyes. "I don't remember," she moaned. *I doan eemembah.*

The blonde man got ready to cut her—not because he was angry with her but because when you let a lady like this get away with one lie it always led to another—and then reconsidered. It was, he decided, perfectly possible that she had temporarily lost her grip on such mundane things as telephone numbers, even those of important clients like Beaumont/Stark. She was in shock. If he had asked her to dial the number of her own agency, she might well have come up just as blank.

But since it was Thad Beaumont and not Rick Cowley they were talking about, he could help.

"Okay," he said. "Okay, sis. You're upset. I understand. I don't know if you believe this or not, but I even sympathize. And you're in luck, because it just so happens I know the number myself. I know it as well as I know my own, you might say. And do you know what? I'm not even going to make you dial it, partly because I don't want to sit here until hell freezes over, waiting for you to get it right, but also because I *do* sympathize. I am going to lean over and dial it myself. Do you know what that means?"

Miriam Cowley shook her head. Her dark eyes appeared to have eaten up most of her face.

"It means I'm going to trust you. But only so far;

only just so far and no further, old girl. Are you listening? Are you getting all this?"

Miriam nodded frantically, her hair flying. God, he loved a woman with a lot of hair.

"Good. That's good. While I dial the phone, sis, you want to keep your eyes right on this blade. It will help you keep your happy thoughts in good order."

He leaned forward and began to pick out the number on the old-fashioned rotary dial. Amplified clicking sounds came from the message recorder beside the phone as he did so. It sounded like a carny Wheel of Fortune slowing down. Miriam Cowley sat with the phone handset in her lap, looking alternately at the razor and the flat, crude planes of this horrible stranger's face.

"Talk to him," the blonde man said. "If his wife answers, tell her it's Miriam in New York and you want to talk to her man. I know your mouth is swollen, but make whoever answers know it's you. Put out for me, sis. If you don't want your face to wind up looking like a Picasso portrait, you put out for me just fine." The last two words came out *jest fahn.*

"What . . . What do I say?"

The blonde man smiled. She was a piece of work, all right. Mighty tasty. All that hair. More stirrings from the area below his belt-buckle. It was getting lively down there.

The phone was ringing. They could both hear it through the answering machine.

"You'll think of the right thing, sis."

There was a click as the phone was picked up. The blonde man waited until he heard Beaumont's voice say hello, and then with the speed of a striking snake he leaned forward and drew the straight-razor down Miriam Cowley's left cheek, pulling open a flap of skin there. Blood poured out in a freshet. Miriam shrieked.

"Hello!" Beaumont's voice barked. "Hello, who is this? Goddammit, is it you?"

Yes, it's me, all right, you son of a bitch, the blonde man thought. It's me and you *know* it's me, don't you?

"Tell him who you are and what's happenin here!" he barked at Miriam. "Do it! Don't make me tell you twice!"

"Who's that?" Beaumont cried. *"What's going on? Who is this?"*

Miriam shrieked again. Blood splattered on the wheat-colored sofa cushions. There wasn't just a single drop of blood on the bodice of her dress now; it was soaked.

"Do what I say or I'll cut your fuckin head off with this thing!"

"Thad there's a man here!" she screamed into the telephone. In her pain and terror, she was enunciating clearly again. *"There's a bad man here! Thad THERE'S A BAD MAN H—"*

"SAY YOUR NAME!" he roared at her, and sliced the straight-razor through the air an inch in front of her eyes.

She cringed back, wailing.

"Who is this? Wh—"

"MIRIAM!" she shrieked, *"OH THAD DON'T LET HIM CUT ME AGAIN DON'T LET THE BAD MAN CUT ME AGAIN DON'T—"*

George Stark swept the straight-razor through the kinked telephone cord. The phone machine uttered one angry bark of static and fell silent.

It was good. It could have been better; he'd wanted to do her, really wanted to have it off with her. It had been a long time since he'd wanted to have it off with a woman, but he had wanted this one, and he wasn't going to get her. There had been too much screaming. The rabbits would be poking their heads out of their holes again, scenting the air for the big predator that was padding around somewhere in the jungle just beyond the glow of their pitiful little electric campfires.

She was still shrieking.

It was clear she had lost all her happy thoughts.

So Stark grabbed her by the hair again, bent her head back until she was staring at the ceiling, shrieking at the ceiling, and cut her throat.

The room fell silent.

"There, sis," he said tenderly. He folded the straight-razor back into its handle and put it into his pocket. Then he reached out his bloody left hand and closed her eyes. The cuff of his shirt was immediately soaked in warm blood because her jugular was still pumping the claret, but the proper thing to do was the proper thing to do. When it was a woman, you closed her eyes. It didn't matter how bad she had been, it didn't matter if she was a junkie whore who had sold her own kids to buy dope, you closed her eyes.

And she was only a small part of it. Rick Cowley was a different story.

And the man who had written the magazine piece.

And the bitch who had taken the pictures, especially that one of the tombstone. A bitch, yes, a right bitch, but he would close *her* eyes, too.

And when they were all taken care of, it would

be time to talk to Thad himself. No intermediaries; *mano a mano*. Time to make Thad see reason. After he had done all of them, he fully expected Thad to be *ready* to see reason. If he wasn't, there were ways to make him see it.

He was, after all, a man with a wife—a very beautiful wife, a veritable queen of air and darkness.

And he had kids.

He held his forefinger in the warm jet of Miriam's blood, and quickly began to print on the wall. He had to go back twice in order to get enough, but the message was up there in short order, printed above the woman's lolling head. She could have read it upside down if her eyes had been open.

And, of course, if she had still been alive.

He leaned forward and kissed Miriam's cheek. "Goodnight, sissy," he said, and left the apartment.

The man across the hall was looking out his door again.

When he saw the tall, blood-smeared blonde man emerge from Miriam's apartment, he slammed the door and locked it.

Wise, George Stark thought, striding down the hall toward the elevator. Very fucking wise.

Meantime, he had to be moving along. He had no time to linger.

There was other business to take care of tonight.

Thirteen

SHEER PANIC

1

For several moments—he never had any idea how long—Thad was in the grip of a panic so utter and complete he was literally unable to function in any way. It was really amazing that he was even able to breathe. Later he would think that the only time he had ever felt remotely like this was when he was ten and he and a couple of friends had decided to go swimming in mid-May. This was at least three weeks earlier than any of them had ever gone swimming before, but it seemed a fine idea all the same; the day was clear and very hot for May in New Jersey, temperatures in the high eighties. The three of them had walked down to Lake Davis, their satiric name for the little pond a mile from Thad's house in Bergenfield. He was the first out of his clothes and into his bathing suit, hence the first into the water. He simply cannonballed in from the bank, and he still thought he might have come close to dying then—just *how* close was not anything he really wanted to know. The *air* that day might have felt like mid-summer, but the *water* felt like that last day in early winter before ice skims itself over the surface. His nervous system had momentarily short-circuited. His breath had stopped dead in his lungs, his heart had stopped in the very act of beating, and when he broke the surface it was as if he were a car with a dead battery and he needed a jumpstart, needed it quick, and didn't know how to do it. He remembered how bright the sunlight had been, making ten thousand gold sparks on the blue-black surface of the water, he remembered Harry Black and Randy Wister standing on the bank, Harry pulling his faded gym-trunks up and over his generous butt, Randy standing there naked with his bathing suit in one hand and yelling *How's the water, Thad?* as he came bursting up, and all he had been able to think was *I'm dying, I'm right here in the sun with my two best friends and it's after school and I have no homework and* Mr. Blandings Builds His Dream House *is going to be on the Early Show tonight and Mom said I could eat in front of the TV but I'll never see it because I'm going to be dead.* What had been easy, uncomplicated breath only seconds before was a clogged athletic sock in his throat, something he could neither push out nor suck in. His heart lay in his chest like a small cold stone. Then it had broken, he sucked in a great, whooping breath, his body rashed out in a billion goose-pimples, and he had answered Randy with the unthinking malicious glee which is the sole province of little boys: *Water's fine! Not too cold! Jump in!* It occurred to him only years later that he could have killed one or both of them, just as he had almost killed himself.

That was how it was now; he was in exactly the same sort of whole-body lock. They had a name for something like this in the army—a cluster fuck. Yes. Good name. When it came to terminology, the army was great. He was sitting here in the middle of a great big cluster fuck. He sat on the chair, not in it but *on* it, leaning forward, the phone still in his hand, staring at the dead eye on the television. He was aware that Liz had come into the doorway, she was asking him first who it was and then what was wrong, and it was like that day at Lake Davis, just like it, his breath a dirty cotton sock in his throat, one that wouldn't go either way, all the lines of communication between brain and heart suddenly down, we are sorry for this unscheduled stop, service will be resumed as soon as possible, or maybe service will *never* be resumed, but either way, please enjoy your stay in beautiful downtown Endsville, the place where all rail service terminates.

Then it just broke, as it had broken that other time, and he took a gasping breath. His heart took two rapid, random galloping beats in his chest and then resumed its regular rhythm . . . although its pace was still fast, much too fast.

That scream. Jesus Christ Our Lord, that *scream.*

Liz was running across the room now, and he was aware that she'd snatched the telephone receiver out of his hand only when he saw her shouting *Hello?* and *Who is this?* into it again and again. Then she heard the hum of the broken connection and put it back down.

"Miriam," he managed to say at last as Liz turned to him. "It was Miriam and she was screaming."

Except in books, I've never killed anyone.

The sparrows are flying.

Down here we call that fool's stuffing.

Down here we call it Endsville.

Gonna hook back north, hoss. You gotta lie me an alibi, because I'm gonna hook back north. Gonna cut me some beef.

"Miriam? Screaming? Miriam *Cowley?* Thad, what's going *on?*"

"It *is* him," Thad said. "I knew it was. I think I knew it almost from the first, and then today . . . this afternoon . . . I had another one."

"Another *what?*" Her fingers pressed against the side of her neck, rubbing hard. "Another blackout? Another trance?"

"Both," he said. "The sparrows again first. I wrote a lot of crazy shit on a piece of paper while I was knocked out. I threw it away, but *her* name was on the sheet, Liz, *Miriam's* name was part of what I wrote this time when I was out . . . and . . ."

He stopped. His eyes were widening, widening.

"What? Thad, what is it?" She seized one of his arms, shook it. *"What is it?"*

"She has a poster in her living room," he said. He heard his voice as though it were someone else's—a voice coming from far away. Over an intercom, perhaps. "A poster from a Broadway musical. *Cats.* I saw it the last time we were there. *Cats,* NOW AND FOREVER. I wrote that down, too. I wrote it because he was *there,* and so I was there, part of me was, part of me was seeing with his eyes . . ."

He looked at her. He looked at her with his wide, wide eyes.

"This is no tumor, Liz. At least, not one that's inside of my body."

"I don't know what you're talking about!" Liz nearly screamed.

"I've got to call Rick," he muttered. Part of his mind seemed to be lifting off, moving brilliantly and talking to itself in images and crude bright symbols. It was this way when he wrote, some-times, but it was the first time he could remember ever being this way in real life—*was* writing real life? he wondered suddenly. He didn't think it was. More like intermission.

"Thad *please!*"

"I've got to warn Rick. He may be in danger."

"Thad, you're not making sense!"

No; of course he wasn't. And if he stopped to explain, he would appear to be making even less . . . and while he paused to confide his fears to his wife, probably accomplishing nothing but causing her to wonder how long it took to get the proper committal papers filled out, George Stark could be crossing the nine city blocks in Manhattan that separated Rick's apartment from his ex-wife's. Sitting in the back of a cab or behind the wheel of a stolen car, hell, sitting behind the wheel of the black Toronado from his dream, for all Thad knew—if you were going to go this far down the path to insanity, why not just say fuck it and go all the way? Sitting there, smoking, getting ready to kill Rick as he had Miriam—

Had he killed her?

Maybe he had just frightened her, left her sobbing and in shock. Or maybe he had hurt her— only, on second thought, make that probably. What had she said? *Don't let him cut me again, don't let the bad man cut me again.* And on paper it had said *cuts.* And . . . hadn't it also said *terminate?*

Yes. Yes, it had. But that had to do with the dream, didn't it? That had to do with Endsville, the place where all rail service terminates . . . didn't it?

He prayed that it did.

He had to get her help, at least had to try, and he had to warn Rick. But if he just called Rick, called him out of a clear blue sky and told him to be on his guard, Rick would want to know why.

What's wrong, Thad? What's happened?

And if he so much as mentioned Miriam's name Rick would be up and off like a shot to her place, because Rick still cared for her. He still cared a hell of a lot. And then he would be the one to find her . . . maybe in pieces (part of Thad's mind tried to shy away from that thought, that *image,* but the rest of his mind was relentless, forcing him to see what pretty Miriam would look like, chopped up like meat on a butcher's counter).

And maybe that was just what Stark was counting on. Stupid Thad, sending Rick into a trap. Stupid Thad, doing his job for him.

But haven't I been doing his job for him all along? Isn't that what the pen name was all about, for Christ's sake?

He could feel his mind jamming up again, softly closing itself into a knot like a charley horse, into a cluster fuck, and he couldn't afford that, just now he couldn't afford that at *all.*

"Thad . . . *please!* Tell me what's going on!"

He took a deep breath and grasped her cold arms in his cold hands.

"It was the same man who killed Homer Gamache and Clawson. He was with Miriam. He was . . . threatening her. I hope that's all he was doing. I don't know. She screamed. The line went dead."

"Oh, Thad! Jesus!"

"There's no time for either of us to have hysterics," he said, and thought, *Although God knows part of me wants to.* "Go upstairs. Get your address book. I don't have Miriam's phone number and address in mine. I think you do."

"What did you mean, you knew it almost from the first?"

"There's no time for that now, Liz. Get your address book. Get it quick. Okay?"

She hesitated a moment longer.

"She may be hurt! Go!"

She turned and ran from the room. He heard the quick, light pad of her feet going upstairs and tried to get his thoughts working again.

Don't call Rick. If it *is* a trap, calling Rick would be a very bad idea.

Okay—we've gotten that far. It's not much, but it's a start. Who, then?

The New York City Police Department? No— they would be full of time-consuming questions—how come a fellow in Maine was reporting a crime in New York, for starters. Not the N.Y.P.D. Another very bad idea.

Pangborn.

His mind seized on the idea. He would call Pangborn first. He would have to be careful what he said, at least for now. What he might or might not decide to say later on—about the blackouts, about the sound of the sparrows, about *Stark*— could take care of itself. For now, Miriam was the important thing. If Miriam was hurt but still alive, it wouldn't do to inject any elements into the situation which might slow Pangborn down. *He* was the one who'd have to call the New York cops. They would act faster and ask fewer questions if word came from one of their own, even if this particular brother cop happened to be up in Maine.

But Miriam first. Pray God she answered the phone.

Liz came flying back into the room with her

address book. Her face was almost as pale as it had been after she had finally succeeded in bringing William and Wendy into the world. "Here it is," she said. She was breathing fast, nearly panting.

This is going to be all right, he thought to say to her, but held it back. He didn't want to say anything which could so easily turn out to be a lie . . . and the sound of Miriam's scream suggested things had gone well past the all-right stage. That for Miriam, at least, things might *never* return to the all-right stage.

There's a man here, there's a bad man here.

Thad thought of George Stark and shuddered a little. He was a very bad man, all right. Thad knew the truth of that better than anyone. He had, after all, built George Stark from the ground up . . . hadn't he?

"We're okay," he said to Liz—that much, at least, was true. *So far,* his mind insisted on adding in a whisper. "Get hold of yourself if you can, babe. Hyperventilating and fainting on the floor won't help Miriam."

She sat down, ramrod straight, staring at him while her teeth gnawed relentlessly at her lower lip. He started to punch Miriam's number. His fingers, shaking a little, stuttered on the second digit, hitting it twice. *You're a great one to be telling people to get hold of themselves.* He drew in another long breath, held it, hit the disconnect button on the phone, and started in again, forcing himself to slow down. He hit the last button and listened to the deliberate clicks of the connection falling into place.

Let her be all right, God, and if she's not entirely all right, if You can't manage that, at least let her be all right enough to answer the telephone. Please.

But the phone didn't ring. There was only the insistent dah-dah-dah of a busy signal. Maybe it really *was* busy; maybe she was calling Rick or the hospital. Or maybe the phone was off the hook.

There was another possibility, though, he thought as he pushed the disconnect button again. Maybe Stark had pulled the phone cord out of the wall. Or maybe

(*don't let the bad man cut me again*)

he had cut it.

As he had cut Miriam.

Razor, Thad thought, and a shudder twisted up his back. That had been another of the words in the stew of them he had written that afternoon. *Razor.*

2

The next half-hour or so was a return to the ominous surrealism he had felt when Pangborn and the two State Troopers had turned up on his doorstep to arrest him for a murder he hadn't even known about. There was no sense of personal threat—no *immediate* personal threat, at least—but the same feeling of walking through a dark room filled with delicate strands of cobweb which brushed across your face, first tickling and ultimately maddening, strands which did not stick but whispered away just before you could grab them.

He tried Miriam's number again, and when it was still busy, he pushed the disconnect button once more and hesitated for just a moment, torn between calling Pangborn and calling an operator in New York to check Miriam's phone. Didn't they have some means of differentiating among a line where someone was talking, one that was off the hook, and one which had been rendered inoperable in some way? He thought they did, but surely the important thing was that Miriam's communication with him had suddenly ceased, and she was no longer reachable. Still, they could find out—*Liz* could find out—if they had two lines instead of just one. *Why* didn't they have two lines? It was *stupid* not to have two lines, wasn't it?

Although these thoughts went through his mind in perhaps two seconds, they seemed to take much longer, and he berated himself for playing Hamlet while Miriam Cowley might be bleeding to death in her apartment. Characters in books— at least in *Stark's* books—never took pauses like this, never stopped to wonder something nonsensical like why they had never had a second telephone line put in for cases where a woman in another state might be bleeding to death. People in books never had to take time out so they could move their bowels, and they never clutched up like this.

The world would be a more efficient place if everyone in it came out of a pop novel, he thought. People in pop novels always manage to keep their thoughts on track as they move smoothly from one chapter to the next.

He dialed Maine directory assistance, and when the operator asked "What city, please?" he foundered for a moment because Castle Rock was a *town*, not a city but a small *town*, county seat or not, and then he thought: *This is panic, Thad. Sheer panic. You've got to get it under control. You mustn't let Miriam die because you panicked.* And he even had time, it seemed, to wonder *why* he couldn't let that happen and to answer the question: he was the only *real* character over whom he had any control at all, and panic was simply not a part of that character's image. At least as he saw it.

Down here we call that bullshit, Thad. Down here we call it fool's—

"Sir?" the operator was prodding. "What city, please?"

Okay. Control.

He took a deep breath, got his shit together, and said, "Castle City." *Christ.* Closed his eyes. And with them still closed, said slowly and clearly: "I'm sorry, operator. Castle *Rock*. I'd like the number for the Sheriff's Office."

There was a lag, and then a robot voice began to recite the number. Thad realized he had no pen or pencil. The robot repeated it a second time, Thad strove mightily to remember it, and the number zipped right across his mind and into blackness again, not even leaving a faint trace behind.

"If you need further assistance," the robot voice was continuing, "please remain on the line and an operator—"

"Liz?" he pleaded. "Pen? Something to write with?"

There was a Bic tucked into her address book and she handed it to him. The operator—the *human* operator—came back on the line. Thad told her he hadn't noted the number down. The operator summoned the robot, who recited once again in her jig-jagging, vaguely female voice. Thad jotted the number on the cover of a book, almost hung up, then decided to double-check by listening to the second programmed recital. The second rendition showed he had transposed two of the numbers. Oh, he was getting right on top of his panic, that was crystal clear.

He punched the disconnect button. Light sweat had broken out all over his body.

"Take it easy, Thad."

"You didn't hear her," he said grimly, and dialed the Sheriff's Office.

The phone rang four times before a bored Yankee voice said, "Castle County Sheriff's Office, Deputy Ridgewick speaking, may I help you?"

"This is Thad Beaumont. I'm calling from Ludlow."

"Oh?" No recognition. None. Which meant more explanations. More cobwebs. The name Ridgewick rang a faint bell. Of course—the officer who had interviewed Mrs. Arsenault and found Gamache's body. Jesus bleeding Christ, how could he have found the old man Thad was supposed to have murdered and not know who he was?

"Sheriff Pangborn came up here to . . . to discuss the Homer Gamache murder with me, Deputy Ridgewick. I have some information on that, and it's important that I speak to him right away."

"Sheriff's not here," Ridgewick said, sounding monumentally unimpressed with the urgency in Thad's voice.

"Well, where *is* he?"

"T'home."

"Give me the number, please."

And, unbelievably: "Oh, I don't know's I should, Mr. Bowman. The Sheriff—Alan, I mean—hasn't had much time off just lately, and his wife has been a trifle poorly. She has headaches."

"I *have* to talk to him!"

"Well," Ridgewick said comfortably, "it's pretty

clear you *think* you do, anyway. Maybe you even *do. Really* do, I mean. Tell you what, Mr. Bowman. Why don't you just lay it out for me and kind of let me be the ju——"

"He came up here to *arrest* me for the murder of Homer Gamache, Deputy, and something else has happened, and if you don't give me his number *right* NOW——"

"Oh, holy *crow!*" Ridgewick cried. Thad heard a faint bang and could imagine Ridgewick's feet coming down off his desk—or, more likely, Pangborn's desk—and landing on the floor as he straightened up in his seat. "Beaumont, not Bowman!"

"Yes, and——"

"Oh, Judas! Judas Priest! The Sheriff—Alan—said if you was to call, I should see you got through right away!"

"Good. Now——"

"Judas *Priest!* I'm a damn lunkhead!"

Thad, who could not have agreed more, said: "Give me his number, please." Somehow, calling upon reserves he'd had no idea he possessed, he managed not to scream it.

"Sure. Just a sec. Uh . . ." An excruciating pause ensued. Seconds only, of course, but it seemed to Thad that the pyramids could have been built during that pause. Built and then torn down again. And all the while, Miriam's life could be draining out on her living-room rug five hundred miles away. *I may have killed her,* he thought, *simply by deciding to call Pangborn and getting this congenital idiot instead of calling the New York Police Department in the first place. Or 911. That's what I probably should have done; dialed 911 and thrown it into their laps.*

Except that option did not seem real, even now. It was the trance, he supposed, and the words he had written while in that trance. He did not think he had foreseen the attack on Miriam . . . but he had, in some dim way, witnessed Stark's *preparations* for the attack. The ghostly cries of those thousands of birds seemed to make this whole crazy thing his responsibility.

But if Miriam died simply because he had been too panicked to dial 911, how would he ever be able to face Rick again?

Fuck that; how would he ever be able to look at *himself* again in a mirror?

Ridgewick the Down-Home Yankee Idiot was back. He gave Thad the Sheriff's number speaking each digit slowly enough for a retarded person to have taken the number down . . . but Thad made him repeat it anyway, in spite of the burning, digging urge to hurry. He was still shaken by how effortlessly he had screwed up the Sheriff's Office number, and what could be done once could be done again.

"Okay," he said. "Thanks."

"Uh, Mr. Beaumont? Sure would appreciate it if you'd kinda soft-pedal any stuff about how I—"

Thad hung up on him without the slightest twinge of remorse and dialed the number Ridgewick had given him. Pangborn would not answer the phone, of course; that was simply too much to hope for on The Night of the Cobwebs. And whoever did answer would tell him (after the obligatory few minutes of verbal ring-around-the-rosy, that was) that the Sheriff had gone out for a loaf of bread and a gallon of milk. In Laconia, New Hampshire, probably, although Phoenix was not entirely out of the question.

He uttered a wild bark of laughter, and Liz looked at him, startled. "Thad? Are you all right?"

He started to answer, then just flapped a hand at her to show he was as the phone was picked up. It wasn't Pangborn; he'd had that much right, anyway. It was a little boy who sounded about ten.

"Hello, Pangborn residence," he piped, "Todd Pangborn speaking."

"Hi," Thad said. He was dimly aware that he was holding the phone receiver much too tightly and tried to loosen his fingers. They creaked but didn't really budge. "My name is Thad—" *Pangborn,* he almost finished, oh Jesus, that would be good, you're on top of this, all right, Thad, you missed your calling, you should have been an air traffic controller. "—Beaumont," he finished after the brief mid-course correction. "Is the Sheriff there?"

No, he had to go to Lodi, California, for beer and cigarettes.

Instead, the boy's voice moved away from the telephone mouthpiece and bugled, "DAAAD! PHONE!" This was followed by a heavy clunk that made Thad's ear ache.

A moment later, O praise God and all His holy Saints, the voice of Alan Pangborn said, "Hello?"

At the sound of that voice, Thad's mental buck fever melted away.

"It's Thad Beaumont, Sheriff Pangborn. There's a lady in New York that may need help very badly right now. It has to do with the matter we were discussing Saturday night."

"Shoot," Alan said crisply, just that, and the relief, oh boy. Thad felt like a picture coming back into focus.

"The woman is Miriam Cowley, my agent's ex-wife." Thad reflected that only a minute ago he undoubtedly would have identified Miriam as "my ex-wife's agent."

"She called here. She was crying, extremely distraught. I didn't even know who she was at first. Then I heard a man's voice in the background. He said for her to tell me who she was and what was going on. She said there was a man in her apartment, threatening to hurt her. To . . ." Thad swallowed. ". . . to cut her. I'd recognized her voice by then, but the man shouted at her, told her if she didn't identify herself he'd cut her fucking head off. Those were his words. 'Do what I say or I'll cut your fucking head off.' Then she said she was Miriam and begged me . . ." He swallowed again. There was a click in his throat, as clear as the letter E sent on a Morse key. "She begged me not to let the bad man do that. Cut her again."

Across from him, Liz was growing steadily whiter. *Don't let her faint,* Thad wished or prayed. *Please don't let her faint now.*

"She was screaming. Then the line went dead. I think he cut it or pulled it out of the wall." Except that was bullshit. He didn't *think* anything. He *knew.* The line had been cut, all right. With a straight-razor. "I tried to get her again, but—"

"What's her address?"

Pangborn's voice was still crisp, still pleasant, still calm. But for the bright line of urgency and command running through it, he might have simply been batting the breeze with an old friend. It was right to call him, Thad thought. Thank God for people who know what they are doing, or at least believe they do. Thank God for people who behave like characters in pop novels. If I had to deal with a Saul Bellow person here, I believe I would lose my mind.

Thad looked below Miriam's name in Liz's book. "Honey, is this a three or an eight?"

"Eight," she said in a distant voice.

"Good. Sit in the chair again. Put your head in your lap."

"Mr. Beaumont? Thad?"

"I'm sorry. My wife is very upset. She looks faint."

"I'm not surprised. You're both upset. It's an upsetting situation. But you're doing well. Just keep it together, Thad."

"Yes." He realized dismally that if Liz fainted, he would have to leave her lying on the floor and plug along until Pangborn had enough information to make a move. *Please don't faint,* he thought again, and looked back at Liz's address book. "Her address is 109 West 84th Street."

"Phone number?"

"I tried to tell you—her phone doesn't—"

"I need the number just the same, Thad."

"Yes. Of course you do." Although he didn't have the slightest idea why. "I'm sorry." He recited the number.

"How long ago was this call?"

Hours, he thought, and looked at the clock over the mantelpiece. His first thought was that it had stopped. Must have stopped.

"Thad?"

"I'm right here," he said in a calm voice which seemed to be coming from someone else. "It was approximately six minutes ago. That's when my communication with her ended. Was broken off."

"Okay, not much time lost. If you'd called N.Y.P.D., they might have had you on hold three times that long. I'll get back to you as quick as I can, Thad."

"Rick," he said. "Tell the police when you talk to them that her ex can't know yet. If the guy's . . . you know, done something to Miriam, Rick will be next on his list."

"You're pretty sure this is the same guy who did Homer and Clawson, aren't you?"

"I am positive." And the words were out and flying down the wire before he could be sure he even wanted to say them: "I think I know who it is."

After the briefest hesitation, Pangborn said: "Okay. Stay by the phone. I'll want to talk to you about this when there's time." He was gone.

Thad looked over at Liz and saw she had slumped sideways in the chair. Her eyes were large and glassy. He got up and went to her quickly, straightened her, tapped her cheeks lightly.

"Which one is it?" she asked him thickly from the gray world of not-quite-consciousness. "Is it Stark or Alexis Machine? Which one, Thad?"

And after a very long time he said, "I don't think there's any difference. I'll make tea, Liz."

3

He was sure they would talk about it. How could they avoid it? But they didn't. For a long time they only sat, looking at each other over the rims of their mugs, and waited for Alan to call back. And as the endless minutes dragged by, it began to seem right to Thad that they not talk—not until Alan called back and told them whether Miriam was dead or alive.

Suppose, he thought, watching her bring her mug of tea to her mouth with both hands and sipping at his own, suppose we were sitting here one night, with books in our hands (we'd look, to an outsider, as if we were reading, and we might be, a little, but what we'd really be doing is savoring the silence as if it were some particularly fine wine, the way only parents of very young children can savor it, because they have so little of it), and *further* suppose that while we were doing that, a meteorite crashed through the roof and landed, smoking and glowing, on the living-room floor. Would one of us go into the kitchen and fill up the floor-bucket with water, douse it before it could light up the carpet, and then just go on reading? No—we'd talk about it. We'd *have* to. The way we have to talk about this.

Perhaps they would begin after Alan called back. Perhaps they would even talk *through* him, Liz listening carefully as Alan asked questions and Thad answered them. Yes—that might be how their own talking would start. Because it seemed to Thad that Alan was the catalyst. In a weird way it seemed to Thad that Alan was the one who had gotten this thing started, even though the Sheriff had only been responding to what Stark had already done.

In the meantime, they sat and waited.

He felt an urge to try Miriam's number again, but didn't dare—Alan might pick that very moment to call back, and would find the Beaumont number busy. He found himself again wishing, in an aimless sort of way, that they had a second line. Well, he thought, wish in one hand, spit in the other.

Reason and rationality told him that Stark could not be out there, ramming around like some weird cancer in human form, killing people. As the country rube in Oliver Goldsmith's *She Stoops to Conquer* was wont to say, it was perfectly unpossible, Diggory.

He was, though. Thad knew he was, and Liz knew it, too. He wondered if Alan would also know when he told him. You'd think not; you'd expect the guy to simply send for those fine young men in their clean white coats. Because George Stark was not real, and neither was Alexis Machine, that fiction within a fiction. Neither of them had ever existed, any more than George Eliot had ever existed, or Mark Twain, or Lewis Carroll, or Tucker Coe, or Edgar Box. Pseudonyms were only a higher form of fictional character.

Yet Thad found it difficult to believe Alan Pangborn would *not* believe, even if he did not want to at first. Thad himself did not want to, yet found himself helpless to do anything else. It was, if you could pardon the expression, inexorably plausible.

"Why doesn't he call?" Liz asked restlessly.

"It's only been five minutes, babe."

"Closer to ten."

He resisted an urge to snap at her—this wasn't the Bonus Round in a TV game-show, Alan would not be awarded extra points and valuable prizes for calling back before nine o'clock.

There *was* no Stark, part of his mind continued to insist upon insisting. The voice was rational but oddly powerless, seeming to repeat this screed not out of any real conviction but only by rote, like a parrot trained to say *Pretty boy!* or *Polly wants a cracker!* Yet it was true, wasn't it? Was he supposed to believe Stark had come BACK FROM THE GRAVE, like a monster in a horror movie? That would be a neat trick, since the man—or un-man—had never been buried, his marker only a *papier-mâché* headstone set up on the surface of an empty cemetery plot, as fictional as the rest of him—

Anyhow, that brings me to the last point . . . or aspect . . . or whatever the hell you want to call it . . . What's your shoe-size, Mr. Beaumont?

Thad had been slouched in his chair, crazily close to dozing in spite of everything. Now he sat up so suddenly he almost spilled his tea. Footprints. Pangborn had said something about—

What footprints are these?

Doesn't matter. We don't even have photos. We've got almost everything on the table . . .

"Thad? What is it?" Liz asked.

What footprints? Where? In Castle Rock, of course, or Alan wouldn't have known about them. Had they perhaps been in Homeland Cemetery, where the neurasthenic lady photographer had shot the picture he and Liz had found so amusing?

"Not a very nice guy," he muttered.

"Thad?"

Then the phone rang, and *both* of them spilled their tea.

4

Thad's hand dived for the receiver . . . then paused for a moment, floating just above it.

What if it's him?

I'm not done with you, Thad. You don't want to fuck

with me, because when you fuck with me, you're fucking with the best.

He made his hand go down, close around the telephone, and bring it to his ear. "Hello?"

"Thad?" It was Alan Pangborn's voice. Suddenly Thad felt very limp, as if his body had been held together with stiff little wires which had just been removed.

"Yes," he said. The word came out sibilant, in a kind of sigh. He drew in another breath. "Is Miriam all right?"

"I don't know," Alan said. "I've given the N.Y.P.D. her address. We should hear quite soon, although I want to caution you that fifteen minutes or half an hour may not seem like a quite soon to you and your wife this evening."

"No. It won't."

"*Is* she all right?" Liz was asking, and Thad covered the phone mouthpiece long enough to tell her that Pangborn didn't know yet. Liz nodded and settled back, still too white but seeming calmer and more in control than before. At least people were doing things now, and it wasn't solely their responsibility anymore.

"They also got Mr. Cowley's address from the telephone company—"

"Hey! They won't—"

"Thad, they won't do *anything* until they know what the Cowley woman's condition is. I told them we had a situation where a mentally unbalanced man might be after a person or persons named in the *People* magazine article about the Stark pen name, and explained the connection the Cowleys had to you. I hope I got it right. I don't know much about writers and even less about their agents. But they do understand it would be wrong for the lady's ex-husband to go rushing over there before they arrive."

"Thank you. Thank you for everything, Alan."

"Thad, N.Y.P.D. is too busy moving on this to want or need further explanations right now, but they *will* want them. I do, too. Who do you think this guy is?"

"That's something I don't want to tell you over the telephone. I'd come to you, Alan, but I don't want to leave my wife and children right now. I think you can understand. You'll have to come here."

"I can't do that," Alan said patiently. "I have a job of my own, and—"

"Is your wife ill, Alan?"

"Tonight she seems quite well. But one of my deputies called in sick, and I've got to sub for him. Standard procedure in small towns. I was just getting ready to leave. What I'm saying is that this is a very bad time for you to be coy, Thad. Tell me."

He thought about it. He'd felt strangely confident that Pangborn would buy it when he heard it. But maybe not over the telephone.

"Could you get up here tomorrow?"

"We'll have to get together tomorrow, certainly," Alan said. His voice was both even and utterly insistent. "But I need whatever you know *tonight*. The fact that the fuzz in New York are going to want an explanation is secondary, as far as I'm concerned. I have my own garden to tend. There are a lot of people here in town who want Homer Gamache's murderer collared, pronto. I happen to be one of them. So don't make me ask you again. It's not so late that I can't get the Penobscot County

D.A. on the phone and ask him to collar you as a material witness in a Castle County murder case. He knows already from the State Police that you're a suspect, alibi or no alibi."

"Would you do that?" Thad asked, bemused and fascinated.

"I would if you made me, but I don't think you will."

Thad's head seemed clearer now; his thoughts actually seemed to be *going* somewhere. It wouldn't really matter, either to Pangborn or to the N.Y.P.D., if the man they were looking for was a psycho who thought he was Stark, or Stark himself . . . would it? He didn't think so, any more than he thought they were going to catch him either way.

"I'm pretty sure it's a psychotic, as my wife said," he told Alan finally. He locked eyes with Liz, tried to send her a message. And he must have succeeded in sending her something, because she nodded slightly. "It makes a weird kind of sense. Do you remember mentioning footprints to me?"

"Yes."

"They were in Homeland, weren't they?" Across the room, Liz's eyes widened.

"How did you know that?" Alan sounded off-balance for the first time. "I didn't tell you that."

"Have you read the article yet? The one in *People?*"

"Yes."

"That's where the woman set up the fake tombstone. That's where George Stark was buried."

Silence from the other end. Then: "Oh shit."

"You get it?"

"I think so," Alan said. "If this guy thinks he's Stark, and if he's crazy, the idea of him starting at

Stark's grave makes a certain kind of sense, doesn't it? Is this photographer in New York?"

Thad started. "Yes."

"Then she might also be in danger?"

"Yes, I . . . well, I never thought of that, but I suppose she might."

"Name? Address?"

"I don't have her address." She had given him her business card, he remembered—probably thinking about the book on which she hoped he would collaborate with her—but he had thrown it away. *Shit.* All he could give Alan was the name. "Phyllis Myers."

"And the guy who actually wrote the story?"

"Mike Donaldson."

"Also in New York?"

Thad suddenly realized he didn't know that, not for sure, and backtracked a little. "Well, I guess I just assumed both of them were—"

"It's a reasonable enough assumption. If the magazine's offices are in New York, they'd stick close, wouldn't they?"

"Maybe, but if one or both of them is free-lance—"

"Let's go back to this trick photo. The cemetery wasn't specifically identified, either in the photo caption or in the body of the story, as Homeland. I'm sure of that. I should have recognized it from the background, but I was concentrating on the details."

"No," Thad said. "I guess it wasn't."

"The First Selectman, Dan Keeton, would have insisted that Homeland not be identified—that would have been a brass-bound condition. He's a very cautious type of guy. Sort of a pill, actually.

I can see him giving permission to do the photos, but I think he would have nixed an ID of the specific cemetery in case of vandalism . . . people looking for the headstone and all of that."

Thad was nodding. It made sense.

"So your psycho either knows you or comes from here," Alan was going on.

Thad had made an assumption of which he was now heartily ashamed: that the Sheriff of a small Maine county where there were more trees than people must be a jerk. This was no jerk; he was certainly running rings around that world champeen novelist Thaddeus Beaumont.

"We have to assume that, at least for the time being, since it seems he had inside information."

"Then the tracks you mentioned *were* in Homeland."

"Sure they were," Pangborn said almost absently. "What are you holding back, Thad?"

"What do you mean?" he asked warily.

"Let's not dance, okay? I've got to call New York with these other two names, and you've got to put on your thinking cap and see if there are any more names I should have. Publishers . . . editors . . . I don't know. Meantime, you tell me the guy we want actually thinks he *is* George Stark. We were theorizing about it Saturday night, blue-skying it, and tonight you tell me it's a stone fact. Then, to back it up, you throw the footprints at me. Either you've made some dizzying leap of deduction based on the facts we have in common, or you know something I don't. Naturally, I like the second alternative better. So give."

But what did he have? Blackout trances which were announced by thousands of sparrows crying in unison? Words that he might have written on a manuscript *after* Alan Pangborn had told him those same words were written on the living-room wall of Frederick Clawson's apartment? More words written on a paper which had been torn to shreds and then fed into the English-Math Building's incinerator? Dreams in which a terrible unseen man led him through his house in Castle Rock and everything he touched, including his own wife, self-destructed? I could call what I believe a known fact of the heart instead of an intuition of the mind, he thought, but there's still no proof, is there? The fingerprints and saliva suggested something was very odd—sure!—but *that* odd?

Thad didn't think so.

"Alan," he said slowly, "you'd laugh. No—I take it back, I know you better than that now. You wouldn't laugh—but I strongly doubt if you would believe me, either. I've been up and down on this, but that's how it shakes out: I really don't think you'd believe me."

Alan's voice came back at once, urgent, imperative, hard to resist.

"Try me."

Thad hesitated, looked at Liz, then shook his head. "Tomorrow. When we can look at each other face to face. Then I will. For tonight you'll just have to take my word that it doesn't matter, that what I've told you is everything of any practical value that I *can* tell you."

"Thad, what I said about having you held as a material witness—"

"If you have to do it, do it. There will be no hard feelings on my part. But I won't go any further than I have right now until I see you, regardless of what you decide."

Silence from Pangborn's end. Then a sigh. "Okay."

"I want to give you a scratch description of the man the police are looking for. I'm not entirely sure it's right, but I think it's close. Close enough to give the cops in New York, anyway. Have you got a pencil?"

"Yes. Give it to me."

Thad closed the eyes God had put in his face and opened the one God had put in his mind, the eye which persisted in seeing even the things he didn't want to look at. When people who had read his books met him for the first time, they were invariably disappointed. This was something they tried to hide from him and could not. He bore them no grudge, because he understood how they felt . . . at least a little bit. If they liked his work (and some professed even to love it), they thought of him beforehand as a guy who was first cousin to God. Instead of a God they saw a guy who stood six-feet-one, wore spectacles, was beginning to lose his hair, and had a habit of tripping over things. They saw a man whose scalp was rather flaky and whose nose had two holes in it, just like their own.

What they could not see was that third eye inside his head. That eye, glowing in the dark half of him, the side which was in constant shade . . . *that* was like a God, and he was glad they could not see it. If they could, he thought many of them would try to steal it. Yes, even if it meant gouging it right out of his flesh with a dull knife.

Looking into the dark, he summoned up his

private image of George Stark—the *real* George
Stark, who looked nothing like the model who
had posed for the jacket photo. He looked for the
shadow-man who had accreted soundlessly over
the years, found him, and began showing him to
Alan Pangborn.

"He's fairly tall," he began. "Taller than me, anyway. Six-three, maybe six-four in a pair of boots.
He's got blonde hair, cut short and neat. Blue eyes.
His long vision is excellent. About five years ago he
took to wearing glasses for close work. Reading and
writing, mostly.

"The reason he gets noticed isn't his height but
his *breadth*. He's not fat, but he's extremely *wide*.
Neck size maybe eighteen-and-a-half, maybe nineteen. He's my age, Alan, but he's not fading the
way I'm starting to or running to fat. He's *strong*.
Like Schwarzenegger looks now that Schwarzenegger has started to build down a little. He works out
with weights. He can pump a bicep hard enough to
pop a sleeve-seam on his shirt, but he's not muscle-
bound.

"He was born in New Hampshire, but following the divorce of his parents, he moved with his
mother to Oxford, Mississippi, where she was
raised. He's lived most of his life there. When he
was younger, he had an accent so thick he sounded
like he came from Dogpatch. A lot of people made
fun of that accent in college—not to his face,
though, you don't make fun of a guy like this to his
face—and he worked hard on getting rid of it. Now
I think the only time you'd be apt to hear cracker in
his voice would be when he gets mad, and I think
people who make him mad are often not available
for testimony later on. He's got a short fuse. He's

violent. He's dangerous. He is, in fact, a practicing psychotic."

"What—" Pangborn began, but Thad overrode him.

"He's quite deeply tanned, and since blonde men usually don't tan all that well, it might be a good point of identification. Big feet, big hands, big neck, wide shoulders. His face looks like somebody talented but in a hurry chopped it out of a hard rock.

"Final thing: he may be driving a black Toronado. I don't know what year. One of the old ones that had a lot of blasting powder under the hood, anyway. Black. It could have Mississippi plates, but he's probably switched them." He paused, then added: "Oh, and there's a sticker on the back bumper. It says HIGH-TONED SON OF A BITCH."

He opened his eyes.

Liz was staring at him. Her face was paler than ever.

There was a long pause on the other end of the line.

"Alan? Are you—"

"Just a sec. I'm writing." There was another, shorter, pause. "Okay," he said at last. "I got it. You can tell me all of this but not who the guy is or your connection with him or how you know him?"

"I don't know, but I'll try. Tomorrow. Knowing his name isn't going to help anyone tonight anyway, because he's using another one."

"George Stark."

"Well, he could be crazy enough to be calling himself Alexis Machine, but I doubt it. Stark is what I think, yeah." He tried to wink at Liz. He did not really believe the mood could be lightened by a wink or anything else, but he tried, anyway. He only succeeded in blinking both eyes, like a sleepy owl.

"There's no way I can persuade you to go on with this tonight, is there?"

"No. There's not. I'm sorry, but there's not."

"All right. I'll get back to you as soon as I can." And he was gone, just like that, no thank-you, no goodbye. Thinking it over, Thad supposed he didn't really rate a thank-you.

He hung up the phone and went to his wife, who sat looking at him as if she had been turned into a statue. He took her hands—they were very cold—and said, "This is going to be all right, Liz. I swear it is."

"Are you going to tell him about the trances when you talk to him tomorrow? The sound of the birds? How you heard it when you were a kid, and what it meant then? The things you wrote?"

"I'm going to tell him everything," Thad said. "What he chooses to pass on to the other authorities . . ." He shrugged. "That's up to him."

"So much," she said in a strengthless little voice. Her eyes were still fixed on him—seemed powerless to leave him. "You know so *much* about him. Thad . . . *how?*"

He could only kneel there before her, holding her cold hands. How could he know so much? People asked him that all the time. They used different words to express it—how did you make that up? how did you put that into words? how did you remember that? how did you see that?—but it always came back to the same thing: how did you *know* that?

He didn't know how he knew.

He just did.

"So much," she repeated, and she spoke in the tone of a sleeper who is in the grip of a distressful dream. Then they were both silent. He kept expecting the twins to sense their parents' upset, to wake up and begin crying, but there was only the steady tick of the clock. He shifted to a more comfortable position on the floor by her chair and went on holding her hands, hoping he could warm them up. They were still cold fifteen minutes later when the phone rang.

5

Alan Pangborn was flat and declarative. Rick Cowley was safe in his apartment, and was under police protection. He would soon be on his way to his ex-wife, who would now be his ex-wife forever; the reconciliation of which both had spoken from time to time, and with considerable longing, was never going to happen. Miriam was dead. Rick would make the formal identification at the Borough of Manhattan Morgue on First Avenue. Thad should not expect a call from Rick tonight or attempt to make one himself; Thad's connection with Miriam Cowley's murder had been withheld from Rick "pending developments." Phyllis Myers had been located and was also under police protection. Michael Donaldson was proving a tougher nut, but they expected to have him located and covered by midnight.

"How was she killed?" Thad asked, knowing the answer perfectly well. But sometimes you had to ask. God knew why.

"Throat was cut," Alan said with what Thad suspected was intentional brutality. He followed it up a moment later. "Still sure there's nothing you want to tell me?"

"In the morning. When we can look at each other."

"Okay. I didn't think there was any harm in asking."

"No. No harm."

"The New York City Police have an APB out on a man named George Stark, your description."

"Good." And he supposed it was, although he knew it was also probably pointless. They almost certainly wouldn't find him if he didn't want to be found, and if anyone did, Thad thought that person would be sorry.

"Nine o'clock," Pangborn said. "Make sure you're at home, Thad."

"Count on it."

6

Liz took a tranquilizer and finally fell asleep. Thad drifted in and out of a thin, scratchy doze and got up at quarter past three to use the bathroom. As he was standing there, urinating into the bowl, he thought he heard the sparrows. He tensed, listening, the flow of his water drying up at once. The sound neither grew nor diminished, and after a few moments he realized it was only crickets.

He looked out the window and saw a State Police cruiser parked across the road, dark and silent. He might have thought it was also deserted if he hadn't seen the fitful wink of a cigarette ember. It seemed that he, Liz, and the twins were also under police protection.

Or police guard, he thought, and went back to bed.

Whichever it was, it seemed to provide a little peace of mind. He fell asleep and woke at eight, with no memory of bad dreams. But of course the *real* bad dream was still out there. Somewhere.

Fourteen

FOOL'S STUFFING

1

The guy with the stupid little pussy-tickler mustache was a lot quicker than Stark had expected.

Stark had been waiting for Michael Donaldson in the ninth-floor hallway of the building where Donaldson lived, just around the corner from Donaldson's apartment door. It all would have been easier if Stark could have gotten into the apartment first, as he had done with the bitch, but a single glance was enough to convince him that these locks, unlike hers, had not been put in by Jiminy Cricket. It should have been all right just the same. It was late, and all the rabbits in the warren should have been fast asleep and dreaming of clover. Donaldson himself should have been slow and fuddled—when you came home at quarter of one in the morning, it wasn't from the public library.

Donaldson *did* seem a trifle fuddled, but he was not slow at all.

When Stark stepped around the corner and slashed out with the razor as Donaldson fiddled and diddled with his keyring, he expected to blind the man quickly and efficiently. Then, before he could more than begin a cry, he would open Donaldson's throat, cutting his plumbing at the same time he severed his vocal cords.

Stark did not try to move quietly. He wanted Donaldson to hear him, wanted Donaldson to turn his face toward him. It would make it easier.

Donaldson did what he was supposed to at first. Stark whipped the razor at his face in a short, hard arc. But Donaldson managed to duck a little—not much, but too much for Stark's purposes. Instead of getting his eyes, the straight-razor laid his forehead open to the bone. A flap of skin curled down over Donaldson's eyebrows like a loose strip of wallpaper.

"*HELP!*" Donaldson blatted in a strangled, sheep-like voice, and there went your no-hitter. Fuck.

Stark moved in, holding the straight-razor out in front of his own eyes with the blade slightly turned up, like a matador saluting the bull before the first *corrida*. Okay; it didn't go just according to Hoyle every time. He hadn't blinded the stool-pigeon, but blood was pouring out of the cut on his forehead in what looked like pints, and what little Donaldson *was* seeing would be coming through a sticky red haze.

He slashed at Donaldson's throat and the bastard pulled his head back almost as fast as a rattlesnake recoiling from a strike, *amazing* speed, and Stark found himself admiring the man a little, ridiculous pussy-tickler mustache or not.

The blade cut only air a quarter of an inch from the man's throat and he screamed for help again. The rabbits, who never slept deeply in this city, this maggoty old Big Apple, would be waking up. Stark reversed direction and brought the blade back again, at the same time rising on his toes and thrusting his body forward. It was a graceful, bal-letic movement, and should have finished it. But Donaldson somehow managed to get a hand up in front of his throat; instead of killing him, Stark only administered a series of long, shallow wounds which police pathologists would call defense cuts. Donaldson raised his hand palm out, and the razor passed across the base of all four fingers. He wore a heavy class ring on the third, and so that one sustained no wound. There was a crisp and minute metallic sound—*brinnk!*—*as* the blade ran across it, leaving a tiny scar in the gold alloy. The razor cut the other three fingers deeply, sliding as effortlessly into the flesh as a warm knife slides into butter. Tendons cut, the fingers slumped forward like sleepy puppets, leaving only the ring-finger standing upright, as if in his confusion and horror, Donaldson had forgotten which finger you used when you wanted to flip somebody the bird.

This time when Donaldson opened his mouth he actually *howled,* and Stark knew he could forget about getting out of this one unheard and unnoticed. He'd had every expectation of doing just that, since he didn't have to save Donaldson long enough to make any telephone calls, but it just wasn't happening. But neither did he intend to let Donaldson live. Once you'd started the wetwork, you didn't quit until either it was done or you were.

Stark bored in. They had moved down the corridor almost to the next apartment door by now. He flicked the straight-razor casually sideways to clear the blade. A fine spray of droplets splashed the cream-colored wall.

Farther down the hall a door opened and a man in a blue pajama shirt with his hair in sleep-corkscrews poked his head and shoulders out.

"What's going on?" he cried in a gruff voice

which proclaimed that he didn't care if it was the Pope of Rome out here, the party was *over*.

"Murder," Stark said conversationally, and for just a moment his eyes shifted from the bloody, howling man in front of him to the man in the doorway. Later this man would tell the police that the intruder's eyes were blue. Bright blue. And utterly mad. "Do you want some?"

The door shut so fast it might never have been opened at all.

Panicked though he must be, hurt though he undoubtedly was, Donaldson saw an opportunity when Stark's gaze shifted, even though the diversion was only momentary. He took it. The little bastard really was quick. Stark's admiration grew. The mark's speed and sense of self-preservation were almost enough to outweigh the fucking nuisance he was making of himself.

Had he leaped forward, grappled with Stark, he might have graduated from the nuisance stage to something approaching a real problem. Instead, Donaldson turned to run.

Perfectly understandable, but a mistake.

Stark ran after him, big shoes whispering on the carpet, and slashed at the back of the man's neck, confident that *this* would finally finish it.

But in the instant of time before the straight-razor should have slashed home, Donaldson simultaneously jerked his head forward and somehow *tucked* it, like a turtle pulling into its shell. Stark was beginning to think Donaldson was telepathic. This time what was meant to be the killing strike merely split the scalp above the protective bulge of bone at the back of the neck. It was bloody, but far from fatal.

This was irritating, maddening . . . and edging into the land of the ludicrous.

Donaldson lurched down the corridor, veering from one side to the other, sometimes even banging off the walls like a pinball striking one of those lighted posts that score the player 100,000 points or a free game or some fucking thing. He screamed as he lurched down the hall. He poured blood on the carpet as he lurched down the hall. He left the occasional gory handprint to mark his progress as he lurched down the hall. But he was not yet dying as he lurched down the hall.

No other doors opened, but Stark knew that right now in at least half a dozen apartments, half a dozen fingers were punching (or had already punched) 911 on half a dozen phones.

Donaldson lurched and stumbled onward toward the elevators.

Not angry or frightened, only terribly exasperated, Stark strode after him. Suddenly he thundered: *"Oh why don't you just stop it and* BEHAVE*!"*

Donaldson's current cry for help turned into a shocked squeak. He tried to look around. His feet tangled in each other and he fell sprawling ten feet from where the hallway opened into the small elevator lobby. Even the most nimble of fellows, Stark had found, eventually ran out of happy thoughts if you cut them enough.

Donaldson got to his knees. He apparently meant to crawl to the elevator lobby now that his feet had betrayed him. He looked around with his bloody no-face to see where his attacker was, and Stark launched a kick at the red-drenched ridge of his nose. He was wearing brown loafers and he kicked the goddam pest as hard as he could, hands down at his sides and thrust slightly backward to maintain balance, left foot connecting and then rising in an arc as high as his own forehead. Anyone who had ever seen a football game would have inevitably been reminded of a very good, very strong punt.

Donaldson's head flew backward, smashed into the wall hard enough to cave the plaster into a shallow bowl-shape at that point, and rebounded.

"Finally pulled your batteries, didn't I?" Stark murmured, and heard a door open behind him. He turned and saw a woman with tousled black hair and huge dark eyes looking out of an apartment door almost all the way down the hall. *"GET BACK IN THERE, BITCH!"* he screamed. The door slammed as if it were on a spring.

He bent, grabbed Donaldson's tacky, gruesome hair, twisted his head back, and cut his throat. He thought Donaldson had probably been dead even before his head connected with the wall, and almost certainly after, but it was best to be sure. And besides: when you started cutting, you *finished* cutting.

He stepped back quickly, but Donaldson did not spurt as the woman had. His pump had already quit or was wheezing to a stop. Stark walked rapidly toward the elevators, folding the straight-razor and sliding it back into his pocket.

An arriving elevator binged softly.

It might have been a tenant; going-on-one wasn't really late in the big city, even for a Monday night. All the same, Stark moved rapidly for the large potted plant which occupied the corner of the elevator lobby along with an absolutely useless nonrepresentational painting. He stepped behind the plant. All his radar was pinging loudly. It *could* be someone returning from a post-weekend bout of Disco Fever or the bibulous aftermath of a business dinner, but he didn't believe it would be either. He believed it would be the police. In fact, he knew it.

A cruiser which fortuitously happened to be in the vicinity of the building when one of the residents of this wing telephoned to say that a murder was being committed in the hallway? Possible, but Stark doubted it. It seemed more likely that Beaumont had raised the roof, sissy had been discovered, and this was Donaldson's police protection arriving. Better belated than never.

He slid slowly down the wall with his back against it, the blood-stained sport-coat he was wearing making a husky whispering noise. He did not so much hide as submerge like a submarine going to periscope depth, and the concealment the potted plant offered was at best minimal. If they looked around, they would see him. Stark, however, was betting all their attention would be riveted by Exhibit A there, halfway down the hall. For a few moments, anyway—and that would be enough.

The plant's broad, crisscrossing leaves printed saw-toothed shadows on his face. Stark stared out from between them like a blue-eyed tiger.

The elevator doors opened. There was a muffled exclamation, holy something-or-other, and two uniformed cops rushed out. They were followed by a black guy in a pair of pegged jeans and big old ditty-bop sneakers with Velcro closures. The black guy also wore a t-shirt with cut-off sleeves. PROPERTY OF THE N.Y. YANKEES was printed on the front. He *also* wore a pair of wrap-around pimp shades, and if he wasn't a detective,

Stark was George of the Motherfucking Jungle. When they went undercover, they *always* went too far . . . and then acted self-conscious about it. It was as if they *knew* they were going overboard but simply couldn't help it. This was—or had been meant to be, anyhow—Donaldson's protection, then. There wouldn't have been a detective in a passing squad-car. That was just a little *too* fortuitous. This guy had come along with the door-guards to first question Donaldson and then babysit him.

Sorry, fellows, Stark thought. I think this baby's talking days are over.

He pushed to his feet and walked around the potted plant. Not a single leaf whispered. His feet were soundless on the carpet. He passed less than three feet behind the detective, who was bent over, pulling a .32 from a shin holster. Stark could have booted him a damned good one in the ass if he'd cared to.

He slipped into the open elevator car in the last whisker of time before the door began to slide closed. One of the uniformed cops had caught a flicker of movement—perhaps the door, perhaps Stark himself, and it didn't really matter—out of the corner of his eye and raised his head from Donaldson's body.

"Hey—"

Stark raised one hand and solemnly twiddled his fingers at the cop. Bye-bye. Then the door cut off the hallway tableau.

The street-level lobby was deserted—except for the doorman, who lay comatose beneath his desk. Stark went out, turned the corner, got into a stolen car, and drove away.

2

Phyllis Myers lived in one of the new apartment buildings on the West Side of Manhattan. Her police protection (accompanied by a detective wearing Nike running pants, a New York Islanders sweatshirt with ripped-off sleeves, and wraparound pimp shades) had arrived at half-past ten on the evening of June 6th to find her fuming over a broken date. She was surly at first, but cheered up considerably when she heard that someone who thought he was George Stark might be interested in murdering her. She answered the detective's questions about the Thad Beaumont interview—which she referred to as the Thad Beaumont Shoot—while loading three cameras with fresh film and fiddling with some two dozen lenses. When the detective asked her what she was doing, she gave him a wink and said: "I believe in the Boy Scout motto. Who knows—something might really happen."

After the interview, outside her apartment door, one of the uniforms asked the detective, "Is she for real?"

"Sure," the detective said. "Her problem is that she doesn't really think anything else is. To her, the whole world's just a photograph waiting to happen. What you got in there is a silly bitch who really believes she's always going to be on the right side of the lens."

Now, at three-thirty on the morning of June 7th, the detective was long gone. Two hours or so before, the two men assigned to protect Phyllis Myers had gotten the news of Donaldson's murder on the police radios clipped to their belts.

They were advised to be extremely cautious and extremely vigilant, as the psycho they were dealing with had proved to be both extremely bloodthirsty and extremely quick-witted.

"Cautious is my middle name," said Cop #1.

"That's a coincidence," said Cop #2. "Extremely is mine."

They had been partners for over a year, and they got on well. Now they grinned at each other, and why not? They were two armed, uniformed members of the maggoty old Big Apple's Finest, standing in a well-lit air-conditioned hallway on the twenty-sixth floor of a brand-new apartment building—or maybe it was a condo, who the fuck knew, when Officers Cautious and Extremely were boys, a condo was something a guy with a speech impediment wore on the end of his dingus—and no one was going to creep up on them or jump out of the ceiling on top of them or hose them down with a magic Uzi that never jammed or ran out of ammunition. This was real life, not an 87th Precinct novel or a Rambo movie, and what real life consisted of tonight was a little special duty one hell of a lot softer than riding around in a cruiser, stopping fights in bars until the bars closed, and then stopping them, until the dawn's early light, in shitty little walk-ups where drunk husbands and wives had agreed to disagree. Real life should always consist of being Cautious and Extremely in air-conditioned hallways on hot nights in the city. Or so they firmly believed.

They had progressed this far in their thinking when the elevator door opened and the wounded blind man staggered out of the car and into the corridor.

He was tall, with very broad shoulders. He looked about forty. He was wearing a torn sport-coat and pants which did not match the coat but at least complemented it. More or less, anyway. The first cop, Cautious, had time to think that the sighted person who picked the blind man's clothes must have pretty good taste. The blind man was also wearing big black glasses that were askew on his nose because one of the bows had been snapped clean off. They were not, by any stretch of the imagination, wraparound pimp shades. What they looked like were the sunglasses Claude Rains had worn in *The Invisible Man.*

The blind man was holding both hands out in front of him. The left was empty, just waving aimlessly. In the right he clutched a dirty white cane with a rubber bicycle handgrip on the end. Both hands were covered with drying blood. There were maroon smears of blood drying on the blind man's sport-coat and shirt. If the two cops assigned to guard Phyllis Myers had actually been Extremely Cautious, the whole thing might have struck them as odd. The blind man was hollering about something which had apparently just happened, and from the look of him, something sure *had* happened to him and not a very *nice* thing, either, but the blood on his skin and clothes had already turned brownish. This suggested it had been spilled some time ago, a fact which might have struck officers deeply committed to the concept of Extreme Caution as a trifle off-beat. It might even have hoisted a red flag in the minds of such officers.

Probably not, though. Things just happened too fast, and when things happen fast enough, it stops mattering if you are extremely cautious or extremely reckless—you just have to go with the flow.

At one moment they were standing outside the Myers woman's door, happy as kids on a day when school is cancelled because the boiler went kaflooey; at the next, this bloody blind man was in their faces, waving his dirty white cane. There was no time to think, let alone deduce.

"Po-*leeece!*" the blind man was yelling even before the elevator doors were all the way open. "Doorman says the police are on twenty-six! *Po-leeeece!* Are you here?"

Now he was wallowing his way down the hall, cane swinging from side to side, and WHOCK!, it hit the wall on his left, and *swish,* back it went, and WHOCK!, the wall on his right, and anyone on the goddam floor who wasn't awake already would be soon.

Extremely and Cautious both started forward without so much as exchanging a glance.

"*Po-leeece! Po—*"

"Sir!" Extremely barked. "Hold it! You're going to fall d—"

The blind man jerked his head in the direction of Extremely's voice but did not stop. He plunged onward, waving his empty hand and his dirty white cane, looking a bit like Leonard Bernstein trying to conduct the New York Philharmonic after smoking a vial or two of crack. "*Po-leeece!* They killed my dog! They killed Daisy! PO-LEEECE!"

"Sir—"

Cautious reached for the reeling blind man. The reeling blind man put his empty hand in the left pocket of his sport-coat and came out not with two tickets to the Blind Man's Gala Ball but a .45

revolver. He pointed it at Cautious and pulled the trigger twice. The reports were deafening and toneless in the close hallway. There was a lot of blue smoke. Cautious took the bullets at nearly point-blank range. He went down with his chest caved in like a broken peach-basket. His tunic was scorched and smouldering.

Extremely stared as the blind man pointed the .45 at him.

"Jesus please don't," Extremely said in a very tiny voice. He sounded as if someone had knocked the wind out of him. The blind man fired two more times. There was more blue smoke. He shot very well for a blind man. Extremely flew backward, away from the blue smoke, hit the hall carpet on his shoulder-blades, went through a sudden, shuddery spasm, and lay still.

3

In Ludlow, five hundred miles away, Thad Beaumont turned over restlessly on his side. "Blue smoke," he muttered. "Blue smoke."

Outside the bedroom window, nine sparrows sat on a telephone line. They were joined by half a dozen more. The birds sat, silent and unseen, above the watchers in the State Police car.

"I won't need these anymore," Thad said in his sleep. He made a clumsy pawing motion at his face with one hand and a tossing gesture with the other.

"Thad?" Liz asked, sitting up. "Thad, are you okay?"

Thad said something incomprehensible in his sleep.

Liz looked down at her arms. They were thick with goosebumps.

"Thad? Is it the birds again? Do you hear the birds?"

Thad said nothing. Outside the windows, the sparrows took wing in unison and flew off into the dark, although this was not their time to fly.

Neither Liz nor the two policemen in the State Police cruiser noticed them.

4

Stark tossed the dark glasses and the cane aside. The hallway was acrid with cordite smoke. He had fired four Colt Hi-Point loads which he had dumdummed. Two of them had passed through the cops and had left plate-sized holes in the corridor wall. He walked over to Phyllis Myers's door. He was ready to talk her out if he had to, but she was right there on the other side, and he could tell just listening to her that she would be easy.

"What's going on?" she screamed. "What happened?"

"We've got him, Ms. Myers," Stark said cheerfully. "If you want the picture, get it goddam fast, and just remember later I never said you could take one."

She kept the door on the chain when she opened it, but that was okay. When she placed one wide brown eye to the crack, he put a bullet through it.

Closing her eyes—or closing the one eye still in existence—was not an option, so he turned and started back toward the elevators. He did not linger, but he did not run, either. One apartment door eased open—everyone was opening doors on him tonight, it seemed—and Stark raised the gun at the starey-eyed rabbit face he saw. The door slammed at once.

He pushed the elevator button. The door of the car he'd ridden up in after knocking out his second doorman of the evening (with the cane he had stolen from the blind man on 60th Street) opened at once, as he had expected it would—at this hour of the night, the three elevators were not exactly in great demand. He tossed the gun back over his shoulder. It thumped onto the carpet.

"That went all right," he remarked, got into the elevator car, and rode down to the lobby.

5

The sun was coming up in Rick Cowley's living-room window when the telephone rang. Rick was fifty, red-eyed, haggard, half-drunk. He picked up the telephone with a hand that shook badly. He hardly knew where he was, and his tired, aching mind kept insisting all this was a dream. Had he been, less than three hours ago, down at the borough morgue on First Avenue, identifying his ex-wife's mutilated corpse less than a block from the chic little French restaurant where they took only the clients who were also friends? Were there police outside his door, because the man who had killed Mir might also want to kill him? Were these things true? Surely not. It surely had to be a dream . . . and maybe the phone wasn't really the phone at all but the bedside alarm. As a rule, he hated that fucking thing . . . had thrown it across the room on more than one occasion. But this morning he would kiss it. Hell, he would *French*-kiss it.

But he didn't wake up. Instead he answered the telephone. "Hello?"

"This is the man who cut your woman's throat," the voice in his ear said, and Rick was suddenly wide awake. Any lingering hope he'd had that this was all just a dream dissipated. It was the sort of voice you should only hear in dreams . . . but that is never where you hear it.

"Who are you?" he heard himself asking in a strengthless little voice.

"Ask Thad Beaumont who I am," the man said. "He knows all about it. Tell him I said you're walking around dead. And tell him I'm not done making fool's stuffing yet."

The phone clicked in his ear, there was a moment of silence, and then the vapid hum of an open line.

Rick lowered the telephone into his lap, looked at it, and suddenly burst into tears.

6

At nine that morning, Rick called the office and told Frieda that she and John should go home— they would not be working today, not for the rest of the week. Frieda wanted to know why and Rick was astounded to find himself on the verge of lying to her, as if he had been busted for some nasty and serious crime—child molestation, say—and couldn't bring himself to admit it until the shock was a little less acute.

"Miriam is dead," he told Frieda. "She was killed in her apartment last night."

Frieda drew in her breath in a quick, shocked hiss. "Jesus-God, Rick! Don't joke about things like that! You joke about things like that, they come true!"

"It *is* true, Frieda," he said, and found he was on the edge of tears again. And these—the ones he'd shed at the morgue, the ones he'd shed in the car coming back here, the ones he'd shed when that crazy man called, the ones he was trying not to shed now—these were only the first. Thinking of all the tears in his future made him feel intensely weary. Miriam had been a bitch, but she had also been, in her own way, a *sweet* bitch, and he had loved her. Rick closed his eyes. When he opened them, there was a man looking in at him through the window, even though the window was fourteen stories up. Rick started, then saw the uniform. A window-cleaner. The window-cleaner waved to him from his scaffold. Rick lifted a hand in a token return salute. His hand seemed to weigh somewhere in the neighborhood of eight hundred pounds, and he let it fall back onto his thigh almost as soon as he had raised it.

Frieda was telling him again not to joke, and he felt more weary than ever. Tears, he saw, were only the beginning. He said, "Just a minute, Frieda," and put the phone down. He went to the window to draw the drapes. Crying over the telephone with Frieda at the other end was bad enough; he didn't have to have the goddam window-cleaner watch him do it.

As he reached the window, the man on the scaffold reached into the slash pocket of his coverall to get something. Rick felt a sudden twinge of unease. *Tell him I said you're walking around dead.*

(Jesus—)

The window-cleaner brought out a small sign. It was yellow with black letters. The message was flanked with moronic smiley-smile faces. HAVE A NICE DAY! it read.

Rick nodded wearily Have a nice day. Sure. He drew the drapes and went back to the phone.

7

When he finally convinced Frieda he wasn't joking, she burst into loud and utterly genuine sobs—everyone at the office and all the clients, even that goddam *putz* Ollinger, who wrote the bad science fiction novels and who had apparently dedicated himself to the task of snapping every bra in the Western world, had liked Mir—and, sure enough, Rick cried with her until he finally managed to disengage himself. At least, he thought, I closed the drapes.

Fifteen minutes later, while he was making coffee, the crazy man's call jumped into his head again. There were two cops outside his door, and he hadn't told them a thing. What in hell was wrong with him?

Well, he thought, my ex-wife died, and when I saw her at the morgue it looked like she'd grown an extra mouth two inches below her chin. That might have something to do with it.

Ask Thad Beaumont who I am. He knows all about it.

He had meant to call Thad, of course. But his mind was still in free fall—things had assumed new proportions which he did not, at least as yet, seem capable of grasping. Well, he *would* call Thad.

He would do it just as soon as he told the police about the call.

He *did* tell them, and they were extremely interested. One of them got on his walkie-talkie to police headquarters with the information. When he finished, he told Rick that the Chief of Detectives wanted him to come down to One Police Plaza and talk to them about the call he had received. While he did that, a fellow would pop into his apartment and fit his telephone with a tape-recorder and traceback equipment. In case there were any more calls.

"There probably will be," the second cop told Rick. "These psychos are really in love with the sound of their own voices."

"I ought to call Thad first," Rick said. "He may be in trouble, too. That's the way it sounded."

"Mr. Beaumont has already been placed under police protection up in Maine, Mr. Cowley. Let's go, shall we?"

"Well, I really think—"

"Perhaps you can call him from the Big One. Now—do you have a coat?"

So Rick, confused and not at all sure any of this was real, allowed himself to be led away.

8

When they got back two hours later, one of Rick's escorts frowned at his apartment door and said, "There's no one here."

"So what?" Rick asked wanly. He *felt* wan, like a pane of milky glass you could almost see through. He had been asked a great many questions, and had answered them as well as he could—a difficult task, since so few of them seemed to make any sense.

"If the guys from Communications finished before we got back, they were supposed to wait."

"They're probably inside," Rick said.

"One of them, maybe, but the other one should be out here. It's standard procedure."

Rick took out his keys, shuffled through them, found the right one, and slipped it into the lock. Any problems these fellows might be having with the operating procedure of their colleagues was no concern of his. Thank God; he had all the concerns he could manage this morning. "I ought to call Thad first thing," he said. He sighed and smiled a little. "It isn't even noon and I already feel like the day is never going to e—"

"*Don't do that!*" one of the cops shouted suddenly, and sprang forward.

"Do wha—" Rick began, turning his key, and the door exploded in a flash of light and smoke and sound. The cop whose instincts had triggered just an instant too late was recognizable to his relatives; Rick Cowley was nearly vaporized. The other cop, who had been standing a little farther back and who had instinctively shielded his face when his partner cried out, was treated for burns, concussion, and internal injuries. Mercifully—almost magically—the shrapnel from the door and the wall flew around him in a cloud but never touched him. He would never work for the N.Y.P.D. again, however; the blast struck him stone deaf in an instant.

Inside Rick's apartment, the two technicians from Communications who had come to cook the phones lay dead on the living-room rug. Tacked to the forehead of one with a push-pin was this note:

THE SPARROWS ARE FLYING AGAIN.

Tacked to the forehead of the other was a second message:

MORE FOOL'S STUFFING. TELL THAD.

II

STARK TAKES CHARGE

"Any fool with fast hands can take a tiger by the balls," Machine told Jack Halstead. "Did you know that?"

Jack began to laugh. The look Machine turned on him made him think better of it.

"Wipe that asshole grin off your face and pay attention to me," Machine said. "I am giving you instruction here. Are you paying attention?"

"Yes, Mr. Machine."

"Then hear this, and never forget it. Any fool with fast hands can take a tiger by the balls, but it takes a hero to keep on squeezing. I'll tell you something else, while I'm at it: only heroes and quitters walk away, Jack. No one else. And I am no quitter."

—Machine's Way
by George Stark

Fifteen

STARK DISBELIEF

1

Thad and Liz sat encased in shock so deep and blue
it felt like ice, listening as Alan Pangborn told them
how the early morning hours had gone in New York
City. Mike Donaldson, slashed and beaten to death
in the hallway of his apartment building; Phyllis Myers and two policemen gunned down at her
West Side condo. The night doorman at Myers's
building had been hit with something heavy, and
had suffered a fractured skull. The doctors held out
odds slightly better than even that he would wake
up on the mortal side of heaven. The doorman at
Donaldson's building was dead. The wet-work had
been carried out gangland-style in all cases, with
the hitter simply walking up to his victims and
starting in.

As Alan talked, he referred to the killer repeat-
edly as Stark.

*He's calling him by his right name without even
thinking about it,* Thad mused. Then he shook his
head, a little impatient with himself. You had to
call him something, he supposed, and Stark was
maybe a little better than "the perp" or "Mr. X." It
would be a mistake at this point to think Pangborn
was using the name in any way other than as a convenient handle.

"What about Rick?" he asked when Alan had finished and he was finally able to unlock his tongue.

"Mr. Cowley is alive and well and under police protection." It was quarter of ten in the morning; the explosion which would kill Rick and one of his guardians was still almost two hours away.

"Phyllis Myers was under police protection, too," Liz said. In the big playpen, Wendy was fast asleep and William was nodding out. His head would go down on his chest, his eyes would close . . . then he would jerk his head up again. To Alan he looked comically like a sentry trying not to fall asleep on duty. But each head jerk was a little weaker. Watching the twins, his notebook now closed and in his lap, Alan noticed an interesting thing: every time William jerked his head up in an effort to stay awake, Wendy twitched in her sleep.

Have the parents noticed that? he wondered, and then thought, *Of course they have.*

"That's true, Liz. He surprised them. Police are as prone to surprise as anyone else, you know; they're just supposed to react to it better. On the floor where Phyllis Myers lived, several people along the hall opened their doors and looked out after the shots were fired, and we've got a pretty good idea of what went down from their statements and what the police found at the crime scene. Stark pretended to be a blind man. He hadn't changed his clothes following the murders of Miriam Cowley and Michael Donaldson, which were . . . forgive me, both of you, but they were messy. He comes out of the elevator, wearing dark glasses he probably bought in Times Square or from a pushcart vendor and waving a white cane covered with blood.

God knows where he got the cane, but N.Y.P.D. thinks he also used it to bash the doormen."

"He stole it from a real blind man, of course," Thad said calmly. "This guy is not Sir Galahad, Alan."

"Obviously not. He was probably yelling that he'd been mugged, or maybe that he had been attacked by burglars in his apartment. Either way, he came on to them so fast they didn't have much time to react. They were, after all, a couple of prowl-car cops who were hauled off their beat and stuck in front of this woman's door without much warning."

"But surely they knew that Donaldson had been murdered, too," Liz protested. "If something like that couldn't alert them to the fact the man was dangerous—"

"They also knew Donaldson's police protection had arrived *after* the man had been murdered," Thad said. "They were overconfident."

"Maybe they were, a little," Alan conceded. "I have no way of knowing. But the guys with Cowley know that this man is daring and quite clever as well as homicidal. Their eyes are open. No, Thad—your agent is safe. You can count on it."

"You said there were witnesses," Thad said.

"Oh yeah. Lots of witnesses. At the Cowley woman's place, at Donaldson's, at Myers's. He didn't seem to give a shit." He looked at Liz and said, "Excuse me."

She smiled briefly. "I've heard that one a time or two before, Alan."

He nodded, gave her a little smile, and turned back to Thad.

"The description I gave you?"

"It checks out all down the line," Alan said. "He's big, blonde, got a pretty good tan. So tell me who he is, Thad Give me a name. I've got a lot more than Homer Gamache to worry about now. I've got the goddam Police Commissioner of New York City leaning on me, Sheila Brigham—that's my chief dispatcher—thinks I'm going to be a media star, but it's still Homer I care about. Even more than the two dead police officers who were trying to protect Phyllis Myers, I care about Homer. So give me a name."

"I already have," Thad said.

There was a long silence—perhaps ten seconds. Then, very softly, Alan said, "What?"

"His name is George Stark." Thad was surprised to hear how calm he sounded, even more surprised to find that he *felt* calm . . . unless deep shock and calm felt the same. But the relief of actually saying that—*You have his name, his name is George Stark*—was inexpressible.

"I don't think I understand you," Alan said after another long pause.

"Of course you do, Alan," Liz said. Thad looked at her, startled by the crisp, no-nonsense tone of her voice. "What my husband is saying is that his pseudonym has somehow come to life. The tombstone in the picture . . . what it says on that tombstone where there should be a homily or a little verse is something Thad said to the wire-service reporter who originally broke the story. NOT A VERY NICE GUY. Do you recall that?"

"Yes, but Liz—" He was looking at them both with a kind of helpless surprise, as if realizing for the first time that he had been holding a conversation with people who had lost their minds.

"Save your buts," she said in the same brisk tone. "You'll have plenty of time for buts and rebuttals. You and everyone else. For the time being, just listen to me. Thad wasn't kidding when he said George Stark wasn't a very nice guy. He may have *thought* he was kidding, but he wasn't. I knew it even if he didn't. Not only was George Stark not a very nice guy, he was in fact a *horrible* guy. He made me more nervous with each of the four books he wrote, and when Thad finally decided to kill him, I went upstairs to our bedroom and cried with relief." She looked at Thad, who was staring at her. She measured him with her gaze before nodding. "That's right. I cried. I really cried. Mr. Clawson in Washington was a disgusting little Creepazoid, but he did us a favor, maybe the biggest favor of our married life together, and for that reason I'm sorry he's dead, if for no other."

"Liz, I don't think you really mean—"

"*Don't* tell me what I do and do not *mean!*" she said.

Alan blinked. Her voice remained modulated, not loud enough to waken Wendy or cause William to do more than raise his head one final time before lying down on his side and falling asleep beside his sister. Alan had a feeling that, if not for the kids, he *would* have heard a louder voice, though. Maybe even one turned up to full volume.

"Thad has got some things to tell you now. You need to listen to him very carefully, Alan, and you need to try and believe him. Because if you don't, I'm afraid this man—or whatever he is—will go on killing until he's worked all the way to the bottom of his butcher's bill. I have some very personal reasons for not wanting that to happen. You see, I think Thad and I and our babies may well be on that list."

"All right." His own voice was mild, but his thoughts were clicking over at a rapid rate. He made a conscious effort to push frustration, anger, even wonder aside and consider this mad idea as clearly as he could. Not the question of whether it was true or false—it was, of course, impossible even to consider it as true—but the one of just why they were even bothering to tell such a story in the first place. Was it concocted to hide some imagined complicity in the murders? A real one? Was it even possible that they *believed* it? It seemed impossible that such a pair of well-educated and rational—up to now, anyway—people *could* believe it, but it was as it had been on the day he had come to arrest Thad for Homer's murder; they just didn't give off the faint but unmistakable aroma of people who were lying. *Consciously* lying, he amended to himself. "Go on, Thad."

"All right," Thad said. He cleared his throat nervously and got up. His hand went to his breast pocket and he realized with an amusement that was half-bitter what he was doing: reaching for the cigarettes which had not been there for years now. He stuffed his hands into his pockets and looked at Alan Pangborn as he might look at a troubled advisee who had washed up on the mostly friendly shores of Thad's office.

"Something very odd is going on here. No—it's more than odd. It's terrible and it's inexplicable, but it *is* happening. And it started, I think, when I was just eleven years old."

2

Thad told it all: the childhood headaches, the shrill cries and muddy visions of the sparrows which had heralded the arrival of these headaches, the return of the sparrows. He showed Alan the manuscript page with THE SPARROWS ARE FLYING slashed across it in dark pencil strokes. He told him about the fugue state he had entered at his office yesterday, and what he had written (as well as he could remember it) on the back of the order-form. He explained what had happened to the form, and tried to express the fear and bewilderment which had compelled him to destroy it.

Alan's face remained impassive.

"Besides," Thad finished, "I *know* it's Stark. Here." He made a fist and knocked lightly on his own chest.

Alan said nothing at all for a few moments. He had begun turning his wedding ring on the third finger of his left hand, and this operation seemed to have captured all his attention.

"You've lost weight since you were married," Liz said quietly. "If you don't have that ring sized, Alan, you'll lose it one day."

"I suppose I will." He raised his head and looked at her. When he spoke, it was as if Thad had left the room on some errand and only the two of them were there. "Your husband took you upstairs to his study and showed you this first message from the spirit world after I left . . . is that correct?"

"The only spirit world I know about for sure is the Agency Liquor Store about a mile down the road," Liz said evenly, "but he *did* show me the message after you left, yes."

"*Right* after I left?"

"No—we put the twins to bed, and then, while we were getting ready for bed ourselves, I asked Thad what he was hiding."

"Between the time when I left and the time when he told you about the blackouts and the bird-sounds, there were periods when he was out of your sight? Times when he could have gone upstairs and written the phrase I mentioned to you?"

"I don't remember for sure," she said. "I *think* we were together all that time, but I can't say absolutely. And it wouldn't matter even if I told you he never left my sight, would it?"

"What do you mean, Liz?"

"I mean you'd then assume I was also lying, wouldn't you?"

Alan sighed deeply. It was the only answer either of them really needed.

"Thad isn't lying about this."

Alan nodded his head. "I appreciate your honesty—but since you can't swear he never left you for a couple of minutes, I don't have to accuse you of lying. I'm glad of that. You admit the opportunity may have been there, and I think you'll also admit that the alternative is pretty wild."

Thad leaned against the mantel, his eyes shifting back and forth like the eyes of a man watching a tennis match. Sheriff Pangborn was not saying a thing Thad had not foreseen, and he was pointing out the holes in his story a good deal more kindly than he might have done, but Thad found that he was still bitterly disappointed . . . almost heartsick. That premonition that Alan would believe—somehow just instinctively *believe*—had proved as bogus as a bottle of medicine show cure-all.

"Yes, I admit those things," Liz said evenly.

"As for what Thad claims happened at his office . . . there are no witnesses to either the blackout or to what he claims to have written down. In fact, he didn't mention the incident to you at all until after Ms. Cowley called, did he?"

"No. He did not."

"And so . . ." He shrugged.

"I have a question for you, Alan."

"All right."

"Why would Thad lie? What purpose would it serve?"

"I don't know." Alan looked at her with complete candor. "He may not know himself." He glanced briefly at Thad, then returned his eyes to Liz's. "He may not even *know* he is lying. What I'm saying is pretty flat: this is not the sort of thing any police officer could accept without strong proof. And there is none."

"Thad is telling the truth about this. I understand everything you've said, but I want very badly for you to believe he is telling the truth, too. I want that desperately. You see, I *lived* with George Stark. And I know how Thad was about him as time went on. I'll tell you something that wasn't in *People* magazine. Thad started talking about getting rid of Stark two books before the last one—"

"Three," Thad said quietly from his place by the mantel. His craving for a cigarette had become a dry fever. "I started talking about it after the first one."

"Okay, three. The magazine article made it sound as though this was a pretty recent thing, and that just wasn't true. That's the point I'm trying to make. If Frederick Clawson hadn't come along and forced my husband's hand, I think Thad would still be talking about getting rid of him in the same way. The way an alcoholic or drug addict tells his family and his friends that he'll quit tomorrow . . . or the next day . . . or the day after that."

"No," Thad said. "Not exactly like that. Right church but the wrong pew."

He paused, frowning, doing more than thinking. *Concentrating.* Alan reluctantly gave up the idea that they were lying, or having him on for some weird reason. They were not spending their efforts in order to convince him, or even themselves, but only to articulate how it had been . . . the way men might try to describe a fire-fight long after it was over.

"Look," Thad said finally. "Let's drop the subject of the blackouts and the sparrows and the precognitive visions—if that's what they were—for a minute. If you feel you need to, you can talk to my doctor, George Hume, about the physical symptoms. Maybe the head-tests I took yesterday will show something odd when they come back, and even if they don't, the doctor who performed the operation on me when I was a kid may still be alive and able to talk to you about the case. He may know something that could cast some light on this mess. I can't remember his name right off-hand, but I'm sure it's in my medical records. But right now, all of this psychic shit is a side-track."

This struck Alan as a very odd thing for Thad to say . . . if he *had* planted the one precognitive note and lied about the other. Someone crazy enough to do such a thing—and crazy enough to forget he'd done it, to actually believe the notes were real manifestations of psychic phenomena—would want to talk about nothing else. Wouldn't he? His head was beginning to ache.

"All right," he said evenly, "if what you call 'this psychic shit' is a side-track, then what's the main line?"

"George Stark is the main line," Thad said, and thought: *The line that goes to Endsville, where all rail service terminates.* "Imagine that some stranger moved into your house. Someone you've always been a little bit frightened of, the way Jim Hawkins was always a little bit frightened of the Old Sea-Dog at the Admiral Benbow—have you read *Treasure Island,* Alan?"

He nodded.

"Well, you know the sort of feeling I'm trying to express, then. You're scared of this guy, and you don't like him at all, but you let him stay. You don't run an inn, like in *Treasure Island,* but maybe you think he's a distant relative of your wife's, or something. Do you follow me?"

Alan nodded.

"And finally one day, after this bad guest has done something like slam the salt-cellar against the wall because it's clogged, you say to your wife, 'How long is your idiot second cousin going to hang around, anyway?' And she looks at you and says, '*My* second cousin? I thought he was *your* second cousin!'"

Alan grunted laughter in spite of himself.

"But do you kick the guy out?" Thad went on. "No. For one thing, he's already been in your house for awhile, and as grotesque as it might sound to someone who's not actually in the situation, it seems like he's got . . . squatter's rights, or something. But that isn't the important thing."

Liz had been nodding. Her eyes had the excited, grateful look of a woman who has just been told the word which has been dancing on the tip of her tongue all day long.

"The important thing is how goddamned *scared* of him you are," she said. "Scared of what he might do if you actually told him, flat out, to take his act and put it on the road."

"There you go," Thad said. "You want to be brave and tell him to leave, and not just because you're afraid he might be dangerous, either. It becomes a matter of self-respect. But . . . you keep putting it off. You find *reasons* to put it off. Like it's raining out, and he's less apt to raise the roof about going if you show him the door on a sunny day. Or maybe after you've all had a good night's sleep. You think of a thousand reasons to put it off. You find that, if the reasons sound good enough to yourself, you can retain at least *some* of your self-respect, and some is better than none at all. Some is also better than all of it, if having all of it means you wind up hurt, or dead.

"And maybe not just you."

Liz chimed in again, speaking with the composed and pleasant voice of a woman addressing a gardening club—perhaps on the subject of when to plant corn, or how to tell when your tomatoes will be ready for harvesting. "He was an ugly, dangerous man when he was . . . living with us . . . and he is an ugly, dangerous man now. The evidence suggests that if anything has happened, he's gotten much worse. He's insane, of course, but by his own lights what he's doing is a perfectly reasonable thing: tracking down the people who conspired to kill him and wiping them out, one after another."

"Are you done?"

She looked at Alan, startled, as if his voice had brought her out of a deep private reverie. "What?"

"I asked if you were done. You wanted to have your say, and I want to make sure you got it."

Her calm broke. She fetched a deep sigh and ran her hands distractedly through her hair. "You don't believe it, do you? Not a single word of it."

"Liz," Alan said, "this is just . . . nuts. I'm sorry to use a word like that, but considering the circumstances, I'd say it's the kindest one available. There will be other cops here soon enough. FBI, I imagine—this man can now be considered an interstate fugitive, and that'll bring them into it. If you tell them this story complete with the blackouts and the ghost-writing, you'll hear plenty of less kind ones. If you told me these people had been murdered by a ghost, I wouldn't believe you, either." Thad stirred, but Alan held a hand up and he subsided, at least for the moment. "But I could have come closer to believing a ghost story than this. We're not just talking about a ghost, we're talking about a man who never was."

"How do you explain my description?" Thad asked suddenly. "What I gave you was my private picture of what George Stark looked—*looks*—like. Some of it is in the author-profile sheet Darwin Press has in its files. Some was just stuff I had in my head. I never sat down and deliberately visualized the guy, you know—I just formed, a kind of mental picture over a period of years, the way you form a mental picture of the disc jockey you listen to every morning on your way to work. But if you ever happen to meet the disc jockey, it turns out you had it all wrong, in most cases. It appears I had it mostly right. How do you explain that?"

"I can't," Alan said. "Unless, of course, you're lying about where the description came from."

"You know I'm not."

"Don't assume that," Alan said. He rose, walked over to the fireplace, and jabbed restlessly with the poker at the birch logs piled there. "Not every lie springs from a conscious decision. If a man has persuaded himself he's telling the truth, he can even pass a lie-detector test with flying colors. Ted Bundy did it."

"Come on," Thad snapped. "Stop straining so goddam hard. This is like the fingerprint business all over again. The only difference is that this time I can't just trot out a bunch of corroboration. What *about* the fingerprints, by the way? When you add that in, doesn't it at least suggest that we're telling the truth?"

Alan turned around. He was suddenly angry at Thad . . . at both of them. He felt as if he were being relentlessly driven into a corner, and they had no goddam right to make him feel that way. It was like being the only person at a meeting of the Flat Earth Society who believes the earth is round.

"I can't explain any of that stuff . . . yet," he said. "But in the meantime, maybe you'd like to tell me exactly where this guy—the *real* one—came from, Thad. Did you just sort of give birth to him one night? Did he pop out of a damn sparrow's egg? Did you look like him while you were writing the books that eventually appeared under his name? Exactly how did it go?"

"I don't know how he came to be," Thad said wearily. "Don't you think I'd tell you if I could? So far as I know, or can remember, I was *me* when I wrote *Machine's Way* and *Oxford Blues* and *Sharkmeat*

Pie and *Riding to Babylon.* I don't have the slightest idea when he became a . . . a separate person. He seemed real to me when I was writing as him, but only in the way all the stories I write seem real to me when I'm writing them. Which is to say, I *take* them seriously but I don't believe them . . . except I do . . . then . . ."

He paused and barked a bewildered little laugh.

"All the times I've talked about writing," he said. "Hundreds of lectures, thousands of classes, and I don't believe I ever said a single word about a fiction-writer's grasp of the twin realities that exist for him—the one in the real world and the one in the manuscript world. I don't think I ever even thought about it. And now I realize . . . well . . . I don't even seem to know *how* to think about it."

"It doesn't matter," Liz said. "He didn't *have* to be a separate person until Thad tried to kill him."

Alan turned toward her. "Well, Liz, you know Thad better than anyone else. Did he change from Dr. Beaumont into Mr. Stark when he was working on the crime stories? Did he slap you around? Did he threaten people with a straight-razor at parties?"

"Sarcasm isn't going to make this any easier to discuss," she said, looking at him steadily.

He threw up his hands in exasperation—although he wasn't sure if it was them, himself, or all three of them he was exasperated with. "I'm not being sarcastic, I'm trying to use a little verbal shock-treatment to make you see how crazy you both sound! *You are talking about a goddam pen name coming to life!* If you tell the FBI even *half* of this stuff, they'll be looking up the State of Maine Involuntary Committal laws!"

"The answer to your question is no," Liz said.

"He didn't beat me up or wave a straight-razor around at cocktail parties. But when he was writing as George Stark—and, in particular, when he was writing about Alexis Machine—Thad wasn't the same. When he—opened the door is maybe the best way to put it—when he did that and invited Stark in, he'd become distant. Not cold, not even cool, just distant. He was less interested in going out, in seeing people. He'd sometimes blow off faculty meetings, even student appointments . . . although that was fairly rare. He'd go to bed later at night, and sometimes he'd still be tossing and turning an hour after he did come to bed. When he fell asleep he'd twitch and mutter a lot, as if he were having bad dreams. I asked him on a few occasions if that was the case and he'd say he felt headachy and unrested, but if he'd been having bad dreams, he couldn't remember what they were.

"There was no big personality change . . . but he wasn't the same. My husband quit drinking alcohol some time ago, Alan. He doesn't go to Alcoholics Anonymous or anything, but he quit. With one exception. When one of the Stark novels was finished, he'd get drunk. Then it was as if he were blowing it *all* off, saying to himself, 'The son of a bitch is gone again. At least for awhile, he's gone again. George has returned to his farm in Mississippi. Hooray.' "

"She's got it right," Thad said. "Hooray—that's just what it felt like. Let me sum up what we have if we leave the blackouts and the automatic writing out of the picture entirely. The man you're looking for is killing people I know, people who were, with the exception of Homer Gamache, responsible for 'executing' George Stark . . . in conspiracy with me, of course. He's got my blood-type, which isn't one of the really rare ones, but is still one that only about six people in every hundred have. He conforms to the description I gave you, which was a distillation of my own image of what George Stark would look like if he existed. He smokes the cigarettes I used to smoke. Last, and most interesting, he appears to have fingerprints which are identical to mine. Maybe six in every hundred have type-A blood with a negative Rh factor, but so far as we know, nobody else in this whole green world has my fingerprints. Despite all of this, you refuse to even consider my assertion that Stark is somehow alive. Now, Sheriff Alan Pangborn, you tell me: who is the one who's operating in a fog, so to speak?"

Alan felt the bedrock which he had once believed sure and solid shift a little. It really *wasn't* possible, was it? But . . . if he did nothing else today, he would have to speak to Thad's doctor and start chasing down the medical history. It occurred to him that it would be really wonderful to discover there *hadn't* been any brain tumor, that Thad had either lied about it . . . or hallucinated it. If he could prove the man was a psycho, it would all be so much more comfortable. Maybe—

Maybe *shit*. There *was* no George Stark, there never *had* been any George Stark. He might not be an FBI whiz-kid, but that didn't mean he was gullible enough to fall for *that*. They might collar the crazy bastard in New York City, going after Cowley, probably would, in fact, but if not, the psycho might decide to vacation in Maine this summer. If he did come back, Alan wanted a shot at him. He didn't think swallowing any of this *Twilight Zone* shit would help him if the chance came up. And he didn't want to waste any more time talking about it now.

"Time will tell, I suppose," he said vaguely. "For now, I'd advise you two to stick to the line you took with me last night—this is a guy who *thinks* he's George Stark, and he's crazy enough to have started at the logical place—logical for a crazyman, anyway—the place where Stark was officially buried."

"If you don't at least allow the idea some mental house-room, you're going to be in shit up to your armpits," Thad said. "This guy—Alan, you can't reason with him, you can't plead with him. You could beg him for mercy—if he gave you the time—but it wouldn't do any good. If you ever get close to him with your guard down, he will make sharkmeat pie out of *you.*"

"I'll check with your doctor," Alan said, "and with the doctor who operated on you as a kid. I don't know what good it will do, or what light it might shed on this business, but I'll do it. Otherwise, I guess I'll just have to take my chances."

Thad smiled with no humor whatsoever. "From my standpoint, there's a problem with that. My wife and kids and I will be taking our chances right along with you."

3

Fifteen minutes later a trim blue-and-white panel truck pulled into Thad's driveway behind Alan's car. It looked like a telephone van, and that was what it turned out to be, although the words *maine state police* were written on the side in discreet lower-case letters.

Two technicians came to the door, introduced themselves, apologized for having taken so long (an apology that was wasted on Thad and Liz, since they hadn't known these guys were coming at all), and asked Thad if he had any problem signing the form one of them carried on a clipboard. He scanned it quickly and saw it empowered them to place recording and traceback equipment on his phone. It did not give them blanket permission to use the transcripts obtained in any court proceeding.

Thad scratched his signature in the proper place. Both Alan Pangborn and one of the technicians (Thad bemusedly noticed that he had a telephone-tester slung on one side of his belt, a .45 on the other) witnessed it.

"This traceback stuff really works?" Thad asked several minutes later, after Alan had left for the Orono State Police Barracks. It seemed important to say something; following the return of their document, the technicians had fallen silent.

"Yeah," one of them answered. He had picked the living-room telephone out of its cradle and was rapidly levering off the handset's plastic inner sleeve. "We can trace a call back to its point of origination anywhere in the world. It's not like the old telephone traces you see in the movies, where you have to keep the caller on the line until the trace is done. As long as no one hangs up the phone on this end"—he waggled the phone, which now looked a little like an android demolished by ray-gun fire in a science fiction epic—"we can trace back to the point of origination. Which more often than not turns out to be a pay telephone in a shopping mall."

"You got that right," his partner said. He was

doing something to the telephone jack, which he had removed from its baseboard plug. "You got a phone upstairs?"

"Two of them," Thad said. He was beginning to feel as if someone had pushed him rudely down Alice's rabbit hole. "One in my study and one in the bedroom."

"They on a separate line?"

"No—we just have the one. Where will you put the tape-recorder?"

"Probably down cellar," the first said absently. He was sticking wires from the telephone into a Lucite block which bristled with spring connectors, and there was a wouldja-mind-lettin-us-do-our-job undertone to his voice.

Thad put his arm around Liz's waist and guided her away, wondering if there was *anyone* who could or would understand that not all the tape-recorders and high-tech state-of-the-art Lucite blocks in the world would stop George Stark. Stark was out there, maybe resting up, maybe already on his way.

And if no one would believe him, just what in the hell was he going to do about it? How in the hell was he supposed to protect his family? *Was* there a way? He thought deeply, and when thought accomplished nothing, he simply listened to himself. Sometimes—not always, but sometimes—the answer came that way when it would come no other.

Not this time, though. And he was amused to find himself suddenly, desperately horny. He thought about coaxing Liz upstairs—and then remembered the State Police technicians would shortly be up there, wanting to do more arcane things to his outmoded oneline telephones.

Can't even get laid, he thought. So what *do* we do?

But the answer was simple enough. They waited, that's what they did.

Nor did they have to wait long for the next horrible tidbit: Stark had gotten Rick Cowley after all—booby-trapped his door somehow after ambushing the technicians who had been doing the same thing to Rick's telephone that the men in the living room were doing to the Beaumonts'. When Rick turned his latchkey, the door simply blew up.

It was Alan who brought them the news. He had gotten less than three miles down the road toward Orono when word of the explosion came over the radio. He had turned back immediately.

"You told us Rick was safe," Liz said. Her voice and her eyes were dull. Even her hair seemed to have lost its luster. "You practically guaranteed it."

"I was wrong. I'm sorry."

Alan felt as deeply shocked as Liz Beaumont looked and sounded, but he was trying hard not to let it show. He glanced at Thad, who was looking back at him with a kind of bright-eyed stillness. A humorless little smile lurked just around the edges of Thad's mouth.

He knows just what I am thinking. This was probably not true, but it *felt* true to Alan. *Well . . . maybe not EVERYTHING, but some of it. Quite a bit of it, maybe. It could be that I'm doing a shitty job of covering up, but I don't think that's it. I think it's him. I think he sees too much.*

"You made an assumption that turned out to be wrong, that's all," Thad said. "Happens to the best of us. Maybe you ought to go back and think about George Stark a little more. What do *you* think, Alan?"

"That you could be right," Alan said, and told himself he was only saying that to soothe both of them. But the face of George Stark, as yet unglimpsed except through Thad Beaumont's description, had begun to peer over his shoulder. He couldn't see it as yet, but he could feel it there, looking.

"I want to talk with this Dr. Hurd—"

"Hume," Thad said. "George Hume."

"Thanks. I want to talk to him, so I'll be around. If the FBI *does* show up, would you two like me to drop back later on?"

"I don't know about Thad, but *I'd* like that very much," Liz said.

Thad nodded.

Alan said, "I'm sorry about this whole thing, but the thing I'm sorriest about is promising you something would be okay when it turned out not to be."

"In a situation like this, I guess it's easy to underestimate," Thad said. "I told you the truth— at least, the truth as I understand it—for a simple reason. If it *is* Stark, I think a lot of people are going to underestimate him before this is over."

Alan looked from Thad to Liz and back again. After a long time, during which there was no sound except for Thad's police guard talking together outside the front door (there was another around back), Alan said: "The bitch of it is, you guys really believe this, don't you?"

Thad nodded. "I do, anyway."

"I don't," Liz said, and they both looked at her, startled. "I don't believe. I *know.*"

Alan sighed and stuffed his hands deep into his pockets. "There's one thing *I'd* like to know," he said. "If this is what you say it is . . . I don't believe it, *can't* believe it, I suppose you'd say . . . but if it *is*, what the hell does this guy want? Just revenge?"

"Not at all," Thad said. "He wants the same thing you or I would want if we were in his position. He wants not to be dead anymore. That's all he wants. Not to be dead anymore. I'm the only one who might be able to make that happen. And if I can't, or won't . . . well . . . he can at least make sure he isn't lonely."

Sixteen

GEORGE STARK CALLING

1

Alan had left to talk to Dr. Hume and the FBI agents were just wrapping up their interrogation—if that was the right word for something which seemed so oddly exhausted and desultory—when George Stark rang. The call came less than five minutes after the State Police technicians (who called themselves "wiremen") finally pronounced themselves satisfied with the accessories they had attached to the Beaumont telephones.

They had been disgusted but apparently not very surprised to find that, beneath the state-of-the-art exterior of the Beaumonts' Merlin phones, they were stuck with the town of Ludlow's horse-and-buggy rotary-dial system.

"Man, this is hard to believe," the wireman whose name was Wes said (in a tone of voice which suggested he really would have expected nothing else out here in East Overshoe).

The other wireman, Dave, trudged out to the panel truck to find the proper adapters and any other equipment they might need to put the Beaumonts' telephones in line with law-enforcement as it exists in the latter years of the twentieth century. Wes rolled his eyes and then looked at Thad, as if Thad should have informed him at once that he was still living in the telephone's pioneer era.

Neither wireman spared so much as a glance for the FBI men who had flown up to Bangor from the Boston branch office and then driven heroically through the dangerous wolf- and bear-infested wilderness between Bangor and Ludlow. The FBI men might have existed in an entirely different light-spectrum which State Police wiremen could see no more than infrared or X-rays.

"All the phones in town are this way," Thad said humbly. He was developing a nasty case of acid indigestion. Under ordinary circumstances, it would have made him grouchy and hard to live with. Today, however, he only felt tired and vulnerable and terribly sad.

His thoughts kept turning to Rick's father, who lived in Tucson, and Miriam's parents, who lived in San Luis Obispo. What was old Mr. Cowley thinking about right now? What were the Penningtons thinking? How, exactly, would these people, often mentioned in conversation but never actually met, be managing? How did one cope, not just with the death of one's child, but with the unexpected death of one's *adult* child? How did one cope with the simple, irrational fact of murder?

Thad realized he was thinking of the survivors instead of the victims for one simple, gloomy reason: he felt responsible for *everything*. Why not? If he was not to blame for George Stark, who was? Bobcat Goldthwait? Alexander Haig? The fact that the outdated rotary-dial system still in use here made his phones unexpectedly difficult to tap was just something else to feel guilty about.

"I think that's everything, Mr. Beaumont," one

of the FBI men said. He had been reviewing his notes, apparently as oblivious of Wes and Dave as the two wiremen were of him. Now the agent, whose name was Malone, flipped his notebook closed. It was leather-bound, with his initials discreetly stamped in silver on the lower left-hand corner of the cover. He was dressed in a conservative gray suit, and his hair was parted ruler-straight on the left. "Have you got anything else, Bill?"

Bill, a.k.a. Agent Prebble, flipped his own notebook—also leather-bound, but *sans* initials—closed and shook his head. "Nope. I think that about does it." Agent Prebble was dressed in a conservative brown suit. His hair was also parted ruler-straight on the left. "We may have a few more questions later on in the investigation, but we've got what we need for the time being. We'd like to thank you both for your cooperation." He gave them a big smile, disclosing teeth which were either capped or so perfect they were eerie, and Thad mused: *If we were five, I believe he'd give each of us a TODAY WAS A HAPPY-FACE DAY! certificate to take home and show Mommy.*

"Not at all," Liz said in a slow, distracted voice. She was gently massaging her left temple with the tips of her fingers, as if she were experiencing the onset of a really bad headache.

Probably, Thad thought, *she is.*

He glanced at the clock on the mantel and saw it was just past two-thirty. Was this the longest afternoon of his life? He didn't like to rush to such judgments, but he suspected it was.

Liz stood. "I think I'm going to put my feet up for awhile, if that's okay. I don't feel very chipper."

"That's a good—" *Idea* was of course how he

meant to finish, but before he could, the telephone rang.

All of them looked at it, and Thad felt a pulse begin to triphammer in his neck. A fresh bubble of acid, hot and burning, rose slowly in his chest and then seemed to spread out in the back of his throat.

"Good deal," Wes said, pleased. "We won't have to send someone out to make a test call."

Thad suddenly felt as if he were encased in an envelope of chilly air. It moved with him as he walked toward the telephone, which was now sharing its table with a gadget that looked like a Lucite brick with lights embedded in its side. One of the lights was pulsing in sync with the ringing of the telephone.

Where are the birds? I should be hearing the birds. But there were none; the only sound was the Merlin phone's demanding warble.

Wes was kneeling by the fireplace and putting tools back into a black case which, with its oversized chrome latches, resembled a workman's dinner-bucket. Dave was leaning in the doorway between the living room and the dining room. He had asked Liz if he could have a banana from the bowl on the table, and was now peeling it thoughtfully, pausing every now and then to examine his work with the critical eye of an artist in the throes of creation.

"Get the circuit-tester, why don'tcha?" he said to Wes. "If we need some line clarification, we can do it while we're right here. Might save a trip back."

"Good idea," Wes said, and plucked something with a pistol grip out of the oversized dinner-bucket.

Both men looked mildly expectant and no more.

Agents Malone and Prebble were standing, replacing notebooks, shaking out the knife-edge creases in the legs of their pants, and generally confirming Thad's original opinion: these men seemed more like H&R Block tax consultants than gun-toting G-men. Malone and Prebble seemed totally unaware the phone was ringing at all.

But Liz knew. She had stopped rubbing her temple and was looking at Thad with the wide, haunted eyes of an animal which has been brought to bay. Prebble was thanking her for the coffee and Danish she had supplied, and seemed as unaware of her failure to answer him as he was of the ringing telephone.

What is the matter with you people? Thad suddenly felt like screaming. *What in the hell did you set up all this equipment for in the first place?*

Unfair, of course. For the man they were after to be the first person to phone the Beaumonts after the tap-and-trace equipment had been set up, a bare five minutes after installation was complete, in fact, was just too fortuitous . . . or so they would have said if anyone had bothered to ask them. Things don't happen that way in the wonderful world of law-enforcement as it exists in the latter years of the twentieth century, they would have said. It's another writer calling you up for a nice fresh plot idea, Thad, or maybe someone wants to know if your wife could spare a cup of sugar. But the guy who thinks he's your alter ego? No way, José. Too soon, too lucky.

Except it *was* Stark. Thad could *smell* him. And, looking at his wife, he knew that Liz could, too.

Now Wes was looking at him, no doubt wondering why Thad didn't answer his freshly rigged phone.

Don't worry, Thad thought. *Don't worry, he'll wait. He knows we're home, you see.*

"Well, we'll just get out of your hair, Mrs. Beau—" Prebble began, and Liz said in a calm but terribly pained voice, "I think you'd better wait, please."

Thad picked up the telephone and shouted: "What do you want, you son of a bitch? Just what the fuck do you WANT?"

Wes jumped. Dave froze just as he was preparing to take the first bite from his banana. The heads of the federal agents snapped around. Thad found himself wishing with miserable intensity that Alan Pangborn were here instead of talking to Dr. Hume up in Orono. Alan didn't believe in Stark, either, at least not yet, but at least he was *human.* Thad supposed these others might be, but he had serious doubts as to whether or not they knew he and Liz were.

"It's him, it's him!" Liz was saying to Prebble.

"Oh Jesus," Prebble said. He and the other fearless minion of the law exchanged an utterly nonplussed glance: *What the fuck do we do now?*

Thad heard and saw these things, but was separate from them. Separate even from Liz. There were only Stark and him now. Together again for the first time, as the old vaudeville announcers used to say.

"Cool down, Thad," George Stark said. He sounded amused. "No need to get your panties all in a bunch." It was the voice he had expected. Exactly. Every nuance, right down to the faint Southern slur that turned "get your" into something that was not "getcho" but wanted to be.

The two wiremen put their heads together briefly, and then Dave bolted for the panel truck and the auxiliary telephone. He was still holding his banana. Wes ran for the cellar stairs to check the voice-activated tape-recorder.

The fearless minions of the Effa Bee Eye stood in the middle of the living room and stared. They looked as if they wanted to put their arms about each other for comfort, like babes lost in the woods.

"What do you want?" Thad repeated in a quieter voice.

"Why, just to tell you that it is over," Stark said. "I got the last one this noontime—that little girl who used to work at Darwin Press for the boss of the accounting department?"

Almost, but not quite, *the accountin depawtment.*

"She was the one got that Clawson boy's coffee perkin in the first place," Stark said. "The cops'll find her; she's got a place on Second Avenue way downtown. Some of her's on the floor; I put the rest on the kitchen table." He laughed. "It's been a busy week, Thad. I been hoppin as fast as a one-legged man in an ass-kickin contest. I just called to set your mind at rest."

"It doesn't feel very rested," Thad said.

"Well, give it time, old hoss; give it time. I think I'll head down south, do me some fishing. This city life tires me out." He laughed, a sound so monstrously jolly it made Thad's flesh crawl.

He was lying.

Thad knew this as surely as he knew that Stark had waited until the tap-and-trace equipment was in place to make his call. *Could* he know something like that? The answer was yes. Stark might be calling from somewhere in New York City, but the two of them were tied together by the same invisible but undeniable bond that connected twins. They *were* twins, halves of the same whole, and Thad was terrified to find himself drifting out of his body, drifting along the phone line, not all the way to New York, no, but halfway; meeting the monster at the center of this umbilicus, in western Massachusetts, perhaps, the two of them meeting and merging again, as they had somehow met and merged every time he had put the cover on his typewriter and picked up one of those goddamned Berol Black Beauty pencils.

"You lying fuck!" he cried.

The FBI agents jumped as if they had been goosed.

"Hey, Thad, that's not very nice!" Stark said. He sounded injured. "Did you think I was gonna hurt *you?* Hell, no! I was getting *revenge* for you, boy! I knew I was the one had to do it. I know you got a chicken liver, but I don't hold it against you; it takes all kinds to spin a world as busy as this one. Why in *hail* would I bother to revenge you if I was gonna fix things so you couldn't enjoy it?"

Thad's fingers had gone to the small white scar on his forehead and were rubbing there, rubbing hard enough to redden the skin. He found himself trying—trying desperately—to hold on to himself. To hold on to his own basic *reality.*

He's lying, and I know why, and he knows I know, and he knows it doesn't matter, because no one will believe me. He knows how odd it all looks to them, and he knows they're listening, he knows what they think . . . but he also knows how they think, and that makes him safe. They believe he's a psycho who only thinks he's George Stark, because that's what they have to think. To think in any other way goes against everything they've learned, everything they are. All the fingerprints in the world won't change that. He knows that if he implies he's not George Stark, if he implies that he's finally figured that out, they'll relax. They won't remove the police protection right away . . . but he can speed it up.

"You know whose idea it was to bury you. It was mine."

"No, no!" Stark said easily, and it was almost (but not quite) *Naw, naw!* "You were misled, that's all. When that slimeball Clawson came along, he knocked you for a loop—that's the way it was. Then, when you called up that trained monkey who called himself a literary agent, he gave you some real bad advice. Thad, it was like someone took a big crap on your dining-room table and you called up someone you trusted to ask em what to do about it, and that someone said, 'You haven't got a problem; just put you some pork gravy on it. Shit with pork gravy on it tastes right fine on a cold night.' You never would have done what you did on your own. I know *that,* hoss."

"That's a goddam lie and you know it!"

And suddenly he realized just how perfect this was, and how well Stark understood the people he was dealing with. *He's going to come right out and say it pretty soon. He's going to come right out and say that he isn't George Stark. And they'll believe him when he does. They'll listen to the tape that's turning down in the basement right now, and they'll believe what it says, Alan and everyone else. Because that's not just what they* want *to believe, it's what they* already *believe.*

"I don't know any such thing," Stark said calmly, almost amiably. "I'm not going to bother you anymore, Thad, but let me give you at least one chunk of advice before I go. May do you some good. Don't *you* get thinkin I'm George Stark. That's the mistake *I* made. I had to go and kill a whole bunch of people just to get my head squared around again."

Thad listened to this, thunderstruck. There were things he should be saying, but he couldn't seem to get past this weird feeling of disconnection from his body and his amazement at the pure and perfect *gall* of the man.

He thought of the futile conversation with Alan Pangborn, and wondered again who he was when he made up Stark, who had started off being just another story to him. Where, exactly, was the line of belief? Had he created this monster by losing that line somehow, or was there some other factor, an X-factor which he could not see but only hear in the cries of those phantom birds?

"I don't know," Stark was saying with an easy laugh, "maybe I actually *am* as crazy as they said I was when I was in that place."

Oh good, that's good, get them checking the insane asylums in the South for a tall, broad-shouldered mam with blonde hair. That won't divert all of them, but it will do for a start, won't it?

Thad clenched the phone tight, his head throbbing with sick fury now.

"But I'm not a bit sorry I did it, because I *did* love those books, Thad. When I was . . . there . . . in that loony-bin . . . I think they were the only things kept me sane. And you know something? I feel a lot better now. I know for sure who I am now, and that's something. I believe you could call what I did therapy, but I don't think there's much future in it, do you?"

"Quit lying, goddammit!" Thad shouted.

"We could discuss this," Stark said. "We could discuss it all the way to hell and back, but it'd take awhile. I guess they told you to keep me on the line, didn't they?"

No. They don't need you on the line. And you know that, too.

"Give my best regards to your lovely wife," Stark said, with a touch of what almost sounded like reverence. "Take care of your babies. And you take it easy your own self, Thad. I'm not going to bother you anymore. It's—"

"What about the birds?" Thad asked suddenly. "Do you hear the birds, George?"

There was a sudden silence on the line. Thad seemed to feel a quality of surprise in it . . . as if, for the first time in the conversation, something had not gone according to George Stark's carefully prepared script. He did not know exactly why, but it was as if his nerve-endings possessed some arcane understanding the rest of him did not have. He felt a moment of wild triumph—the sort of triumph an amateur boxer might feel, slipping one past Mike Tyson's guard and momentarily rocking the champ back on his heels.

"George—do you hear the birds?"

The only sound in the room was the tick of the clock on the mantelpiece. Liz and the FBI agents were staring at him.

"I don't know what you're talkin about, hoss," Stark said slowly. "Could be you—"

"No," Thad said, and laughed wildly. His fingers continued to rub the small white scar, shaped vaguely like a question mark, on his forehead. "No, you *don't* know what I'm talking about, do you?

Well, you listen to *me* for a minute, George. *I* hear the birds. I don't know what they mean yet . . . but I will. And when I do . . ."

But that was where the words stopped. When he did, what would happen? He didn't know.

The voice on the other end said slowly, with great deliberation and emphasis: "Whatever you are talking about, Thad, it doesn't matter. *Because this is over now.*"

There was a click. Stark was gone. Thad almost *felt* himself being yanked back along the telephone line from that mythical meeting-place in western Massachusetts, yanked along not at the speed of sound or light but at that of thought, and thumped rudely back into his own body, Stark naked again.

Jesus.

He dropped the phone and it hit the cradle askew. He turned around on legs which felt like stilts, not bothering to replace it properly.

Dave rushed into the room from one direction, Wes from another.

"*It worked perfect!*" Wes screamed. The FBI agents jumped once more. Malone made an "Eeek!" noise very much like the one attributed to women in comic strips who have just spotted mice. Thad tried to imagine what these two would be like in a confrontation with a gang of terrorists or shotgun-toting bank-robbers and couldn't do it. Maybe I'm just too tired, he thought.

The two wiremen did a clumsy little dance, slapping each other on the back, and then raced out to the equipment van together.

"It was him," Thad said to Liz. "He said he wasn't, but it was him. *Him.*"

She came to him then and hugged him tightly and he needed that—he hadn't known how badly until she did it.

"I know," she whispered in his ear, and he put his face into her hair and closed his eyes.

2

The shouting had wakened the twins; they were both crying lustily upstairs. Liz went to get them. Thad started to follow her, then returned to set the telephone properly into its cradle. It rang at once. Alan Pangborn was on the other end. He had stopped in at the Orono State Police Barracks to have a cup of coffee before his appointment with Dr. Hume, and had been there when Dave the wire-man radioed in with news of the call and the pre-liminary trace results. Alan sounded very excited.

"We don't have a complete trace yet, but we know it was New York City, area code 212," he said. "Five minutes and we'll have the location nailed down."

"It was him," Thad repeated. "It was Stark. He said he wasn't, but that's who it was. Someone has to check on the girl he mentioned. The name is probably Darla Gates."

"The slut from Vassar with the bad nasal habits?"

"Right," Thad said. Although he doubted if Darla Gates would be worrying about her nose much anymore, one way or the other. He felt intensely weary.

"I'll pass the name on to the N.Y.P.D. How you doing, Thad?"

"I'm all right."

"Liz?"

"Never mind the bedside manner just now, okay? Did you hear what I said? It was him. No matter what he said, it was *him*."

"Well . . . why don't we just wait and see what comes of the trace?"

There was something in his voice Thad hadn't heard there before. Not the sort of cautious incredulity he'd evinced when he first realized the Beaumonts were talking about George Stark as a real guy, but actual embarrassment. It was a realization Thad would happily have spared himself, but it was simply too clear in the Sheriff's voice. Embarrassment, and of a very special sort—the kind you felt for someone too distraught or stupid or maybe just too self-insensitive to feel it for himself. Thad felt a twinkle of sour amusement at the idea.

"Okay, we'll wait and see," Thad agreed. "And while we're waiting and seeing, I hope you'll go ahead and keep your appointment with my doctor."

Pangborn was replying, something about making another call first, but all of a sudden Thad didn't much care. The acid was percolating up from his stomach again, and this time it was a volcano. Foxy George, he thought. They think they see through him. He *wants* them to think that. He is *watching* them see through him, and when they go away, far enough away, foxy old George will arrive in his black Toronado. And what am I going to do to stop him?

He didn't know.

He hung up the telephone, cutting off Alan Pangborn's voice, and went upstairs to help Liz change the twins and dress them for the afternoon.

And he kept thinking about how it had felt, how it had felt to be somehow trapped in a telephone line running beneath the countryside of western Massachusetts, trapped down there in the dark with foxy old George Stark. It had felt like Endsville.

3

Ten minutes later the phone rang again. It stopped halfway through the second ring, and Wes the wireman called Thad to the phone. He went downstairs to take the call.

"Where are the FBI agents?" he asked Wes.

For a moment he really expected Wes to say, *FBI agents? I didn't see any FBI agents.*

"Them? They left." Wes gave a big shrug, as if to ask Thad if he had expected anything else. "They got all these computers, and if someone doesn't play with them, I guess someone else wonders how come there's so much down-time, and they might have to take a budget cut, or something."

"Do they *do* anything?"

"Nope," Wes said simply. "Not in cases like these. Or if they do, I've never been around when they did it. They write stuff down; they do that. Then they put it in a computer someplace. Like I said."

"I see."

Wes looked at his watch. "Me'n Dave are out of here, too. Equipment'll run on its own. You won't even get a bill."

"Good," Thad said, going to the phone. "And thank you."

"No problem. Mr. Beaumont?"

Thad turned.

"If I was to read one of your books, would you say I'd do better with one you wrote under your own name, or one under the other guy's name?"

"Try the other guy," Thad said, picking up the phone. "More action."

Wes nodded, sketched a salute, and went out.

"Hello?" Thad said. He felt as if he should have a telephone grafted onto the side of his head soon. It would save time and trouble. With recording and traceback equipment attached, of course. He could carry it around in a back-pack.

"Hi, Thad. Alan. I'm still at the State Police Barracks. Listen, the news is not so good on the phone trace. Your friend called from a telephone kiosk in Penn Station."

Thad remembered what the other wireman, Dave, had said about installing all that expensive high-tech equipment in order to trace a call back to a bank of phones in a shopping mall somewhere. "Are you surprised?"

"No. Disappointed, but not surprised. We hope for a slip, and believe it or not, we usually get one, sooner or later. I'd like to come over tonight. That okay?"

"Okay," Thad said, "why not? If things get dull, we'll play bridge."

"We expect to have voice-prints by this evening."

"So you get his voice-print. So what?"

"Not print. *Prints.*"

"I don't—"

"A voice-print is a computer-generated graphic which accurately represents a person's vocal qualities," Pangborn said. "It doesn't have anything to do with *speech,* exactly—we're not interested in accents, impediments, pronunciation, that sort of thing. What the computer synthesizes is pitch and tone—what the experts call head voice—and timbre and resonance, which is known as chest or gut voice. They are verbal fingerprints, and like fingerprints, no one has ever found two which are exactly alike. I'm told that the difference in the voiceprints of identical twins is much wider than the difference in their fingerprints."

He paused.

"We've sent a high-resolution copy of the tape we got to FOLE in Washington. What we'll get is a comparison of your voice-print and *his* voice-print. The guys at the State Police barracks here wanted to tell me I was crazy. I could see it in their faces, but after the fingerprints and your alibi, no one quite had the nerve to come right out and say it."

Thad opened his mouth, tried to speak, couldn't, wet his lips, tried again, and still couldn't.

"Thad? Are you hanging up on me again?"

"No," he said, and all at once there seemed to be a cricket in the middle of his voice. "Thank you, Alan."

"No, don't say that. I know what you're thanking me for, and I don't want to mislead you. All I'm trying to do is follow standard investigatory procedure. The procedure is a little odd in this case, granted, because the circumstances are a little odd. That doesn't mean you should make unwarranted assumptions. Get me?"

"Yes. What's FOLE?"

"F—? Oh. The Federal Office of Law Enforcement. Maybe the only good thing Nixon did the whole damn time he was in the White House. It's mostly made up of computer banks that serve as a central clearing-house for the local law-enforcement agencies . . . and the program-crunchers who run them, of course. We can access the fingerprints of almost anyone in America convicted of a felony crime since 1969 or so. FOLE also supplies ballistics reports for comparison, blood-typing on felons where available, voice-prints, and computer-generated pictures of suspected criminals."

"So we'll see if my voice and his——?"

"Yes. We should have it by seven. Eight if there's heavy computer traffic down there."

Thad was shaking his head. "We didn't sound anything alike."

"I heard the tape and I know that," Pangborn said. "Let me repeat: a voice-print has absolutely nothing to do with *speech*. Head voice and gut voice, Thad. There's a big difference."

"But——"

"Tell me something. Do Elmer Fudd and Daffy Duck sound the same to you?"

Thad blinked. "Well . . . no."

"Not to me, either," Pangborn said, "but a guy named Mel Blanc does both of them . . . not to mention the voices of Bugs Bunny, Tweety Bird, Foghorn Leghorn, and God knows how many others. I've got to go. See you tonight, okay?"

"Yes."

"Between seven-thirty and nine, all right?"

"We'll look for you, Alan."

"Okay. However this goes, I'll be heading back to The Rock tomorrow, and barring some unforeseen break in the case, there I will remain."

"The finger, having writ, moves on, right?" Thad said, and thought: *That's what he's counting on, after all.*

"Yeah—I've got lots of other fish to fry. None

are as big as this one, but the people of Castle County pay my salary for fryin em. You know what I mean?" This seemed to Thad to be a serious question and not just a placeholder in the conversation.

"Yes. I do know." *We both do. Me . . . and foxy George.*

"I'll have to go, but you'll see a State Police cruiser parked out in front of your house twenty-four hours a day until this thing is over. Those guys are tough, Thad. And if the cops in New York let down their guards a little, the Bears you got watching out for you won't. No one is going to underestimate this spook again. No one is going to forget you, or leave you and your family to cope with this on your own. People will be working on this case, and while they do, other people will be watching out for you and yours. You understand that, don't you?"

"Yes. I understand." And thought: *Today. Tomorrow. Next week. Maybe next month. But next year? No way. I know it. And he knows it, too. Right now they don't completely believe what he said about coming to his senses and laying off. Later on, they will . . . as the weeks pass and nothing happens, it will become more than politic for them to believe it; it will also become economic. Because George and I know how the world goes rolling around the sun in its accustomed groove, just as we know that, as soon as everybody is busy frying those other fish, George will show up and fry me. US.*

4

Fifteen minutes later, Alan was still in the Orono State Police Barracks, still on the telephone, and still on hold. There was a click on the line. A young woman spoke to him in a slightly apologetic tone. "Can you hold a little longer, Chief Pangborn? The computer is having one of its slow days."

Alan considered telling her he was a Sheriff, not a Chief, and then didn't bother. It was a mistake everyone made. "Sure," he said.

Click.

He was returned to Hold, that latter-twentieth-century version of limbo.

He was sitting in a cramped little office all the way to the rear of the Barracks; any farther back and he would have been doing business in the bushes. The room was filled with dusty files. The only desk was a grammar-school refugee, the type with a sloping surface, a hinged lid, and an inkwell. Alan balanced it on his knees and swung it idly back and forth that way. At the same time he turned the piece of paper on the desk around and around. Written on it in Alan's small, neat hand were two pieces of information: *Hugh Pritchard* and *Bergenfield County Hospital, Bergenfield, New Jersey.*

He thought of his last conversation with Thad, half an hour ago. The one where he had told him all about how the brave State Troopers were going to protect him and his wife from the bad old crazyman who thought he was George Stark, if the bad old crazyman showed up. Alan wondered if Thad had believed it. He doubted it; he guessed that a man who wrote fiction for a living would have a keen nose for fairy-tales.

Well, they would try to protect Thad and Liz; give them that. But Alan kept remembering something which had happened in Bangor in 1985.

A woman had requested and had received police

protection after her estranged husband had beaten her severely and threatened to come back and kill her if she went through with her plans for a divorce. For two weeks, the man had done nothing. The Bangor P.D. had been about to cancel the watch when the husband showed up, driving a laundry truck and wearing green fatigues with the laundry's name on the back of the shirt. He had walked up to the door, carrying a bundle of laundry. The police might have recognized the man, even in the uniform, if he had come earlier, when the watch order was fresh, but that was moot; they hadn't recognized him when he *did* show up. He knocked on the door, and when the woman opened it, her husband pulled a gun out of his pants pocket and shot her dead. Before the cops assigned to her had fully realized what was happening, let alone got out of their car, the man had been standing on the stoop with his hands raised. He had tossed the smoking gun into the rose bushes. "Don't shoot me," he'd said calmly. "I'm finished." The truck and the uniform, it turned out, had been borrowed from an old drinking buddy who didn't even know the perp had been fighting with his wife.

The point was simple: if someone wanted you badly enough, and if that someone had just a little luck, he would get you. Look at Oswald; look at Chapman; look what this fellow Stark had done to those people in New York.

Click.

"Are you still there, Chief?" the female voice from Bergenfield County Hospital asked brightly.

"Yes," he said. "Still right here."

"I have the information you requested," she said. "Dr. Hugh Pritchard retired in 1978. I have an address and telephone number for him in the town of Fort Laramie, Wyoming."

"May I have it, please?"

She gave it to him. Alan thanked her, hung up, and dialed the number. The telephone uttered half a ring, and then an answering machine cut in and began spieling its recorded announcement into Alan's ear.

"Hello, this is Hugh Pritchard," a gravelly voice said. *Well,* Alan thought, *the guy hasn't croaked, anyway—that's a step in the right direction.* "Helga and I aren't in right now. I'm probably playing golf; God knows what *Helga's* up to." There was an old man's rusty chuckle. "If you've got a message, please leave it at the sound of the tone. You've got about thirty seconds."

Bee-eep!

"Dr. Pritchard, this is Sheriff Alan Pangborn," he said. "I'm a law-enforcement officer in Maine. I need to talk to you about a man named Thad Beaumont. You removed a lesion from his brain in 1960, when he was eleven. Please call me collect at the Orono State Police Barracks—207-555-2121. Thank you."

He finished in a mild sweat. Talking to answering machines always made him feel like a contestant on *Beat the Clock.*

Why are you even bothering with all this?

The answer he had given Thad was a simple one: procedure. Alan himself could not be satisfied with such a pat answer, because he knew it *wasn't* procedure. It might have been—conceivably—if this Pritchard had operated on the man calling himself *Stark,*

(except he's not anymore now he says he knows who he really is)

but he hadn't. He had operated on *Beaumont,* and in any case, that had been twenty-eight long years ago.

So why?

Because none of it was right, that was why. The fingerprints weren't, the blood-type obtained from the cigarette ends wasn't, the combination of cleverness and homicidal rage which their man had displayed wasn't, Thad's and Liz's insistence that the pen name was real wasn't. That most of all. That was the assertion of a couple of lunatics. And now he had something else which wasn't right. The State Police accepted the man's assertion that he now understood who he really was without a qualm. To Alan, it had all the authenticity of a three-dollar bill. It screamed trick, ruse, runaround.

Alan thought maybe the man was still coming.

But none of that answers the question, his mind whispered. *Why are you bothering with all this? Why are you calling Fort Laramie, Wyoming, and chasing down an old doc who probably doesn't remember Thad Beaumont from a hole in the wall?*

Because I don't have anything better to do, he answered himself irritably. *Because I can call from here without the town selectmen bitching about the goddam long-distance charges. And because* THEY *believe it—Thad and Liz. It's crazy, all right, but they seem sane enough otherwise . . . and, goddammit,* THEY *believe it. That doesn't mean I do.*

And he didn't.

Did he?

The day passed slowly. Dr. Pritchard didn't call back. But the voice-prints came in shortly after eight o'clock, and the voice-prints were amazing.

5

They weren't what Thad had expected at all.

He had expected a sheet of graph paper covered with spiky mountains and valleys which Alan would try to explain. He and Liz would nod wisely, as people did when someone was explaining a thing too complex for them to understand, knowing that if they *did* ask questions, the explanations which followed would be even *less* comprehensible.

Instead, Alan showed them two sheets of plain white paper. A single line ran across the middle of each. There were a few groups of spike-points, always in pairs or trios, but for the most part, the lines were peaceful (if rather irregular) sine-waves. And you only had to look from one to the other with the naked eye to see that they were either identical or very close to it.

"That's it?" Liz asked.

"Not quite," Alan said. "Watch." He slid one sheet on top of the other. He did this with the air of a magician performing an exceptionally fine trick. He held the two sheets up to the light. Thad and Liz stared at the doubled sheets.

"They really are," Liz said in a soft, awed voice. "They're just the same."

"Well . . . not quite," Alan said, and pointed at three spots where the voice-print line on the under-sheet showed through the tiniest bit. One of these show-throughs was above the line on the top sheet, the other two below. In all three cases, the show-through was in places where the line spiked. The sine-wave itself seemed to match perfectly. "The differences are in Thad's print, and they come only at stress-points." Alan tapped each show-through in turn. "Here: 'What do you want, you son of a bitch, just what the fuck do you want.' And here: 'That's a goddam lie and you know it.' And, finally, here: 'Quit lying, goddammit.' Right now everyone's focusing on these three minute differences, because they want to hang onto their assumption that no two voice-prints are ever alike. But the fact is, there *weren't* any stress-points in Stark's part of the conversation. The bastard stayed cool, calm, and collected all the way through."

"Yeah," Thad said. "He sounded like he was drinking lemonade."

Alan put the voice-prints down on an endtable. "Nobody at State Police Headquarters *really* believes these are two different voice-prints, even with the minute differences," he said. "We got the prints back from Washington very fast. The reason I'm so late is because, after the expert in Augusta saw them, he wanted a copy of the tape. We sent it down on an Eastern Airlines commuter flight out of Bangor and they ran it through a gadget called an audio enhancer. They use it to tell if someone actually spoke the words under investigation or if they're listening to a voice which was on tape."

"Is it live or is it Memorex?" Thad said. He was sitting by the fireplace, drinking a soda.

Liz had returned to the playpen after looking at the voice-prints. She was sitting cross-legged on the floor, trying to keep William and Wendy from rapping their heads together as they examined each other's toes. "Why did they do that?"

Alan cocked a thumb at Thad, who was grinning sourly. "Your husband knows."

Thad asked Alan, "With the little differences in

the spikes, they can at least *kid* themselves that two different voices were speaking, even if they know better—that was your point, wasn't it?"

"Uh-huh. Even though I've never heard of voice-prints even remotely as close as these." He shrugged. "Granted, my experience with them isn't as wide as the guys at FOLE who study them for a living, or even the guys in Augusta who are more or less general practitioners—voice-prints, fingerprints, footprints, tire-prints. But I *do* read the literature, and I was there when the results came back, Thad. They are kidding themselves, yes, but they're not doing it very hard."

"So they've got three small differences, but they're not enough. The problem is that my voice was stressed and Stark's wasn't. So they went to this enhancer thing hoping for a fall-back position. Hoping, in fact, that Stark's end of the conversation would turn out to be a tape-recording. Made by me." He cocked an eyebrow at Alan. "Do I win the stewing chicken?"

"Not only that, you win the glassware for six and the free trip to Kittery."

"That's the craziest thing I ever heard," Liz said flatly.

Thad laughed without much humor. "The whole thing is crazy. They thought I might have changed my voice, like Rich Little . . . or Mel Blanc. The idea is that I made a tape in my George Stark voice, building in pauses where I could reply, in my own voice, in front of witnesses. Of course I'd have to buy a gadget that could hook a cassette tape-recorder into a pay telephone. There *are* such things, aren't there, Alan?"

"You bet. Available at fine electronics supply

houses everywhere, or just dial the 800 number that will appear on your screen, operators are standing by."

"Right. The only other thing I'd need would be an accomplice—someone I trusted who would go to Penn Station, attach the tape-player to a phone in the bank which looked like it was doing the least business, and dial my house at the proper time. Then—" He broke off. "How was the call paid for? I forgot about that. It wasn't collect."

"Your telephone credit card number was used," Alan said. "You obviously gave it to your accomplice."

"Yeah, obviously. I only had to do two things once this shuck-and-jive got started. One was to make sure I answered the telephone myself. The other was to remember my lines and plug them into the correct pauses. I did very well, wouldn't you say, Alan?"

"Yeah. Fantastic."

"My accomplice hangs up the telephone when the script says he should. He unhooks the tape-player from the phone, tucks it under his arm—"

"Hell, slips it into his pocket," Alan said. "The stuff they've got now is so good even the CIA buys at Radio Shack."

"Okay, he slips it into his pocket and just walks away. The result is a conversation where I am both seen and heard to be talking to a man five hundred miles away, a man who *sounds* different—who sounds, in fact, just the tiniest bit Southern-fried—but has the same voice-print as I do. It's the fingerprints all over again, only better." He looked at Alan for confirmation.

"On second thought," Alan said, "make that an all-expense-paid trip to Portsmouth."

"Thank you."

"Don't mention it."

"That's not just crazy," Liz said, "it's utterly incredible. I think all those people should have their heads—"

While her attention was diverted, the twins finally succeeded in knocking their own heads together and began to cry lustily. Liz picked up William. Thad rescued Wendy.

When the crisis passed, Alan said, "It's incredible, all right. You know it, I know it, and they know it, too. But Conan Doyle had Sherlock Holmes say at least one thing that still holds true in crime detection: when you eliminate all the impossible explanations, whatever is left is your answer . . . no matter how improbable it may be."

"I think the original was a little more elegant," Thad said.

Alan grinned. "Screw you."

"You two may find this funny, but I don't," Liz said. "Thad would have to be crazy to do something like that. Of course, the police may think we're both crazy."

"They don't think any such thing," Alan replied gravely, "at least not at this point, and they won't, as long as you go on keeping your wilder tales to yourselves."

"What about *you,* Alan?" Thad asked. "We've spilled *all* the wild tales to you—what do *you* think?"

"Not that you're crazy. All of this would be a lot simpler if I did believe it. I don't know *what's* going on."

"What did you get from Dr. Hume?" Liz wanted to know.

"The name of the doctor who operated on Thad when he was a kid," Alan said. "It's Hugh Pritchard—does that ring a bell, Thad?"

Thad frowned and thought it over. At last he said, "I think it does . . . but I might only be kidding myself. It was a long time ago."

Liz was leaning forward, bright-eyed; William goggled at Alan from the safety of his mother's lap. "What did Pritchard tell you?" she asked.

"Nothing. I got his answering machine—which allows me to deduce that the man is still alive—and that's all. I left a message."

Liz settled back in her chair, clearly disappointed.

"What about my tests?" Thad asked. "Did Hume have anything back? Or wouldn't he tell you?"

"He said that when he had the results, you'd be the first to know," Alan said. He grinned. "Dr. Hume seemed rather offended at the idea of telling a County Sheriff *anything.*"

"That's George Hume," Thad said, and smiled. "Crusty is his middle name."

Alan shifted in his seat.

"Would you like something to drink, Alan?" Liz asked. "A beer or a Pepsi?"

"No thanks. Let's go back to what the State Police do and do not believe. They *don't* believe either of you is involved, but they reserve the right to believe you *might* be. They know they can't hang last night's and this morning's work on you, Thad. An accomplice, maybe—the same one, hypothetically, who would have worked the tape-recorder gag—but not you. You were here."

"What about Darla Gates?" Thad asked quietly. "The girl who worked in the comptroller's office?"

"Dead. Mutilated pretty badly, as he suggested, but shot once through the head first. She didn't suffer."

"That's a lie."

Alan blinked at him.

"He didn't let her off so cheaply. Not after what he did to Clawson. After all, she was the original stoolie, wasn't she? Clawson dangled some money in front of her—it couldn't have been very much, judging from the state of Clawson's finances—and she obliged by letting the cat out of the bag. So don't tell me he shot her before he cut her and that she didn't suffer."

"All right," Alan said. "It wasn't like that. Do you want to know how it *really* was?"

"No," Liz said immediately.

There was a moment of heavy silence in the room. Even the twins seemed to feel it; they looked at each other with what seemed to be great solemnity. At last Thad asked, "Let me ask you again: what do *you* believe? What do you believe now?"

"I don't have a theory. I know you didn't tape Stark's end of the conversation, because the enhancer didn't detect any tape-hiss, and when you jack up the audio, you can hear the Penn Station loudspeaker announcing that the *Pilgrim* to Boston is now ready for boarding on Track Number Three. The *Pilgrim did* board on Track Three this afternoon. Boarding started at two-thirty-six p.m., and that's right in line with your little chat. But I didn't even need that. If the conversation had been taped on Stark's end, either you or Liz would have asked me what the enhancing process showed as soon as I brought it up. Neither of you did."

"All this and you still don't believe it, do you?"

Thad said. "I mean, it's got you rocking and rolling—enough so you really *are* trying to chase down Dr. Pritchard—but you really can't get all the way to the middle of what's happening, can you?" He sounded frustrated and harried even to himself.

"The guy himself admitted he wasn't Stark."

"Oh yes. He was very sincere about it, too." Thad laughed.

"You act as though that doesn't surprise you."

"It doesn't. Does it surprise *you?*"

"Frankly, yes. It does. After going to such great pains to establish the fact that you and he share the same fingerprints, the same voice-prints—"

"Alan, stop a second," Thad said.

Alan did, looking at Thad inquiringly.

"I told you this morning that I thought George Stark was doing these things. Not an accomplice of mine, not a psycho who has somehow managed to invent a way to wear other people's fingerprints— between his murderous fits and identity fugues, that is—and you didn't believe me. Do you now?"

"No, Thad. I wish I could tell you differently, but the best I can do is this: I believe that you believe." He shifted his gaze to take in Liz. "*Both* of you."

"I'll settle for the truth, since anything less is apt to get me killed," Thad said, "and my family along with me, more likely than not. At this point it does my heart good just to hear you say you don't have a theory. It's not much, but it's a step forward. What I was trying to show you is that the fingerprints and voice-prints don't make a difference, and Stark knows it. You can talk all you want about throwing away the impossible and accepting whatever is left, no matter how improbable, but it doesn't work that way. You don't accept *Stark,* and *he's* what's left when you eliminate the rest. Let me put it this way, Alan: if you had this much evidence of a tumor in your brain, you would go into the hospital and have an operation, even if the odds were good you'd not come out alive."

Alan opened his mouth, shook his head, and snapped it shut again. Other than the clock and the soft babble and coo of the twins, there was no sound in the living room, where Thad was rapidly coming to feel he had spent his entire adult life.

"On one hand you have enough hard evidence to make a strong circumstantial court case," Thad resumed softly. "On the other, you have the unsubstantiated assertion of a voice on the phone that he's 'come to his senses,' that he 'knows who he is now.' Yet you're going to ignore the evidence in favor of the assertion."

"No, Thad. That's not true. I'm not accepting *any* assertions right now—not yours, not your wife's, and least of all the ones made by the man who called on the phone. All my options are still open."

Thad jerked a thumb over his shoulder at the window. Beyond the gently wavering drapes, they could see the State Police car that belonged to the Troopers who were watching the Beaumont house.

"What about *them?* Are all *their* options still open? I wish to Christ you were staying here, Alan—I'd take you over an *army* of State Troopers, because you've at least got one eye half-open. Theirs are stuck shut."

"Thad—"

"Never mind," Thad said. "It's true. You know it . . . *and he knows it, too.* He'll wait. And when everybody decides it's over and the Beaumonts are safe, when all the police fold their tents and move on, George Stark will come here."

He paused, his face a dark and complicated study. Alan saw regret, determination, and fear at work in that face.

"I'm going to tell you something now—I'm going to tell both of you. I know exactly what he wants. He wants me to write another novel under the Stark byline—probably another novel about Alexis Machine. I don't know if I could do that, but if I thought it would do any good, I'd try. I'd trash *The Golden Dog* and start tonight."

"Thad, no!" Liz cried.

"Don't worry," he said. "It would kill me. Don't ask me how I know that; I just do. But if my death was the end of it, I still might try. But I don't think it would be. Because I don't really think he is a man at all."

Alan was silent.

"So!" Thad said, speaking with the air of a man bringing an important piece of business to a close. "That's where matters stand. I can't, I won't, I mustn't. That means he'll come. And when he comes, God knows what will happen."

"Thad," Alan said uncomfortably, "you need a little perspective on this, that's all. And when you get it, most of it will just . . . blow away. Like a milkweed puff. Like a bad dream in the morning."

"It isn't perspective we need," Liz said. They looked at her and saw she was crying silently. Not a lot, but the tears were there. "What we need is for someone to turn him *off*."

6

Alan returned to Castle Rock early the next morning, arriving home shortly before two o'clock. He crept into the house as quietly as possible, noticing that Annie had once again neglected to activate the burglar alarm. He didn't like to hassle her about it—her migraines had become more frequent lately—but he supposed he would have to, sooner or later.

He started upstairs, shoes held in one hand, moving with a smoothness that made him seem almost to float. His body possessed a deep grace, the exact opposite of Thad Beaumont's clumsiness, which Alan rarely showed; his flesh seemed to know some arcane secret of motion which his mind found somehow embarrassing. Now, in this silence, there was no need to hide it, and he moved with a shadowy ease that was almost macabre.

Halfway up the stairs he paused . . . and went back down again. He had a small den off the living room, not much more than a broom-closet furnished with a desk and some bookshelves, but adequate for his needs. He tried not to bring his work home with him. He did not always succeed in this, but he tried very hard.

He closed the door, turned on the light, and looked at the telephone.

You're not really going to do this, are you? he asked himself. *I mean, it's almost midnight, Rocky Mountain Time, and this guy is not just a retired doctor, he's a retired* NEUROSURGEON. *You wake him up and he's apt to chew you a new asshole.*

Then Alan thought of Liz Beaumont's eyes—her

dark, frightened eyes—and decided he *was* going to do it. Perhaps it would even do some good; a call in the dead of night would establish the fact that this was serious business, and get Dr. Pritchard thinking. Then Alan could call him back at a more reasonable hour.

Who knows, he thought without much hope (but with a trace of humor), *maybe he MISSES getting calls in the middle of the night.*

Alan took the scrap of paper from the pocket of his uniform blouse and dialed Hugh Pritchard's number in Fort Laramie. He did it standing up, setting himself for a blast of anger from that gravelly voice.

He need not have worried; the answering machine cut in after the same fraction of a ring, and delivered the same message.

He hung up thoughtfully and sat down behind his desk. The gooseneck lamp cast a round circle of light on the desk's surface, and Alan began to make a series of shadow animals in its glow—a rabbit, a dog, a hawk, even a passable kangaroo. His hands possessed that same deep grace which owned the rest of his body when he was alone and at rest; beneath those eerily flexible fingers, the animals seemed to march in a parade through the tiny spotlight cast by the hooded lamp, one flowing into the next. This little diversion had never failed to fascinate and amuse his children, and it often set his own mind at rest when it was troubled.

It didn't work now.

Dr. Hugh Pritchard is dead. Stark got him, too.

That was impossible, of course; he supposed he could swallow a ghost if someone put a gun to his head, but not some malignant Superman of a ghost who crossed whole continents in a single bound. He could think of several good reasons why someone might turn on his answering machine at night. Not the least of them was to keep from being disturbed by late-calling strangers such as Sheriff Alan J. Pangborn, of Castle Rock, Maine.

Yeah, but he's dead. He and his wife, too. What was her name? Helga. "I'm probably playing golf; God knows what Helga's up to." *But I know what Helga's up to; I know what you're both up to. You're up to your cut throats in blood, that's what I think, and there's a message written on your living-room wall out there in Big Sky Country. It says* THE SPARROWS ARE FLYING AGAIN.

Alan Pangborn shuddered. It was crazy, but he shuddered anyway. It twisted through him like a wire.

He dialed Wyoming Directory Assistance, got the number for the Fort Laramie Sheriff's Office, and made another call. He was answered by a dispatcher who sounded half-asleep. Alan identified himself, told the dispatcher whom he had been trying to contact and where he lived, and then asked if they had Dr. Pritchard and his wife in their vacation file. If the doctor and his wife *had* gone off on holiday—and it was getting to be that season—they would probably have informed the local law and asked them to keep an eye on the house while it was empty.

"Well," Dispatch said, "why don't you give me your number? I'll call you back with the information."

Alan sighed. This was just more standard operating procedure. More bullshit, not to put too fine a point on it. The guy didn't want to give out the information until he was sure Alan was what he said he was.

"No," he said. "I'm calling from home, and it's the middle of the night—"

"It's not exactly high noon here, Sheriff Pangborn," Dispatch answered laconically.

Alan sighed. "I'm sure that's true," he said, "and I'm also sure that your wife and kids aren't asleep upstairs. Do this, my friend: call the Maine State Police Barracks in Oxford, Maine—I'll give you the number—and verify my name. They can give you my LAWS ID number. I'll call back in ten minutes or so, and we can exchange passwords."

"Shoot it to me," Dispatch said, but he didn't sound happy about it. Alan guessed he might have taken the man away from the late show or maybe this month's *Penthouse.*

"What's this about?" Dispatch asked after he had read back the Oxford State Police Barracks phone number.

"Murder investigation," Alan said, "and it's hot. I'm not calling you for my health, pal." He hung up.

He sat behind his desk and made shadow animals and waited for the minute hand to circle the face of the clock ten times. It seemed very slow. It had only gone around five times when the study door opened and Annie came in. She was wearing her pink robe and looked somehow ghostly to him; he felt that shudder wanting to work through him again, as if he had looked into the future and seen something there which was unpleasant. Nasty, even.

How would I feel if it was me he was after? he wondered suddenly. *Me and Annie and Toby and Todd?*

How would I feel if I knew who he was . . . and nobody would believe me?

"Alan? What are you doing, sitting down here so late?"

He smiled, got up, kissed her easily. "Just waiting for the drugs to wear off," he said.

"No, really—is it this Beaumont business?"

"Yeah. I've been trying to chase down a doctor who may know something about it. I keep getting his answering machine, so I called the Sheriff's Office to see if he's in their vacation file. The man on the other end is supposedly checking my *bona fides*." He looked at Annie with careful concern. "How are you, honey? Headache tonight?"

"No," she said, "but I heard you come in." She smiled. "You're the world's quietest man when you want to be, Alan, but you can't do a thing about your car."

He hugged her.

"Do you want a cup of tea?" she asked.

"God, no. A glass of milk, if you want to get one."

She left him alone and came back a minute later with the milk. "What's Mr. Beaumont like?" she asked. "I've seen him around town, and his wife comes into the shop once in awhile, but I've never spoken to him." The shop was You Sew and Sew, owned and operated by a woman named Polly Chalmers. Annie Pangborn had worked there part-time for four years.

Alan thought about it. "I like him," he said at last. "At first I didn't—I thought he was a cold fish. But I was seeing him under difficult circumstances. He's just . . . distant. Maybe it's because of what he does for a living."

"I liked both of his books very much," Annie said.

He raised his eyebrows. "I didn't know you'd read him."

"You never asked, Alan. Then, when the story broke about the pen name, I tried one of the *other* ones." Her nose wrinkled in displeasure.

"No good?"

"*Terrible.* Scary. I didn't finish it. I never would have believed the same man wrote both books."

Guess what, babe? Alan thought. *He doesn't believe it, either.*

"You ought to get back to bed," he said, "or you'll wake up with another pounder."

She shook her head. "I think the Headache Monster's gone again, at least for a while." She gave him a look from beneath lowered lashes. "I'll still be awake when you come up . . . if you're not too long, that is."

He cupped one breast through the pink robe and kissed her parted lips. "I'll be up just as fast as I can."

She left, and Alan saw that more than ten minutes had passed. He called Wyoming again and got the same sleepy dispatcher.

"Thought you'd forgot me, my friend."

"Not at all," Alan said.

"Mind giving me your LAWS number, Sheriff?"

"109-44-205-ME."

"I guess you're the genuine article, all right. Sorry to put you through this rigamarole so late, Sheriff Pangborn, but I guess you understand."

"I do. What can you tell me about Dr. Pritchard?"

"Oh, he and his wife are in the vacation file, all

right," Dispatch said. "They're in Yellowstone Park, camping, until the end of the month."

There, Alan thought. *You see? You're down here jumping at shadows in the middle of the night. No cut throats. No writing on the wall. Just two old folks on a camping trip.*

But he was not much relieved, he found. Dr. Pritchard was going to be a hard man to get hold of, at least for the next couple of weeks.

"If I needed to get a message to the guy, do you think I could do it?" Alan asked.

"I'd think so," Dispatch said. "You could call Park Services at Yellowstone. They'll know where he is, or they should. It might take awhile, but they'd probably get him for you. I've met him a time or two. He seems like a nice enough old fella."

"Well, that's good to know," Alan said. "Thanks for your time."

"Don't mention it—it's what we're here for." Alan heard the faint rattle of pages, and could imagine this faceless man picking up his *Penthouse* again, half a continent away.

"Goodnight," he said.

"Goodnight, Sheriff."

Alan hung up and sat where he was for a moment, looking out the small den window into the darkness.

He is out there. Somewhere. And he's still coming.

Alan wondered again how he would feel if it were his own life—and the lives of Annie and his children—at stake. He wondered how he would feel if he knew that, and no one would believe what he knew.

You're taking it home with you again, dear, he heard Annie say in his mind.

And it was true. Fifteen minutes ago he had been convinced—in his nerve-endings, if not in his head—that Hugh and Helga Pritchard were lying dead in a pool of blood. It wasn't true; they were sleeping peacefully under the stars in Yellowstone National Park tonight. So much for intuition; it had a way of just fading out on you.

This is the way Thad's going to feel when we find out what's really going on, he thought. *When we find out that the explanation, as bizarre as it may turn out to be, conforms to all the natural laws.*

Did he really believe that?

Yes, he decided—he really did. In his head, at least. His nerve-endings were not so sure.

Alan finished his milk, turned off the desk-lamp, and went upstairs. Annie was still awake, and she was gloriously naked. She folded him into her arms, and Alan gladly allowed himself to forget everything else.

7

Stark called again two days later. Thad Beaumont was in Dave's Market at the time.

Dave's was a mom-and-pop store a mile and a half down the road from the Beaumont house. It was a place to go when running to the supermarket in Brewer was just too much of a pain in the ass.

Thad went down that Friday evening to get a six-pack of Pepsi, some chips, and some dip. One of the Troopers watching over the family rode with him. It was June 10th, six-thirty in the evening, plenty of light left in the sky. Summer, that beautiful green bitch, had ridden into Maine again.

The cop sat in the car while Thad went in. He got his soda and was inspecting the wild array of dips (you had your basic clam, and if you didn't like that, you had your basic onion) when the telephone rang.

He looked up at once, thinking: *Oh. Okay.*

Rosalie behind the counter picked it up, said hello, listened, then held the phone out to him, as he had known she would. He was again swallowed by that dreamy feeling of *presque vu.*

"Telephone, Mr. Beaumont."

He felt quite calm. His heart had stumbled over a beat, but only one; now it was jogging along at its usual rate. He was not sweating.

And there were no birds.

He felt none of the fear and fury he'd felt three days earlier. He didn't bother asking Rosalie if it was his wife, wanting him to pick up a dozen eggs or maybe a carton of o.j. while he was here. He knew who it was.

He stood by the Megabucks computer with its bright green screen announcing there had been no winner last week and this week's lottery jackpot was four million dollars. He took the phone from Rosalie and said, "Hello, George."

"Hello, Thad." The soft brush-stroke of Southern accent was still there, but the overlay of country bumpkin was entirely gone—Thad only realized how strongly yet subtly Stark had managed to convey that feeling of "Hail*fahr,* boys, I ain't too bright but I shore did get away with it, didn't I, hyuck, hyuck, hyuck?" when he heard its complete absence here.

But of course now it's just the boys, Thad thought. *Just a coupla white novelists standin around, talkin.*

"What do you want?"

"You know the answer to that. There's no need for us to play games, is there? It's a little bit late for that."

"Maybe I just want to hear you say it out loud." That feeling was back, that weird feeling of being sucked out of his body and pulled down the telephone line to someplace precisely between the two of them.

Rosalie had taken herself down to the far end of the counter, where she was removing packs of cigarettes from a pile of cartons and re-stocking the long cigarette dispenser. She was ostentatiously not listening to Thad's end of the conversation in a way that was almost funny. There was no one in Ludlow—this end of town, anyway—who wasn't aware that Thad was under police guard or police protection or police some-damn-thing, and he didn't have to hear the rumors to know they had already begun to fly. Those who didn't think he was about to be arrested for drug-trafficking no doubt believed it was child abuse or wife-beating. Poor old Rosalie was down there trying to be good, and Thad felt absurdly grateful. He also felt as if he were looking at her through the wrong end of a powerful telescope. He was down the telephone line, down the rabbit hole, where there was no white rabbit but only foxy old George Stark, the man who could not be there but somehow was, all the same.

Foxy old George, and down here in Endsville all the sparrows were flying again.

He fought the feeling, fought hard.

"Go on, George," he said, a little surprised by the rough edge of fury in his voice. He was dazed, caught in a powerful undertow of distance and unreality . . . but God, he sounded so awake and aware! "Say it right out loud, why don't you?"

"If you insist."

"I do."

"It's time to start a new book. A new Stark novel."

"I don't think so."

"Don't say that!" The edge in that voice was like a whiplash loaded with tiny pellets of shot. "I've been drawing you a picture, Thad. I've been drawing it *for* you. Don't make me draw it *on* you."

"You're dead, George. You just don't have the sense to lie down."

Rosalie's head turned a little; Thad glimpsed one wide eye before she turned hurriedly back to the cigarette racks again.

"*You just watch your mouth!*" Real fury in that voice. But was there something more? Was there fear? Pain? Both? Or was he only fooling himself?

"What's wrong, George?" he jeered suddenly. "Are you losing some of your happy thoughts?"

There was a pause, then. That had surprised him, thrown him off-stride, at least momentarily. Thad was sure of that. But why? What had done it?

"Listen to me, buddy-roo," Stark said at last. "I'll give you a week to get started. Don't think you can bullshit me, because you can't." Except the last word was really *cain't*. Yes, George was upset. It might cost Thad a great deal before this was over, but for the time being he felt only savage gladness. He had gotten through. It seemed he was not the only one that felt helpless and dreamily vulnerable during these nightmarishly intimate conversations; he had hurt Stark, and that was utterly fine.

Thad said, "That much is true. There's no bullshit between us. Whatever else there may be, there's none of that."

"You got an idea," Stark said. "You had it before that damn kid even thought about blackmailing you. The one about the wedding and the armored-car score."

"I threw away my notes. I'm done with you."

"No, those were *my* notes you threw away, but it doesn't matter. You don't need notes. It'll be a good book."

"You don't understand. George Stark is *dead.*"

"*You're* the one don't understand," Stark replied. His voice was soft, deadly, emphatic. "You got a week. And if you haven't got at least thirty pages of manuscript, I'll be coming for you, hoss. Only it won't start with you—that'd be too easy. That'd be *entirely* too easy. I'll take your kids first, and they will die slow. I'll see to it. I know how. They won't know what's happening, only that they're dying in agony. But you'll know, and I'll know, and your wife will know. I'll take her next . . . only before I take her, I'll *take* her. You know what I mean, old hoss. And when they're gone, I'll do you, Thad, and you'll die like no man on earth ever died before."

He stopped. Thad could hear him panting harshly in his ear, like a dog on a hot day.

"You didn't know about the birds," Thad said softly. "That much is true, isn't it?"

"Thad, you're not making sense. If you don't start pretty soon, a lot of people are gonna get hurt. Time is runnin out."

"Oh, I'm paying attention," Thad said. "What I'm wondering is how you could have written what you did on Clawson's wall and then on Miriam's *and not know about it.*"

"You better stop talkin trash and start makin sense, my friend," Stark said, but Thad could sense bewilderment and some rough fear just under the surface of that voice. "There wasn't anything written on their walls."

"Oh yes. Yes there was. And do you know what, George? I think maybe the reason you don't know about that is because *I* wrote it. I think part of me was *there*. Somehow part of me was there, watching you. I think I'm the only one of us who knows about the sparrows, George. I think maybe *I* wrote it. You want to think about that . . . think about it *hard* . . . before you start pushing me."

"Listen to me," Stark said with gentle force. "Hear me real good. First your kids . . . then your wife . . . then you. Start another book, Thad. It's the best advice I can give you. Best advice you ever got in y'damn life. Start another book. I'm not dead."

A long pause. Then, softly, very deliberately:

"And I don't want to *be* dead. So you go home and you sharpen y'pencils, and if you need any inspiration, think about how your little babies would look with their faces full of glass.

"There ain't no goddam birds. Just forget about em and start writin."

There was a click.

"Fuck you," Thad whispered into the dead line, and slowly hung up the phone.

Seventeen

WENDY TAKES A FALL

1

The situation would have resolved itself in some way or other no matter what happened—Thad was sure of that. George Stark wasn't simply going to go away. But Thad came to feel, and not without justification, that Wendy's tumble from the stairs two days after Stark called him at Dave's Market set just what course the situation would take for good and all.

The most important result was that it finally showed him a course of action. He had spent those two days in a sort of breathless lull. He found it difficult to follow even the most simple-minded TV program, impossible to read, and the idea of writing seemed roughly akin to the idea of faster-than-light travel. Mostly he wandered from one room to the next, sitting for a few moments, and then moving on again. He got under Liz's feet and on her nerves. She wasn't sharp with him about it, although he guessed she had to bite her tongue on more than one occasion to keep from giving him the verbal equivalent of a paper-cut.

Twice he set out to tell her about the second call from Stark, the one where foxy George had told him exactly what was on his mind, secure in the knowledge that the line wasn't tapped and they were speaking privately. On both occasions he had stopped, aware that he could do nothing but upset her more.

And twice he had found himself up in his study, actually holding one of those damned Berol pencils he had promised never to use again and looking at a fresh, cellophane-wrapped pile of the notebooks Stark had used to write his novels.

You got an idea . . . The one about the wedding and the armored-car score.

And that was true. Thad even had a title, a good one: *Steel Machine.* Something else was true, too: part of him really wanted to write it. That itch was there, like that one place on your back you can't quite reach when you need to scratch.

George would scratch it for you.

Oh yes. George would be *happy* to scratch it for him. But something would happen to him, because things had changed now, hadn't they? What, exactly, would that thing be? He didn't know, perhaps *couldn't* know, but a frightening image kept recurring to him. It was from that charming, racist children's tale of yore, *Little Black Sambo.* When Black Sambo climbed the tree and the tigers couldn't get him, they became so angry that they bit each other's tails and raced faster and faster around the tree until they turned into butter. Sambo gathered the butter up in a crock and took it home to his mother.

George the alchemist, Thad had mused, sitting in his study and tapping an unsharpened Berol Black Beauty against the edge of the desk. *Straw into gold. Tigers into butter. Books into best-sellers. And Thad into . . . what?*

He didn't know. He was *afraid* to know. But *he*

would be gone, *Thad* would be gone, he was sure of that. There might be somebody living here who *looked* like him, but behind that Thad Beaumont face there would be another mind. A sick, brilliant mind.

He thought the new Thad Beaumont would be a good deal less clumsy . . . and a good deal more dangerous.

Liz and the babies?

Would Stark leave them alone if he did make it into the driver's seat?

Not him.

He had considered running, as well. Packing Liz and the twins into the Suburban and just going. But what good would that do? What good when Foxy Old George could look out through Dumb Old Thad's eyes? It wouldn't matter if they ran to the end of the earth; they would get there, look around, and see George Stark mushing after them behind a team of huskies, his straight-razor in his hand.

He considered and, even more rapidly and decisively, dismissed the idea of calling Alan Pangborn. Alan had told them where Dr. Pritchard was, and his decision not to try to get a message through to the neurosurgeon—to wait until Pritchard and his wife returned from their camping trip—told Thad all he needed to know about what Alan believed . . . and, more important, what he did not believe. If he told Alan about the call he'd received in Dave's, Alan would think he was making it up. Even if Rosalie confirmed the fact that he had received a call from *someone* at the market, Alan would go on not believing. He and all the other police officers who had invited themselves to this particular party had a big investment in not believing.

So the days passed slowly, and they were a kind of white time. Just after noon on the second day, Thad jotted *I feel as if I'm in a mental version of the horse latitudes* in his journal. It was the only entry he had made in a week, and he began to wonder if he would ever make another one. His new novel, *The Golden Dog,* was sitting dead in the water. That, he supposed, went almost without saying. It was very hard to make up stories when you were afraid a bad man—a *very* bad man—was going to show up and slaughter your whole family before starting in on you.

The only time he could recall being at such a loss with himself had been in the weeks after he had quit drinking—after he'd pulled the plug on the booze-bath he'd wallowed in following Liz's miscarriage and before Stark appeared. Then, as now, there had been the feeling that there was a problem, but it was as unapproachable as one of those water-mirages you see at the end of a flat stretch of highway on a hot afternoon. The harder he ran toward the problem, wanting to attack it with both hands, dismantle it, destroy it, the faster it receded, until he was finally left, panting and breathless, with that bogus ripple of water still mocking him at the horizon.

These nights he slept badly, and dreamed George Stark was showing him his own deserted house, a house where things exploded when he touched them and where, in the last room, the corpses of his wife and Frederick Clawson were waiting. At the moment he got there, all the birds would begin to fly, exploding upward from trees and telephone lines and electricity poles, thousands of them, millions of them, so many that they blotted out the sun.

Until Wendy fell on the stairs, he felt very much like fool's stuffing himself, just waiting for the right murderous somebody to come along, tuck a napkin into his collar, pick up his fork, and begin to eat.

2

The twins had been crawling for some time, and for the last month or so they had been pulling themselves up to a standing position with the aid of the nearest stable (or, in some cases, unstable) object—a chair-leg was good, as was the coffee-table, but even an empty cardboard carton would serve, at least until the twin in question put too much weight on it and it crumpled inward or turned turtle. Babies are capable of getting themselves into divine messes at any age, but at the age of eight months, when crawling has served its purpose and walking has not quite been learned, they are clearly in the Golden Age of Mess-Making.

Liz had set them out on the floor to play in a bright patch of sun around quarter of five in the afternoon. After ten minutes or so of confident crawling and shaky standing (the latter accompanied by lusty crows of accomplishment to their parents and to each other), William pulled himself up on the edge of the coffee-table. He glanced around and made several imperious gestures with his right arm. These gestures reminded Thad of old newsfilm showing *Il Duce* addressing his constituency from his balcony. Then William seized his mother's teacup and managed to pour the lees all over himself before toppling backward onto his bottom. The tea was fortunately cold, but William held onto the cup and managed to rap it against his mouth smartly enough to make his lower lip bleed a little. He began to wail. Wendy promptly joined in.

Liz picked him up, examined him, rolled her eyes at Thad, and took him upstairs to soothe him and then clean him up. "Keep an eye on the princess," she said as she went.

"I will," Thad said, but he had discovered and would shortly rediscover that, in the Golden Age of Mess-Making, such promises often amount to little. William had managed to snatch Liz's teacup from under her very nose, and Thad saw that Wendy was going to fall from the third stair-riser just a moment too late to save her the tumble.

He had been looking at a news magazine—not reading it but thumbing idly through it, glancing every now and then at a picture. When he was finished, he went over to the large knitting basket by the fireplace which served as a sloppy sort of magazine-rack to put it back and get another. Wendy was crawling across the floor, her tears forgotten before they were entirely dry on her chubby cheeks. She was making the breathy little *rum-rum-rum* sound both of them uttered when crawling, a sound that sometimes made Thad wonder if they associated all movement with the cars and trucks they saw on TV. He squatted, put the magazine on top of the pile in the basket, and thumbed through the others, finally selecting a month-old *Harper's* for no particular reason. It occurred to him that he was behaving quite a bit like a man in a dentist's office waiting for a tooth extraction.

He turned around and Wendy was on the stairs. She had crawled up to the third one and was now rising shakily to her feet, holding onto one of the spindles which ran between the rail of the bannister and the floor. As he looked at her she spied him and gave a particularly grandiloquent arm-gesture and a grin. The sweep of her arm sent her chubby body swaying forward over the short drop.

"Jesus," he said under his breath, and as he rose to his feet, knees popping dryly, he saw her take a step forward and let go of the spindle. *"Wendy, don't do that!"*

He nearly leaped across the room, and almost made it. But he was a clumsy man, and one of his feet caught on the leg of the armchair. It fell over, and Thad went sprawling. Wendy fell outward and forward with a startled little squawk. Her body turned slightly in midair. He grabbed for her from his knees, trying to make a saving catch, and missed by a good two feet. Her right leg struck the first stair-riser, and her head struck the carpeted floor of the living room with a muffled thud.

She screamed, and he had time to think how terrifying a baby's cry of pain is, and then he had swept her into his arms.

Overhead, Liz called out, "Thad?" in a startled voice, and he heard the thump-thump of her slippered feet running down the hall.

Wendy was trying to cry. Her first yell of pain had expelled all but the tidal air from her lungs, and now came the paralyzing, eternal moment when she struggled to unlock her chest and draw in breath for the next whoop. It would bludgeon the eardrums when it finally came.

If it came.

He held her, looking anxiously into her twisted, blood-engorged face. It had gone a color which was almost puce, except for the red mark like a very large comma on her forehead. *God, what if she passes out? What if she strangles to death, unable to pull in breath and utter the cry locked in her flat little lungs?*

"Cry, damn it!" he shouted down at her. God, her purple face! Her bulging stricken eyes! "*Cry!*"

"Thad!" Liz sounded *very* scared now, but she also seemed very distant. In those few eternal seconds between Wendy's first cry and her struggle to free the second one and so go on breathing, George Stark was driven totally out of Thad's mind for the first time in the last eight days. Wendy drew in a great convulsive breath and began to whoop. Thad, trembling with relief, hugged her to his shoulder and began to stroke her back gently, making shushing sounds.

Liz came pounding downstairs, a struggling William clasped against her side like a small bag of grain. "What happened? Thad, is she all right?"

"Yes. She took a tumble from the third stair up. She's fine now. Once she started crying. At first it was like . . . like she just locked up." He laughed shakily and traded Wendy for William, who was now bellowing in sympathetic harmony with his sister.

"Weren't you watching her?" Liz asked reproachfully. She was automatically swinging her body back and forth at the hips, rocking Wendy, trying to soothe her.

"Yes . . . no. I went over to get a magazine. Next thing I knew, she was on the stairs. It was like Will and the teacup. They're just so damned . . . eely. Is her head all right, do you think? She hit on the carpet, but she hit hard."

Liz held Wendy at arm's length for a moment,

looked at the red mark, then kissed it gently. Wendy's sobs were already beginning to diminish in volume.

"I think it's okay. She'll have a bump for a day or two, that's all. Thank God for the carpet. I didn't mean to jump on you, Thad. I know how quick they are. I'm just . . . I feel like I'm going to have my period, only it's all the time now."

Wendy's sobs were winding down to sniffles. Accordingly, William also began to dry up. He reached out a chubby arm and snatched at his sister's white cotton t-shirt. She looked around. He cooed, then babbled at her. To Thad, their babbling always sounded a little eerie: like a foreign language which had been speeded up just enough so you couldn't quite tell which one it was, let alone understand it. Wendy smiled at her brother, although her eyes were still streaming tears and her cheeks were wet with them. She cooed and babbled in reply. For a moment it was as if they were holding a conversation in their own private world—the world of twins.

Wendy reached out and caressed William's shoulder. They looked at each other and went on cooing.

Are you all right, sweet one?

Yes; I hurt myself, dear William, but not badly.

Will you want to stay home from the Stadleys' dinner-party, dear heart?

I should think not, although you are very thoughtful to ask.

Are you quite sure, my dear Wendy?

Yes, darling William, no damage has been done, although I greatly fear I have shit in my diapers.

Oh sweetheart, how TIRESOME!

Thad smiled a little, then looked at Wendy's leg. "That's going to bruise," he said. "In fact, it looks like it's started already."

Liz offered him a little smile. "It will heal," she said. "And it won't be the last."

Thad leaned forward and kissed the tip of Wendy's nose, thinking how fast and how furiously these storms blew in—not three minutes ago he had been afraid she might die from lack of oxygen—and how fast they blew back out again. "No," he agreed. "God willing, it won't be the last."

3

By the time the twins got up from their late naps at seven that evening, the bruise on Wendy's upper thigh had turned a dark purple. It had an odd and distinctive mushroom shape.

"Thad?" Liz said from the other changing-table. "Look at this."

Thad had removed Wendy's nap-diaper, slightly dewy but not really wet, and dropped it into the diaper-bucket marked HERS. He carried his naked daughter over to his son's changing-table to see what Liz wanted him to see. He looked down at William and his eyes widened.

"What do you think?" she asked quietly. "Is that weird, or what?"

Thad looked down at William for a long time. "Yeah," he said at last. "That's pretty weird."

She was holding their wriggling son on the changing-table with a hand on his chest. Now she looked sharply around at Thad. "Are you okay?"

"Yes," Thad said. He was surprised at how calm

he sounded to himself. A large white light seemed to have gone off, not in front of his eyes, like a flash-gun, but behind them. Suddenly he thought he understood about the birds—a little—and what the next step should be. Just looking down at his son and seeing the bruise on his leg, identical in shape, color, and location to the one on Wendy's leg, had made him understand that. When Will had grabbed Liz's teacup and upended it all over himself, he had sat down hard on his butt. So far as Thad knew, William hadn't done anything to his leg at all. Yet there it was—a sympathetic bruise on the upper thigh of his right leg, a bruise which was almost mushroom-shaped.

"You *sure* you're okay?" Liz persisted.

"They share their bruises, too," he said, looking down at William's leg.

"Thad?"

"I'm fine," he said, and brushed her cheek with his lips. "Let's get Psycho and Somatic dressed, what do you say?"

Liz burst out laughing. "Thad, you're crazy," she said.

He smiled at her. It was a slightly peculiar, slightly distant smile. "Yeah," he said. "Crazy like a fox."

He took Wendy back to her changing-table and began to diaper her.

Eighteen

AUTOMATIC WRITING

1

He waited until Liz had gone to bed before going up to his study. He paused outside their bedroom door for a minute or so on his way, listening to the regular ebb and flow of her breathing, assuring himself that she was asleep. He wasn't at all sure that what he was going to try would work, but if it did, it might be dangerous. Extremely dangerous.

His study was one large room—a renovated barn loft—which had been divided into two areas: the "reading room," which was a book-lined area with a couch, a reclining chair, and track lighting, and, at the far end of the long room, his work-area. This part of the study was dominated by an old-fashioned business desk without a single feature to redeem its remarkable ugliness. It was a scarred, battered, uncompromisingly utilitarian piece of furniture. Thad had owned it since he was twenty-six, and Liz sometimes told people he wouldn't let it go because he secretly believed that it was his own private Fountain of Words. They would both smile when she said this, as if they really believed it was a joke.

Three glass-shaded lights hung down over this dinosaur, and when Thad turned on only these lights, as he did now, the savage, overlapping cir-cles of light they made on the desk's littered landscape made it seem as if he were about to play some strange version of billiards there—what the rules for play on such a complex surface might be it was impossible to tell, but on the night after Wendy's accident, the tight set of his face would have convinced an observer that the game would be for very high stakes, whatever the rules.

Thad would have agreed with that one hundred per cent. It had, after all, taken him over twenty-four hours to work his courage up to this.

He looked at the Remington Standard for a moment, a vague hump under its cover with the stainless-steel return lever sticking out from the left side like a hitchhiker's thumb. He sat down in front of it, drummed his fingers restlessly on the edge of the desk for a few moments, then opened the drawer to the left of the typewriter.

This drawer was both wide and deep. He took his journal out of it, then opened the drawer all the way to its stop. The mason jar in which he kept the Berol Black Beauties had rolled all the way to the back, spilling pencils as it went. He took it out, set it in its accustomed place, then gathered up the pencils and put them back into it.

He shut the drawer and looked at the jar. He had tossed it in the drawer after that first fugue, during which he had used one of the Black Beauties to write THE SPARROWS ARE FLYING AGAIN on the manuscript of *The Golden Dog*. He had never intended to use one again . . . yet he had been fooling with one just a couple of nights ago and here they were, sitting where they had sat during the dozen or so years when Stark had lived with him, lived *in* him. For long periods Stark would be quiet, hardly there at all. Then an idea would strike and foxy old George would leap out of his head like a crazed jack-in-the-box. *Ka-POP!* Here I am, Thad! Let's go, old hoss! Saddle up!

And every day for about three months thereafter Stark would leap out promptly at ten o'clock every day, weekends included. He would pop out, seize one of the Berol pencils, and commence writing his crazed nonsense—the crazed nonsense which paid the bills Thad's own work could not pay. Then the book would be done and George would disappear again, like the crazy old man who had woven straw into gold for Rapunzel.

Thad took out one of the pencils, looked at the teeth-marks lightly tattooed on the wooden barrel, and then dropped it back into the jar. It made a tiny *clink!* sound.

"My dark half," he muttered.

But was George Stark his? Had he *ever* been his? Except for the fugue, or trance, or whatever it had been, he had not used one of these pencils, not even to make notes, since writing *The End* at the bottom of the last page of the last Stark novel, *Riding to Babylon.*

There had been nothing to use them *for,* after all; they were George Stark's pencils and Stark was dead . . . or so he had assumed. He supposed he would have gotten around to throwing them out in time.

But now it seemed he had a use for them after all.

He reached toward the wide-mouthed jar, then pulled his hand back, as if from the side of a furnace which glows with its own deep and jealous heat.

Not yet.

He took the Scripto pen from his shirt pocket, opened his journal, uncapped the pen, hesitated, and then wrote.

If William cries, Wendy cries. But I've discovered the link between them is much deeper and stronger than that. Yesterday Wendy fell down the stairs and earned a bruise—a bruise that looks like a big purple mushroom. When the twins got up from their naps, William had one, too. Same location, same shape.

Thad lapsed into the self-interview style which characterized a good part of his journal. As he did so, he realized this very habit—this way of finding a path to the things he really thought—suggested yet another form of duality . . . or perhaps it was only another aspect of a single split in his mind and spirit, something which was both fundamental and mysterious.

Question: If you took slides of the bruises on my children's legs, then overlaid them, would you end up with what looked like a single image?

Answer: Yes, I think you would. I think it is like the fingerprints. I think it is like the voice-prints.

Thad sat quietly for a moment, tapping the end of the pen against the journal page, considering this. Then he leaned forward again and began to write more quickly.

Question: Does William KNOW *he has a bruise?*

Answer: No. I don't think he does.

Question: Do I know what the sparrows are, or what they mean?

Answer: No.

Question: But I do know there ARE *sparrows. I know that much, don't I? Whatever Alan Pangborn or anyone else may believe, I know there* ARE *sparrows, and I know that they are flying again, don't I?*

Answer: Yes.

Now the pen was racing over the page. He had not written so quickly or unselfconsciously in months.

Question: Does Stark know there are sparrows?

Answer: No. He said he doesn't, and I believe him.

Question: Am I SURE *I believe him?*

He stopped again, briefly, and then wrote:

Stark knows there is SOMETHING. *But William must know there is something, too—if his leg is bruised, it must hurt. But Wendy gave him the bruise when she fell downstairs. William only knows he has a hurt place.*

Question: Does Stark know he has a hurt place? A vulnerable place?

Answer: Yes. I think he does.

Question: Are the birds mine?

Answer: Yes.

Question: Does that mean that when he wrote THE SPARROWS ARE FLYING AGAIN *on Clawson's wall and Miriam's wall, he didn't know what he was doing and didn't remember it when he was done?*

Answer: Yes.

Question: Who wrote about the sparrows? Who wrote it in blood?

Answer: The one who knows. The one to whom the sparrows belong.

Question: Who is the one who knows? Who owns the sparrows?

Answer: I am the knower. I am the owner.

Question: Was I there? Was I there when he murdered them?

He paused again, briefly. *Yes,* he wrote, and then: *No. Both. I didn't have a fugue when Stark killed either Homer Gamache or Clawson, at least not that I remember. I think that what I know . . . what I* SEE . . . *may be growing.*

Question: Does he see you?

Answer: I don't know. But . . .

"He must," Thad muttered.

He wrote: *He must know me. He must see me. If he really* DID *write the novels, he has known me for a long time. And his own knowing, his own seeing, is also growing. All that traceback and recording equipment didn't faze foxy old George a bit, did it? No—of course not. Because foxy old George knew it would be there. You don't spend almost ten years writing crime fiction without finding out about stuff like that. That's one reason it didn't faze him. But the other one's even better, isn't it? When he wanted to talk to me, talk to me privately, he knew exactly where I'd be and how to get hold of me, didn't he?*

Yes. Stark had called the house when he wanted to be overheard, and he had called Dave's Market when he didn't. Why had he wanted to be overheard in the first case? Because he had a message to send to the police he knew would be listening— that he wasn't George Stark and *knew* he wasn't . . . and that he was done killing, he wasn't coming after Thad and Thad's family. And there was another reason, too. He wanted Thad to see the voice-prints he knew they would make. He knew the police wouldn't believe their evidence, no matter how incontrovertible it seemed . . . but Thad would.

Question: How did he know where I'd be?

And that was a mighty good question, wasn't it? That was right up there with such questions as how can two different men share the same fingerprints and voice-prints and how can two different babies have exactly the same bruise . . . especially when only one of the babies in question happened to bump her leg.

Except he knew that similar mysteries were well-documented and accepted, at least in cases where twins were involved; the bond between identicals was even more eerie. There had been an article about it in one of the news magazines a year

or so ago. Because of the twins in his own life, Thad
had read the article closely.

There was the case of identical twins who were
separated by an entire continent—but when one of
them broke his left leg, the other suffered excruciating pains in his own left leg without even knowing
something had happened to his sib. There were the
identical girls who had developed their own special
language, a language known and understood by no
one else on earth. These twin girls had never learned
English in spite of their identical high IQs. What
need for English had they? They had each other . . .
and that was all they wanted. And, the article said,
there were the twins who, separated at birth, were
reunited as adults and found they had both married
on the same day of the same year, women with the
same first name and strikingly similar looks. Fur-
thermore, both couples had named their first sons
Robert. Both Roberts had been born in the same
month and in the same year.

Half and half.

Criss and cross.

Snick and snee.

"Ike and Mike, they think alike," Thad muttered. He reached out and circled the last line he
had written:

Question: How did he know where I'd be?

Below this he wrote:

*Answer: Because the sparrows are flying again. And
because we are twins.*

He turned to a fresh page in his journal and laid
the pen aside. Heart thumping hard, skin freezing
with fear, he reached out a trembling right hand and
pulled one of the Berol pencils from the jar. It seemed
to burn with a low and unpleasant heat in his hand.

Time to go to work.

Thad Beaumont leaned over the blank page, paused, and then printed THE SPARROWS ARE FLYING AGAIN in large block letters at the top.

2

What, exactly, did he mean to do with the pencil?

But he knew that, too. He was going to try and answer the last queston, the one so obvious he hadn't even bothered to write it down: Could he consciously induce the trance state? Could he *make* the sparrows fly?

The idea embodied a form of psychic contact he had read about but had never seen demonstrated: automatic writing. The person attempting to contact a dead soul (or a living one) by this method held a pen or pencil loosely in his hand with the tip on a blank sheet of paper and simply waited for the spirit—pun most definitely intended—to move him. Thad had read that automatic writing, which could be practiced with the aid of a Ouija board, was often approached as a kind of lark, a party-game, even, and that this could be extremely dangerous—that it could, in fact, lay the practitioner wide open to some form of possession.

Thad had neither believed nor disbelieved this when reading it; it seemed as foreign to his own life as the worship of pagan idols or the practice of trepanning to relieve headaches. Now it seemed to have its own deadly logic. But he would have to summon the sparrows.

He thought of them. He tried to summon up the image of all those birds, all those *thousands* of birds,

sitting on roofpeaks and telephone wires beneath a
mild spring sky, waiting for the telepathic signal
to take off.

And the image came . . . but it was flat and
unreal, a kind of mental painting with no life in it.
When he began writing it was often like this—a
dry and sterile exercise. No, it was worse than that.
Starting off always felt a little obscene to him, like
French-kissing a corpse.

But he had learned that, if he kept at it, if he
simply kept pushing the words along the page,
something else kicked in, something which was
both wonderful and terrible. The words as individ-
ual units began to disappear. Characters who were
stilted and lifeless began to limber up, as if he had
kept them in some small closet overnight and they
had to loosen their muscles before they could begin
their complicated dances. Something began to
happen in his *brain;* he could almost feel the shape
of the electrical waves there changing, losing their
prissy goose-step discipline, turning into the soft,
sloppy delta waves of dreaming sleep.

Now Thad sat hunched over his journal, pencil in hand, and tried to make this happen. As the
moments spun themselves out and nothing did
happen, he began to feel more and more foolish.

A line from the old *Rocky and Bullwinkle* cartoon show got into his head and refused to leave:
Eenie-meenie-chili-beanie, the spirits are about to speak!
What in God's name was he going to say to Liz if
she showed up and asked him what he was doing
here with a pencil in his hand and a blank sheet of
paper in front of him, at just a few minutes before
midnight? That he was trying to draw the bunny
on the matchbook and win a scholarship to the

Famous Artists School in New Haven? Hell, he didn't even *have* one of those matchbooks.

He moved to put the pencil back, and then paused. He had turned in his chair a little so he was looking out the window to the left of his desk.

There was a bird out there, sitting on the window-ledge and looking in at him with bright black eyes.

It was a sparrow.

As he watched, it was joined by another.

And another.

"Oh my God," he said in a trembling, watery voice. He had never been so terrified in his life . . . and suddenly that sensation of *going* filled him again. It was as it had been when he spoke to Stark on the telephone, but now it was stronger, much stronger.

Another sparrow landed, jostling the other three aside for place, and beyond them he saw a whole line of birds sitting on top of the carriage-house where they kept the lawn equipment and Liz's car. The antique weathervane on the carriage-house's single gable was covered with them, swinging beneath their weight.

"Oh my God," he repeated, and he heard his voice from a million miles away, a voice which was filled with horror and terrible wonder. "Oh my dear God, they're real—*the sparrows are real.*"

In all his imaginings he had never suspected this . . . but there was no time to consider it, no mind to consider it *with*. Suddenly the study was gone, and in its place he saw the Ridgeway section of Bergenfield, where he had grown up. It lay as silent and deserted as the house in his Stark nightmare; he found himself peering at a silent suburb in a dead world.

Yet it was not entirely dead, because the roof of every house was lined with twittering sparrows. Every TV antenna was freighted with them. Every tree was filled with them. They queued upon every telephone line. They sat on the tops of parked cars, on the big blue mailbox which stood at the corner of Duke Street and Marlborough Lane, and on the bike-rack in front of the Duke Street Convenience Store, where he had gone to buy milk and bread for his mother when he was a boy.

The world was filled with sparrows, waiting for the command to fly.

Thad Beaumont lolled back in his office chair, a thin froth spilling from the corners of his mouth, feet twitching aimlessly, and now all the windows of the study were lined with sparrows, looking in at him like strange avian spectators. A long, gargling sound escaped his mouth. His eyes rolled up in his head, revealing bulging, glistening whites.

The pencil touched the sheet and began to write.

SIS

it scrawled across the top line. It dropped two lines, made the L-shaped indent-mark that was characteristic of each new Stark paragraph, and wrote:

⌐ The woman began to slip away from the door. She did this almost at once, even before the door had stopped its short inward swing, but it was too late. My hand shot out through the two-inch gap between the door and the jamb and clamped over her hand.

The sparrows flew.

All at once they all took flight, the ones in his head from that long-ago Bergenfield, and the ones outside his Ludlow home . . . the *real* ones. They flew up into two skies: a white spring sky in the year 1960, and a dark summer sky in the year 1988.

They flew and they were gone in a ruffling blast of wings.

Thad sat up . . . but his hand was still nailed to the pencil, being pulled along.

The pencil was writing by itself.

I made it, he thought dazedly, wiping spit and froth from his mouth and chin with his left hand. *I made it . . . and I wish to God I had let it alone. What* is *this?*

He stared down at the words pouring out of his fist, his heart thumping so hard he felt the pulse, high and fast, in his throat. The sentences spilling out on the blue lines were in his own handwriting—but then, *all* of Stark's novels had been written in his hand. *With the same fingerprints, the same taste in cigarettes, and exactly the same vocal characteristics, it would be odder if it were someone else's handwriting,* he thought.

His handwriting, just as it had been all the other times, but where were the *words* coming from? Not from his own head, that was certain; there was nothing up there right now but terror overlaid with loud, roaring confusion. And there was no feeling in his hand anymore. His right arm seemed to end roughly three inches above his wrist. There was not even a remote sense of pressure in his fingers, although he could see he was gripping the Berol tightly enough to turn his thumb and first two fingers white at the tips. It was as if he had been given a healthy shot of Novocain.

He reached the bottom of the first sheet. His unfeeling hand tore it back, his unfeeling palm raced up the journal's binding, creasing the page flat, and began to write again.

> *Miriam Cowley opened her mouth to scream. I had been standing just inside the door, waiting patiently for just over four hours, not drinking coffee, not smoking cigarettes (I'd wanted one, and would have one as soon as it was over, but before, the smell might have alerted her). I reminded myself to close her eyes after cutting her throat.*

Thad realized with mounting horror that he was reading an account of Miriam Cowley's murder . . . and this time it was not a broken, confused stew of words, but the coherent, brutal narration of a man who was, in his own horrid way, an extremely effective writer—effective enough so that millions of people had bought his fiction.

George Stark's nonfiction debut, he thought sickly.

He had done exactly what he had set out to do: had made contact, had somehow tapped into Stark's mind, just as Stark must somehow have tapped into Thad's own mind. But who would have guessed what monstrous, unknown forces he would touch in doing so? Who *could* have guessed? The sparrows—and the realization that the sparrows were *real*—had been bad, but this was worse. Had he thought both the pencil and the notebook were warm to the touch? No wonder. This man's mind was a fucking furnace.

And now—Jesus! Here it was! Unrolling out of his own fist! Jesus Christ!

("You're thinking you could brain me with that thing, aren't you, dis?" I asked her. "let me tell you something — that's not a happy thought. and you know what happens to people who lose their happy thoughts, don't you?" (The tears were running down his cheeks now.)

What's wrong, George? Are you losing some of your happy thoughts?

No *wonder* it had stopped the black-hearted son of a bitch for a moment when he had said that. If this was the way it really had been, then Stark had used the same phrase before killing Miriam.

I WAS *tapped into his mind during the murder—I* WAS. *That's why I used that phrase during the conversation we had at Dave's.*

Here was Stark forcing Miriam to call Thad, dialing the number for her because she was too terrified to remember it, although there were weeks when she must have dialed it half a dozen times. Thad found this forgetfulness and Stark's understanding of it both horrible and persuasive. And now Stark was using his razor to—

But he didn't want to read that, wouldn't read that. He pulled his arm up, lifting his numb hand along with it like a lead weight. The instant the pencil's contact with the notebook was broken, feeling flooded back into the hand. The muscles were cramped, and the side of his second finger ached dully; the barrel of the pencil had left an indentation which was now turning red.

He looked down at the scrawled page, full of horror and a dumb species of wonder. The last thing on earth he wanted to do was to put that pencil back down again, to complete that obscene circuit between Stark and himself again . . . but he hadn't gotten into this just to read Stark's first-hand account of Mir Cowley's murder, had he?

Suppose the birds come back?

But they wouldn't. The birds had served their purpose. The circuit he had achieved was still whole and functioning. Thad had no idea how he knew that, but he *did* know.

Where are you, George? he thought. *How come I don't feel you? Is it because you are as unaware of my presence as I am of yours? Or is it something else? Where the fuck* ARE *you?*

He held the thought in the front of his mind, trying to visualize it as a bright red neon sign. Then he gripped the pencil again and began lowering it toward his journal.

As soon as the tip of the pencil touched the paper, his hand rose again and flipped to a blank sheet. The palm flattened the turned sheet along the crease as it had done once before. Then the pencil returned to the paper, and wrote:

> ("It doesn't matter," Machine told Jack Rangely. "All places are the same." He paused. "Except maybe home. And I'll know that when I get there."

All places are the same. He recognized that line first, then the whole quote. It was from the first chapter of Stark's first novel, *Machine's Way.*

The pencil had stopped of its own accord this time. He raised it and looked down at the scribbled words, cold and prickling. *Except maybe home. And I'll know that when I get there.*

In *Machine's Way,* home had been Flatbush Avenue, where Alexis Machine had spent his childhood, sweeping up in the billiard parlor of his diseased alcoholic father. Where was home in *this* story?

Where is home? he thought at the pencil, and slowly lowered it to the paper again.

The pencil made a quick series of sloping m-shapes. It paused, then moved again.

Home is where the start is

the pencil wrote below the birds.

A pun. Did it mean anything? Was the contact really still there, or was he fooling himself now? He hadn't been fooling himself about the birds, and he hadn't been fooling himself during that first frenzied spate of writing, he knew that, but the feeling of heat and compulsion seemed to have abated. His hand still felt numb, but how tightly he was gripping the pencil—and that was very tightly indeed, judging from the mark on the side of his finger—could have something to do with that. Hadn't he read in that same piece on automatic writing that people often fooled themselves with the Ouija board—that in most cases it was guided not by the spirits but by the subconscious thoughts and desires of the operator?

Home is where the start is. If it was still Stark, and if the pun had some meaning, it meant here, in this house, didn't it? Because George Stark had been born here.

Suddenly part of the damned *People* magazine article floated into his mind.

"I rolled a sheet of paper into my typewriter . . . and

then I rolled it right back out again. I've typed all my books, but George Stark apparently didn't hold with typewriters. Maybe because they didn't have typing classes in any of the stone hotels where he did time."

Cute. Very cute. But it had only a second-cousinship with the actual facts, didn't it? It wasn't the first time Thad had told a story that had only a tenuous relationship to the truth, and he supposed it wouldn't be the last—assuming he lived through this, of course. It wasn't exactly lying; it wasn't even embroidering the truth, strictly speaking. It was the almost unconscious act of fictionalizing one's own life, and Thad didn't know a single writer of novels or short stories who didn't do it. You didn't do it to make yourself look better than you'd actually been in any given situation; sometimes that happened, but you were just as apt to relate a story that cast you in a bad light or made you look comically stupid. What was the movie where some newspaperman had said, "When you've got a choice between truth and legend, print the legend"? *The Man Who Shot Liberty Valance,* maybe. It might make for shitty and immoral reporting, but it made for wonderful fiction. The overflow of make-believe into one's own life seemed to be an almost unavoidable side-effect of story-telling—like getting calluses on the pads of your fingers from playing the guitar, or developing a cough after years of smoking.

The facts of Stark's birth were actually quite different from the *People* version. There had been no mystic decision to write the Stark novels longhand, although time had turned it into a kind of ritual. And when it came to ritual, writers were as superstitious as professional athletes. Baseball players might wear the same socks day after day or cross themselves before stepping into the batter's box if they were hitting well; writers, when successful, were apt to follow the same patterns until they became rituals in an effort to ward off the literary equivalent of a batting slump . . . which was known as writer's block.

George Stark's habit of writing his novels longhand had begun simply because Thad forgot to bring any fresh ribbons for the Underwood in his little office at the summer house in Castle Rock. He'd had no typewriter ribbons, but the idea had been too hot and promising to wait, so he had rooted through the drawers of the little desk he kept down there until he found a notebook and some pencils and—

In those days we used to get down to the place at the lake a lot later in the summer, because I taught that three-week block course—what was it called? Creative Modes. Stupid damned thing. It was late June that year, and I remember going up to the office and discovering there weren't any ribbons. Hell, I remember Liz bitching that there wasn't even any coffee—

Home is where the start is.

Talking to Mike Donaldson, the guy from *People* magazine, telling the semi-fictional story of George Stark's genesis, he had switched the location to the big house here in Ludlow without even thinking about it—because, he supposed, Ludlow was where he did most of his writing and it was perfectly normal to set the scene here—especially if you *were* setting a scene, *thinking* of a scene, the way you did when you were making a piece of fiction. But it wasn't here that George Stark had made his debut; not here that he had first used Thad's eyes to look out at the world, although it was here that he had done most of his work both as Stark and as himself, it was here that they lived most of their odd dual lives.

Home is where the start is.

In this case, home must mean Castle Rock. Castle Rock, which also happened to be the location of Homeland Cemetery. Homeland Cemetery, which was where, in Thad's mind if not in Alan Pangborn's, George Stark had first appeared in his murderous physical incarnation, about two weeks ago.

Then, as if it were the most natural progression in the world (and for all he knew, it might have been), another question occurred to him, one that was so basic and occurred so spontaneously that he heard himself mutter it aloud, like a shy fan at a meet-the-author tea: "Why do you want to go back to writing?"

He lowered his hand until the tip of the pencil touched the paper. That numbness flowed back over it and into it, making it feel as if it were immersed in a stream of very cold, very clear water.

Once more the hand's first act was to rise again and turn to a fresh page in the journal. It came back down, creased the turned sheet flat . . . but this time the writing did not begin at once. Thad had time to think that the contact, whatever it was, had been broken in spite of the numbness, and then the pencil jerked in his hand as if it were a live thing itself . . . alive but badly wounded. It jerked, making a mark like a sleepy comma, jerked again, making a dash, and then wrote

*George Stark   George Stark George
George Stark   There are no birds*

before coming to rest like a wheezy piece of machinery.

Yes. You can write your name. And you can deny the sparrows. Very good. But why do you want to go back to writing? Why is it so important? Important enough to kill people?

∟*If I don't I'll die*

the pencil wrote.

"What do you mean?" Thad muttered, but he felt a wild hope explode in his head. Could it possibly be that simple? He supposed that it *could* be, especially for a writer who had no business existing in the first place. Christ, there were enough *real* writers who couldn't exist unless they were writing, or felt they couldn't . . . and in the case of men like Ernest Hemingway, it really came down to the same thing, didn't it?

The pencil trembled, then drew a long, scrawling line below the last message. It looked weirdly like the voice-print.

"Come *on*," Thad whispered. "What the hell do you mean?"

∟*Falling* APART

the pencil wrote. The letters were stilted, reluctant. The pencil jerked and wavered between his fingers, which were wax-white. *If I exert much more pressure,* Thad thought, *it's just gonna snap off.*

*losing losing necessary COHESION
there are no birds THERE ARE NO FUCKING BIRDS
oh you son of a bitch get out of
my head*

Suddenly his arm flew up. At the same time his numb hand flicked the pencil with the agility of a stage-magician manipulating a card, and instead of holding it between his fingers most of the way down its barrel, he was gripping the pencil in his fist like a dagger.

He brought it down—*Stark* brought it down—and suddenly the pencil was buried in the web of flesh between the thumb and first finger of his left hand. The graphite tip, somewhat dulled by the writing Stark had done with it, passed almost all the way through it. The pencil snapped. A bright puddle of blood filled the depression the pencil's barrel had dragged into his flesh, and suddenly the force which had gripped him was gone. Red pain raved up from his hand, which lay on his desk with the pencil jutting out of it.

Thad threw his head back and clamped his teeth shut against the agonized howl which fought to escape his throat.

3

There was a small bathroom off the study, and when Thad felt able to walk, he took his monstrously throbbing hand there and examined the wound under the harsh glare of the overhead fluorescent tube. It looked like a bullet-wound—a perfectly round hole rimmed with a flaring black smudge. The smudge looked like gunpowder, not graphite. He turned his hand over and saw a bright red dot, the size of a pinprick, on the palm side. The tip of the pencil.

That's how close it came to going all the way through, he thought.

He ran cold water over and into the wound until his hand was numb, then took the bottle of hydrogen peroxide from the cabinet. He found he could not hold the bottle in his left hand, so he pressed it against his body with his left arm in order to get the cap off. Then he poured disinfectant into the hole in his hand, watching the liquid turn white and foam, gritting his teeth against the pain.

He put the hydrogen peroxide back and then took down the few bottles of prescription medicine in the cabinet one by one, examining their labels. He had had terrible back-spasms after a fall he had taken while cross-country skiing two years ago, and good old Dr. Hume had given him a prescription for Percodan. He had taken only a few of them; he had found the pills fucked up his sleep-cycle and made it hard for him to write.

He finally discovered the plastic vial hiding behind a can of Barbasol shaving cream that had to be at least a thousand years old. Thad pried the vial's cap off with his teeth and shook one of the pills out onto the side of the sink. He debated adding a second, and decided against it. They were strong.

And maybe they're spoiled. Maybe you can end this

wild night of fun with a good convulsion and a trip to the
hospital—how about that?

But he decided to take the chance. There really
wasn't even a question—the pain was immense,
incredible. As for the hospital . . . he looked at the
wound in his hand again and thought, *Probably I*
should go and have this looked at, but I'll be goddamned
if I will. I've had enough people looking at me like I was
crazy in the last few days to last me a lifetime.

He scooped up another four Percodans, stuffed
them into his pants pocket, and returned the vial
to the medicine cabinet shelf. Then he covered the
wound with a Band-Aid. One of the round spots
did the trick. *Looking at that little circle of plastic,*
he thought, *you'd have no idea how badly the damned*
thing hurts. He set a bear-trap for me. A bear-trap in his
mind, and I walked right into it.

Was that really what had happened? Thad didn't
know, not for sure, but he knew one thing: he did
not want a repeat performance.

4

When he had himself under control again—or
something approaching it—Thad returned his
journal to his desk drawer, turned off the lights in
the study, and went down to the second floor. He
paused on the landing, listening for a moment. The
twins were quiet. So was Liz.

The Percodan, apparently not too old to work,
began to kick in and the pain in Thad's hand began
to back off a little. If he inadvertently flexed it, the
low throb there turned into a scream, but if he was
careful of it, it wasn't too bad.

Oh, but it's going to hurt in the morning, buddy . . . and what are you going to tell Liz?

He didn't know, exactly. Probably the truth . . . or some of it, anyway. She had gotten very skilled, it seemed, at picking up on his lies.

The pain was better, but the after-effects of the sudden shock—*all* the sudden shocks—still lingered, and he thought it would be some time yet before he could sleep. He went down to the first floor and peeked out at the State Police cruiser parked in the driveway through the sheers drawn across the big living-room window. He could see the firefly flicker of two cigarettes inside.

They're sitting there just as cool as a pair of summer cucumbers, he thought. *The birds didn't bother them any, so maybe there really* WEREN'T *any, except in my head. After all, these guys get paid to be bothered.*

It was a tempting idea, but the study was on the other side of the house. Its windows could not be seen from the driveway. Neither could the carriage-house. So the cops couldn't have seen the birds, anyway. Not, at least, when they began to roost.

But what about when they all flew away? You want to tell me they didn't hear that? You saw at least a hundred of them, Thad—maybe two or three hundred.

Thad went outside. He had hardly done more than open the kitchen screen door before both Troopers were out of the car, one on each side. They were big men who moved with the silent speed of ocelots.

"Did he call again, Mr. Beaumont?" the one who had gotten out on the driver's side asked. His name was Stevens.

"No—nothing like that," Thad said. "I was writing in my study when I thought I heard a whole bunch of birds take off. It freaked me out a little. Did you guys hear that?"

Thad didn't know the name of the cop who had gotten out on the passenger side. He was young and blonde, with one of those round, guileless faces which radiate good nature. "Heard em and saw em both," he said. He pointed to the sky, where the moon, a little past the first quarter, hung above the house. "They flew right across the moon. Sparrows. Quite a flock of em. They hardly ever fly at night."

"Where do you suppose they came from?" Thad asked.

"Well, I tell you," the Trooper with the round face said, "I don't know. I flunked Bird Surveillance."

He laughed. The other Trooper did not. "Feeling jumpy tonight, Mr. Beaumont?" he asked.

Thad looked at him levelly. "Yes," he said. "I've been feeling jumpy *every* night, just lately."

"Could we do anything for you just now, sir?"

"No," Thad said. "I think not. I was just curious about what I heard. Goodnight, you guys."

"Night," the round-faced Trooper said.

Stevens only nodded. His eyes were bright and expressionless below the wide brim of his Trooper's Stetson.

That one thinks I'm guilty, Thad thought, going back up the walk. *Of what? He doesn't know. Probably doesn't care. But he's got the face of a man who believes everyone is guilty of something. Who knows? Maybe he's even right.*

He closed the kitchen door and locked it

behind him. He went back into the living room and looked out again. The Trooper with the round face had retreated back into the cruiser, but Stevens was still standing on the driver's side, and for a moment Thad had the impression that Stevens was looking directly into his eyes. It couldn't be, of course; with the sheers drawn, Stevens would see only an indistinct dark shape . . . if he saw anything at all.

Still, the impression lingered.

Thad drew the drapes over the sheers and went to the liquor cabinet. He opened it and took out a bottle of Glenlivet, which had always been his favorite tipple. He looked at it for a long moment and then put it back. He wanted a drink very badly, but this would be the worst time in history to start drinking again.

He went out to the kitchen and poured himself a glass of milk, being very careful not to bend his left hand. The wound had a brittle, hot feel.

He came in vague, he thought, sipping the milk. *It didn't last long—he sharpened up so fast it was scary—but he came in vague. I think he was asleep. He might have been dreaming of Miriam, but I don't think so. What I tapped into was too coherent to be a dream. I think it was memory. I think it was George Stark's subconscious Hall of Records, where everything is neatly written down and then filed in its own slot. I imagine that if he tapped my subconscious—and for all I know, maybe he already has—he'd find the same sort of thing.*

He sipped his milk and looked at the pantry door.

I wonder if I could tap into his WAKING *thoughts . . . his conscious thoughts.*

He thought the answer was yes . . . but he also thought it would render him vulnerable again. And next time it might not be a pencil in the hand. Next time it might be a letter-opener in the neck.

He can't. He needs me.

Yeah, but he's crazy. Crazy people are not always hip to their own best interests.

He looked at the pantry door and thought about how he could go in there . . . and from there outside again, on the other side of the house.

Could I make him do something? The way he made me do something?

He could not answer that one. At least not yet. And one failed experiment might kill him.

Thad finished his milk, rinsed his glass, and put it into the dish drainer. Then he went into the pantry. Here, between shelves of canned goods on the right and shelves of paper goods on the left, was a Dutch door leading out to the wide expanse of lawn which they called the back yard. He unlocked the door, pushed both halves open, and saw the picnic table and the barbecue out there, standing silent sentinel. He stepped out onto the asphalt walk which ran around this side of the house and finally joined the main walk in front.

The walk glimmered like black glass in the chancy light of the half-moon. He could see white splotches on it at irregular intervals.

Sparrow-shit, not to put too fine a point on it, he thought.

Thad walked slowly up the asphalt path until he was standing directly below his study windows. An Orinco truck came over the horizon and pelted down Route 15 toward the house, casting a momentary bright light across the lawn and the asphalt walk. In this brief light, Thad saw the corpses of two sparrows lying on the walk—tiny heaps of feathers with trifurcate feet sticking out of them. Then the truck was gone. In the moonlight, the bodies of the dead birds became irregular patches of shadow once again—no more than that.

They were real, he thought again. *The sparrows were real.* That blind, revolted horror returned, making him feel somehow unclean. He tried to make his hands into fists, and his left responded with a wounded bellow. What little relief he had gotten from the Percodan was already passing.

They were here. They were real. How can that be?

He didn't know.

Did I call them, or did I create them out of thin air?

He didn't know that, either. But he felt sure of one thing: the sparrows which had come tonight, the real sparrows which had come just before the trance had swallowed him, were only a fraction of all *possible* sparrows. Perhaps only a microscopic fraction.

Never again, he thought. *Please—never again.*

But he suspected that what he wanted did not matter. That was the real horror; he had touched some terrible paranormal talent in himself, but he could not control it. The very idea of control in this matter was a joke.

And he believed that before this was over, they would be back.

Thad shuddered and went back to the house. He slipped into his own pantry like a burglar, then locked the door behind him and took his throbbing hand up to bed. Before he went, he swallowed another Percodan, washing it down with water from the kitchen tap.

Liz did not wake when he lay down beside her. Some time later he escaped into three hours of grainy, fitful sleep in which nightmares flew and circled around him, always just out of reach.

Nineteen

STARK MAKES A PURCHASE

1

Waking up wasn't like waking up.

When you came right down to it, he didn't think he had *ever* really been awake or asleep, at least in the way normal people used those words. In a way it was as if he were always asleep, and only moved from one dream to another. In that way, his life—what little of it he remembered—was like a nest of Chinese boxes that never ended, or like peering into an endless hall of mirrors.

This dream was a nightmare.

He came slowly out of sleep knowing he hadn't really been asleep at all. Somehow Thad Beaumont had managed to capture him for a little while; had managed to bend him to his will for a little while. Had he said things, *revealed things,* while Beaumont had been in control of him? He had a feeling he might have done . . . but he also felt quite sure Beaumont would not know how to interpret those things, or how to tell the important things he might have said from the things that didn't matter.

He also came out of sleep to pain.

He had rented a two-room "efficiency" in the East Village, just off Avenue B. When he opened his eyes he was sitting at the lopsided kitchen table with an open notebook in front of him. A rivulet of bright blood ran across the faded oilcloth which covered the table, and there was nothing very surprising about that, because there was a Bic pen sticking out of the back of his right hand.

Now the dream began to come back.

That was how he had been able to drive Beaumont out of his mind, the only way he had been able to break the bond the cowardly shit had somehow forged between them. Cowardly? Yes. But he was also *sly,* and it would be a bad idea to forget that. A very bad idea, indeed.

Stark could vaguely remember dreaming that Thad was with him, in his bed—they were talking together, whispering together, and at first this had seemed both pleasant and oddly comforting—like talking with your brother after lights out.

Except they were doing more than *talking,* weren't they?

What they had been doing was *exchanging secrets* . . . or, rather, Thad was asking him questions and Stark found himself answering. It was *pleasant* to answer, it was *comforting* to answer. But it was also alarming. At first his alarm was centered on the birds—why did Thad keep asking him about *birds?* There *were* no birds. Once, perhaps . . . a long, long time ago . . . but not anymore. It was just a mind-game, a puny effort to freak him out. Then, little by little, his sense of alarm became entwined with his almost exquisitely attuned survival instinct—it grew sharper and more specific as he continued trying to struggle awake. He felt as if he were being held underwater, drowned . . .

So, still in that half-waking, half-dreaming

state, he had gone into the kitchen, opened the notebook, and picked up the ballpoint pen. Thad hadn't tipped to any of that; why should he have? Wasn't he also writing five hundred miles away? The pen wasn't right, of course—didn't even feel right in his hand—but it would do. For now.

Falling APART, he had watched himself write, and by then he had been very close to the magic mirror that divided sleep from wakefulness, and he struggled to impose his own thoughts upon the pen, his own will upon what would and would not appear on the blankness of the paper, but it was hard, good God, good Christ, it was so damned *hard.*

He had bought the Bic pen and half a dozen notebooks in a stationery shop right after he had arrived in New York City; had done it even before renting the wretched "efficiency." There were Berol pencils in the shop, and he had wanted to buy *them,* but he hadn't. Because, no matter whose mind it was that had driven the pencils, it had been Thad Beaumont's hand which held them, and he needed to know if that was a bond he could break. So he had left the pencils and had taken the pen instead.

If he could write, if he could write *on his own,* all would be well and he wouldn't need the wretched, whining creature up in Maine at all. But the pen had been useless to him. No matter how hard he tried, no matter how mightily he concentrated, the only thing he had been able to write was his own name. He had written it over and over again: George Stark, George Stark, George Stark, until, at the bottom of the sheet, they were not recognizable words at all but only the jittery scribbles of a preschooler.

Yesterday he had gone to a branch of the New

York Public Library and had rented an hour's time on one of the grim gray electric IBMs in the Writing Room. The hour had seemed to last a thousand years. He sat in a carrel which was enclosed on three sides, fingers trembling on the keys, and typed his name, this time in capital letters: GEORGE STARK, GEORGE STARK, GEORGE STARK.

Break it! he had screamed at himself. *Type something else, anything else, just break it!*

So he had tried. He had bent over the keys, sweating, and typed: *The quick brown fox jumped over the lazy dog.*

Only when he looked up at the paper, he saw that what he had written was *The george George Stark george starked over the starky stark.*

He had felt an urge to rip the IBM right off its bolts and go rampaging through the room with it, swinging the typewriter like a barbarian's mace, splitting heads and breaking backs: if he could not create, let him uncreate!

Instead, he had controlled himself (with a mighty effort) and had walked out of the library, crumpling the useless sheet of paper in one strong hand as he went and dropping it into a litter basket on the sidewalk. He remembered now, with the Bic pen in his hand, the utter blind rage he had felt at discovering that without Beaumont he couldn't write anything but his own name.

And the fear.

The panic.

But he still *had* Beaumont, didn't he? Beaumont might think it was the other way around, but maybe . . . maybe Beaumont was in for one large fucking surprise.

losing, he wrote, and Jesus, he couldn't tell Beaumont any *more*—what he had written already was bad enough. He made a mighty effort to seize control of his traitor hand. To *wake up.*

necessary COHESION, his hand wrote, as if to amplify the previous thought, and suddenly Stark saw himself stabbing Beaumont with the pen. He thought: *And I can do it, too: I don't think* you *could, Thad, because when it comes down to it, you're just a long drink of milk, aren't you? But when it comes to the sticking point . . . I can handle it, you bastard. It's time you learned that, I think.*

Then, even though this was like a dream within a dream, even though he was gripped by that horrible, vertiginous feeling of being out of control, some of his savage and unquestioning self-confidence returned and he was able to pierce the shield of sleep. In that triumphant moment of breaking the surface before Beaumont could drown him, he seized control of the pen . . . and was finally able to *write* with it.

For a moment—and it was only a moment—there was a sensation of *two* hands grasping two writing instruments. The feeling was too clear, too real, to be anything *but* real.

there are no birds, he wrote—the first real sentence he had *ever* written as a physical being. It was terribly hard to write; only a creature of supernatural determination could have suffered through the effort. But once the words were out, he felt his control strengthen. The grip of that other hand weakened, and Stark laid his own grip over it, showing no mercy or hesitation.

Drown for awhile, he thought. *See how* you *like it.*

In a rush quicker and far more satisfying than even the most powerful orgasm, he wrote: THERE

ARE NO FUCKING BIRDS *Oh you son of a bitch get out of my* HEAD!

Then, before he could think about it—thinking might have provoked fatal hesitation—he swept the Bic pen around in a short, shallow arc. The steel tip plunged into his right hand . . . and, hundreds of miles north, he could feel Thad Beaumont sweeping a Berol Black Beauty pencil around and plunging it into his *left* hand.

That was when he woke up—when they *both* woke up—for real.

2

The pain was sizzling and enormous—but it was also liberating. Stark screamed, turning his sweaty head against his arm to muffle the sound, but it was a scream of joy and exhilaration as well as pain.

He could feel Beaumont stifling his own scream in his study up there in Maine. The awareness Beaumont had created between them did not break; it was more like a hastily-tied knot which gave way under the pressure of a final tremendous yank. Stark sensed, almost *saw,* the probe the treacherous bastard had sent wriggling into his head while he slept now twisting and twitching and slithering away.

Stark reached out, not physically, but with his mind, and seized that disappearing tail of Thad's mental probe. In the eye of Stark's own mind it looked like a worm, a fat white maggot deliriously stuffed with offal and decay.

He thought of making Thad grab another pencil from the mason jar and use it to stab himself again—in the eye this time. Or perhaps he would have him drive the pencil's point deep into his ear, rupturing the eardrum and digging for the soft meat of the brain beyond. He could almost hear Thad's scream. He would not be able to muffle *that* one.

Then he stopped. He didn't want Beaumont dead.

At least not yet.

Not until Beaumont had taught him how to live on his own.

Stark slowly relaxed his fist, and as he did, he felt the fist in which he held Beaumont's essence—the mental fist, which had proved every bit as quick and merciless as his physical one—also open. He felt Beaumont, the plump white maggot, slip away, squealing and moaning.

"Only for now," he whispered, and turned to the other necessary business. He closed his left hand around the pen jutting out of his right hand. He drew it smoothly out. Then he dropped it into the wastebasket.

3

There was a bottle of Glenlivet standing on the stainless-steel dish-drainer by the sink. Stark picked it up and walked into the bathroom. His right hand swung by his side as he walked, splattering dime-sized droplets of blood on the warped and faded linoleum. The hole in his hand was about half an inch above the ridge of the knuckles and slightly to the right of the third one. It was perfectly round. The stain of the black ink around the edge of the hole, combined with the internal bleeding and trauma, made it look like a gunshot wound. He tried to flex the hand. The fingers moved . . . but the sickening wave of pain that resulted was too great for further experimentation.

He pulled the chain depending from the fixture above the medicine cabinet mirror, and the unshaded sixty-watt bulb came on. He used his right arm to hold the bottle of whiskey clamped against his side so he could unscrew the cap. Then he held his wounded hand splayed out over the basin. Was Beaumont doing the same thing in Maine? He doubted it. He doubted if Beaumont had the guts to clean up his own mess. He would undoubtedly be on his way to the hospital by now.

Stark tipped whiskey into the wound, and a bolt of pure, steely pain leaped up his arm to his shoulder. He saw the whiskey bubbling in the wound, saw little threads of blood in the amber, and had to bury his face against the sweat-soaked arm of his shirt again.

He thought the pain would never fade, but at last it began to.

He tried to put the bottle of whiskey on the shelf bolted to the tile wall below the mirror. His hand was shaking too badly for this operation to stand much chance of success, so he set it on the rust-splotched tin floor of the shower stall instead. He would want a drink in a minute.

He raised the hand to the light and peered into the hole. He could see the bulb through it, but dimly—it was like looking through a red filter bleared with some kind of membranous muck. He hadn't driven the pen all the way through his hand, but it had been damned close. Maybe Beaumont had done better.

He could always hope.

He held his hand under the cold water tap, splaying the fingers to draw the hole as wide open as possible, then steeled himself for the pain. It was bad at first—he had to strain another scream through teeth which were clenched and lips which were pressed together in a thin white line—but then the hand grew numb and it was better. He forced himself to hold it under the tap for a full three minutes. Then he turned the faucet off and held it up to the light again.

The glow of the bulb through the hole was still there, but now it was dim and distant. The wound was closing up. His body seemed to have amazing powers of regeneration, and that was rather amusing, because at the same time he was falling apart. Losing cohesion, he had written. And that was close enough.

He looked at his face fixedly in the wavery, spotted mirror on the medicine chest for thirty seconds or more, then shook himself back to awareness with a physical jerk. Looking at his face, so well-known and familiar and yet so new and strange, always made him feel as if he were falling into a hypnotic trance. He supposed if he looked at it long enough, he would do just that.

Stark opened the medicine cabinet, swinging the mirror and his repulsively fascinating face aside. There was an odd little collection of items in the chest: two disposable razors, one used; bottles of make-up; a compact; several wedges of fine-grained sponge, ivory-colored where they had not been stained a slightly darker color by face-powder;

a bottle of generic aspirin. No Band-Aids. Band-Aids were like cops, he thought—never one around when you really needed one. That was all right, though—he would disinfect the wound with some more whiskey (after disinfecting his insides with a healthy wallop, that was) and then wrap it in a handkerchief. He didn't think it would turn septic; he seemed immune to infection. He also found this amusing.

He used his teeth to uncap the aspirin bottle, spat the cap into the basin, then upended the bottle and shook half a dozen pills into his mouth. He took the whiskey out of the shower stall and washed the aspirins down with a slug. The booze hit his stomach and opened its comforting blossom of heat there. Then he used some more on his hand.

Stark went into the bedroom and opened the top drawer of a bureau which had seen better—much better—days. It and an ancient sofa-bed were the only pieces of furniture in the room.

The top drawer was the only one with anything in it save newspaper liners from the *Daily News:* three pairs of undershorts still in the store wrapper, two pairs of socks with the manufacturer's label still banded around them, a pair of Levi's, and a Hav-a-Hank, also still in its wrapper. He tore the cellophane open with his teeth and tied the Hav-a-Hank around his hand. Amber whiskey soaked through the thin cloth, then one small bloom of blood. Stark waited to see if the bloom would spread, but it didn't. Good deal. A very good deal.

Had Beaumont been able to pick up any *sensory* input? he wondered. Did he, maybe, know that George Stark was currently sheltering in a cruddy little East Village apartment in a cheesy building where the roaches looked big enough to steal the welfare checks? He didn't think so, but it made no sense to take chances when he didn't have to. He had promised Thad a week to decide, and although he was now all but positive that Thad had no plans to start writing as Stark again, he would see that Thad got all the time he had been promised.

He was a man of his word, after all.

Beaumont was probably going to need a little inspiration. One of those little propane torches you could buy in hardware stores turned on the soles of his kids' feet for a couple of seconds ought to do the trick, Stark thought, but that was for later. For the time being he would play a waiting game . . . and while he did, it wouldn't hurt to start drifting north. To get a little field position, you might say. There was, after all, his car—the black Toronado. It was in storage, but that didn't mean it had to *stay* in storage. He could leave New York City tomorrow morning. But before he did, he had a purchase to make . . . and right now he ought to use some of the cosmetics in the bathroom cabinet.

4

He took out the little jars of liquid make-up, the powder, the sponges. He took another hefty drink from the bottle before starting. His hands were steady again, but his right throbbed nastily. This did not particularly upset him; if his was throbbing, Beaumont's must be screaming.

He faced himself in the mirror, touched the arc

of skin under his left eye with his left finger, then ran it down his cheek to the corner of his mouth. "Losing cohesion," he muttered, and oh boy, that certainly was the truth.

When Stark had first looked at his face—kneeling outside Homeland Cemetery, gazing into a mud-puddle whose still and scummy surface had been lit by the round white moon of a nearby streetlamp—he had been satisfied. It was exactly as it had appeared in the dreams he'd had while imprisoned in the womblike dungeon of Beaumont's imagination. He had seen a conventionally handsome man whose features were a little too broad to attract much attention. Had the forehead not been quite so high, the eyes not so far apart, it might have been the sort of face that would make women turn their heads for a second look. A *perfectly* nondescript face (if there is such a thing) may attract attention just because there is no one feature to catch the eye before the eye dismisses it and moves on; its utter ordinariness may trouble that eye, and cause it to return for a second glance. The face Stark had seen for the first time with real eyes in the mud-puddle missed that degree of plainness by a comfortable margin. He had thought it the perfect face, one no one would be able to describe afterward. Blue eyes . . . a tan that might seem the tiniest bit odd on one with such fair hair . . . and that was it! That was all! The witness would be forced to move on to the broad shoulders which were really the most distinguishing thing about him . . . and the world was full of broad-shouldered men.

Now everything had changed. Now his face had become decidedly strange . . . and if he did not begin writing again soon, it would become more than strange. It would become grotesque.

Losing cohesion, he thought again. *But you're going to put a stop to that, Thad. When you start the book about the armored-car job, what's happening to me will start to reverse itself. I don't know how I know that, but I do know it.*

It had been two weeks since he had seen himself for the first time in that puddle, and his face had undergone a steady degeneration since then. It had been subtle at first, so subtle that he had been able to persuade himself it was only his imagination . . . but, as the changes began to speed up, that position had become untenable and he had been forced to retreat from it. Seeing a photograph of him taken then and one taken now might have made someone think of a man who had been exposed to some weird radiation or corrosive chemical substance. George Stark seemed to be experiencing a spontaneous breakdown of all his soft tissues at the same time.

The crow's feet around the eyes, ordinary marks of middle age which he had seen in the puddle, were now deep grooves. His lids had grown droopy and had taken on the rough texture of crocodile skin. His cheeks had begun to take on a similar seamed and cracked look. The rims of the eyes themselves had grown reddish, giving him the sorrowful look of a man who didn't know it was time to take his nose out of the bottle. Deep lines had carved themselves in the flesh of his face from the corners of his lips to the line of his jaw, giving his mouth the disquietingly hinged look of a ventriloquist's dummy. His blonde hair, fine to begin with, had grown finer still, drawing back from his temples and showing the pink skin of his pate. Liverspots had appeared on the backs of his hands.

He could have abided all this without resorting to make-up. He only looked old, after all, and old age was hardly remarkable. His strength seemed unimpaired. Plus, there was that unshakable surety that once he and Beaumont started writing again—writing as George Stark, that was—the process would reverse itself.

But now his teeth had grown loose in his gums. And there were sores, too.

He had noticed the first one inside his right elbow three days ago—a red patch with a lace of dead white skin around the edges. It was the sort of blemish he associated with pellagra, which had been endemic in the deep South even into the 1960s. The day before yesterday he had seen another one, on his neck this time, below the lobe of his left ear. Two more yesterday, one on his chest between his nipples, the other below his navel.

Today the first one had appeared on his face, at the right temple.

They didn't hurt. There was a dull, deep-seated itch, but that was all . . . at least, as far as sensation went. But they spread rapidly. His right arm was now a dull, swollen red from the fold of his elbow halfway to his shoulder. He had made the mistake of scratching, and the flesh had given way with sickening ease. A mixture of blood and yellowish pus had oozed out along the trenches his fingernails had left, and the wounds gave off a ghastly, gassy smell. Yet it was not infection. He would have sworn to that. It was more like . . . damp-rot.

Looking at him now, someone—even a trained medical person—would probably have guessed grass-fire melanoma, perhaps caused by exposure to high-level radiation.

Still, the sores did not worry him greatly. He supposed they would multiply in number, spread in area, join each other, and eventually eat him alive . . . if he let them. Since he didn't intend to let that happen, there was no need for them to worry him. But he couldn't be just another face in the crowd if the features on that face were transforming themselves into an erupting volcano. Hence, the make-up.

He applied the liquid foundation carefully with one of the sponge wedges, spreading it up from cheekbones to temples, eventually covering the dull red lump beyond the end of his right brow and the new sore just beginning to poke through the skin over his left cheekbone. A man wearing pancake make-up looked like only one thing on God's earth, Stark had discovered, and that was a man wearing pancake make-up. Which was to say, either an actor in a TV soap opera or a guest on the Donahue show. But anything was an improvement on the sores, and the tan mitigated some of the phony effect. If he stayed in the gloom or was seen in artificial lighting, it was hardly noticeable at all. Or so he hoped. There were other reasons to stay out of direct sunlight, as well. He suspected the sun actually accelerated the disastrous chemical reaction going on inside him. It was almost as if he were turning into a vampire. But that was all right; in a way, he had always been one. *Besides—I'm a night-person, always have been; that's just my nature.*

This made him grin, and the grin exposed teeth like fangs.

He screwed the cover back on the liquid

make-up and began to powder. *I can smell myself,* he thought, *and pretty soon other people are going to be able to smell me, too—a thick, unpleasant smell, like a can of potted meat that's spent the day standing in the sun. This is not good, friends and dear hearts. This is not good at all.*

"You *will* write, Thad," he said, looking at himself in the mirror. "But with luck, you won't have to do it for long."

He grinned more widely, exposing an incisor which had gone dark and dead.

"I'm a quick study."

5

At half-past ten the next day, a stationer on Houston Street sold three boxes of Berol Black Beauty pencils to a tall, broad-shouldered man wearing a checked shirt, blue-jeans, and very large sunglasses. The man was also wearing pancake make-up, the stationer observed—probably the remains of a night spent tomcatting around in the leather bars. And from the way he smelled, the stationer thought he had done a little more than just splash on the old English Leather; he smelled as if he had *bathed* in it. The cologne didn't disguise the fact that the broad-shouldered dude smelled filthy. The stationer thought briefly—*very* briefly—about making a wisecrack, and then thought again. The dude smelled bad but looked strong. Also, the transaction was mercifully brief. After all, it was just pencils the fruitcake was buying, not a Rolls-Royce Corniche.

Best to leave ill enough alone.

6

Stark made a brief stop back at the East Village "efficiency" to stuff his few belongings into the packsack he had bought in an Army-Navy store on his first day in the maggoty old Big Apple. If not for the bottle of Scotch, he probably would not have bothered to return at all.

On his way up the crumbling front steps, he passed the small bodies of three dead sparrows without noticing them.

He left Avenue B on foot . . . but he didn't walk for long. A determined man, he had discovered, can always find a ride if he really needs one.

Twenty

OVER THE DEADLINE

1

The day Thad Beaumont's week of grace ended felt more like a day in late July than one in the third week of June. Thad drove the eighteen miles to the University of Maine under a sky the color of hazy chrome, the air-conditioner in the Suburban going full blast in spite of the havoc it wreaked on the gas mileage. There was a dark brown Plymouth behind him. It never got closer than two car-lengths and never dropped back farther than five. It rarely allowed another car to come between itself and Thad's Suburban; if one did happen to ease its way into the two-car parade at an intersection or the school-zone in Veazie, the brown Plymouth passed quickly . . . and if this didn't look almost immediately feasible, one of Thad's guardians would pull the cover off the blue bubble on the dashboard. A few flashes from that would do the trick.

Thad drove mostly with his right hand, using his left only when he absolutely had to. The hand was better now, but it still hurt like hell if he bent or flexed it too ruthlessly, and he found himself counting down the last few minutes of the last hour before he could swallow another Percodan.

Liz hadn't wanted him to go up to the University

today, and the State Police assigned to the Beaumonts hadn't wanted him to, either. For the State boys, the issue was simple: they hadn't wanted to split their watch team. With Liz, things were a little more complex. What she *talked* about was his hand; he might open the wound trying to drive, she said. What was in her eyes was quite different. Her eyes had been full of George Stark.

Just what in the hell do you have to go up to the shop for today, anyway? she had wanted to know—and this was a question he had had to prepare himself for, because the semester was over, had been for some time now, and he wasn't teaching any summer classes. What he'd settled on, finally, were the Honors folders.

Sixty students had applied for Eh-7A, the Department's Honors course in creative writing. This was over twice the number that had applied for the previous fall semester's Honors writing course, but (elementary, my dear Watson) last fall the world—including that part of it majoring in English at the University of Maine—had not known that boring old Thad Beaumont also just happened to be funky George Stark.

So he had told Liz that he wanted to pull those files and start going through them, winnowing the sixty applicants down to fifteen students—the maximum he could take on (and probably fourteen more than he could actually teach) in a creative writing course.

She had, of course, wanted to know why he couldn't put it off, at least until July, and had reminded him (also of course) that he had put it off until mid-August the year before. He had gone back to the big leap in applications, then added virtuously that he didn't want last summer's laziness to become a habit.

At last she had stopped protesting—not because his arguments had convinced her, he thought, but because she could see he meant to go, no matter what. And she knew as well as he did that they would *have* to start going out again, sooner or later—hiding in the house until someone killed or collared George Stark wasn't a very palatable option. But her eyes had still been full of a dull, questioning fear.

Thad had kissed her and the twins and left quickly. She looked as if she might start crying soon, and if he was still home when she did that, he would *stay* home.

It wasn't the Honors folders, of course.

It was the deadline.

He had awakened this morning full of his own dull fear, a feeling as unpleasant as a belly cramp. George Stark had called on the evening of June 10th and had given him a week to get going on the novel about the armored-car heist. Thad had still done nothing about starting . . . although he saw how the book could go more clearly with each passing day. He had even dreamed about it a couple of times. It made a nice break from touring his own deserted house in his sleep and having things explode when he touched them. But this morning his first thought had been, *The deadline. I'm over the deadline.*

That meant it was time to talk to George again, as little as he wanted to do that. It was time to find out just how angry George was. Well . . . he supposed he knew the answer to that one. But it was just possible that, if he was *very* angry, out-of-control angry, and if Thad could goad him until he was all the way out of control, foxy old George might just make a mistake and let something slip.

Losing cohesion.

Thad had a feeling that George had *already* let something slip when he allowed Thad's intruding hand to write those words in his journal. If he could only be sure of what they meant, that was. He had an idea . . . but he wasn't *sure.* And a mistake at this point could mean more than just *his* life.

So he was on his way to the University, on his way to his office in the English-Math Building. He was on his way there not to collect the Honors files—although he would—but because there was a telephone there, one that wasn't tapped, and because something had to be done. He was over the deadline.

Glancing down at his left hand, which rested on the steering wheel, he thought (not for the first time during this long, long week) that the telephone was not the only way to get in touch with George. He had proved that . . . but the price had been very high. It was not just the excruciating agony of plunging a sharpened pencil into the back of his hand, or the horror of watching while his out-of-control body hurt itself at the command of Stark—foxy old George, who seemed to be the ghost of a man who had never been. He had paid the *real* price in his mind. The real price had been the coming of the sparrows; the terror of realizing that the forces at work here were much greater and even more incomprehensible than George Stark himself.

The sparrows, he had become more and more sure, meant death. But for whom?

He was terrified that he might have to risk the sparrows in order to get in touch with George Stark again.

And he could see them coming; he could see them arriving at that mystic halfway point where the two of them were linked, that place where he would eventually have to wrestle George Stark for control of the one soul they shared.

He was afraid he knew who would win in a struggle at that place.

2

Alan Pangborn sat in his office at the rear of the Castle County Sheriff's Office, which occupied one wing of the Castle Rock Municipal Building. It had been a long, stressful week for him, too . . . but that was nothing new. Once summer really started to roll in The Rock, it got this way. Law-enforcement from Memorial Day to Labor Day was always insane in Vacationland.

There had been a gaudy four-car smashup on Route 117 five days ago, a booze-inspired wreck that had left two people dead. Two days later, Norton Briggs had hit his wife with a frying pan, knocking her flat on the kitchen floor. Norton had hit his wife a great many licks during the turbulent twenty years of their marriage, but this time he apparently believed he had killed her. He wrote a brief note, long on remorse and short on grammar, then took his own life with a .38 revolver. When his wife, no Rhodes Scholar herself, woke up and found the cooling corpse of her tormentor lying beside her, she had turned on the gas oven and stuck her head into it. The paramedics from Rescue Services in Oxford had saved her. Barely.

Two kids from New York had wandered away from their parents' cottage on Castle Lake and had gotten lost in the woods, just like Hansel and Gretel. They had been found eight hours later, scared but all right. John LaPointe, Alan's number-two deputy, was not in such good shape; he was home with a raving case of poison ivy he had contracted during the search. There had been a fist-fight between two summer people over the last copy of the Sunday *New York Times* at Nan's Luncheonette; another fist-fight in the parking-lot of the Mellow Tiger; a weekend fisherman had torn off half of his right ear while trying to make a fancy cast into the lake; three cases of shoplifting; and a small dope bust at Universe, Castle Rock's billiard parlor and video game arcade.

Just your typical small-town week in June, a sort of grand opening celebration for summer. Alan had had barely enough time to drink a whole cup of coffee at one sitting. And still, he had found his mind turning to Thad and Liz Beaumont again and again . . . to them, and to the man who was haunting them. That man had also killed Homer Gamache. Alan had made several calls to the New York City cops—there was a certain Lieutenant Reardon who was probably very sick of him by now—but they had nothing new to report.

Alan had come in this afternoon to an unexpectedly peaceful office. Sheila Brigham had nothing to report from dispatch, and Norris Ridgewick was snoozing in his chair out in the bullpen area, feet cocked up on his desk. Alan should have wakened him—if Danforth Keeton, the First Selectman, came in and saw Norris cooping like that, he would have a cow—but he just didn't have the heart to do it. It had been a busy week for Norris, too. Norris had been in charge of scraping up the road-toads after the smash out on 117, and he had done a damned good job, fluttery stomach and all.

Alan now sat behind his desk, making shadow animals in a patch of sun which fell upon the wall . . . and his thoughts turned once more to Thad Beaumont. After getting Thad's blessing, Dr. Hume in Orono had called Alan to tell him that Thad's neurological tests were negative. Thinking of this now, Alan's mind turned once more to Dr. Hugh Pritchard, who had operated on Thad when Thaddeus Beaumont was eleven and a long way from famous.

A rabbit hopped across the patch of sun on the wall. It was followed by a cat; a dog chased the cat.

Leave it alone. It's crazy.

Sure it was crazy. And sure, he could leave it alone. There would be another crisis to handle here before long; you didn't have to be psychic to know that. It was just the way things went during the summer here in The Rock. You were kept so busy that most times you couldn't think, and sometimes it was *good* not to think.

An elephant followed the dog, swinging a shadow trunk which was actually Alan Pangborn's left forefinger.

"Ah, fuck it," he said, and pulled the telephone over to him. At the same time his other hand was digging his wallet out of his back pocket. He punched the button which automatically dialed the State Police Barracks in Oxford and asked dispatch there if Henry Payton, Oxford's O.C. and

C.I.D. man, was in. It turned out he was. Alan had time to think that the State Police must also be having a slow day for a change, and then Henry was on the line.

"Alan! What can I do for you?"

"I was wondering," Alan said, "if you'd like to call the Head Ranger at Yellowstone National Park for me. I could give you the number." He looked at it with mild surprise. He had gotten it from directory assistance almost a whole week before, and written it on the back of a business card. His facile hands had dug it out of his wallet almost on their own.

"Yellowstone!" Henry sounded amused. "Isn't that where Yogi Bear hangs out?"

"Nope," Alan said, smiling. "That's *Jellystone*. And the bear isn't suspected of anything, anyway. At least, as far as I know. I need to talk to a man who's on a camping vacation there, Henry. Well . . . I don't know if I actually *need* to talk to him or not, but it would set my mind at rest. It feels like unfinished business."

"Does it have to do with Homer Gamache?"

Alan shifted the phone to his other ear and walked the business card on which he had written the Yellowstone Head Ranger's number absently across his knuckles.

"Yes," he said, "but if you ask me to explain, I'm going to sound like a fool."

"Just a hunch?"

"Yes." And he was surprised to find he *did* have a hunch—he just wasn't sure what it was about. "The man I want to talk to is a retired doctor named Hugh Pritchard. He's with his wife. The Head Ranger probably knows where they are—I understand you have to register when you come in—and I'm guessing it's probably in a camping area with access to a telephone. They're both in their seventies. If *you* called the Head Ranger, he'd probably pass the message on to the guy."

"In other words, you think a National Park Ranger might take the Officer Commanding of a State Police Troop more seriously than a dipshit County Sheriff."

"You have a very diplomatic way of putting things, Henry."

Henry Payton laughed delightedly. "I *do*, don't I? Well, I'll tell you what, Alan—I don't mind doin a little business for you, as long as you don't want me to wade in any deeper, and as long as you—"

"No, this is it," Alan said gratefully. "This is all I want."

"Wait a minute, I'm not done. As long as you understand I can't use our WATS line here to make the call. The Captain looks at those statements, my friend. He looks very closely. And if he saw this one, I think he might want to know why I was spendin the taxpayer's money to stir your stew. You see what I'm sayin?"

Alan sighed resignedly. "You can use my personal credit card number," he said, "and you can tell the Head Ranger to have Pritchard call collect. I'll red-line the call and pay for it out of my own pocket."

There was a pause on the other end, and when Henry spoke again, he was more serious. "This really means something to you, doesn't it, Alan?"

"Yes. I don't know why, but it does."

There was a second pause. Alan could feel Henry Payton struggling not to ask questions. At last, Henry's better nature won. Or perhaps, Alan thought, it was only his more practical nature. "Okay," he said. "I'll make the call, and tell the Head Ranger that you want to talk to this Hugh Pritchard about an ongoing murder investigation in Castle County, Maine. What's his wife's name?"

"Helga."

"Where they from?"

"Fort Laramie, Wyoming."

"Okay, Sheriff; here comes the hard part. What's your telephone credit card number?"

Sighing, Alan gave it to him.

A minute later he had the shadow-parade marching across the patch of sunlight on the wall again.

The guy will probably never call back, he thought, *and if he does, he won't be able to tell me a goddam thing I can use—how could he?*

Still, Henry had been right about one thing: he had a hunch. About *something*. And it wasn't going away.

3

While Alan Pangborn was speaking to Henry Payton, Thad Beaumont was parking in one of the faculty slots behind the English-Math Building. He got out, being careful not to bang his left hand. For a moment he just stood there, digging the day and the unaccustomed dozy peace of the campus.

The brown Plymouth pulled in next to his Suburban, and the two big men who got out dispelled any dream of peace he might have been on the verge of building.

"I'm just going up to my office for a few minutes," Thad said. "You could stay down here, if you wanted." He eyed two girls strolling by, probably on their way to East Annex to sign up for summer courses. One was wearing a halter top and blue shorts, the other an almost non-existent mini with no back and a hem that was a strong man's heart-beat away from the swell of her buttocks. "Enjoy the scenery."

The two State cops had turned to follow the girls' progress as if their heads were mounted on invisible swivels. Now the one in charge—Ray Garrison or Roy Harriman, Thad wasn't sure which—turned back and said regretfully, "Sure would like to, sir, but we better come up with you."

"Really, it's just the second floor—"

"We'll wait out in the hall."

"You guys don't know how much all of this is starting to depress me," Thad said.

"Orders," Garrison-or-Harriman said. It was clear that Thad's depression—or happiness, for that matter—meant less than zero to him.

"Yeah," Thad said, giving it up. "Orders."

He headed for the side door. The two cops followed him at a distance of a dozen paces, looking more like cops in their streetclothes than they ever had in their uniforms, Thad suspected.

After the still, humid heat, the air conditioning struck Thad with a wallop. All at once his shirt felt as if it were freezing to his skin. The building, so full of life and racket during the September-to-May academic year, felt a little creepy on this week-end afternoon at the end of spring. It would fill up to maybe a third of its usual hustle and bustle on Monday, when the first three-week summer session started, but for today, Thad found himself feeling a trifle relieved to have his police guard with him. He thought the second floor, where his office was, might be entirely deserted, which would at least allow him to avoid the necessity of explaining his large, watchful friends.

It turned out not to be entirely deserted, but he got off easily just the same. Rawlie DeLesseps was wandering down the hallway from the Department common room toward his own office, drifting in his usual Rawlie DeLesseps way . . . which meant he looked as if he might have recently sustained a hard blow to the head which had disrupted both his memory and his motor control. He moved dreamily from one side of the corridor to the other in mild loops, peering at the cartoons, poems, and announcements tacked to the bulletin boards on the locked doors of his colleagues. He *might* have been on his way to his office—it *looked* that way—but even someone who knew him well would probably have declined to make book on it. The stem of an enormous yellow pipe was clamped between his dentures. The dentures were not quite as yellow as the pipe, but they were close. The pipe was dead, had been since late 1985, when his doctor had forbidden him to smoke it following a mild heart attack. *I never liked to smoke that much anyway,* Rawlie would explain in his gentle, distracted voice when someone asked him about the pipe. *But without the bit in my teeth . . . gentlemen, I would not know where to go or what to do if I were lucky enough to arrive there.* Most times he gave the impression of not knowing where to go or what to do anyway . . . as he did now. Some people knew Rawlie for years before discovering he was not at all the absent-minded educated fool he seemed to be. Some never discovered it at all.

"Hello, Rawlie," Thad said, picking through his keys.

Rawlie blinked at him, shifted his gaze to scan the two men behind Thad, dismissed them, and returned his gaze to Thad once more.

"Hello, Thaddeus," he said. "I didn't think you were teaching any summer courses this year."

"I'm not."

"Then what can have possessed you to come here, of all places, on the first *bona fide* dog day of summer?"

"Just picking up some Honors files," Thad said. "I'm not going to be here any longer than I have to, believe me."

"What did you do to your hand? It's black and blue all the way to the wrist."

"Well," Thad said, looking embarrassed. The story made him sound like a drunk or an idiot, or both . . . but it still went down a lot easier than the truth would have done. Thad had been dourly amused to find that the police accepted it as easily as Rawlie did now—there had not been a single question about how or why he had managed to slam his own hand in the door of his bedroom closet.

He had instinctively known exactly the right story to tell—even in his agony he had known that. He was *expected* to do clumsy things—it was part of his character. In a way, it was like telling the interviewer from *People* (God rest his soul) that George Stark had been created in Ludlow instead of Castle Rock, and that the reason Stark wrote in longhand was because he had never learned to type.

He hadn't even tried to lie to Liz . . . but he had insisted she keep quiet about what had really happened, and she had agreed to do so. Her only concern had been extracting a promise from him that he would not try to contact Stark again. He had given the promise willingly enough, although he knew it was one he might not be able to keep. He suspected that, on some deep level of her mind, Liz knew that, too.

Rawlie was now looking at him with real interest. "In a closet door," he said. "Marvelous. Were you perhaps playing hide and seek? Or was it some strange sexual rite?"

Thad grinned. "I gave up strange sexual rites around 1981," he said. "Doctor's advice. Actually, I just wasn't paying attention to what I was doing. The whole thing is sort of embarrassing."

"I imagine so," Rawlie said . . . and then winked. It was a very subtle wink, a bare flutter of one puffed and wrinkled old eyelid . . . but it was very definitely there. Had he thought he had fooled Rawlie? Pigs might fly.

Suddenly a new thought occurred to Thad. "Rawlie, do you still teach that Folk Myth seminar?"

"Every fall," Rawlie agreed. "Don't you read your own Department's catalogue, Thaddeus? Dowsing, witches, holistic remedies, Hex Signs of the Rich and Famous. It's as popular now as ever. Why do you ask?"

There was an all-purpose answer to that question, Thad had discovered; one of the best things about being a writer was that you always had an answer to *Why do you ask?* "Well, I have a story idea," he said. "It's still in the exploration stage, but it's got possibilities, I think."

"What did you want to know?"

"Do sparrows have any significance in American superstition or folk myth that you know of?"

Rawlie's furrowing brow began to resemble the topography of some alien planet which was clearly inimical to human life. He gnawed on the stem of his pipe. "Nothing occurs right off the top of my head, Thaddeus, although . . . I wonder if that's really why you're interested."

Pigs might fly, Thad thought again: "Well . . . maybe not, Rawlie. Maybe not. Maybe I just said that because my interest is nothing I could explain in a hurry." His eyes flicked briefly to his watchdogs, then returned to Rawlie's face. "I'm a bit pressed for time right now."

Rawlie's lips quivered in the faintest ghost of a smile. "I understand, I think. Sparrows . . . such common birds. Too common to have any deep superstitious connotations, I'd think. Yet . . . now that I think about it . . . there *is* something. Except I associate it with whippoorwills. Let me check. Will you be here awhile?"

"Not more than half an hour, I'm afraid."

"Well, I might find something right away in Barringer's book. *Folklore of America.* It's really not much more than a cookbook of superstitions, but it comes in handy. And I could always call you."

"Yes. You could always do that."

"Lovely party you and Liz threw for Tom Carroll," Rawlie said. "Of course, you and Liz *always* throw the best parties. Your wife is much too charming to *be* a wife, Thaddeus. She should be your mistress."

"Thanks. I guess."

"Gonzo Tom," Rawlie continued fondly. "It's hard to believe Gonzo Tom Carroll has sailed into the Gray Havens of retirement. I've been listening to him cut those trumpet-blast farts of his in the next office for better than twenty years. I suppose the next fellow will be quieter. Or at least more discreet."

Thad laughed.

"Wilhelmina also enjoyed herself," Rawlie said. His eyelids drooped roguishly. He knew perfectly well how Thad and Liz felt about Billie.

"That's fine," Thad said. He found Billie Burks and the concept of enjoyment mutually exclusive . . . but since she and Rawlie had formed part of a badly needed alibi, he supposed he should be glad she had come. "And if anything occurs to you about that other thing . . ."

"Sparrows and their place in the Invisible World. Yes indeed." Rawlie nodded to the two policemen behind Thad. "Good afternoon, gentlemen." He skirted them and continued on down to his office with a little more purpose. Not much, but a little.

Thad looked after him, bemused.

"What was *that?*" Garrison-or-Harriman asked.

"DeLesseps," Thad murmured. "Chief grammarian and amateur folklorist."

"Looks like the kind of guy who might need a map to find his way home," the other cop said.

Thad moved to the door of his office and unlocked it. "He's more alert than he looks," he said, and opened the door.

He wasn't aware that Garrison-or-Harriman was beside him, one hand inside his specially tailored Tall Fella sport-coat, until he had flicked on the overhead lights. Thad felt a moment of belated fear, but the office was empty, of course—empty and so neat, after the soft and steady fallout of an entire year's clutter, that it looked dead.

For no reason that he could place, he felt a sudden and nearly sickening wave of homesickness and emptiness and loss—a mix of feelings like a deep, unexpected grief. It was like the dream. It was as if he had come here to say goodbye.

Stop being so goddam foolish, he told himself, and another part of his mind replied quietly: *Over the deadline, Thad. You're over the deadline, and I think you might have made a very bad mistake in not at least trying to do what the man wants you to do. Short-term relief is better than no relief at all.*

"If you want coffee, you can get a cup in the common room," he said. "The pot will be full, if I know Rawlie."

"Where's that?" Garrison-or-Harriman's partner asked.

"Other side of the hall, two doors up," Thad said, unlocking the files. He turned and gave them a grin that felt crooked on his face. "I think you'll hear me if I scream."

"Just make sure you *do* yell, if something happens," Garrison-or-Harriman said.

"I will."

"I could send Manchester here for the coffee," Garrison-or-Harriman said, "but I get the feeling that you're asking for a little privacy."

"Well, yeah. Now that you mention it."

"That's fine, Mr. Beaumont," he said. He looked at Thad seriously, and Thad suddenly remembered that his name was Harrison. Just like the ex-Beatle. Stupid to have forgotten it. "You just want to remember those people in New York died from an overdose of privacy."

Oh? I thought Phyllis Myers and Rick Cowley died in the company of the police. He thought of saying this out loud and then didn't. These men were, after all, only trying to do their duty.

"Lighten up, Trooper Harrison," he said. "The building's so quiet today a barefoot man would make echoes."

"Okay. We'll be across the hall in the what-do-you-call-it."

"Common room."

"Right."

They left, and Thad opened the file marked HNRS APPS. In his mind's eye he kept seeing Rawlie DeLesseps dropping that quick, unobtrusive wink. And listening to that voice telling him he was over the deadline, that he had crossed to the dark side. The side where the monsters were.

4

The phone sat there and didn't ring.

Come on, he thought at it, stacking the Honors folders on the desk beside his University-supplied IBM Selectric. *Come on, come on, here I am, standing right next to a phone with no bug on it, so come on, George, give me a call, give me a ring, give me the scoop.*

But the phone only sat there and didn't ring.

He realized he was looking into a file cabinet that wasn't just pruned but entirely empty. In his preoccupation he had pulled *all* the folders, not just the ones belonging to Honors students interested in taking creative writing. Even the Xeroxes of those who wanted to take Transformational Grammar, which was the Gospel according to Noam Chomsky, translated by that Dean of the Dead Pipe, Rawlie DeLesseps.

Thad went to the door and looked out. Harrison and Manchester were standing in the door of the Department common room, drinking coffee. In their ham-sized fists, the mugs looked the size of demitasse cups. Thad raised his hand. Harrison raised his in return and asked him if he would be much longer.

"Five minutes," Thad said, and both cops nodded.

He went back to his desk, separated the creative writing files from the others, and began to replace the latter in the file drawer, doing it as slowly as possible, giving the phone time to ring. But the phone just went on sitting there. He heard one ring someplace far down the corridor, the sound muffled by a closed door, somehow ghostly in the building's unaccustomed summer silence. *Maybe George got the wrong number,* he thought, and uttered a little laugh. The fact was, George wasn't going to call. The fact was, he, Thad, had been wrong. Apparently George had some other trick up his sleeve. Why should he be surprised? Tricks were George Stark's *spécialité de la maison.* Still, he had been so *sure,* so goddamned *sure*—

"Thaddeus?"

He jumped, almost spilling the contents of the last half a dozen files onto the floor. When he was sure they weren't going to slip out of his grasp, he turned around. Rawlie DeLesseps was standing just outside the door. His large pipe poked in like a horizontal periscope.

"Sorry," Thad said. "You threw a jump into me, Rawlie. My mind was ten thousand miles away."

"Someone calling for you on my phone," Rawlie said amiably. "Must have gotten the number wrong. Lucky I was in."

Thad felt his heart begin to beat slow and hard— it was as if there were a snare-drum inside his chest, and someone had begun to whack it with a great deal of measured energy.

"Yes," Thad said. "That was very lucky."

Rawlie gave him an appraising glance. The blue eyes under his puffy, slightly reddened lids were so alive and inquisitive they were almost rude, and certainly at odds with his cheerful, bumbling, absent-minded-professor manner. "Is everything quite all right, Thaddeus?"

No, Rawlie. These days there's a mad killer out there who's partly me, a fellow who can apparently take over my body and make me do fun things like sticking pencils into myself, and I consider each day which concludes with me still sane a victory. Reality is out of joint, good buddy.

"All right? Why wouldn't everything be all right?"

"I seem to detect the faint but unmistakably ferrous odor of irony, Thad."

"You're mistaken."

"Am I? Then why do you look like a deer caught in a pair of headlights?"

"*Rawlie—*"

"And the man I just spoke to sounds like the sort of salesman you buy something from on the phone just to make sure he'll never visit your home in person."

"It's nothing, Rawlie."

"Very well." Rawlie didn't look convinced.

Thad left his office and headed down the hall toward Rawlie's.

"Where are you off to?" Harrison called after him.

"Rawlie has a call for me in his office," he explained. "The phone numbers up here are all sequential. The guy must have gotten the numbers bolloxed."

"And just happened to get the only other faculty member here today?" Harrison asked skeptically.

Thad shrugged and kept on walking.

Rawlie DeLesseps' office was cluttered, pleasant, and still inhabited by the smell of his pipe—two years' abstinence apparently did not make up for some thirty years of indulgence. It was dominated by a dart-board with a photograph of Ronald Reagan mounted on it. An encyclopedia-sized volume, Franklin Barringer's *Folklore of America,* lay open on Rawlie's desk. The telephone was off the hook, lying on a stack of blank blue-books. Looking at the handset, Thad felt the old dread fall over him in its familiar stifling folds. It was like being bundled in a blanket that badly needs to be washed. He turned his head, sure he would see all three of them—Rawlie, Harrison, and Manchester—lined up in the doorway like sparrows on a telephone wire. But the office doorway was empty, and from somewhere down the hall, he could hear the soft rasp of Rawlie's voice. He had buttonholed Thad's guard-dogs. Thad doubted that he had done it by accident.

He picked up the telephone and said, "Hello, George."

"You've had your week," the voice on the other end said. It was Stark's voice, but Thad wondered if the voice-prints would match so exactly now. Stark's voice wasn't the same. It had grown hoarse and rough, like the voice of a man who had spent too much time hollering at some sporting event.

"You had your week and you haven't done doodly-squat."

"Right you are," Thad said. He felt very cold. He had to expend a conscious effort to keep from shivering. That cold seemed to be coming out of the telephone itself, oozing out of the holes in the earpiece like icicles. But he was also very angry. "I'm not going to do it, George. A week, a month, ten years, it's all the same to me. Why not accept it? You're dead, and dead you will stay."

"You're wrong, old hoss. If you want to be dead wrong, y'all just keep goin."

"Do you know what you sound like, George?" Thad asked. "You sound like you're falling apart. That's why you want me to start writing again, isn't it? Losing cohesion, that's what you wrote. You're biodegrading, right? It won't be long before you just crumble to bits, like the wonderful one-hoss shay."

"None of that matters to you, Thad," the hoarse voice replied. It went from a scabrous drone to a harsh sound like gravel falling out of the back of a dump-truck to a squeaking whisper—as if the vocal cords had given up functioning altogether for the space of a phrase or two—and then back to the drone again. "None of what's going on with me is your concern. That's nothing but a distraction to you, buddy. You just want to get going by night-fall, or you're going to be one sorry son of a bitch. And you won't be the only one."

"I don't—"

Click! Stark was gone. Thad looked at the telephone handset thoughtfully for a moment, then replaced it in the cradle. When he turned around, Harrison and Manchester were standing there.

5

"Who was it?" Manchester asked:

"A student," Thad said. At this point he wasn't even sure why he was lying. The only thing he was really sure of was that he had a terrible feeling in his guts. "Just a student. As I thought."

"How did he know you'd be in?" Harrison asked. "And how come he called on this gentleman's phone?"

"I give up," Thad said humbly. "I'm a Russian deep-cover agent. It was really my contact. I'll go quietly."

Harrison wasn't angry—or, at least, he did not appear to be angry. The look of slightly tired reproach he sent Thad's way was a good deal more effective than anger. "Mr. Beaumont, we're trying to give you and your wife a help. I know that having a couple of fellows trail after you wherever you go can get to be a pain in the ass after awhile, but we really *are* trying to give you a help."

Thad felt ashamed of himself . . . but not ashamed enough to tell the truth. That bad feeling was still there, the feeling that things were going to go wrong, that maybe they already *had* gone wrong. And something else, as well. A light, fluttery feeling along his skin. A wormy feeling *inside* his skin. Pressure at his temples. It wasn't the sparrows; at least, he didn't think it was. All the same, some mental barometer he hadn't even been aware of was falling. Nor was this the first time he'd felt it. There had been a sensation similar to this, although not as strong, when he was on the way to Dave's Market eight days ago. He had felt it in his own office while he had been getting the files. A low, jittery feeling.

It's Stark. He's with you somehow, in you. He's watching. If you say the wrong thing, he'll know. And then somebody will suffer.

"I apologize," he said. He was aware that Rawlie DeLesseps was now standing behind the two policemen, watching Thad with quiet, curious eyes. He would have to start lying now, and the lies came so naturally and smoothly to mind that, for all he knew, they might have been planted there by George Stark himself. He wasn't entirely sure Rawlie would go along, but it was a little late to worry about that. "I'm on edge, that's all."

"Understandable," Harrison said. "I just want you to realize we're not the enemy, Mr. Beaumont."

Thad said, "The kid who phoned knew I was here because he was coming out of the bookstore when I drove by. He wanted to know if I was teaching a summer writing course. The faculty telephone directory is divided into departments, the members of each department listed in alphabetical order. The print is very fine, as anyone who has ever tried to use it will testify."

"It's a very naughty book that way," Rawlie agreed around his pipe. The two policemen turned to look at him for a moment, startled. Rawlie favored them with a solemn, rather owlish nod.

"Rawlie follows me in the directory listings," Thad said. "We don't happen to have any faculty member whose last name begins with C this year." He glanced at Rawlie for a moment, but Rawlie had taken his pipe from his mouth and appeared to be inspecting its fire-blackened bowl with close attention. "As a result," Thad finished, "I'm always getting his calls and he's always getting mine. I told this kid he was out of luck; I'm off until fall."

Well, that was that. He had a feeling he might have overexplained the situation a little, but the real question was when Harrison and Manchester had gotten to the doorway of Rawlie's office and how much they had overheard. One did not ordinarily tell students applying for writing courses that they were biodegrading, and that they would soon just crumble to bits.

"I wish *I* was off until fall," Manchester sighed. "Are you about done, Mr. Beaumont?"

Thad breathed an interior sigh of relief and said, "I just have to put back the files I won't be needing."

(and a note you have to write a note to the secretary)

"And, of course, I have to write a note to Mrs. Fenton," he heard himself saying. He didn't have the slightest idea why he was saying this; he only knew he had to. "She's the English Department secretary."

"Do we have time for another cup of coffee?" Manchester asked.

"Sure. Maybe even a couple of cookies, if the barbarian hordes left any," he said. That feeling that things were out of joint, that things were wrong and going wronger all the time, was back and stronger than ever. Leave a note for Mrs. Fenton? Jesus, *that* was a laugh. Rawlie must be choking on his pipe.

As Thad left Rawlie's office, Rawlie asked: "Can I speak to you for a minute, Thaddeus?"

"Sure," Thad said. He wanted to tell Harrison and Manchester to leave them alone, he would be right up, but recognized—reluctantly—that such a remark was not exactly the sort of thing you said when you wanted to allay suspicions. And Harrison, at least, had his antennae up. Maybe not quite all the way just yet, but almost.

Silence worked better, anyway. As he turned to Rawlie, Harrison and Manchester strolled slowly up the hall. Harrison spoke briefly to his partner, then stood in the doorway of the Department common room while Manchester hunted up the cookies. Harrison had them in sight, but Thad thought they were out of earshot.

"That was quite a tale about the faculty directory," Rawlie remarked, putting the chewed stem of his pipe back in his mouth. "I believe you have a great deal in common with the little girl in Saki's 'The Open Window,' Thaddeus—romance at short notice seems to be your specialty."

"Rawlie, this isn't what you think it is."

"I don't have the slightest idea *what* it is," Rawlie said mildly, "and while I admit to a certain amount of human curiosity, I'm not sure I really want to know."

Thad smiled a little.

"And I *did* get the clear feeling that you'd forgotten Gonzo Tom Carroll on purpose. He may be retired, but last time I looked, he still came between us in the current faculty directory."

"Rawlie, I better get going."

"Indeed," Rawlie said. "You have a note to write to Mrs. Fenton."

Thad felt his cheeks grow a bit warm. Althea Fenton, the English Department secretary since 1961, had died of throat cancer in April.

"The only reason I held you at all," Rawlie went on, "was to tell you that I may have found what you were looking for. About the sparrows."

Thad felt his heartbeat jog. "What do you mean?"

Rawlie led Thad back inside the office and picked up Barringer's *Folklore of America*. "Sparrows, loons, and especially whippoorwills are psychopomps," he said, not without some triumph in his voice. "I *knew* there was something about whippoorwills."

"Psychopomps?" Thad said doubtfully.

"From the Greek," Rawlie said, "meaning those who conduct. In this case, those who conduct human souls back and forth between the land of the living and the land of the dead. According to Barringer, loons and whippoorwills are outriders of the living; they are said to gather near the place where a death is about to occur. They are not birds of ill omen. Their job is to guide newly dead souls to their proper place in the afterlife."

He looked at Thad levelly.

"Gatherings of sparrows are rather more ominous, at least according to Barringer. Sparrows are said to be the outriders of the deceased."

"Which means—"

"Which means their job is to guide lost souls back into the land of the living. They are, in other words, the harbingers of the living dead."

Rawlie took his pipe from his mouth and looked at Thad solemnly.

"I don't know what your situation is, Thaddeus, but I suggest caution. Extreme caution. You look like a man who is in a lot of trouble. If there's anything I can do, please tell me."

"I appreciate that, Rawlie. You've done as much as I could hope for just by keeping quiet."

"In that, at least, you and my students seem to be in perfect agreement." But the mild eyes looking at Thad over the pipe were concerned. "You'll take care of yourself?"

"I will."

"And if those men are following you around to help you in that endeavor, Thaddeus, it might be wise to take them into your confidence."

It would be wonderful if he could, but his confidence in them wasn't the issue. If he really *did* open his mouth, they would have precious little confidence in *him*. And even if he *did* trust Harrison and Manchester enough to talk to them, he would not dare say anything until that wormy, crawling feeling inside his skin went away. Because George Stark was watching him. And he was over the deadline.

"Thanks, Rawlie."

Rawlie nodded, told him again to take care of himself, and then sat down behind his desk.

Thad walked back to his own office.

6

And, of course, I have to write a note to Mrs. Fenton.

He paused in the act of putting back the last of the files he'd pulled by mistake and looked at his beige IBM Selectric. Just lately he seemed almost hypnotically aware of all writing instruments, great and small. He had wondered on more than one occasion over the last week if there were a different version of Thad Beaumont inside each one, like evil genies lurking inside a bunch of bottles.

I have to write a note to Mrs. Fenton.

But these days one would more properly use a Ouija board than an electric typewriter to get in touch with the late great Mrs. Fenton, who had made coffee so strong it could almost walk and talk, and why had he said that, anyway? Mrs. Fenton had been the furthest thing from his mind.

Thad dropped the last of the non-writing Honors files into the file-cabinet, closed the drawer, and looked at his left hand. Underneath the bandage, the web of flesh between his thumb and forefinger had suddenly begun to burn and itch. He rubbed his hand against the leg of his pants, but that only seemed to make the itch worse. And now it was throbbing as well. That sensation of deep, baking heat intensified.

He looked out his office window.

Across Bennett Boulevard, the telephone wires were lined with sparrows. More sparrows stood on the roof of the infirmary, and as he watched, a fresh batch landed on one of the tennis courts.

They all seemed to be looking at him.

Psychopomps. The harbingers of the living dead.

Now a flock of sparrows whirled down like a cyclone of burned leaves and landed on the roof of Bennett Hall.

"No," Thad whispered in a shaky voice. His back was hard with gooseflesh. His hand itched and burned.

The typewriter.

He could get rid of the sparrows and the burning, maddening itch in his hand only by using the typewriter.

The instinct to sit down in front of it was too strong to deny. Doing it seemed horribly natural, somehow, like wanting to stick your hand in cold water after you had burned it.

I have to write a note to Mrs. Fenton.

You just want to get going by nightfall, or you're going to be one sorry son of a bitch. And you won't be the only one.

That itchy, wormy feeling under his skin was getting steadily stronger. It radiated out from the hole in his hand in waves. His eyeballs seemed to be pulsing in perfect sync with that feeling. And in the eye of his mind, the vision of the sparrows intensified. It was the Ridgeway section of Bergenfield; Ridgeway under a mild white spring sky; it was 1960; the whole world was dead except for these terrible, common birds, these psychopomps, and as he watched, they all took wing. The sky went dark with their great, wheeling mass. The sparrows were flying again.

Outside Thad's window, the sparrows on the wires, the infirmary, and Bennett Hall flew upward together in a whir of wings. A few early students paused in their walk across the quad to watch the flock bank left across the sky and disappear into the west.

Thad did not see this. He saw nothing but the neighborhood of his childhood somehow transformed into the weird dead country of a dream. He sat down in front of the typewriter, sinking deeper into the twilit world of his trance as he did so. Yet one thought held firm. Foxy George could make him sit down and twiddle the keys of the IBM, yes, but he wouldn't write the book, no matter what . . . and if he held to that, foxy old George would either fall apart or simply whiff out of existence, like a candle-flame. He knew that. He *felt* it.

His hand seemed to be *whamming* in and out now, and he felt that, if he could see it, it would look like the paw of a cartoon character—Wile E. Coyote, perhaps—after it had been hit with a sledgehammer. It wasn't pain, exactly; it was more like the I'm-going-to-go-crazy-soon feeling you get when the middle of your back, the one place you can never quite reach, starts to itch. Not a surface itch, but that nerve-deep, throbbing itch that makes you clamp your teeth together.

But even that seemed distant, unimportant.

He sat down at the typewriter.

7

The moment he turned the machine on, the itch went away . . . and the vision of the sparrows went with it.

Yet the trance held, and at the center of it was some harsh imperative; there was something which needed to be written, and he could feel his whole body yelling at him to get to it, do it, get it done. In its own way, it was much worse than either the vision of the sparrows or the itch in his hand. This itch seemed to be emanating from a place deep in his mind.

He rolled a sheet of paper into the typewriter, then just sat there for a moment, feeling distant and lost. Then he laid his fingers in the touch-typist's "home" position on the middle row of keys, although he had given up touch-typing years ago.

They trembled there for a moment, and then all but the index fingers withdrew. Apparently when Stark did type, he did it the same way Thad himself did—hunt and peck. He would, of course; the typewriter was not his instrument of choice.

There was a distant tug of pain when he moved the fingers of his left hand, but that was all. His index fingers typed slowly, but it still didn't take long for the message to form itself on the white sheet. It was chillingly brief. The Letter Gothic type-ball whirled and produced six words in capitals:

GUESS WHERE I CALLED FROM, THAD?

The world suddenly swam back into sharp focus. He had never felt such dismay, such horror, in his whole life. God, of course—it was so right, so *clear.*

The son of a bitch called from my house! He's got Liz and the twins!

He started to get up, with no idea of where he meant to go. He was not even aware that he was doing it until his hand flared with pain, like a smouldering torch which is swung hard through the air to produce a bright bloom of fire. His lips peeled back from his teeth and he made a low groaning noise. He dropped back into the chair in front of the IBM, and before he knew what was happening, his hands had groped their way back to the keys and were slamming at them again.

Five words this time:

TELL ANYBODY AND THEY DIE

He stared at the words dully. As soon as he typed the final E, everything cut off suddenly—it was as if he were a lamp and someone had pulled his plug. No more pain in his hand. No more itch. No more wormy, watched feeling under his skin.

The birds were gone. That dim, entranced feeling was gone. And Stark was gone, too.

Except he wasn't really gone at all, was he? No.

Stark was keeping house while Thad was gone. They had left two Maine State Troopers watching the place, but that didn't matter. He had been a fool, an incredible fool, to think a couple of cops could make a difference. A squad of Delta Force Green Berets wouldn't have made a difference. George Stark wasn't a man; he was something like a Nazi Tiger tank which just happened to look human.

"How's it going?" Harrison asked from behind him.

Thad jumped as if someone had poked a pin into the back of his neck . . . and that made him think of Frederick Clawson, Frederick Clawson who had butted in where he had no business . . . and had committed suicide by telling what he knew.

TELL ANYBODY AND THEY DIE

glared up at him from the sheet of paper in the typewriter.

He reached out, tore the sheet from the roller, and crumpled it up. He did this without looking around to see how close Harrison was—that would have been a bad mistake. He tried to look casual. He didn't feel casual; he felt insane. He waited for Harrison to ask him what he had written, and why he was in such a hurry to get it out of the typewriter. When Harrison didn't say anything, Thad did.

"I think I'm done. Hell with the note. I'll have these files back before Mrs. Fenton knows they're gone, anyway." That much, at least, was true . . . unless Althea happened to be looking down from heaven. He got up, praying his legs wouldn't betray him and spill him back into his chair. He was relieved to see Harrison was standing in the doorway, not looking at him at all. A moment ago Thad would have sworn the man was breathing down the back of his neck, but Harrison was eating a cookie and peering past Thad at the few students who were idling across the quad.

"Boy, this place sure is dead," the cop said.

My family may be, too, before I get home.

"Why don't we go?" he asked Harrison.

"Sounds good to me."

Thad started for the door. Harrison looked at him, bemused. "Jeepers-creepers," he said. "Maybe there's something to that absent-minded-professor stuff after all."

Thad blinked at him nervously, then looked down and saw he was still holding the crumpled ball of paper in one hand. He tossed it toward the wastebasket, but his unsteady hand betrayed him. It struck the rim and bounced off. Before he could bend over and grab it, Harrison had moved past him. He picked up the ball of paper and tossed it casually from one hand to the other. "You gonna walk out without the files you came for?" he asked. He pointed at the creative writing Honors files, which were sitting beside the typewriter with a red rubber band around them. Then he went back to tossing the ball of paper with Stark's last two messages on it from one hand to the other, right-left, left-right, back and forth, follow the bouncing ball. Thad could see a snatch of letters on one of the crimps: ELL ANYBODY AND THEY DI.

"Oh. Those. Thanks."

Thad picked the files up, then almost dropped them. Now Harrison would uncrumple the ball of paper in his hand. He would do that, and although Stark wasn't watching him right now—Thad was pretty sure he wasn't, anyway—he would be checking back in soon. When he did, he would know. And when he knew, he would do something unspeakable to Liz and the twins.

"Don't mention it." Harrison tossed the crumpled ball of paper toward the wastebasket. It rolled almost all the way around the rim and then went in. "Two points," he said, and stepped out into the hall so Thad could close the door.

8

He went downstairs with his police escort trailing behind him. Rawlie DeLesseps popped out of his office and told him to have a good summer, if he didn't see Thad again. Thad wished him the same in a voice which, to his own ears, at least, sounded normal enough. He felt as if he were on autopilot. The feeling lasted until he got to the Suburban. As he tossed the files in on the passenger side, his eye was caught by the pay telephone on the other side of the parking lot.

"I'm going to call my wife," he told Harrison. "See if she wants anything at the store."

"Should have done it upstairs," Manchester said. "Would have saved yourself a quarter."

"I forgot," Thad said. "Maybe there *is* something to that absent-minded-professor stuff."

The two cops exchanged an amused glance and got into their Plymouth, where they could run the air conditioning and watch him through the windshield.

Thad felt as if all his insides had turned to jumbled glass. He fished a quarter out of his pocket and dropped it into the slot. His hand was shaking and he got the second number wrong. He hung up the phone, waited for his quarter to come back, and then tried again, thinking, *Christ, it's like the night Miriam died. Like that night all over again.*

It was the kind of *déjà vu* he could have done without.

The second time he got it right and stood there with the handset pressed so tightly against his ear that it hurt. He tried consciously to relax his stance. He mustn't let Harrison and Manchester know something was wrong—above all else, he must not do that. But he couldn't seem to unlock his muscles.

Stark picked up the telephone on the first ring. "Thad?"

"What have you done to them?" Like spitting out dry balls of lint. And in the background he could hear both twins howling their heads off. Thad found their cries strangely comforting. They were not the hoarse whoops that Wendy had made when she tumbled down the stairs; they were bewildered cries, angry cries, perhaps, but not *hurt* cries.

Liz, though—where was Liz?

"Not a thing," Stark replied, "as you can hear for yourself. I haven't harmed a hair of their precious little heads. Yet."

"Liz," Thad said. He was suddenly overcome with lonely terror. It was like being immersed in a long, cold comber of surf.

"What about her?" The teasing tone was grotesque, insupportable.

"Put her on!" Thad barked. "If you expect me to ever write another goddam word under your name, *you put her on!"* And there was a part of his mind, apparently unmoved by even such an extreme of terror and surprise as this, which cautioned: *Watch your face, Thad. You're only three-quarters turned away from the cops. A man doesn't scream into the telephone when he's phoning home to ask his wife if she's got enough eggs.*

"Thad! Thad, old hoss!" Stark sounded injured, but Thad knew with horrible and maddening certainty that the son of a bitch was grinning. "You got one hell of a bad opinion of me, buddy-roo. I mean it's *low,* son! Cool your jets, here she is."

"Thad? Thad, are you there?" She sounded harried and afraid, but not panicked. Not quite.

"Yes. Honey, are you okay? Are the kids?"

"Yes, we're okay. We . . ." The last word trailed off a bit. Thad could hear the bastard telling her something, but not what it was. She said yes, okay, and was back on the phone. Now she sounded close to tears. "Thad, you've got to do what he wants."

"Yes. I know that."

"But he wants me to tell you that you can't do it here. The police will come here soon. He . . . Thad, he says he killed the two that were watching the house."

Thad closed his eyes.

"I don't know how he did it, but he says he did . . . and I . . . I believe him." Now she *was* crying. Trying not to, knowing it would upset Thad and knowing if he was upset he might do something dangerous. He clutched the phone, ground it against his ear, and tried to look casual.

Stark, murmuring in the background again. And Thad caught one of the words. *Collaboration.* Incredible. Fucking incredible.

"He's going to take us away," she said. "He says you'll know where we're going. Remember Aunt Martha? He says you should lose the men that are with you. He says he knows you can do it, because *he* could. He wants you to join us by dark tonight. He says—" She uttered a frightened sob. Another one got started, but she managed to swallow it back. "He says you're going to collaborate with him, that with you and him both working on it, it will be the best book ever. He—"

Murmur, murmur, murmur.

Oh Thad wanted to hook his fingers into George Stark's evil neck and choke until his fingers popped through the skin and into the son of a bitch's throat.

"He says Alexis Machine's back from the dead and bigger than ever." Then, shrilly: "*Please* do what he says, Thad! He's got guns! And he's got a blowtorch! A little blowtorch! He says if you try anything funny—"

"Liz—"

"Please, Thad, do what he says!"

Her words faded off as Stark took the telephone away from her.

"Tell me something, Thad," Stark said, and now there was no teasing in his voice. It was dead serious. "Tell me something, and you want to make it believable and sincere, buddy-roo, or they'll pay for it. Do you understand me?"

"Yes."

"You sure? Because she was telling the truth about the blowtorch."

"Yes! *Yes,* goddammit!"

"What did she mean when she told you to

remember Aunt Martha? Who the fuck is that? Was it some kind of code, Thad? Was she trying to put one over on me?"

Thad suddenly saw the lives of his wife and children hanging by a single thin thread. This was not metaphor; this was something he could *see*. The thread was ice-blue, gossamer, barely visible in the middle of all the eternity there might be. Everything now came down to just two things—what he said, and what George Stark believed.

"Is the recording equipment off the phones?"

"Of course it is!" Stark said. "What do you take me for, Thad?"

"Did *Liz* know that when you put her on?"

There was a pause, and then Stark said: "All she had to do was look. The wires are layin right on the goddam floor."

"But did she? Did she look?"

"Stop beatin around the bush, Thad."

"She was trying to tell me where you're going without saying the words," Thad told him. He was striving for a patient, lecturing tone—patient, but a little patronizing. He couldn't tell if he was getting it or not, but he supposed George would let him know one way or the other, and quite soon. "She meant the summer house. The place in Castle Rock. Martha Tellford is Liz's aunt. We don't like her. Whenever she'd call and say she was coming to visit, we'd fantasize about just running away to Castle Rock and hiding at the summer house until she died. Now *I've* said it, and if they've got wireless recording equipment on our phone, George, it's on your own head."

He waited, sweating, to see if Stark would buy this . . . or if the thin thread which was the only thing between his loved ones and forever would snap.

"They don't," Stark said at last, and his voice sounded relaxed again. Thad fought the need to lean against the side of the telephone kiosk and close his eyes in relief. *If I ever see you again, Liz,* he thought, *I'll wring your neck for taking such a crazy chance.* Except he supposed what he would really do when and if he saw her again would be to kiss her until she couldn't breathe.

"Don't hurt them," he said into the telephone. "Please don't hurt them. I'll do whatever you want."

"Oh, I know it. I know you will, Thad. And we're gonna do it together. At least, to start with. You just get moving. Shake your watchdogs and get your ass down to Castle Rock. Get there as fast as you can, but don't move so fast you attract attention. That'd be a mistake. You might think about swapping cars, but I'm leaving the details up to you—after all, you're a creative guy. Get there before dark, if you want to find them alive. Don't fuck up. You dig me? Don't fuck up and don't try anything cute."

"I won't."

"That's right. You won't. What you're gonna do, hoss, is play the game. If you screw up, all you're gonna find when you get there is bodies and a tape of your wife cursing your name before she died."

There was a click. The connection was broken.

9

As he was getting back into the Suburban, Manchester unrolled the passenger window of the

Plymouth and asked if everything was okay at home. Thad could see by the man's eyes that this was more than an idle question. He had seen something on Thad's face after all. But that was okay; he thought he could deal with that. He was, after all, a creative guy, and his mind seemed to be moving with its own ghastly-silent speed now, like that Japanese bullet-train. The question presented itself again: lie or tell the truth? And as before, it was really no contest.

"Everything's fine," he said. His tone of voice was natural and casual. "The kids are cranky, that's all. And that makes Liz cranky." He let his voice rise a little. "You two guys have been acting antsy ever since we left the house. Is there something happening I should know about?"

He had enough conscience, even in this desperate situation, to feel a little twinge of guilt at that. Something was happening all right—but he was the one who knew, and he wasn't telling.

"Nope," Harrison said from behind the wheel, leaning forward to speak past his partner. "We can't reach Chatterton and Eddings at the house, that's all. Might have gone inside."

"Liz said she'd just made some fresh iced tea," Thad said, lying giddily.

"That's it, then," Harrison said. He smiled at Thad, who felt another, slightly stronger, throb of conscience. "Maybe there'll be some left when we get there, huh?"

"Anything's possible." Thad slammed the Suburban's door and poked the ignition key into its slot with a hand that seemed to have no more feeling than a block of wood. Questions whirled around in his head, doing their own complicated and not particularly lovely gavotte. Were Stark and his family off for Castle Rock yet? He hoped so—he wanted them solid-gone before the news that they had been snatched went out along the nets of police communication. If they were in Liz's car and someone spotted it, or if they were still close to or in Ludlow, there could be bad trouble. Killing trouble. It was horribly ironic that he should be hoping Stark would make a clean getaway, but that was exactly the position he was in.

And, speaking of getaways, how was he going to lose Harrison and Manchester? That was another good question. Not by outrunning them in the Suburban, that was for sure. The Plymouth they were driving looked like a dog with its dusty finish and blackwall tires, but the rough idle of its motor suggested it was all roadrunner under the hood. He supposed he *could* ditch them—he already had an idea of how and where it could be done—but how was he going to keep from being discovered again while he made the hundred-and-sixty-mile drive to The Rock?

He didn't have the slightest idea . . . he only knew he would have to do it somehow.

Remember Aunt Martha?

He had fed Stark a line of bull about what that meant, and Stark had swallowed it. So the bastard's access to his mind wasn't complete. Martha Tellford was Liz's aunt, all right, and they had joked, mostly in bed, about running away from her, but they had talked about running to exotic places like Aruba or Tahiti . . . because Aunt Martha knew all about the summer house in Castle Rock. She had visited them there much more frequently than she had visited them in Ludlow. And Aunt Martha Tellford's favorite place in Castle Rock was the dump. She was a card-carrying, dues-paying member of the NRA, and what she liked to do at the dump was shoot rats.

"If you want her to leave," Thad could remember telling Liz once, "you'll have to be the one to tell her." That conversation had also taken place in bed, toward the end of Aunt Martha's interminable visit in the summer of—had it been '79 or '80? It didn't matter, he supposed. "She's *your* aunt. Besides, I'm afraid that if I told her, she might use that Winchester of hers on *me.*"

Liz had said, "I'm not sure that being blood kin would cut much ice, either. She gets a look in her eyes . . ." She had mock-shivered next to him, he remembered, then giggled and poked him in the ribs. "Go on. God hates a coward. Tell her we're conservationists, even when it comes to dumprats. Walk right up to her, Thad, and say, 'Bug out, Aunt Martha! You've shot your last rat at the dump! Pack your bags and just bug out!' "

Of course, neither of them had told Aunt Martha to bug out; she had kept on with her daily expeditions to the dump, where she shot dozens of rats (and a few seagulls when the rats ran for cover, Thad suspected). Finally the blessed day came when Thad drove her to the Portland Jetport and put her on a plane back to Albany. At the gate, she had given him her oddly disconcerting man's double-pump handshake—as if she were closing a business deal instead of saying goodbye—and told him she just might favor them with a visit the following year. "Goddam good shooting," she'd said.

"Must have gotten six or seven dozen of those little germbags."

She never *had* come back, although there had been one close shave (*that* impending visit had been averted by a merciful last-minute invitation to go to Arizona instead, where, Aunt Martha had informed them over the phone, there was still a bounty on coyotes).

In the years since her last visit, "Remember Aunt Martha" had become a code-phrase like "Remember the *Maine.*" It meant one of them should get the .22 out of the storage shed and shoot some particularly boring guest, as Aunt Martha had shot the rats at the dump. Now that he thought about it, Thad believed Liz had used the phrase once during the *People* magazine interview-and-photo sessions. Hadn't she turned to him and murmured, "I wonder if that Myers woman remembers Aunt Martha, Thad?"

Then she had covered her mouth and started giggling.

Pretty funny.

Except it wasn't a joke now.

And it wasn't shooting rats at the dump now.

Unless he had it all wrong, Liz had been trying to tell him to come after them and kill George Stark. And if she wanted him to do that, Liz, who cried when she heard about homeless animals being "put to sleep" at the Derry Animal Shelter, must think there was no other solution. She must think there were only two choices now: death for Stark . . . or death for her and the twins.

Harrison and Manchester were looking at him curiously, and Thad realized he had been sitting behind the wheel of the idling Suburban, lost in thought, for nearly a full minute. He raised his hand, sketched a little salute, backed out, and turned toward Maine Avenue, which would take him off-campus. He tried to start thinking about how he was going to get away from these two before they heard the news that their colleagues were dead over their police-band radio. He tried to think, but he kept hearing Stark telling him that if he screwed up, all he would find when he got to the summer place in Castle Rock would be their bodies and a tape of Liz cursing him before she died.

And he kept seeing Martha Tellford, sighting down the barrel of her Winchester, which had been one hell of a lot bigger than the .22 he kept in the locked storage shed of the summer place, aiming at the plump rats scurrying among the piles of refuse and the low orange dump-fires. He realized suddenly that he *wanted* to shoot Stark, and not with a .22, either.

Foxy George deserved something bigger.

A howitzer might be the right size.

The rats, leaping up against the galaxy-shine of broken bottles and crushed cans, their bodies first twisting, then splattering as the guts and fur flew.

Yes, watching something like that happen to George Stark would be very fine.

He was gripping the steering-wheel too hard, making his left hand ache. It actually seemed to moan deep in its bones and joints.

He relaxed—tried to, anyway—and felt in his breast pocket for the Percodan he had brought along, found it, dry-swallowed it.

He began thinking about the school-zone intersection in Veazie. The one with the four-way stop sign.

And he began to think about what Rawlie DeLesseps had said, too. Psychopomps, Rawlie had called them.

The emissaries of the living dead.

Twenty-one

STARK TAKES CHARGE

1

He had no trouble planning what he wanted to do and how he wanted to do it, even though he had never actually been in Ludlow in his life.

Stark had been there often enough in his dreams.

He drove the stolen rag-tag Honda Civic off the road and into a rest area a mile and a half down the road from the Beaumont house. Thad had gone up to the University, and that was good. Sometimes it was impossible to tell what Thad was doing or thinking, although he could almost always catch the flavor of his emotions if he strained.

If he found it very difficult to get in touch with Thad, he simply began to handle one of the Berol pencils he'd bought in the Houston Street stationer's.

That helped.

Today it would be easy. It would be easy because, whatever Thad might have told his watchdogs, he had gone to the University for one reason and one reason only: because he was over the deadline, and he believed Stark would try to get in touch with him. Stark intended to do just that. Yes indeed.

He just didn't plan to do it the way Thad expected.

And certainly not from a *place* Thad expected.

It was almost noon. There were a few picnickers in the rest area, but they were at the tables on the grass or gathered around the small stone barbecues down by the river. No one looked at Stark as he got out of the Civic and walked away. That was good, because if they had seen him, they certainly would have remembered him.

Remember, yes.

Describe, no.

As he strode across the asphalt and then set off up the road toward the Beaumont house on foot, Stark looked a great deal like H. G. Wells's Invisible Man. A wide swath of bandage covered his forehead from eyebrows to hairline. Another swath covered his chin and lower jaw. A New York Yankees baseball cap was jammed down on his head. He wore sunglasses, a quilted vest, and black gloves on his hands.

The bandages were stained with a yellow, pussy material that oozed steadily through the cotton gauze like gummy tears. More of the yellow stuff dribbled out from behind the Foster Grant sunglasses. From time to time he wiped it off his cheeks with the gloves, which were thin imitation kid. The palms and fingers of these gloves were sticky with the drying ooze. Under the bandages, much of his skin had sloughed off. What remained was not precisely human flesh; it was, instead, dark, spongy stuff that wept almost constantly. This waste matter looked like pus but had a dark, unpleasant smell—like a combination of strong coffee and India ink.

He walked with his head bent slightly forward. The occupants of the few cars which came toward him saw a man in a ball-cap with his head held down against the glare and his hands stuffed into his pockets. The shadow of the cap's visor would defeat all but the most insistent glances, and if they had looked more closely, they would have seen only the bandages. The cars which came from behind and passed him going north had nothing but his back to get a good look at, of course.

Closer in toward the twin cities of Bangor and Brewer, this walk would have been a bit more difficult. Closer in you had your suburbs and housing developments. The Beaumonts' part of Ludlow was still far enough out in the country to qualify as a rural community—not the sticks, but definitely not part of either of the big towns. The houses sat on lots large enough, in some cases, to qualify as fields. They were divided one from another not by hedges, those avatars of suburban privacy, but by narrow belts of trees and, sometimes, meandering rock walls. Here and there satellite dishes loomed grimly on the horizon, looking like the advance outposts of some alien invasion.

Stark strode along the shoulder of the road until he passed the Clarks' house. Thad's was the next up. He cut across the far corner of the Clarks' front yard, which was more hay than grass. He glanced once at the house. The shades were pulled against the heat, and the garage door was tightly shut. The Clark place looked more than mid-morning deserted; it had the forlorn air of houses which have been empty for some time. There was no tattletale pile of newspapers inside the screen door, but Stark believed nevertheless that the Clark family was probably off on an early summer vacation, and that was just fine with him.

He entered the stand of trees between the two

properties, stepped over the crumbled remnant of a rock wall, and then sank down to one knee. For the first time he was looking directly at the house of his stubborn twin. There was a police cruiser parked in the driveway, and the two cops who belonged to it were standing in the shade of a nearby tree, smoking and talking. Good.

He had what he needed; the rest was cake and ice cream. Yet he lingered a moment longer. He did not think of himself as an imaginative man—at least not outside the pages of the books he had had a vital part in creating—nor an emotional one, so he was a little startled by the dull coal of rage and resentment he felt smouldering in his gut.

What right did the son of a bitch have to refuse him? What goddam right? Because he had been real first? Because Stark did not know just how, why, or when he himself had become real? That was bullshit. As far as George Stark was concerned, seniority cut zero ice in this matter. He had no responsibility to lie down and die without a murmur of protest, as Thad Beaumont seemed to think he should do. He had a responsibility to himself—that was simple survival. Nor was that all.

He had his loyal fans to think of as well, didn't he?

Look at that house. Just *look* at it. A roomy New England Colonial, maybe one wing shy of qualifying for mansionhood. Big lawn, sprinklers twirling busily to keep it green. A wooden stake fence running along one side of the bright black driveway—the sort of fence Stark guessed was supposed to be "picturesque." There was a breezeway between the house and the garage—a *breezeway,* by God! And inside, the place was furnished in graceful (or maybe they called it gracious) Colonial style to match the outside—a long oak table in the dining room, high handsome bureaus in the rooms upstairs, and chairs that were delicate and pleasing to the eye without being precious; chairs you could admire and still dare to sit on. Walls that were not papered but painted and then stencilled. Stark had seen all these things, seen them in the dreams Beaumont hadn't even known he was having when he had been writing as George Stark.

Suddenly he wanted to burn the charming white house to the ground. Touch a match to it— or maybe the flame of the propane torch he had in the pocket of the vest he was wearing—and burn it flat to the foundation. But not until he had been inside. Not until he had smashed the furniture, shat upon the living-room rug, and wiped the excrement across those carefully stencilled walls in crude brown smears. Not until he had taken an axe to those oh-so-precious bureaus and reduced them to kindling.

What right did Beaumont have to children? To a beautiful woman? What right, exactly, did Thad Beaumont have to live in the light and be happy while his dark brother—who had made him rich and famous when he would otherwise have lived poor and expired in obscurity—died in darkness like a diseased mongrel in an alley?

None, of course. No right at all. It was just that Beaumont had *believed* in that right, and still, in spite of everything, continued to believe in it. But the belief, not George Stark from Oxford, Mississippi, was the fiction.

"It's time for your first big lesson, buddy-roo," Stark murmured in the trees. He found the clips holding the bandage around his forehead, removed them, and tucked them away in his pocket for later. Then he began to unwind the bandage, the layers growing wetter as they got closer to his strange flesh. "It's one you'll never, ever forget. I guaran-fucking-tee it."

2

It was nothing but a variation on the white-cane scam he'd run on the cops in New York, but that was perfectly okay with Stark; he was a firm believer in the idea that if you happened on a good gag, you should go on using it until you used it up. These cops presented no problem, anyway, unless he got sloppy; they had been on duty for better than a week now, the surety growing in them every day that the crazy guy had been telling the truth when he'd said he was just going to pick up his marbles and go home. The only wild card was Liz—if she happened to be looking out the window when he wasted the pigs, it could complicate things. But it was still a few minutes shy of noon; she and the twins would either be taking naps or getting ready to take them. Regardless of how it went, he was confident things would work out.

In fact, he was sure of it.

Love would find a way.

3

Chatterton lifted his boot to butt his cigarette—he planned to put the stub in the cruiser's ashtray once it was dead; Maine State Police did not litter the driveways of the taxpayers—and when he looked up the man with the skinned face was there, lurching slowly up the driveway. One hand waved slowly at him and Jack Eddings for help; the other was bent behind his back and looked broken.

Chatterton almost had a heart-attack.

"Jack!" he shouted, and Eddings turned. His mouth dropped open.

"—*help me*—" the man with the skinned face croaked. Chatterton and Eddings ran toward him.

If they had lived, they might have told their fellow officers that they thought the man had been in a car crash, or had been burned by an explosive backlash of gas or kerosene, or that he might have fallen face-first into one of those pieces of farm machinery which decide, every now and then, to reach out and tomahawk their owners with their blades, choppers, or cruel, whirling spokes.

They might have told their fellow officers any of these things, but at that moment they were really thinking of nothing at all. Their minds had been sponged clean by horror. The left side of the man's face seemed almost to be *boiling,* as if, after the skin had been stripped off, someone had poured a powerful carbolic acid solution over the raw meat. Sticky, unthinkable fluid ran down hillocks of proud flesh and rolled through black cracks, sometimes overspilling in gruesome flash floods.

They thought nothing; they simply reacted.

That was the beauty of the white-cane trick.

"—*help me*—"

Stark allowed his feet to tangle together and fell forward. Yelling something incoherent to his partner, Chatterton reached out to grab the wounded man before he could fall. Stark looped his right arm around the State Policeman's neck and brought his left hand out from behind his back. There was a surprise in it. The surprise was the pearl-handled straight-razor. The blade glittered feverishly in the humid air. Stark rammed it forward and it split Chatterton's right eyeball with an audible pop. Chatterton screamed and clapped a hand to his face. Stark ran his hand into Chatterton's hair, jerked his head back, and slit his throat from ear to ear. Blood burst from his muscular neck in a red shout. All of this happened in four seconds.

"What?" Eddings inquired in a low and weirdly studious tone of voice. He was standing flat-footed about two feet behind Chatterton and Stark. "What?"

One of his dangling hands was hanging beside the butt of his service revolver, but one quick glance convinced Stark that the pig had no more idea that his gun was in reach than he had of the population of Mozambique. His eyes were bulging. He didn't know what he was looking at, or who was bleeding. *No, that isn't true,* Stark thought, *he thinks it's me. He stood there and watched me cut his partner's throat, but he thinks* I'm *the one bleeding because half my face is gone, and that isn't* really *why—it's me bleeding,* has *to be, because he and his partner, they're the police. They're the heroes of this movie.*

"Here," he said, "hold this for me, will you?" And shoved Chatterton's dying body backward at his partner.

Eddings uttered a high-pitched little scream. He tried to step away, but he was too late. The two-hundred-pound sack of dying bull that was Tom Chatterton sent him reeling back against the police-car. Loose hot blood poured down into his upturned face like water from a busted shower-head. He screamed and flailed at Chatterton's body. Chatterton spun slowly away and grabbed blindly at the car with the last of his strength. His left hand hit the hood, leaving a splattered handprint. His right grabbed weakly at the radio antenna and snapped it off. He fell into the driveway holding it in front of his one remaining eye like a scientist with a specimen too rare to relinquish even *in extremis.*

Eddings caught a blurred glimpse of the skinned man coming in low and hard and tried to draw back. He struck the car.

Stark sliced upward, splitting the crotch of Eddings' beige Trooper uniform, splitting his scrotal sac, drawing the razor up and out in a long, buttery stroke. Eddings' balls, suddenly untethered from each other, swung back against his inner thighs like heavy knots on the end of an unravelling sash-cord. Blood stained his pants around the zipper. For a moment he felt as if someone had jammed a handful of ice cream into his groin . . . and then the pain struck, hot and full of ragged teeth. He screamed.

Stark snapped the razor out, wicked-quick, at Eddings' throat, but Eddings managed somehow to get a hand up and the first stroke only split his palm in half. Eddings tried to roll to the left, and that exposed the right side of his neck.

The naked blade, pale silver in the day's hazy light, whickered through the air again, and this time it went where it was supposed to go. Eddings sank to his knees, hands between his legs. His beige pants had turned bright red almost to the knees. His head drooped, and now he looked like the object of a pagan sacrifice.

"Have a nice day, motherfucker," Stark said in a conversational voice. He bent over, tangled his hand in Eddings' hair, and jerked his head back, baring the neck for the final stroke.

4

He opened the back door of the cruiser, lifted Eddings by the neck of his uniform shirt and the bloody seat of his trousers, and tossed him in like a sack of grain. Then he did the same with Chatterton. The latter must have weighed close to two hundred and thirty pounds, with his equipment belt and the .45 on his belt thrown in, but Stark handled him as if he were a bag stuffed with feathers. He slammed the door, then shot a glance full of bright curiosity at the house.

It was silent. The only sounds were the crickets in the high grass beside the driveway and the low, strawlike *whick! whick! whick!* of the lawnsprinklers. To this there was added the sound of an oncoming truck—an Orinco tanker. It roared by at sixty, headed north. Stark tensed and lowered himself slightly behind the side of the police cruiser when he saw the truck's big brake lights flare red for an instant. He uttered a single grunt of laughter when they went out again and the tanker disappeared over the next hill, accelerating again. The driver had glimpsed the State Police cruiser parked in the Beaumont driveway, had checked his speedometer, and had thought speed-trap. The most natural thing in the world. He needn't have worried; this speed-trap was closed forever.

There was a lot of blood in the driveway, but puddled on the bright black asphalt, it could have been water . . . unless you got very close. So that was okay. And even if it wasn't, it would have to do.

Stark folded the straight-razor, held it in one sticky hand, went over to the door. He saw neither the little drift of dead sparrows lying by the stoop, nor the live ones which now lined the roofpeak of the house and sat in the apple tree by the garage, watching him silently.

In a minute or two, Liz Beaumont came downstairs, still half-asleep from her midday nap, to answer the doorbell.

5

She didn't scream. The scream was there, but the stripped face looking at her when she opened the door locked it deep inside her, froze it, denied it, cancelled it, buried it alive. Unlike Thad, she'd had no dreams of George Stark she could remember, but they might have been there all the same, deep in the fastnesses of her unconscious mind, because this glaring, grinning face seemed almost an expected thing, for all its horror.

"Hey lady, wanna buy a duck?" Stark asked through the screen. He grinned, exposing a great many teeth. Most of them were now dead. The sunglasses turned his eyes into big black sockets. Goo dripped from his cheek and jawline and splattered on the vest he was wearing.

Belatedly, she tried to close the door. Stark

rammed a gloved fist through the screen and slammed it back open again. Liz stumbled away, trying to scream. She couldn't. Her throat was still locked up.

Stark came in and closed the door.

Liz watched him walk slowly toward her. He looked like a decayed scarecrow which had somehow come to life. The grin was the worst, because the left half of his upper lip appeared not just decayed or decaying, but chewed away. She could see gray-black teeth, and the sockets where, until recently, other teeth had been.

His gloved hands stretched out toward her.

"Hello, Beth," he said through that terrible grin. "Please excuse the intrusion, but I was in the neighborhood and thought I'd drop by. I'm George Stark, and I'm pleased to meet you. More pleased, I think, than you could possibly know."

One of his fingers touched her chin . . . caressed it. The flesh beneath the black leather felt spongy, unsteady. At that moment she thought of the twins, sleeping upstairs, and her paralysis broke. She turned and fled for the kitchen. Somewhere in the roaring confusion of her mind she saw herself snatching one of the butcher-knives from the magnetized runners over the counter and plunging it deep into that obscene caricature of a face.

She heard him after her, quick as the wind.

His hand brushed the back of her blouse, hunting for purchase, and slipped off.

The kitchen door was the sort that swings back and forth. It was propped open with a wooden wedge. She kicked at the wedge on the run, knowing that if she missed it or only knocked it aslant, there wouldn't be a second chance. But she hit it dead-square with one slippered foot, feeling an instant of bright pain in her toes. The wedge flew across the kitchen floor, which was so brightly waxed that she could see the whole room in it, hung upside down. She felt Stark groping for her again. She reached behind her and raked the door shut. She heard the thud as it hit him. He yelled, furious and surprised but unhurt. She groped for the knives—

—and Stark grabbed her by the hair and the back of her blouse. He jerked her backward and spun her around. She heard the rough purr of parting cloth and thought incoherently: *If he rapes me oh Jesus if he rapes me I'll go crazy—*

She hammered at his grotesque face with her fists, knocking the sunglasses first askew and then off. The flesh below his left eye had sagged and fallen away like a dead mouth, exposing the whole bloodshot bulge of the eyeball.

And he was *laughing.*

He grabbed her hands and forced them down. She twisted one free, brought it up, and scratched at his face. Her fingers left deep grooves from which blood and pus began to flow sluggishly. There was little or no sense of resistance; she might as well have torn at a piece of flyblown meat. And now she was making a sound—she wanted to shriek, to articulate her horror and fear before they choked her, but the most she was able to manage was a series of hoarse, distressed barks.

He snatched her free hand out of the air, brought it down, forced both hands behind her, and encircled the wrists with his own hand. It was spongy but as unyielding as a manacle. He lifted his other hand to the front of her blouse and cupped a breast.

Her flesh moaned at his touch. She closed her eyes and tried to pull away.

"Oh, quit that," he said. He was not grinning on purpose now, but the left side of his mouth grinned anyway, frozen in its own decayed rictus. "Quit it, Beth. For your own good. It turns me on when you fight. You don't want me turned on. I guarantee it. I think we ought to have a Platonic relationship, you and I.

"At least for now."

He squeezed her breast harder, and she felt the ruthless strength under the decay, like an armature of articulated steel rods embedded in soft plastic.

How can he be so strong? How can he be so strong when he looks like he's dying?

But the answer was obvious. He wasn't human. She didn't think he was really even *alive.*

"Or maybe you *do* want it?" he asked. "Is that it? Do you want it? Do you want it right now?" His tongue, black and red and yellow, its surface blasted with strange cracks like those in a drying floodplain, poked out of his snarling, smiling mouth and wiggled at her.

She stopped struggling at once.

"Better," Stark said. "Now—I'm going to let go of you, Bethie my dear, my sweet one. When I do that, the urge to run the hundred-yard dash in five seconds flat is going to come over you again. That's natural enough; we hardly know each other, and I am aware that I don't look my best. But before you do anything foolish, I want you to remember the two cops outside—they're dead. And I want you to think of your bambinos, sleeping peacefully upstairs. Children need their rest, don't they? Especially very *small* children, very *defenseless* children, like yours. Do you understand? Do you follow me?"

She nodded dumbly. She could smell him now. It was a horrible, meaty aroma. *He's rotting,* she thought. *Rotting away right in front of me.*

It had become very clear to her why he so desperately wanted Thad to start writing again.

"You're a vampire," she said hoarsely. "A goddam vampire. And he's put you on a diet. So you break in here. You terrorize me and threaten my babies. You're a fucking coward, George Stark."

He let go of her and pulled first the left glove and then the right one smooth and tight again. It was a prissy yet oddly sinister bit of business.

"I hardly think that's fair, Beth. What would *you* do if you were in my position? What would you do, for instance, if you were stranded on an island without anything to eat or drink? Would you strike poses of languor and sigh prettily? Or would you fight? Do you really blame me for wanting something so simple as survival?"

"*Yes!*" she spat at him.

"Spoken like a true partisan . . . but you may change your mind. You see, the price of partisanship can run higher than you know right now, Beth. When the opposition is cunning and dedicated, the price can go right out of sight. You may find yourself more enthusiastic about our collaboration than you'd ever think possible."

"Dream on, motherfucker!"

The right side of his mouth rose, the eternally smiling left side hitched a little higher, and he favored her with a ghoul-grin she supposed was meant to be engaging. His hand, sickeningly gelid under the thin glove, slid down her forearm in a caress. One finger pressed suggestively into her left palm for an instant before dropping away. "This is no dream, Beth—I assure you. Thad and I are going to collaborate on a new Stark novel . . . for awhile. Put another way, Thad's going to give me a push. I'm like a stalled car, you see. Only instead of vapor-lock, I've got writer's block. That's all. That's the only problem there is, I judge. Once I get rolling, I'll put her in second, pop the clutch, and *vrooom!* Off I go!"

"You're crazy," she whispered.

"Yep. But so was Tolstoy. So was Richard Nixon, and they elected *that* greasy dawg President of the United States." Stark turned his head and looked out the window. Liz heard nothing, but all of a sudden he seemed to be listening with all his concentration, striving to pick up some faint, almost inaudible sound.

"What do you—" she began.

"Hush your mouth a second, hon," Stark told her. "Just put a sock in it."

Faintly, she heard the sound of a flock of birds taking wing. The sound was impossibly distant, impossibly beautiful. Impossibly *free.*

She stood there looking at him, her heart pounding too fast, wondering if she could break loose from him. He wasn't exactly in a trance, or anything like that, but his attention was certainly diverted. She could run, maybe. If she could get a gun—

His rotten hand stole around one of her wrists again.

"I can get inside your man and look out, you know. I can *feel* him thinking. I can't do that with you, but I can look at your face and make some real good guesses. Whatever you're thinking right now, Beth, you want to remember those cops . . . and your kids. You do that, it's gonna help you keep this in perspective."

"Why do you keep calling me that?"

"What? Beth?" He laughed. It was a nasty sound, as if he'd gotten gravel caught in his throat. "It's what *he'd* call you, if he was smart enough to think of it, you know."

"You're cr—"

"Crazy, I know. This is charmin, darlin, but we'll have to defer your opinions on my sanity until later. Too much happening right now. Listen: I have to call Thad, but not at his office. Phone there might be tapped. *He* doesn't think it is, but the cops might have done it without telling him. Your man is a trusting sort of fellow. I'm not."

"How can you—"

Stark leaned toward her and spoke very slowly and carefully, as a teacher might speak to a slow first-grader. "I want you to stop pickin this bone with me, Beth, and answer my questions. Because if I can't get what I need out of *you,* maybe I can get it out of your twins. I realize they can't talk yet, but maybe I can teach them. A little incentive does wonders."

He was wearing a quilted vest over his shirt in spite of the heat, the kind with many zippered pockets favored by hunters and hikers. He pulled down one of the side zippers where some cylindrical object bulged the polyester quilting. He took out a small gas torch. "Even if I can't teach em to talk, I bet I could teach em to sing. I bet I could teach em to sing just like a couple of larks. You might not want to face that music, Beth."

She tried to take her gaze away from the torch, but it wouldn't go. Her eyes followed it helplessly as he switched it back and forth from one gloved hand to the other. Her eyes seemed nailed to the nozzle.

"I'll tell you anything you want to know," she said, and thought: *For now.*

"That's good of you," he said, and stowed the gas torch back in its pocket. The vest pulled a little to the side when he did it, and she saw the butt of a very big handgun. "Very sensible, too, Beth. Now listen. There's somebody else there today, in the English Department. I can see him as clearly as I can see you right now. Short little fella, white hair, got a pipe in his mouth almost as big as he is. What's his name?"

"It sounds like Rawlie DeLesseps," she said drearily. She wondered how he could know Rawlie was there today . . . and decided she didn't really want to know.

"Could it be anyone else?"

Liz thought it over briefly and then shook her head. "It must be Rawlie."

"Have you got a faculty directory?"

"There's one in the telephone table drawer. In the living room."

"Good." He had slipped past her almost before she realized he was moving—the oily cat-grace of this decaying piece of meat made her feel a little sick—and plucked one of the long knives from the magnetized runners. Liz stiffened. Stark glanced at her and that caught-gravel sound came from his throat again. "Don't worry, I ain't gonna cut you. You're my good little helper, aren't you? Come on."

The hand, strong but unpleasantly spongy, slid

around her wrist again. When she tried to pull away, it only tightened. She stopped pulling at once and allowed him to lead her.

"Good," he said.

He took her into the living room, where she sat on the sofa and hugged her knees in front of her. Stark glanced at her, nodded to himself, and then turned his attention to the telephone. When he determined that there was no alarm wire—and that was sloppy, just sloppy—he slashed the cords the State Police had added: the one going to the trace-back gadget and the one that went down to the voice-activated recorder in the basement.

"You know how to behave, and that's very important," Stark said to the top of Liz's bent head. "Now, listen. I'm gonna find this Rawlie DeLesseps' number and have a brief little pow-wow with Thad. And while I do that, you're gonna go upstairs and pack whatever duds and other things your babies will need down at your summer place. When you're finished, roust em and bring em on down here."

"How did you know they were—"

He smiled a little at her look of surprise. "Oh, I know your schedule," he said. "I know it better than you do, maybe. You get em up, Beth, and get em ready, and bring em down here. I know the lay-out of the house as well as I know your schedule, and if you try to get away from me, honey, I will know. There's no need to dress em; just pack what they'll need and bring em down in their didies. You can dress em later, after we're on our merry way."

"Castle Rock? You want to go to Castle Rock?"

"Uh-huh. But you don't need to think about

that now. All you need to think about right now is that if you're longer than ten minutes by my watch, I'll have to come upstairs to see what's keeping you." He looked at her levelly, the dark glasses creating skull-like eyesockets below his peeling, oozing brow. "And I'll come with my little blowtorch lit and ready for action. You understand?"

"I . . . yes."

"Above all, Beth, you want to remember one thing. If you cooperate with me, you are going to be all right. And your children will be all right." He smiled again. "Bein a good mother like you are, I suspect that's much more important to you. I only want you to know better than to try gettin clever with me. Those two State cops are out there in the back of their bubblemobile, drawing flies, because they had the bad luck to be on the tracks when my express was comin through. There's a bunch of dead cops in New York City who had the same sort of bad luck . . . as you well know. The way to help yourself, and your kids—and Thad, too, because if he does what I want, he's gonna be fine—is to stay dumb and helpful. You understand?"

"Yes," she said hoarsely.

"You may get an idea. I know how that can happen when a person feels like his back's to the wall. But if you *do* get one, you want to shoo that idea right away. You want to remember that, although I may not look so hot, my ears are *great*. If you try to open a window, I'll hear it. If you try to take out a screen, I'll hear *that*. Bethie, I'm a man who can hear the angels singin in heaven and the devils screamin in the deepest holes of hell. You have to ask yourself if you dare take the chance. You're a

smart woman. I think you'll make the right decision. Move, girl. Get goin."

He was looking at his watch, actually timing
her. And Liz bounded for the stairs on legs which
felt nerveless.

6

She heard him speak briefly on the telephone downstairs. There was a long pause, and then he began to
speak again. His voice changed. She didn't know
who he had talked to before the pause—Rawlie
DeLesseps, maybe—but when he began to speak
again, she was almost positive Thad was on the
other end. She couldn't make out the words and
didn't dare go to the extension phone, but she was
still sure it was Thad. There was no time for eaves-
dropping, anyway. He had asked her to ask herself
if she dared chance crossing him. She did not.

She threw diapers into the diaper-bag, clothes
into a suitcase. She swept the creams, baby powder,
Handi-Wipes, diaper pins, and other odds and ends
into a shoulder-bag.

The conversation had ended downstairs. She was
heading for the twins, about to wake them, when
he called up to her.

"Beth! It's time!"

"I'm *coming!*" She lifted Wendy, who began to
cry sleepily.

"I want you down here—I'm expecting a telephone call, and you're the sound effects." But
she barely heard this last. Her eyes were fixed on
the plastic diaper-pin caddy on top of the twins'
bureau.

Lying beside the caddy was a bright pair of sewing scissors.

She put Wendy back in her crib, threw a glance at the door, and then hurried across to the bureau. She took the scissors and two of the diaper pins. She stuck the pins in her mouth like a woman making a dress, and unzipped her skirt. She pinned the scissors to the inside of her panties, then zipped the skirt again. There was a small bulge where the handle of the scissors and the heads of the pins were. She didn't think an ordinary man would notice, but George Stark was not an ordinary man. She left her blouse hanging out. Better.

"Beth!" The voice was on the verge of being angry now. Worse, it was coming from halfway up the stairs and she had never even heard him, although she would have said it was impossible to use the main staircase in this old place without producing all sorts of creaks and groans.

Just then the telephone rang.

"You get them down here now!" he screamed up at her, and she hurried to rouse William. She had no time to be gentle, and as a result she had a baby squalling at top volume in each arm when she came downstairs. Stark was on the telephone and she expected that he would be even more furious at the noise. On the contrary, he looked quite pleased . . . and then she realized that if he was talking to Thad, he should be pleased. He could hardly have done better if he had brought his own sound-effects record.

The ultimate persuader, she thought, and felt a flash of powerful hate for this rotten creature who had no business existing but who refused to disappear.

Stark was holding a pencil in one hand, tapping the eraser end gently on the edge of the telephone table, and she realized with a little shock of recognition that it was a Berol Black Beauty. *One of Thad's pencils,* she thought. *Has he been in the study?*

No—of course he hadn't been in the study, nor was it one of Thad's pencils. They had never been Thad's pencils, not really—he just bought them sometimes. The Black Beauties belonged to Stark. He had used the pencil to write something in block letters on the back of the faculty directory. As she neared him she could read two sentences. GUESS WHERE I CALLED FROM, THAD? read the first one. The second was brutally direct: TELL ANYBODY AND THEY DIE.

As if to confirm this, Stark said: "Not a thing, as you can hear for yourself. I haven't harmed a hair of their precious little heads."

He turned toward Liz and winked at her. It was somehow the most hideous thing of all—as if they were in on this together. Stark was twirling his sunglasses between the thumb and forefinger of his left hand. His eyeballs glared out of his face like marbles in the face of a melting wax statue.

"Yet," he added.

He listened, then grinned. Even if his face had not been decomposing almost before her eyes, that grin would have struck her as teasing and vicious.

"What about her?" Stark asked in a voice which was almost lilting, and that was when her anger got on top of her fear and she thought for the first time of Aunt Martha and the rats. She wished Aunt Martha were here now, to take care of this particular rat. She had the scissors, but that didn't mean he would give her the opening she would need to use them. But Thad . . . *Thad* knew about Aunt Martha. And the idea winked into her mind.

7

When the conversation was over and Stark had hung up, she asked him what he meant to do.

"Move fast," he said. "It's my specialty." He held out his arms. "Give me one of the kids. Don't matter which one."

She shrank away from him, reflexively hugging both babies tighter to her breasts. They had quieted down, but at her convulsive hug, both began to whimper and wriggle again.

Stark looked at her patiently. "I don't have time to argue with you, Beth. Don't make me persuade you with this." He patted the cylindrical bulge in the pocket of the hunting vest. "I'm not going to hurt your kids. In a funny sort of way, you know, I'm their daddy, too."

"*Don't you say that!*" she shrieked at him, drawing away farther still. She trembled on the edge of flight.

"You get control of yourself, woman."

The words were flat, accentless, and deadly cold. They made her feel as if she had been slapped across the face with a bag of cold water.

"Get hip, sweetheart. I have to go outside and move that cop-car into your garage. I can't have you running down the road in the other direction while I do it. If I'm holding one of your kids—as collateral, so to speak—I won't have to worry about that. I mean what I say about bearing you and them no ill will . . . and even if I did, what good would I do myself by hurting one of your kids? I need your cooperation. That's not the way to get it. Now you give one of them over right now, or I'll hurt them both—not kill them but hurt them, really hurt them—and you'll be the one to blame."

He held out his arms. His ruined face was stern and set. Looking at it, she saw that no argument would sway him, no plea would turn him. He would not even listen. He would just do what he had threatened.

She walked toward him, and when he tried to take Wendy her arm tightened again, balking him for a moment. Wendy began to sob harder. Liz relaxed, letting the girl go, and began to cry again herself. She looked into his eyes. "If you hurt her, I'll kill you."

"I know you'd try," Stark said gravely. "I have great respect for motherhood, Beth. You think I am a monster, and maybe you're right. But real monsters are never without feelings. I think in the end it's that, and not how they look, that makes them so scary. I'm not going to hurt this little one, Beth. She's safe with me . . . as long as you cooperate."

Liz now held William in both arms . . . and the circle her arms made had never felt so empty to her. Never in her life had she been so convinced she had made a mistake. But what else was there to do?

"Besides . . . look!" Stark cried, and there was something in his voice that she could not, would not credit. The tenderness she believed she heard *had* to be counterfeit, only more of his monstrous teasing. But he was looking down at Wendy with a profound and disturbing attention . . . and Wendy was looking up at him, rapt, no longer crying. "The little one doesn't know how I look. She's not scared of me a bit, Beth. Not a bit."

She watched in silent horror as he raised his right hand. He had stripped off the gloves and she could see a heavy gauze bandage across it, exactly where Thad was wearing a bandage over the back of his left hand. Stark opened his fist, closed it, opened it again. It was clear from the tightening of his jaw that flexing his hand caused him some pain, but he did it, anyway.

Thad does that, he does it just that way, oh my God he does it JUST THAT SAME WAY—

Wendy now appeared to be totally calm. She gazed up into Stark's face, studying him with close attention, her cool gray eyes on Stark's muddy blue ones. With the skin fallen away beneath them, his eyes looked as if they might fall out at any moment and dangle on his cheeks by their stalks.

And Wendy waved back.

Hand open; hand closed; hand open.

A Wendy-wave.

Liz felt movement in her arms, looked down, and saw that William was looking at George Stark with the same rapt blue-gray gaze. He was smiling.

William's hand opened; closed; opened.

A William-wave.

"No," she moaned, almost too low to hear. "Oh God, no, please don't let this be happening."

"You see?" Stark said, looking up at her. He was grinning his frozen Sardonicus grin at her, and the most horrible thing about it was her understanding that he was trying to be gentle . . . and could not be. "You see? They like me, Beth. They *like* me."

8

Stark carried Wendy out to the driveway after putting his dark glasses on again. Liz ran to the window and looked after them anxiously. Part of her was positive he intended to hop into the police cruiser and drive away with her baby on the seat beside him and the two dead State Troopers in the back.

But for a moment he did nothing—simply stood there in hazy sunshine by the driver's door, head down, the baby cradled in his arms. He remained in that motionless position for some time, as if speaking seriously to Wendy, or perhaps praying. Later, when she had more information, she decided he had been trying to get in touch with Thad again, perhaps to read his thoughts and divine whether he intended to do what Stark wanted him to do or if he had plans of his own.

After about thirty seconds of this, Stark lifted his head, shook it briskly as if to clear it, then got into the cruiser and started it up. *The keys were in the ignition,* she thought dully. *He didn't even have to hot-wire it, or whatever they do. That man has got the luck of the devil.*

Stark drove the cruiser into the garage and cut the motor. Then she heard the car door slam and he came back out, pausing long enough to hit the button that sent the door rumbling down on its tracks.

A few moments later he was in the house again and handing Wendy back to her.

"You see?" he asked. "She's fine. Now tell me about the people next door. The Clarks."

"The Clarks?" she asked, feeling extraordinarily stupid. "Why do you want to know about them? They're in Europe this summer."

He smiled. It was, in a way, the most hideous thing yet, because under more ordinary circumstances it would have been a smile of genuine pleasure . . . and quite a winning one, she suspected. And didn't she feel just an instant of attraction? A freakish flicker? It was insane, of course, but did that mean she could deny it? Liz didn't think so, and she even understood why it might be. After all, she had married this man's closest relative.

"Wonderful!" he said. "Couldn't be better! And do they have a car?"

Wendy began to cry. Liz looked down and saw her daughter looking at the man with the rotten face and the bulging marble eyes, holding her small and pleasantly chubby arms out. She was not crying because she was afraid of him; she was crying because she wanted to go back to him.

"Isn't that sweet!" Stark said. "She wants to come back to Daddy."

"Shut up, you monster!" she spat at him.

Foxy George Stark threw his head back and laughed.

9

He gave her five minutes to pack a few more things for herself and the twins. She told him it would be impossible to get together half of what they'd need in that length of time, and he told her to do the best she could.

"You're lucky I'm giving you any more time at all, Beth, under the circumstances—there are two dead cops in your garage and your husband knows what's going on. If you want to take the five minutes debating the point with me, that's your choice. You're already down to . . ." He glanced at his watch, then smiled at her. "Four-and-a-half."

So she did what she could, pausing once while tossing jars of baby food into a shopping bag to look at her children. They were sitting side by side on the floor, playing an idle sort of pat-a-cake with each other and looking at Stark. She was dreadfully afraid she knew what they were thinking about.

Isn't that sweet.

No. She wouldn't think about it. She wouldn't think about it but it was all she *could* think about: Wendy, crying and holding out her pudgy little arms. Holding them out to the murderous stranger.

They want to go back to Daddy.

He was standing in the kitchen doorway, watching her, smiling, and she wanted to use the scissors right then. She had never in her life wanted anything so badly. "Can't you give me a hand?" she cried angrily at him, gesturing at the two bags and the cooler she had filled.

"Of course, Beth," he said. He took one of the bags for her. His other hand, the left, he kept free.

10

They crossed the side yard, passed through the little greenbelt between properties, and then walked across the Clarks' yard to their driveway. Stark insisted that she move fast, and she was panting by the time they stopped in front of the closed garage door. He had offered to take one of the twins, but she'd refused.

He set down the cooler, took his wallet from his back pocket, removed a narrow strip of metal which tapered to a point, and slipped it into the lock of the garage door. He turned it first to the right and then back to the left, one ear cocked. There was a click and he smiled.

"Good," he said. "Even Mickey Mouse locks on garage doors can be a pain in the ass. Big springs. Hard to tip them over. This one's as tired as an old whore's twat at daybreak, though. Lucky for us." He turned the handle and shoved. The door rumbled up on its tracks.

The garage was hot as a haymow, and the Clarks' Volvo wagon was even hotter inside. Stark bent beneath the dashboard, exposing the back of his neck to her as she sat in the passenger seat. Her fingers twitched. It would only take a second to rip the scissors free, but that could still be too long. She had seen how quickly he reacted to the unexpected. It did not really surprise her that his reflexes were as fast as those of a wild animal, since that was what he was.

He raked down a bunch of wires from behind the dash, then produced a bloody straight-razor from his front pocket. She shivered a little and had to swallow twice, fast, to stifle a gag-reflex. He unfolded the blade, bent down again, stripped insulation from two of the wires, and touched the bare copper cores together. There was a sliver of blue spark, and then the engine began to turn over. A moment later the car was running.

"Well, all *right!*" George Stark crowed. "Let's roll, what do you *say?*"

The twins giggled together and waved their hands at him. Stark waved gaily back. As he backed the car out of the garage, Liz reached stealthily behind Wendy, who was sitting on her lap, and touched the rounds that were the fingerholes of the scissors. Not now, but soon. She had no intention of waiting for Thad. She was too uneasy about what this dark creature might decide to do to the twins in the meantime.

Or to her.

As soon as he was sufficiently distracted, she intended to free the scissors from their hiding place and bury them in his throat.

III

THE COMING OF THE PSYCHOPOMPS

"The poets talk about love," Machine said, running the straight-razor back and forth along the strop in a steady, hypnotic rhythm, "and that's okay. There is love. The politicians talk about duty, and that's okay, too. There is duty. Eric Hoffer talks about post-modernism. Hugh Hefner talks about sex. Hunter Thompson talks about drugs, and Jimmy Swaggart talks about God the Father Almighty, maker of heaven and earth. Those things all exist and they are all okay. Do you know what I mean, Jack?"

"Yeah, I guess so," Jack Rangely said. He really didn't know, didn't have the slightest idea, but when Machine was in this sort of mood, only a lunatic would argue with him.

Machine turned the straight-razor's edge down and suddenly slashed the strop in two. A long section fell to the pool-hall floor like a severed tongue. "But what I talk about is doom," he said. "Because, in the end, doom is all that counts."

—*Riding to Babylon*
by George Stark

Twenty-two

THAD ON THE RUN

1

Pretend it's a book you're writing, he thought as he turned left onto College Avenue, leaving the campus behind. *And pretend you're a character in that book.*

It was a magic thought. His mind had been filled with roaring panic—a kind of mental tornado in which fragments of some possible plan spun like chunks of uprooted landscape. But at the idea that he could pretend it was all a harmless fiction, that he could move not only himself but the other characters in this story (characters like Harrison and Manchester, for instance) around the way he moved characters on paper, in the safety of his study with bright lights overhead and either a cold can of Pepsi or a hot cup of tea beside him . . . at this idea, it was as if the wind howling between his ears suddenly blew itself out. The extraneous shit blew away with it, leaving him with the pieces of his plan lying around . . . pieces he found he was able to put together quite easily. He discovered he had something which might even work.

It better work, Thad thought. *If it doesn't, you'll wind up in protective custody and Liz and the kids will most likely wind up dead.*

But what about the sparrows? Where did the sparrows fit?

He didn't know. Rawlie had told him they were psychopomps, the harbingers of the living dead, and that fit, didn't it? Yes. Up to a point, anyway. Because foxy old George was alive again, but foxy old George was also dead . . . dead and rotting. So the sparrows fit in . . . but not all the way. If the sparrows had guided George back from

(the land of the dead)

wherever he had been, how come George himself knew nothing about them? How come he did not remember writing that phrase, THE SPARROWS ARE FLYING AGAIN, in blood on the walls of two apartments?

"Because *I* wrote it," Thad muttered, and his mind flew back to the things he had written in his journal while he had been sitting in his study, on the edge of a trance.

Question: Are the birds mine?
Answer: Yes.
Question: Who wrote about the sparrows?
Answer: The one who knows . . . I am the knower. I am the owner.

Suddenly all the answers trembled almost within his grasp—the terrible, unthinkable answers. Thad heard a long, shaky sound emerging from his own mouth. It was a groan.

Question: Who brought George Stark back to life?
Answer: The owner. The knower.

"I didn't *mean* to!" he cried.

But was that true? Was it really? Hadn't there always been a part of him in love with George Stark's simple, violent nature? Hadn't part of him always admired George, a man who didn't stumble over things or bump into things, a man who never looked weak or silly, a man who would never have to fear the demons locked away in the liquor cabinet? A man with no wife or children to consider, with no loves to bind him or slow him down? A man who had never waded through a shitty student essay or agonized over a Budget Committee meeting? A man who had a sharp, straight answer to all of life's more difficult questions?

A man who was not afraid of the dark because he *owned* the dark?

"*Yes, but he's a* BASTARD!" Thad screamed into the hot interior of his sensible American-made four-wheel-drive car.

Right—and part of you finds that SO *attractive, doesn't it?*

Perhaps he, Thad Beaumont, had not really created George . . . but was it not possible that some longing part of him had allowed Stark to be *recreated?*

Question: If I own the sparrows, can I use them?

No answer came. It *wanted* to come; he could feel its longing. But it danced just out of his reach, and Thad found himself suddenly afraid that he himself—some Stark-loving part of him—might be holding it off. Some part that didn't want George to die.

I am the knower. I am the owner. I am the bringer.

He paused at the Orono traffic light and then was heading out along Route 2, toward Bangor and Ludlow beyond.

Rawlie was a part of his plan—a part of it which he at least understood. What would he do if he actually managed to shake the cops following him only to find that Rawlie had already left his office?

He didn't know.

What would he do if Rawlie was there but refused to help him?

He didn't know that, either.

I'll burn those bridges when and if I come to them.

And he would be coming to them soon enough.

He was passing Gold's on the right, now. Gold's was a long, tubular building constructed of pre-fab aluminum sections. It was painted a particularly offensive shade of aqua and was surrounded by a dozen acres of junked-out cars. Their windshields glittered in the hazy sunlight in a galaxy of white starpoints. It was Saturday afternoon—had been for almost twenty minutes now. Liz and her dark kidnapper would be on their way to The Rock. And, although there would be a clerk or two selling parts to weekend mechanics in the pre-fab building where Gold's did its retail business, Thad could reasonably hope that the junkyard itself would be unattended. With nearly twenty thousand cars in varying states of decay roughly organized into dozens of zig-zagging rows, he should be able to hide the Suburban . . . and he *had* to hide it. High-shouldered, boxy, gray with brilliant red sides, it stuck out like a sore thumb.

SLOW SCHOOL ZONE, the sign coming up read. Thad felt a hot wire poke into his gut. This was it.

He checked the rearview mirror and saw the Plymouth was still riding two cars back. It wasn't as good as he could have wished, but it was probably as good as it was going to get. For the rest, he would have to depend on luck and surprise. They weren't expecting him to make a break; why would he? And for a moment he thought of not doing it. Suppose he just pulled over instead? And when they pulled up behind him and Harrison got out to ask what was wrong, he would say: *Plenty. Stark's got my family. The sparrows are still flying, you see.*

"Thad, he says he killed the two that were watch-

ing the house. I don't know how he did it, but he says he did . . . and I . . . I believe him."

Thad believed him, too. That was the hell of it. And that was the reason he couldn't just stop and ask for help. If he tried anything funny, Stark would know. He didn't think Stark could read his thoughts, at least not the way aliens read thoughts in comic books and science fiction movies, but he *could* "tune in" on Thad . . . could get a very good idea of what he was up to. He might be able to prepare a little surprise for George—if he was able to clarify his idea about the goddam birds, that was— but for now he intended to play it by the script.

If he could, that was.

Here was the school intersection and the four-way stop. It was far too busy, as always; for years there had been fender-benders at this intersection, mostly caused by people who simply couldn't grok the idea of a four-way stop where everybody took turns, and just went bashing through instead. A spate of letters, most of them written by worried parents, demanding that the town put in a stop-light at the intersection, followed each accident, and a statement from the Veazie selectmen saying a stop-light was "under consideration" would follow *that* . . . and then the issue would simply go to sleep until the next fender-bender.

Thad joined the line of cars waiting to cross southbound, checked to make sure the brown Plymouth was still two cars back, then watched the your-turn-to-curtsey-my-turn-to-bow action at the intersection. He saw a car filled with blue-haired ladies almost crash into a young couple in a Datsun Z, saw the girl in the Z shoot the blue-haired ladies the bird, and saw that he himself would cross north-south just before a long Grant's Dairy tanker crossed east-west.

That was an unexpected break.

The car in front of him crossed, and Thad was up. The hot wire poked into his belly again. He checked the rearview mirror a final time. Harrison and Manchester were still two cars back.

A pair of cars criss-crossed in front of him. On his left, the milk-tanker moved into position. Thad took a deep breath and rolled the Suburban sedately through the intersection. A pick-up truck, north-bound toward Orono, passed him in the other lane.

On the far side, he was gripped by an almost irresistible urge—a *need*—to tromp the pedal to the metal and blast the Suburban up the road. Instead, he went rolling along at a calm and perfectly school-zone-legal fifteen miles an hour, eyes glued to the rearview mirror. The Plymouth was still waiting in line to cross, two cars back.

Hey, milk-truck! he thought, concentrating, really bearing down, as if he could make it come by simple force of will . . . as he made people and things come and go in a novel by force of will. *Milk-truck, come now!*

And it *did* come, rolling across the intersection in slow, silver dignity, like a mechanized dowager.

The moment it blotted out the dark brown Plymouth in his rearview mirror, Thad did floor the Suburban's gas pedal.

2

There was a right turn half a block up. Thad took it and roared up a short street at forty, praying no little kid would pick this instant to chase his rubber ball out into the road.

He had a nasty moment when it seemed the street must be a dead end, then saw he could make another right after all—the cross-street had been partially blocked by the high line of hedge which belonged to the house on the corner.

He made a California stop at the T-junction, then swerved right with the tires wailing softly. A hundred and eighty yards farther up, he made another right and scooted the Suburban back down to this street's intersection with Route 2. He had worked his way back to the main road about a quarter of a mile north of the four-way stop. If the milk-truck had blocked his right turn from view, as he hoped, the brown Plymouth was still heading south along 2. They might not even know anything was wrong yet . . . although Thad seriously doubted that Harrison was that dumb. Manchester maybe, but not Harrison.

He cut a left, scooting into a break in traffic so narrow that the driver of a Ford in the southbound lane had to hit his brakes. The Ford's driver shook his fist at Thad as Thad cut across his bows and headed back down toward Gold's Junkyard, the pedal again stamped to the floor. If a roving cop happened to observe him not just breaking the speed limit but apparently trying to disintegrate it, that was just too bad. He couldn't afford to linger. He had to get this vehicle, which was just too big and too bright, off the road as fast as he could.

It was half a mile back to the automobile junkyard. Thad drove most of it with his eyes on the rear-view mirror, looking for the Plymouth. It was still nowhere to be seen when he turned left into Gold's.

He rolled the Suburban slowly through an open gate in the chainlink fence. A sign, faded red letters on a dirty white background, read EMPLOYEES ONLY BEYOND THIS POINT! On a weekday he would have been spotted almost at once, and turned back. But it was Saturday, and now well into the lunch-hour to boot.

Thad drove down an aisle lined with wrecked cars stacked up two and sometimes three deep. The ones on the bottom had lost their essential shapes and seemed to be melting slowly into the ground. The earth was so black with oil you would have believed nothing could grow there, but rank green weeds and huge, silently nodding sunflowers sprouted in cheesy clusters, like survivors of a nuclear holocaust. One large sunflower had grown up through the broken windshield of a bakery truck lying on its back like a dead dog. Its hairy green stem had curled like a knotted fist around the stump of a wheel, and a second fist clung to the hood ornament of the old Cadillac which lay on top of the truck. It seemed to stare at Thad like the black-and-yellow eye of a dead monster.

It was a large and silent Detroit necropolis, and it gave Thad the creeps.

He made a right turn, then a left. Suddenly he could see sparrows everywhere, perched on roofs and trunks and greasy amputated engines. He saw a trio of the small birds bathing in a hubcap filled with water. They did not fly away as he approached but stopped what they were doing and watched him with their beady black eyes. Sparrows lined the top of a windshield which leaned against the side of an old Plymouth. He passed within three feet of them.

They fluttered their wings nervously but held their positions as he passed.

The harbingers of the living dead, Thad thought. His hand went to the small white scar on his forehead and began to rub it nervously.

Looking through what appeared to be a meteorhole in the windshield of a Datsun as he passed it, he observed a wide splash of dried blood on the dashboard.

It wasn't a meteor that made that hole, he thought, and his stomach turned over slowly and giddily.

A congregation of sparrows sat on the Datsun's front seat.

"What do you want with me?" he asked hoarsely. "What in God's name do you want?"

And in his mind he seemed to hear an answer of sorts; in his mind he seemed to hear the shrill single voice of their avian intelligence: *No, Thad— what do YOU want with US? You are the owner. You are the bringer. You are the knower.*

"I don't know jack shit," he muttered.

At the end of this row, space was available in front of a late-model Cutlass Supreme—someone had amputated its entire front end. He backed the Suburban in and got out. Looking from one side of the narrow aisle to the other, Thad felt a little bit like a rat in a maze. The place smelled of oil and the higher, sourer odor of transmission fluid. There were no sounds but the faraway drone of cars on Route 2.

The sparrows looked at him from everywhere— a silent convocation of small brown-black birds.

Then, abruptly, they took wing all at once— hundreds of them, perhaps a thousand. For a moment the air was harsh with the sound of their wings. They flocked across the sky, then banked west—in the direction where Castle Rock lay. And abruptly he began to feel that crawling sensation again . . . not so much on his skin as *inside* it.

Are we trying to have a little peek, George?

Under his breath he began to sing a Bob Dylan song: "John Wesley Harding . . . was a friend to the poor . . . he travelled with a gun in every hand . . ."

That crawling, itching sensation seemed to increase. It found and centered upon the hole in his left hand. He could have been completely wrong, engaging in wishful thinking and no more, but Thad seemed to sense anger . . . and frustration.

"All along the telegraph . . . his name it did resound . . ." Thad sang under his breath. Ahead, lying on the oily ground like the twisted remnant of some steel statue no one had ever really wanted to look at in the first place, was a rusty motor-mount. Thad picked it up and walked back to the Suburban, still singing snatches of "John Wesley Harding" under his breath and remembering his old raccoon buddy of the same name. If he could camouflage the Suburban by beating on it a little, if he could give himself even an extra two hours, it could mean the difference between life and death to Liz and the twins.

"All along the countryside . . . sorry, big guy, this hurts me more than it does you . . . he opened many a door . . ." He threw the motor-mount at the driver's side of the Suburban, bashing a dent as deep as a washbasin in it. He picked up the motor-mount again, walked around to the front of the Suburban, and pegged it at the grille hard enough to strain his shoulder. Plastic splintered and flew.

Thad unlatched the hood and raised it a little, giving the Suburban the dead-alligator smile which seemed to be the Gold's version of automotive *haute couture.*

". . . but he was never known to hurt an honest man . . ."

He picked up the motor-mount again, observing as he did so that fresh blood had begun to stain the bandage on his wounded hand. Nothing he could do about it now.

". . . with his lady by his side, he took a stand . . ."

He threw the mount a final time, sending it through the windshield with a heavy crunch, which—absurd as it might be—pained his heart.

He thought the Suburban now looked enough like the other wrecks to pass muster.

Thad started walking up the row. He turned right at the first intersection, heading back toward the gate and the retail parts shop beyond it. He had seen a pay telephone on the wall by the door when he drove in. Halfway there he stopped walking and stopped singing. He cocked his head. He looked like a man straining to catch some small sound. What he was really doing was listening to his body, auditing it.

The crawling itch had disappeared.

The sparrows were gone, and so was George Stark, at least for the time being.

Smiling a little, Thad began to walk faster.

3

After two rings, Thad began to sweat. If Rawlie was still there, he should have picked up his phone by now. The faculty offices in the English-Math Building were just not that big. Who else could he call? Who the hell else *was* there? He could think of no one.

Halfway through the third ring, Rawlie picked up his phone. "Hello, DeLesseps."

Thad closed his eyes at the sound of that smoke-roughened voice and leaned against the cool metal side of the parts shop for a moment.

"Hello?"

"Hi, Rawlie. It's Thad."

"Hello, Thad." Rawlie did not seem terribly surprised to hear from him. "Forget something?"

"No. Rawlie, I'm in trouble."

"Yes." Just that, and not a question. Rawlie spoke the word and then just waited.

"You know those two"—Thad hesitated for a moment—"those two fellows who were with me?"

"Yes," Rawlie said calmly. "The police escort."

"I ditched them," Thad said, then took a quick glance over his shoulder at the sound of a car rumbling onto the packed dirt which served as Gold's customer parking area. For a moment he was so sure it was the brown Plymouth that he actually *saw* it . . . but it was some sort of foreign car, what he had taken at first for brown was a deep red dulled by road-dust, and the driver was just turning around. "At least I *hope* I've ditched them." He paused. He had come to the place where the only choice was to jump or not to jump, and he had no time to delay the decision. When you came right down to it, there really wasn't any decision, either, because he had no choice. "I need help, Rawlie. I need a car they don't know."

Rawlie was silent.

"You said if there was anything you could do for me, I should ask."

"I'm aware of what I said," Rawlie replied mildly. "I also recall saying that if those two men were following you around in a protective capacity, you might be wise to give them as much help as you could." He paused. "I think I can infer you chose not to take my advice."

Thad came very close to saying, *I couldn't, Rawlie. The man who has my wife and our babies would only kill them, too.* It wasn't that he didn't dare tell Rawlie what was going on, that Rawlie would think he was crazy if he did; college and university professors have much more flexible views on the subject of craziness than most other people, and sometimes they have no view of it at all, preferring to think of people as either dull (but sane), rather eccentric (but sane), or *very* eccentric (but still quite sane, old boy). He kept his mouth shut because Rawlie DeLesseps was one of those men so inner-directed that Thad could probably say nothing at all which would persuade him . . . and anything which came out of his mouth might only damage his case. But, inner-directed or not, the grammarian had a good heart . . . he was brave, in his way . . . and Thad believed Rawlie was more than a little interested in what was going on with Thad, his police escort, and his odd interest in sparrows. In the end he simply believed—or only hoped—that it was in his best interest to keep quiet.

Still, it was hard to wait.

"All right," Rawlie said at last. "I'll loan you my car, Thad."

Thad closed his eyes and had to stiffen his knees

to keep them from buckling. He wiped his neck under his chin and his hand came away wet with sweat.

"But I hope you'll have the decency to stand good for any repairs if it comes back . . . wounded," Rawlie said. "If you're a fugitive from justice, I doubt very much if my insurance company will pay."

A fugitive from justice? Because he had slipped out from under the gaze of the cops who couldn't possibly protect him? He didn't know if that made him a fugitive from justice or not. It was an interesting question, one he would have to consider at a later date. A later date when he wasn't half out of his mind with worry and fear.

"You know I would."

"I have one other condition," Rawlie said.

Thad closed his eyes again. This time in frustration. "What's that?"

"I want to know all about this when it's over," Rawlie said. "I want to know why you were really so interested in the folk meanings of sparrows, and why you turned white when I told you what psychopomps were and what it is they are supposed to do."

"Did I turn white?"

"As a sheet."

"I'll tell you the whole story," Thad promised. He grinned a little. "You may even believe some of it."

"Where are you?" Rawlie asked.

Thad told him. And asked him to come as quickly as he could.

4

He hung up the telephone, walked back through the gate in the chain-link fence, and sat down on the wide bumper of a schoolbus which had, for some reason, been chopped in half. It was a good place to wait, if waiting was what you had to do. He was hidden from the road, but he could see the dirt parking area of the parts department simply by leaning forward. He looked around for sparrows and didn't see a one—only a large, fat crow picking listlessly at shiny bits of chrome in one of the aisles running between the junked cars. The thought that he had finished his second conversation with George Stark only a little over half an hour ago made him feel mildly unreal. It seemed that hours had passed since then. In spite of the steady pitch of anxiety to which he was tuned, he felt sleepy, as if it were bedtime.

That itching, crawling sensation began to invade him again about fifteen minutes after his conversation with Rawlie. He sang those snatches of "John Wesley Harding" he still remembered, and after a minute or two the feeling passed.

Maybe it's psychosomatic, he thought, but he knew that was bullshit. The feeling was George trying to punch a keyhole into his mind, and as Thad grew more aware of it he became more sensitive to it. He supposed it would work the other way, too. And he supposed that, sooner or later, he might have to try to *make* it work the other way . . . but that meant trying to call the birds, and that wasn't a thing he was looking forward to. And there was something else, too—the last time he'd succeeded at peeking in on George Stark, he'd wound up with a pencil sticking out of his left hand.

The minutes crawled by with exquisite slowness. After twenty-five of them, Thad began to be afraid Rawlie had changed his mind and wasn't coming. He left the bumper of the dismembered bus and stood in the gateway between the automobile graveyard and the parking area, heedless of who might see him from the road. He began to wonder if he dared try hitchhiking.

He decided to try Rawlie's office again instead and was halfway to the pre-fab parts building when a dusty Volkswagen beetle pulled into the lot. He recognized it at once and broke into a run, thinking with some amusement about Rawlie's insurance concerns. It looked to Thad as if he could total the VW and pay for the damage with a case of returnable soda bottles.

Rawlie pulled up beside the end of the parts building and got out. Thad was a little surprised to see that his pipe was lit, and giving off great clouds of what would been *extremely* offensive smoke in a closed room.

"You're not supposed to smoke, Rawlie," was the first thing he could think of to say.

"You're not supposed to run," Rawlie returned gravely.

They looked at each other for a moment and then burst into surprised laughter.

"How will you get home?" Thad asked. Now that it had come down to this—just jumping into Rawlie's little car and following the long and winding road down to Castle Rock—he seemed to have nothing left in his store of conversation but *non sequiturs*.

"Call a cab, I imagine," Rawlie said. He eyed

the glittering hills and valleys of junked cars. "I'd guess they must come out here quite frequently to pick up fellows who are rejoining the Great Unhorsed."

"Let me give you five dollars—"

Thad pulled his wallet from his back pocket, but Rawlie waved him away. "I'm loaded, for an English teacher in the summertime," he said. "Why, I must have more than forty dollars. It's a wonder Billie lets me walk around without a Brinks guard." He puffed at his pipe with great pleasure, removed it from his mouth, and smiled at Thad. "But I'll get a receipt from the cab-driver and present it to you at the proper moment, Thad, never fear."

"I'd started to think that maybe you weren't going to come."

"I stopped at the five-and-ten," Rawlie said. "Picked up a couple of things I thought you might like to have, Thaddeus." He leaned back into the beetle (which sagged quite noticeably to the left on a spring which was either broken or would be soon) and, after some time spent rummaging, muttering, and puffing out fresh clouds of smog, brought out a paper bag. He handed the bag to Thad, who looked in and saw a pair of sunglasses and a Boston Red Sox baseball cap which would cover his hair quite nicely. He looked up at Rawlie, absurdly touched.

"Thank you, Rawlie."

Rawlie waved a hand and gave Thad a sly and slanted little smile. "Maybe I'm the one who should thank *you*," he said. "I've been looking for an excuse to stoke up the old stinker for the last ten months. Things would come along from time to time—my youngest son's divorce, the night I lost fifty bucks playing poker at Tom Carroll's house—but nothing seemed quite . . . apocalyptic enough."

"This is apocalyptic, all right," Thad said, and shivered a little. He looked at his watch. It was pushing one o'clock. Stark had at least an hour on him, maybe more. "I have to be going, Rawlie."

"Yes—it's urgent, isn't it?"

"I'm afraid so."

"I have one other thing—I stuck it in my coat pocket so I wouldn't lose it. This didn't come from the five-and-ten. I found it in my desk."

Rawlie began to rummage methodically through the pockets of the old checked sport-coat he wore winter and summer.

"If the oil light comes on, swing in someplace and get a jug of Sapphire," he said, still hunting. "That's the recycled stuff. Oh! Here it is! I was starting to think I'd left it back at the office after all."

He took a tubular piece of peeled wood from his pocket. It was about as long as Thad's forefinger and hollow. A notch had been cut in one end. It looked old.

"What is it?" Thad asked, taking it when Rawlie held it out. But he already knew, and he felt another block of whatever unthinkable thing it was that he was building slide into place.

"It's a bird-call," Rawlie said, studying him from above the shimmering bowl of his pipe. "If you think you can use it, I want you to take it."

"Thank you," Thad said, and put the bird-call into his breast pocket with a hand which was not quite steady. "It might come in handy."

Rawlie's eyes widened beneath the tangled hedge of his brows. He took the pipe from his mouth.

"I'm not sure you'll need it," he said in a low, unsteady voice.

"What?"

"Look behind you."

Thad turned, knowing what Rawlie had seen even before he saw it himself.

There were not hundreds of sparrows now, or thousands; the dead cars and trucks stacked on the back ten acres of Gold's Junkyard and Auto Supply were *carpeted* with sparrows. They were everywhere . . . and Thad had not heard a single one of them come.

The two men looked at the birds with four eyes. The birds looked back with twenty thousand . . . or perhaps forty thousand. They did not make a sound. They only sat on hoods, windows, roofs, exhaust-pipes, grilles, engine blocks, universal joints, and frames.

"Jesus Christ," Rawlie said hoarsely. "The psychopomps . . . what does it mean, Thad? What does it mean?"

"I think I'm just starting to know," Thad said.

"My God," Rawlie said. He lifted his hands above his head and clapped them loudly. The sparrows did not move. And they had no interest in Rawlie; it was only Thad Beaumont they were looking at.

"Find George Stark," Thad said in a quiet voice— really not much more than a whisper. "George Stark. Find him. *Fly!*"

The sparrows rose into the hazy blue sky in a black cloud, wings whirring with a sound that was like thunder turned to thinnest lace, throats cheeping. Two men who had been standing just inside the doorway of the retail parts shop ran out to look. Overhead, the single black mass banked and turned, as the other, smaller, flock had done, and headed west.

Thad looked up at them, and for a moment this reality merged with the vision which marked the onset of his trances; for a moment past and present were one, entwined in some strange and gorgeous pigtail.

The sparrows were gone.

"Christ Almighty!" a man in a gray mechanic's coverall was bellowing. "Did you see those birds? Where'd all those fucking *birds* come from?"

"I have a better question," Rawlie said, looking at Thad. He was in control of himself again, but it was clear he had been badly shaken. "Where are they *going?* You know, don't you, Thad?"

"Yes, of course," Thad muttered, opening the VW's door. "I have to go, too, Rawlie—I really have to. I can't thank you enough."

"Be careful, Thaddeus. Be very careful. No man controls the agents of the afterlife. Not for long— and there is always a price."

"I'll be as careful as I can."

The VW's stick-shift protested, but finally gave up and went into gear. Thad paused long enough to put on the dark glasses and the baseball cap, then raised his hand to Rawlie and pulled out.

As he turned onto Route 2, he saw Rawlie trudging toward the same pay telephone he had used himself, and Thad thought: *Now I've GOT to keep Stark out. Because now I have a secret. I may not be able to control the psychopomps, but for a little while at least I own them—or they own me—and he must not know that.*

He found second gear, and Rawlie DeLesseps' Volkswagen began to shudder itself into the largely unexplored realms of speed above thirty-five miles an hour.

Twenty-three

TWO CALLS FOR
SHERIFF PANGBORN

1

The first of the two calls which sent Alan Pang-born back into the heart of the thing came just after three o'clock, while Thad was pouring three quarts of Sapphire Motor Oil into Rawlie's thirsty Volkswagen at an Augusta service station. Alan himself was on his way to Nan's for a cup of coffee.

Sheila Brigham poked her head out of the dispatcher's office and yelled, "Alan? Collect call for you—do you know somebody named Hugh Pritchard?"

Alan swung back. "Yes! Take the call!"

He hurried into his office and picked up the phone just in time to hear Sheila accepting the charges.

"Dr. Pritchard? Dr. Pritchard, are you there?"

"Yes, right here." The connection was a pretty good one, but Alan still had a moment of doubt—this man didn't sound seventy. Forty, maybe, but not seventy.

"Are you the Dr. Hugh Pritchard who used to practice in Bergenfield, New Jersey?"

"Bergenfield, Tenafly, Hackensack, Englewood, Englewood Heights . . . hell, I doctored heads all the way to Paterson. Are you the Sheriff Pangborn who's been trying to get hold of me? My wife and I were way the hell and gone over to Devil's Knob. Just got back. Even my aches have aches."

"Yes, I'm sorry. I want to thank you for calling, Doctor. You sound much younger than I expected."

"Well, that's fine," Pritchard said, "but you should see the rest of me. I look like an alligator walking on two legs. What can I do for you?"

Alan had considered this and decided on a careful approach. Now he cocked the telephone between his ear and his shoulder, leaned back in his chair, and the parade of shadow animals commenced on the wall.

"I'm investigating a murder here in Castle County, Maine," he said. "The victim was a local man named Homer Gamache. There may be a witness to the crime, but I am in a very delicate situation with this man, Dr. Pritchard. There are two reasons why. First, he's famous. Second, he's exhibiting symptoms with which you were once familiar. I say so because you operated on him twenty-eight years ago. He had a brain tumor. I'm afraid that if this tumor has recurred, his testimony may not be very believ—"

"Thaddeus Beaumont," Pritchard interrupted at once. "And whatever symptoms he may be suffering, I doubt very much if it's a recurrence of that old tumor."

"How did you know it was Beaumont?"

"Because I saved his life back in 1960," Pritchard said, and added with an unconscious arrogance: "If not for me, he wouldn't have written a single book, because he would have been dead before his twelfth birthday. I've followed his career with some interest ever since he almost won that National Book Award for his first novel. I took one look at the photograph on the jacket and knew it was the same guy. The face had changed, but the eyes were the same. Unusual eyes. Dreamy, I should have called them. And of course I knew that he lived in Maine, because of the recent article in *People*. It came out just before we went on vacation."

He paused for a moment and then said something so stunning and yet so casual that Alan could not respond for a moment.

"You say he may have witnessed a murder? You sure you don't really suspect he may have committed one?"

"Well . . . I . . ."

"I only wonder," Pritchard went on, "because people with brain tumors often do very peculiar things. The peculiarity of the acts seems to rise in direct ratio to the intelligence of the man or woman so afflicted. But the boy didn't have a brain tumor at all, you know—at least, not in the usually accepted sense of the term. It was an unusual case. Extremely unusual. I've read of only three similar cases since 1960—two of them since I retired. Has he had the standard neurological tests?"

"Yes."

"And?"

"They were negative."

"I'm not surprised." Pritchard fell silent for a few moments, then said: "You're being less than honest with me, young man, aren't you?"

Alan stopped making shadow animals and sat forward in his chair. "Yes, I suppose I am. But I very badly want to know what you mean when you say Thad Beaumont didn't have a brain tumor in 'the usually accepted sense of the term.' I know all about the confidentiality rule in doctor-patient relationships, and I don't know if you can trust a man you're talking to for the first time—and over the phone, at that—but I hope you'll believe me when I say that I'm on Thad's side here, and I'm sure he would want you to tell me what I want to know. And I can't take the time to have him call you and give you the go-ahead, Doctor—I need to know *now*."

And Alan was surprised to find that this was true—or he believed it to be true. A funny tenseness had begun to creep over him, a feeling that things were happening. Things he didn't know about . . . but soon would.

"I have no problem with telling you about the case," Pritchard said calmly. "I have thought, on many occasions, that I ought to get in touch with Beaumont myself, if only to tell him what happened at the hospital shortly after his surgery was complete. I felt it might interest him."

"What was that?"

"I'll get to it, I assure you. I didn't tell his parents what the operation had uncovered because it didn't matter—not in any practical way—and I didn't want anything more to do with them. With his father in particular. That man should have been born in a cave and spent his life hunting woolly mammoths. I decided at the time to tell them what they wanted to hear and get shut of them as fast as I could. Then, of course, time itself became a factor. You lose touch with your patients. I thought of writing to him when Helga showed me that first book, and I've thought of it on several occasions since then, but I also felt he might not believe me . . . or wouldn't care . . . or that he might think I was a crackpot. I don't know any famous people, but I pity them—I suspect they must live defensive, disorganized, fearful lives. It seemed easier to let sleeping dogs lie. Now this. As my grandchildren would say, it's a bummer."

"What was wrong with Thad? What brought him to you?"

"Fugues. Headaches. Phantom sounds. And finally—"

"Phantom sounds?"

"Yes—but you must let me tell it in my own way, Sheriff." Again Alan heard that unconscious arrogance in the man's voice.

"All right."

"Finally there was a seizure. The problems were all being caused by a small mass in the prefrontal lobe. We operated, assuming it was a tumor. The tumor turned out to be Thad Beaumont's twin."

"What!"

"Yes, indeed," Pritchard said. He sounded as if the unalloyed shock in Alan's voice rather pleased him. "This is not entirely uncommon—twins are often absorbed *in utero*, and in rare cases the absorption is incomplete—but the *location* was unusual, and so was the growth-spurt of the foreign tissue. Such tissue almost always remains inert. I believe that Thad's problems may have been caused by the early onset of puberty."

"Wait," Alan said. "Just wait." He had read the phrase "his mind reeled" a time or two in books, but this was the first time he had ever experienced such a feeling himself. "Are you telling me that Thad was a twin, but he . . . he somehow . . . somehow *ate* his brother?"

"Or sister," Pritchard said. "But I suspect it was a brother, because I believe absorption is much more rare in cases of fraternal twins. That's based on statistical frequency, not hard fact, but I do believe it. And since identicals are always the same sex, the answer to your question is yes. I believe the fetus Thad Beaumont once was ate his brother in his mother's womb."

"Jesus," Alan said in a low voice. He could not remember hearing anything so horrible—or so *alien*—in his entire life.

"You sound revolted," Dr. Pritchard said cheerfully, "but there is really no need to be, once you put the matter in its proper context. We're not talking about Cain rising up and slaying Abel with a rock. This was not an act of murder; it's just that some biological imperative we don't understand went to work here. A bad signal, perhaps, triggered by something in the mother's endocrine system. We aren't even talking about fetuses, if we speak exactly; at the time of absorption, there would have been two conglomerates of tissue in Mrs. Beaumont's womb, probably not even humanoid. Living amphibians, if you will. And one of them—the larger, the stronger—simply swarmed over the weaker, enfolded it . . . and incorporated it."

"It sounds fucking insectile," Alan muttered.

"Does it? I suppose so, a little. At any rate, the absorption was not complete. A little of the other twin retained its integrity. This alien matter—I can think of no other way to put it—wound up entwined in the tissue which became Thaddeus Beaumont's brain. And for some reason, it became active not long after the boy turned eleven. It began to grow. There was no room at the inn. Therefore, it was necessary to excise it like a wart. Which we did, very successfully."

"Like a wart," Alan said, sickened, fascinated.

All sorts of ideas were flying in his mind. They were dark ideas, as dark as bats in a deserted church steeple. Only one was completely coherent: *He is two men—he has* ALWAYS *been two men. That's what any man or woman who makes believe for a living must be. The one who exists in the normal world . . . and the one who creates worlds. They are two. Always at least two.*

"I would remember such an unusual case no matter what," Pritchard was saying, "but something happened just before the boy woke up that was perhaps even more unusual. Something I have always wondered about."

"What was it?"

"The Beaumont boy heard birds before each of his headaches," Pritchard said. "That in itself was not unusual; it's a well-documented occurrence in cases of brain tumor or epilepsy. It is called sensory precursor syndrome. But shortly after the operation, there was an odd incident concerning *real* birds. Bergenfield County Hospital was, in fact, attacked by sparrows."

"What do you mean?"

"It sounds absurd, doesn't it?" Pritchard seemed quite pleased with himself. "It isn't the kind of thing I'd even talk about, except that it was an extremely well-documented event. There was even a story about it on the front page of the Bergenfield *Courier*, with a picture. At just past two in the afternoon on October 28th, 1960, an extremely large flock of sparrows flew into the west side of County Hospital. That is the side where the Intensive Care Unit was in those days, and of course that was where the Beaumont boy was taken following his operation.

"A great many windows were broken, and the maintenance men cleared away better than three hundred dead birds following the incident. An ornithologist was quoted in the *Courier's* article, as I recall—he pointed out that the west side of the building was almost wholly glass, and theorized that the birds might have been attracted by the bright sunlight reflected on that glass."

"That's crazy," Alan said. "Birds only fly into glass when they can't see it."

"I believe the reporter conducting the interview mentioned that, and the ornithologist pointed out that flocking birds seem to share a group telepathy which unites their many minds—if birds can be said to *have* minds—into one. Rather like foraging ants. He said that if one of the flock decided to fly into the glass, the rest probably just followed along. I wasn't at the hospital when it happened—I'd finished with the Beaumont boy, checked to make sure his vites were stable—"

"Vites?"

"Vital signs, Sheriff. Then I left to play golf. But I understand that those birds scared the bejabbers out of everyone in the Hirschfield Wing. Two people were cut by flying glass. I could accept the ornithologist's theory, but it still made a ripple in my mind . . . because I knew about young Beaumont's sensory precursor, you see. Not just birds, but specific birds: sparrows."

"The sparrows are flying again," Alan muttered in a distracted, horrified voice.

"I beg your pardon, Sheriff?"

"Nothing. Go on."

"I questioned him about his symptoms a day later. Sometimes there is localized amnesia about sensory precursors following an operation which removes the cause, but not in this case. He remembered perfectly well. He *saw* the birds as well as heard them. Birds everywhere, he said, all over the houses and lawns and streets of Ridgeway, which was the section of Bergenfield where he lived.

"I was interested enough to check his charts, and match them with the reports of the incident. The flock of sparrows hit the hospital at about two-oh-five. The boy woke up at two-ten. Maybe even a little earlier." Pritchard paused and then added: "In fact, one of the ICU nurses said she believed it was the sound of the breaking glass that woke him up."

"Wow," Alan said softly.

"Yes," Pritchard said. "Wow is right. I haven't spoken of that business in years, Sheriff Pangborn. Does any of it help?"

"I don't know," Alan said honestly. "It might. Dr. Pritchard, maybe you didn't get it all—I mean, if you didn't, maybe it's started growing again."

"You said he'd had tests. Was one of them a CAT-scan?"

"Yes."

"And he was X-rayed, of course."

"Uh-huh."

"If those tests showed negative, then it's because there's nothing to show. For my part, I believe we *did* get it all."

"Thank you, Dr. Pritchard." He had a little trouble forming the words; his lips felt numb and strange.

"Will you tell me what has happened in greater detail when this matter has resolved itself, Sheriff?

I've been very frank with you, and it seems a small favor to ask in return. I'm very curious."

"I will if I can."

"That's all I ask. I will let you get back to your job, and I will return to my vacation."

"I hope you and your wife are having a good time."

Pritchard sighed. "At my age, I have to work harder and harder to have just a mediocre time, Sheriff. We used to love camping, but I think next year we'll stay home."

"Well, I sure appreciate you taking the time to return my call."

"It was my pleasure. I miss my work, Sheriff Pangborn. Not the mystique of surgery—I never cared much for that—but the *mystery*. The mystery of the mind. That was very exciting."

"I imagine it was," Alan agreed, thinking he would be very happy if there were a little less mental mystery in his life right now. "I'll be in touch if and when things . . . clarify themselves."

"Thank you, Sheriff." He paused and then said: "This is a matter of great concern to you, isn't it?"

"Yes. Yes it is."

"The boy I remember was very pleasant. Scared, but pleasant. What sort of man is he?"

"A good one, I think," Alan said. "A trifle cold, maybe, and a trifle distant, but a good man for all that." And he repeated: "I think."

"Thank you. I'll let you get on with your business. Goodbye, Sheriff Pangborn."

There was a click on the line, and Alan replaced the receiver slowly. He leaned back in his chair, folded his limber hands, and made a large black bird flap slowly across the patch of sun on his office wall. A line from *The Wizard of Oz* occurred to him and went clanging around in his mind: "I *do* believe in spooks, I *do* believe in spooks, I *do*, I *do*, I *do* believe in spooks!" That had been the Cowardly Lion, hadn't it?

The question was, what did *he* believe?

It was easier for him to think of things he *didn't* believe. He didn't believe Thad Beaumont had murdered anybody. Nor did he believe Thad had written that cryptic sentence on anyone's wall.

So how had it gotten there?

Simple. Old Dr. Pritchard just flew east from Fort Laramie, killed Frederick Clawson, wrote THE SPARROWS ARE FLYING AGAIN on his wall, then flew on up to New York from D.C., picked Miriam Cowley's lock with his favorite scalpel, and did the same thing to her. He operated on them because he missed the mystery of surgery.

No, of course not. But Pritchard wasn't the only one who knew about Thad's—what had he called it?—his sensory precursor. It hadn't been in the *People* article, true, but—

You're forgetting the fingerprints and the voice-prints. You're forgetting Thad's and Liz's calm, flat assertion that George Stark is real; that he's willing to commit murder in order to STAY real. And now you're trying like hell not to examine the fact that you are starting to believe it all might be true. You talked to them about how crazy it would be to believe not just in a vengeful ghost, but in the ghost of a man who never was. But writers INVITE ghosts, maybe; along with actors and artists, they are the only totally accepted mediums of our society. They make worlds that never were, populate them with people who never existed, and then invite us to join them in their fantasies. And we do it, don't we? Yes. We PAY to do it.

Alan knotted his hands tightly, extended his pinkie fingers, and sent a much smaller bird flying across the sunny wall. A sparrow.

You can't explain the flock of sparrows that hit Bergenfield County Hospital almost thirty years ago any more than you can explain how two men can have the same fingerprints and voice-prints, but now you know that Thad Beaumont shared his mother's womb with someone else. With a stranger.

Hugh Pritchard had mentioned the early onset of puberty.

Alan Pangborn suddenly found himself wondering if the growth of that alien tissue coincided with something else.

He wondered if it had begun to grow at the same time Thad Beaumont began to write.

2

The intercom on his desk beeped, startling him. It was Sheila again. "Fuzzy Martin's on line one, Alan. He wants to talk to you."

"*Fuzzy?* What in hell's name does he want?"

"I don't know. He wouldn't tell me."

"Jesus," Alan said. "That's all I need today."

Fuzzy had a large chunk of property out on Town Road #2, about four miles from Castle Lake. The Martin place had once been a prosperous dairy farm, but that had been in the days when Fuzzy had been known by his proper Christian name, Albert, and was still holding the whiskey jug instead of the other way around. His kids were grown, his wife had given him up as a bad job ten years ago, and now Fuzzy presided alone over twenty-seven acres of fields which were going slowly but steadily back to the wild. On the west side of his property, where Town Road #2 wound by on its way to the lake, the house and barn stood. The barn, which had once been home to forty cows, was a huge building, its roof now deeply swaybacked, its paint peeling, most of the windows blocked with squares of cardboard. Alan and Trevor Hartland, the Castle Rock Fire Chief, had been waiting for the Martin house, the Martin barn, or the Martin both to burn down for the last four years or so.

"Do you want me to tell him you're not here?" Sheila asked. "Clut just came in—I could give it to him."

Alan actually considered this for a moment, then sighed and shook his head. "I'll talk to him, Sheila. Thanks."

He picked up the telephone and cocked it between his ear and his shoulder.

"Chief Pangborn?"

"This is the Sheriff, yes."

"This is Fuzzy Martin, out on Number Two. Might have a problem out here, Chief."

"Oh?" Alan drew the second telephone on the desk closer to him. This was a direct line to the other offices in the Municipal Building. The tip of his finger skated around the square keypad with the number 4 stamped on it. All he had to do was pick up the receiver and push the button to get Trevor Hartland. "What kind of problem is that?"

"Well, Chief, I'll be dipped in shit if I edzackly know. I'd call it Grand Car Thievery, if it was a car I knew. But t'wasn't. Never seen it before in m'life. But it came out of my barn just the same." Fuzzy spoke with that deep and somehow satiric

Maine accent that turned a simple word like barn into something that sounded almost like a bray of laughter: *baaa'n.*

Alan pushed the inter-office telephone back to its normal place. God favored fools and drunks—a fact he had learned well in his many years of police work—and it seemed that Fuzzy's house and barn were still standing in spite of his habit of flicking live cigarette butts here, there, and everywhere while he was drunk. *Now all I have to do,* Alan thought, *is sit here until he unravels whatever the problem is. Then I can figure out—or try to—if it's in the real world or only inside whatever is left of Fuzzy's mind.*

He caught his hands flying another sparrow across the wall and made them stop.

"What car was it that came out of your barn, Albert?" Alan asked patiently. Almost everyone in The Rock (including the man himself) called Albert Fuzzy, and Alan might try it himself after he'd been in town another ten years. Or maybe twenty.

"Just told you I never seen it before," Fuzzy Martin said in a tone that said oh you damned fool so clearly he might as well have spoken it. "That's why I'm callin you, Chief. Sure wasn't one of mine."

A picture at last began to form in Alan's mind. With his cows, his kids, and his wife gone, Fuzzy Martin didn't need a whole lot of hard cash—the land had been his free and clear, except for taxes, when he inherited it from his dad. What money Fuzzy did see came from various odd sources. Alan believed, almost knew, in fact, that a bale or two of marijuana joined the hay in Fuzzy's barn loft every couple of months or so, and that was just one of Fuzzy's little scams. He had thought from time to time that he ought to make a serious effort to bust Fuzzy for possession with intent to sell, but he doubted if Fuzzy even smoked the stuff, let alone had brains enough to sell it. Most likely he just collected a hundred or two hundred dollars every now and again for providing storage space. And even in a little burg like Castle Rock, there were more important things to do than busting drunks for holding weed.

Another of Fuzzy's storage services—this a legal one, at least—was keeping cars in his barn for summer people. When Alan first came to town, Fuzzy's barn had been a regular parking garage. You could go in there and see as many as fifteen cars—most of them summer cars owned by people who had places on the lake—stored where the cows used to spend their winters. Fuzzy had knocked out the partitions to make one big garage and there the summer cars waited out the long months of fall and winter in the sweet hay-smelling shadows, their bright surfaces dulled by the steady fall of old chaff from the loft, parked bumper to bumper and side to side.

Over the years, Fuzzy's car-storage business had fallen off radically. Alan supposed that word of his careless smoking habits had gotten around and that had done it. No one wants to lose their car in a barn-fire, even if it's just an old lag you kept around to run errands when summer came. The last time he had been out to Fuzzy's, Alan had seen only two cars in the barn: Ossie Brannigan's '59 T-Bird—a car which would have been a classic if it hadn't been so rusted out and beat-to-shit—and Thad Beaumont's old Ford Woody wagon.

Thad again.

Today it seemed that all roads led back to Thad Beaumont.

Alan sat up straighter in his chair, unconsciously pulling the telephone closer to him.

"It wasn't Thad Beaumont's old Ford?" he asked Fuzzy now. "You're sure?"

" 'Course I'm sure. This wasn't no Ford, and it sure as hell wasn't any Woody wagon. It was a black Toronado."

Another flare went off in Alan's mind . . . but he wasn't quite sure why. Someone had said something to him about a black Toronado, and not long ago. He couldn't think just who or when, not now . . . but it would come to him.

"I just happened to be in the kitchen, gettin myself a cool drink of lemonade," Fuzzy was going on, "when I seen that car backin out of the barn. First thing I thought of was how I don't store no car like that. *Second* thing I thought of was how anybody got it in there in the first place, when there's a big old Kreig padlock on the barn door and I got the only key to it on my ring."

"What about the people with cars stored in there? They don't have keys?"

"No, sir!" Fuzzy seemed offended by the very idea.

"You didn't happen to get the license plate number, did you?"

"You're damn tooting I got it!" Fuzzy cried. "Got the goddam ole Jeezly b'noc'lars right there on the kitchen windowsill, ain't I?"

Alan, who had been in the barn on inspection tours with Trevor Hartland but never in Fuzzy's kitchen (and had no plans to make such a trip soon, thanks), said: "Oh, yeah. The binoculars. I forgot about them."

"Well, I didn't!" Fuzzy said with happy truculence. "You got a pencil?"

"I sure do, Albert."

"Chief, why don't you just call me Fuzzy, like everyone else?"

Alan sighed. "Okay, Fuzzy. And while we're at it, why don't you just call me Sheriff?"

"Whatever you say. Now do you want this plate number or not?"

"Shoot."

"First off, it was a Mississippi plate," Fuzzy said with something like triumph in his voice. "What the hell do you think of *that?*"

Alan didn't know exactly *what* he thought of it . . . except a third flare had gone off in his head, this one even brighter than the others. A Toronado. And Mississippi. Something about Mississippi. And a town. Oxford? Was it Oxford? Like the one two towns over from here?

"I don't know," Alan said, and then, supposing it was the thing Fuzzy wanted to hear: "It sounds pretty suspicious."

"Ain't you Christing right!" Fuzzy crowed. Then he cleared his throat and became businesslike. "Okay. Miss'ippi plate 62284. You got that, Chief?"

"62284."

"62284, ayuh, you can take that to the fuckin bank. Suspicious! Oh, ayuh! That's just what *I* thought! Jesus ate a can of beans!"

At the image of Jesus chowing down on a can of B&M beans, Alan had to cover the telephone for another brief moment.

"So," Fuzzy said, "what action you gonna take, Chief?"

I am going to try and get out of this conversation with my sanity intact, Alan thought. *That's the first thing I'm going to do. And I'm going to try and remember who mentioned—*

Then it came to him in a flash of cold radiance that made his arms crown with gooseflesh and stretched the flesh on the back of his neck as tight as a drumhead.

On the phone with Thad. Not long after the psycho called from Miriam Cowley's apartment. The night the killing-spree had really started.

He heard Thad saying, *He moved from New Hampshire to Oxford, Mississippi with his mother . . . he's lost all but a trace of his Southern accent.*

What else had Thad said when he had been describing George Stark over the telephone?

Final thing: he may be driving a black Toronado. I don't know what year. One of the old ones with a lot of blasting powder under the hood, anyway. Black. It could have Mississippi plates, but he's undoubtedly switched them.

"I guess he was a little too busy to do that," Alan muttered. The gooseflesh was still crawling over his body with its thousand tiny feet.

"What was that, Chief?"

"Nothing, Albert. Talking to myself."

"My mom useta say that meant you was gonna get some money. Maybe I ought to start doin it myself."

Alan suddenly remembered that Thad had added something else—one final detail.

"Albert—"

"Call me Fuzzy, Chief. Told you."

"Fuzzy, was there a bumper sticker on the car you saw? Did you maybe notice—"

"How the hell did you know about that? You got a hot-sheet on that motor, Chief?" Fuzzy asked eagerly.

"Never mind the questions, Fuzzy. This is police business. Did you see what it said?"

" 'Course I did," Fuzzy Martin said. "HIGH-TONED SON OF A BITCH, that's what it said. Can you believe that?"

Alan hung up the phone slowly, believing it, but telling himself it proved nothing, nothing at all . . . except that maybe Thad Beaumont was as crazy as a bedbug. It would just be plain stupid to think that what Fuzzy had seen proved anything . . . well, anything *supernatural,* for want of a better word . . . was going on.

Then he thought of the voice-prints and the fingerprints, he thought of hundreds of sparrows crashing into the windows of Bergenfield County Hospital, and he was overcome with a fit of violent shivering that lasted almost a full minute.

3

Alan Pangborn was neither a coward nor a super-stitious countryman who forked the sign of the evil eye at crows and kept his pregnant womenfolk away from the fresh milk because he was afraid they would clabber it. He was not a rube; he was not sus-ceptible to the blandishments of city slickers who wanted to sell famous bridges cheap; he had not been born yesterday. He believed in logic and rea-sonable explanations. So he waited out his flock of shivers and then he pulled his Rolodex over in front of him and found Thad's telephone number. He observed with wry amusement that the number on the card and the one in his head matched. Apparently Castle Rock's distinguished "writer fella" had remained even more firmly fixed in his mind— some part of it, anyway—than he had thought.

It has *to have been Thad in that car. If you eliminate the nutty stuff, what other alternative is there? He described it. What was the old radio quiz show?* Name It and Claim It.

Bergenfield County Hospital was, in fact, attacked by sparrows.

And there were other questions—far too many.

Thad and his family were under protection from the Maine State Police. If they had decided to pack up and come down here for the weekend, the State boys should have given him a call—partially to alert him, partially as a gesture of courtesy. But the State Police would have tried to dissuade Thad from making such a trip, now that they had their protective surveillance down to routine up there in Ludlow. And if the trip had been of the spur-of-the-moment kind, their efforts to change his mind would have been even more strenuous.

Then there was what Fuzzy had *not* seen— namely, the back-up car or cars that would have been assigned the Beaumonts if they decided to put on their travelling shoes anyway . . . as they *could* have done; they weren't, after all, prisoners.

People with brain tumors often do very peculiar things.

If it was Thad's Toronado, and if he had been out at Fuzzy's to get it, *and* if he had been alone, that led to a conclusion Alan found very unpalatable, because he had taken a qualified liking to Thad. That conclusion was that he had deliberately ditched both his family and his protectors.

The State Police still should have called me, if that was the case. They'd put out an APB, and they'd know damned well this is one of the places he'd be likely to come.

He dialed the Beaumont number. It was picked up on the first ring. A voice he didn't know answered. Which was only to say he could not put a name to the voice. That he was speaking to an officer of the law was something he knew from the first syllable.

"Hello, Beaumont residence."

Guarded. Ready to drive a wedge of questions into the next gap if the voice happened to be the right one . . . or the wrong one.

What's happened? Pangborn wondered, and on the heels of that: *They're dead. Whoever's out there has killed the whole family, as quickly, effortlessly, and with as little mercy as he showed the others. The protection, the interrogations, the traceback equipment . . . it was all for nothing.*

Not even a hint of these thoughts showed in his voice as he answered.

"This is Alan Pangborn," he said crisply. "Sheriff, Castle County. I was calling for Thad Beaumont. To whom am I speaking?"

There was a pause. Then the voice replied, "This is Steve Harrison, Sheriff. Maine State Police. I was going to call you. Should have done it at least an hour ago. But things here . . . things here are fucked all the way to the ionosphere. Can I ask why you called?"

Without a pause for thought—that would certainly have changed his response—Alan lied. He did it without asking himself why he was doing it. That would come later.

"I called to check in with Thad," he said. "It's

been awhile, and I wanted to know how they're doing. I gather there's been trouble."

"Trouble so big you wouldn't believe it," Harrison said grimly. "Two of my men are dead. We're pretty sure Beaumont did it."

We're pretty sure Beaumont did it.

The peculiarity of the acts seems to rise in direct ratio to the intelligence of the man or woman so afflicted.

Alan felt *déjà vu* not just stealing into his mind but marching over his whole body like an invading army. Thad, it always came back to Thad. Of course. He was intelligent, he was peculiar, and he was, by his own admission, suffering from symptoms which suggested a brain tumor.

The boy didn't have a brain tumor at all, you know.

If those tests showed negative, then it's because there's nothing to show.

Forget the tumor. The sparrows are what you want to be thinking about now—because the sparrows are flying again.

"What happened?" he asked Trooper Harrison.

"He cut Tom Chatterton and Jack Eddings damned near to pieces, that's what happened!" Harrison shouted, startling Alan with the depth of his fury. "He's got his family with him, and I *want* that son of a bitch!"

"What . . . how did he get away?"

"I don't have the time to go into it," Harrison said. "It's a sorry fucking story, Sheriff. He was driving a red-and-gray Chevrolet Suburban, a god-damn whale on wheels, but we think he must have ditched it someplace and switched. He's got a summer place down there. You know the locale and the layout, right?"

"Yes," Alan said. His mind was racing. He

looked at the clock on the wall and saw it was a minute or so shy of three-forty. Time. It all came back to time. And he realized he hadn't asked Fuzzy Martin what time it had been when he saw the Toronado rolling out of his barn. It hadn't seemed important at the moment. Now it did. "What time did you lose him, Trooper Harrison?"

He thought he could feel Harrison fuming at that, but when he answered, he did so without anger or defensiveness, "Around twelve-thirty. He must have taken awhile to switch cars, if that's what he did, and then he went to his house in Ludlow—"

"Where was he when you lost him? How far away from his house?"

"Sheriff, I'd like to answer all your questions, but there's no time. The point is, if he's headed for his place down there—it seems unlikely, but the guy's crazy, so you never know—he won't have arrived yet, but he'll be there soon. Him and his whole fam' damly. It would be very nice if you and a couple of your men were there to greet him. If something pops, you radio Henry Payton at the Oxford State Police Barracks and we'll send more back-up than you've ever seen in your life. *Don't try to apprehend him yourself under any circumstances.* We're assuming the wife's been taken hostage, if she's not dead already, and that goes double for the kids."

"Yes, he'd have to have taken his wife by force if he killed the Troopers on duty, wouldn't he?" Alan agreed, and found himself thinking, *But you'd make them part of it if you could, wouldn't you? Because your mind is made up and you're not going to change it. Hell, man, you're not even going to* think, *straight or otherwise, until the blood dries on your friends.*

There were a dozen questions he wanted to ask, and the answers to those would probably produce another four dozen—but Harrison was right about one thing. There wasn't time.

He hesitated for a moment, wanting very badly to ask Harrison about the most important thing of all, wanting to ask the jackpot question: was Harrison sure Thad had had *time* to get to his house, kill the men on guard there, and spirit his family away, all before the first reinforcements arrived? But to ask the question would be to claw at the painful wound this Harrison was trying to deal with right now, because buried in the question was that condemning, irrefutable judgment: *You lost him. Somehow you lost him. You had a job to do and you fucked it up.*

"Can I depend on you, Sheriff?" Harrison asked, and now his voice didn't sound angry, only tired and harried, and Alan's heart went out to him.

"Yes. I'll have the place covered almost immediately."

"Good man. And you'll liaise with the Oxford Barracks?"

"Affirmative. Henry Payton's a friend."

"Beaumont is dangerous, Sheriff. *Extremely* dangerous. If he does show up, you watch your ass."

"I will."

"And keep me informed." Harrison broke the connection without saying goodbye.

4

His mind—the part of it that busied itself with protocol, anyway—awoke and started asking questions . . . or trying to. Alan decided he didn't have time for protocol. Not in any of its forms. He was simply going to keep all possible circuits open and proceed. He had a feeling things had reached the point where some of those circuits would soon begin to close of their own accord.

At least call some of your own men.

But he didn't think he was ready to do that, either. Norris Ridgewick, the one he would have called, was off duty and out of town. John LaPointe was still laid up with poison ivy. Seat Thomas was out on patrol. Andy Clutterbuck was here, but Clut was a rookie and this was a nasty piece of work.

He would roll this one on his own for awhile.

You're crazy! Protocol screamed in his mind.

"I might be getting there, at that," Alan said out loud. He looked up Albert Martin's number in the phone book and called him back to ask the questions he should have asked the first time.

5

"What time did you see the Toronado backing out of your barn, Fuzzy?" he asked when Martin answered, and thought: *He won't know. Hell, I'm not entirely sure he knows how to tell time.*

But Fuzzy promptly proved him a liar. "Just a cunt's hair past three, Chief." Then after a considering pause:

" 'Scuse my Fran-kais."

"You didn't call until—" Alan glanced at the day-sheet, where he had logged Fuzzy's call without even thinking about it. "Until three-twenty-eight."

"Had to think her over," Fuzzy said. "Man should always look before he leaps, Chief, at least that's the way I see her. Before I called you, I went down to the barn to see if whoever got the car was up to any other ructions in there."

Ructions, Alan thought, bemused. *Probably checked the bale of pot in the loft while you were at it, didn't you, Fuzzy?*

"Had he been?"

"Been what?"

"Up to any other ructions."

"Nope. Don't believe so."

"What condition was the lock in?"

"Open," Fuzzy said pithily.

"Smashed?"

"Nope. Just hangin in the hasp with the arm popped up."

"Key, do you think?"

"Don't know where the sonofawhore could've come by one. I think he picked it."

"Was he alone in the car?" Alan asked. "Could you tell that?"

Fuzzy paused, thinking it over. "I couldn't tell for sure," he said at last. "I know what you're thinkin, Chief—if I could make out the breed o' plate and read that smart-ass sticker, I ought to been able to make out how many folks was in it. But the sun was on the glass, and I don't think it was ordinary glass, either. I think it had some tint to it. Not a whole lot, but some."

"Okay, Fuzzy. Thanks. We'll check it out."

"Well, he's gone from here," Fuzzy said, and then added in a lightning flash of deduction: "But he must be *somewhere.*"

"That's very true," Alan said. He promised to

tell Fuzzy "how it all warshed out" and hung up. He pushed away from his desk and looked at the clock.

Three, Fuzzy had said. *Just a cunt's hair past three. 'Scuse my Fran-kais.*

Alan didn't think there was any way Thad could have gotten from Ludlow to Castle Rock in three hours short of rocket travel, not with a side-trip back to his house thrown in for good measure—a little side-trip during which, incidentally, he had kidnapped his wife and kids and killed a couple of State Troopers. Maybe if it had been a straight shot right from Ludlow, but to come from someplace else, stop in Ludlow, and then get here in time to pick a lock and drive away in a Toronado he just happened to have conveniently stashed in Fuzzy Martin's barn? No way.

But suppose someone *else* had killed the Troopers at the Beaumont house and snatched Thad's people? Someone who didn't have to mess around losing a police escort, switching vehicles, and making side-trips? Someone who had simply piled Liz Beaumont and her twins into a car and headed for Castle Rock? Alan thought *they* could have gotten here in time for Fuzzy Martin to have seen them at just past three. They could have done it without even breathing hard.

The police—read Trooper Harrison, at least for the time being—thought it had to be Thad, but Harrison and his *compadres* didn't know about the Toronado.

Mississippi plates, Fuzzy had said.

Mississippi was George Stark's home state, according to Thad's fictional biography of the man. If Thad was schizo enough to think he was Stark, at least some of the time, he might well have provided himself with a black Toronado to enhance the illusion, or fantasy, or whatever it was . . . but in order to get plates, he'd not only have to have visited Mississippi, he'd have to claim residency there.

That's dumb. He could have stolen some Mississippi plates. Or bought an old set. Fuzzy didn't say anything about what year the tags were—from the house he probably couldn't have read them, anyway, not even with binoculars.

But it wasn't Thad's car. Couldn't have been. Liz would have known, wouldn't she?

Maybe not. If he's crazy enough, maybe not.

Then there was the locked door. How could Thad have gotten into the barn without breaking the lock? He was a writer and a teacher, not a cracksman.

Duplicate key, his mind whispered, but Alan didn't think so. If Fuzzy *was* storing wacky tobaccy in there from time to time, Alan thought Fuzzy would be pretty careful of where he left his keys lying around, no matter how careless he was of his cigarette ends.

And one final question, the killer: How come Fuzzy had never seen that black Toronado before, if it had been in his barn all along? How could that be?

Try this, a voice in the back of his mind whispered as he grabbed his hat and left the office. *This is a pretty funny idea, Alan. You'll laugh. You'll laugh like hell. Suppose Thad Beaumont was right all the way from the jump? Suppose there really is a monster named George Stark running around out there . . . and the elements of his life, the elements Thad created, come into being when he needs them?* WHEN *he needs them, but not always* WHERE *he needs them. Because they'd always show up at places connected to the primary creator's life. So Stark would have to get his car out of storage where Thad stores his, just like he had to start from the graveyard where Thad symbolically buried him. Don't you love it? Isn't it a scream?*

He didn't love it. It wasn't a scream. It wasn't even remotely funny. It drew an ugly scratch not just across everything he believed but across the way he had been taught to *think.*

He found himself remembering something Thad had said. *I don't know who I am when I'm writing.* That wasn't exact, but it was close. *And what's even more amazing, it never occurred to me to wonder until now.*

"You were *him,* weren't you?" Alan said softly. "You were him and he was you and that's the way the killer grew, pop goes the weasel."

He shivered and Sheila Brigham looked up from her typewriter at the dispatcher's desk in time to see it. "It's too hot to do that, Alan. You must be coming down with a cold."

"Coming down with something, I guess," Alan said. "Cover the telephone, Sheila. Relay anything small to Seat Thomas. Anything big to me. Where's Clut?"

"I'm in here!" Clut's voice came drifting out of the john.

"I expect to be back in forty-five minutes or so!" Alan yelled at him. "You got the desk until I get back!"

"Where you going, Alan?" Clut came out of the men's room tucking in his khaki shirt.

"The lake," Alan said vaguely, and left before either Clut or Sheila could ask any more questions . . . or before he could reflect on what he was doing. Leaving without a stated destination in a situation like this was a very bad idea. It was asking for more than trouble; it was asking to get killed.

But what he was thinking

(the sparrows are flying)

simply couldn't be true. *Couldn't.* There had to be a more reasonable explanation.

He was still trying to convince himself of this as he drove his prowl-car out of town and into the worst trouble of his life.

6

There was a rest area on Route 5 about a half a mile from Fuzzy Martin's property. Alan turned in, operating on something which was half hunch and half whim. The hunch part was simple enough: black Toronado or no black Toronado, they hadn't come down here from Ludlow on a magic carpet. They must have driven. Which meant there had to be a ditched car around someplace. The man he was hunting had ditched Homer Gamache's truck in a roadside parking area when he was through with it, and what a perp would do once he would do again.

There were three vehicles parked in the turn-around: a beer truck, a new Ford Escort, and a road-dusty Volvo.

As he got out of the prowler-car, a man in green fatigues came out of the men's convenience and walked toward the cab of the beer truck. He was short, dark-haired, narrow-shouldered. No George Stark here.

"Officer," he said, and gave Alan a little salute. Alan nodded at him and walked down to where three elderly ladies were sitting at one of the picnic tables, drinking coffee from a Thermos and talking.

"Hello, Officer," one of them said. "Can we do something for you?" *Or did we maybe do something wrong?* the momentarily anxious eyes asked.

"I just wondered if the Ford and the Volvo up there belonged to you ladies," Alan said.

"The Ford is mine," a second said. "We all came in that. I don't know anything about a Volvo. Is it that sticker thing? Did that sticker thing run out again? My son is supposed to take care of that sticker thing, but he's *so* forgetful! Forty-three years old, and I still have to tell him ev—"

"The sticker's fine, ma'am," Alan said, smiling his best The Policeman Is Your Friend smile. "None of you happened to see the Volvo drive in, did you?"

They shook their heads.

"Have you seen anyone else during the last few minutes who might belong to it?"

"No," the third lady said. She looked at him with bright little gerbil's eyes. "Are you on the scent, Officer?"

"Pardon, ma'am?"

"Tracking a criminal, I mean."

"Oh," Alan said. He felt a moment of unreality. Exactly what was he doing here? Exactly what had he been thinking to *get* here? "No, ma'am. I just like Volvos." Boy, that sounded intelligent. That sounded just . . . fucking . . . *crackerjack.*

"Oh," the first lady said. "Well, we haven't seen anyone. Would you like a cup of coffee, Officer? I believe there's just about one good one left."

"No, thank you," Alan said. "You ladies have a nice day."

"You too, Officer," they chorused in an almost perfect three-part harmony. It made Alan feel more unreal than ever.

He walked back up to the Volvo. Tried the driver's side door. It opened. The inside of the car had a hot attic feel. It had been sitting here awhile. He looked in the back and saw a packet, a little bigger than a Sweet 'n Low packet, on the floor. He leaned between the seats and picked it up.

HANDI-WIPE, the packet said, and he felt someone drop a bowling-ball in his stomach.

It doesn't mean anything, the voice of Protocol and Reason spoke up at once. *At least, not necessarily. I know what you're thinking: you're thinking babies. But, Alan, they give those things out at the roadside stands when you buy fried chicken, for heaven's sake.*

All the same . . .

Alan stuck the Handi-Wipe in one of the pockets of his uniform blouse and got out of the car. He was about to close the door, and then leaned in again. He tried to look under the dashboard and couldn't quite do it on his feet. He had to get down on his knees.

Someone dropped another bowling-ball. He made a muffled sound—the sound of a man who has been hit quite hard.

The ignition wires were hanging down, their copper cores bare and slightly kinked. The kink, Alan knew, came from being braided together. The Volvo had been hot-wired, and very efficiently from the look of it. The driver had grasped the wires above the bare cores and pulled them apart again to cut the engine when they had parked here.

So it was true . . . some of it, at least. The big question was how much. He was beginning to feel like a man edging closer and closer to a potentially lethal drop.

He went back to his prowl-car, got in, started it up, and took the microphone off its prong.

What's true? Protocol and Reason whispered. God, that was a maddening voice. *That someone is at the Beaumonts' lake house? Yes—that might be true. That someone named George Stark backed that black Toronado out of Fuzzy Martin's barn? Come on, Alan.*

Two thoughts occurred to him almost simultaneously. The first was that, if he contacted Henry Payton at the State Police Barracks in Oxford, as Harrison had told him to do, he might *never* know how this came out. Lake Lane, where the Beaumonts' summer house was located, was a dead end. The State Police would tell him not to approach the house on his own—not a single officer, not when they suspected the man who was holding Liz and the twins of at least a dozen murders. They would want him to block off the road *and no more* while they sent out a fleet of cruisers, maybe a chopper, and, for all Alan knew, a few destroyers and fighter-planes.

The second thought was about Stark.

They weren't thinking about Stark; they didn't even *know* about Stark.

But what if Stark was real?

If that was the case, Alan was coming to believe that sending a bunch of State Troopers who didn't know any better up Lake Lane would be like marching men into a meat-grinder.

He put the microphone back on its prong. He was going in, and he was going in alone. It might be wrong, probably was, but it was what he was going to do. He could live with the thought of his own stupidity; God knew he had done it before. What he couldn't live with was even the possibility that he might have caused the deaths of a woman and two infants by making a radio-call for back-up before he knew the real nature of the situation.

Alan pulled out of the rest area and headed for Lake Lane.

Twenty-four

THE COMING OF
THE SPARROWS

1

Thad avoided the turnpike on the way down (Stark had instructed Liz to use it, cutting half an hour off their time), and so he had to go through either Lewiston-Auburn or Oxford. L.A., as the natives called it, was a much bigger metropolitan area . . . but the State Police Barracks was in Oxford.

He chose Lewiston-Auburn.

He was waiting at an Auburn traffic light and checking his rearview mirror constantly for police cars when the idea he'd first grasped clearly while talking to Rawlie at the auto junkyard struck him again. This time it was not just a tickle; it was something like a hard open-handed blow.

I am the knower. I am the owner. I am the bringer.

It's magic we are dealing with here, Thad thought, *and any magician worth his salt has got to have a magic wand. Everyone knows that. Luckily, I know just where such an item may be had. Where, in fact, they sell them by the dozen.*

The nearest stationer's store was on Court Street, and now Thad diverted in that direction. He was sure there were Berol Black Beauty pencils at the house in Castle Rock, and he was equally sure Stark had brought his own supply, but he didn't want them. What he wanted were pencils Stark had never touched, either as a part of Thad or as a separate entity.

Thad found a parking space half a block down from the stationer's, killed the engine of Rawlie's VW (it died hard, with a wheeze and several lunging chugs), and got out. It was good to get away from the ghost of Rawlie's pipe and into the fresh air for awhile.

At the stationer's he bought a box of Berol Black Beauty pencils. The clerk told him to be his guest when Thad asked if he could use the pencil-sharpener on the wall. He used it to sharpen six of the Berols. These he put in his breast pocket, lining it from side to side. The leads stuck up like the warheads of small, deadly missiles.

Presto and abracadabra, he thought. *Let the revels commence.*

He walked back to Rawlie's car, got in, and just sat there for a moment, sweating in the heat and softly singing "John Wesley Harding" under his breath. Almost all of the words had come back. It was really amazing what the human mind could do under pressure.

This could be very, very dangerous, he thought. He found that he didn't care so much for himself. He had, after all, brought George Stark into the world, and he supposed that made him responsible for him. It didn't seem terribly fair; he didn't think he had created George with any evil intent. He couldn't see himself as either of those infamous doctors, Mssrs. Jekyll and Frankenstein, in spite of what might be happening to his wife and children. He had not set out to write a series of novels which would make a great deal of money, and he had certainly not set out to create a monster. He had only been trying to feel a way around the block that had dropped into his path. He had only wanted to find a way to write another good story, because doing that made him happy.

Instead, he had caught some sort of supernatural disease. And there were diseases, lots of them, that found homes in the bodies of people who had done nothing to deserve them—fun things like cerebral palsy, muscular dystrophy, epilepsy, Alzheimer's—but once you got one, you had to deal with it. What was the name of that old radio quiz show? *Name It and Claim It?*

This could be very dangerous for Liz and the kids, though, his mind insisted, reasonably enough.

Yes. Brain surgery could be dangerous, too . . . but if you had a tumor growing in there, what choice did you have?

He'll be looking. Peeking. The pencils are okay; he might even be flattered. But if he senses what you plan to do with them, or if he finds out about the birdcall . . . if he guesses about the sparrows . . . hell, if he even guesses there's something to guess . . . then you're in deep shit.

But it could work, another part of his mind whispered. *Goddammit, you know it could work.*

Yes. He did know it. And because the deepest part of his mind insisted that there was really nothing else to do or try, Thad started the VW and pointed it toward Castle Rock.

Fifteen minutes later he had left Auburn behind and was out in the country again, heading west toward the Lakes Region.

2

For the last forty miles of the trip, Stark talked steadily about *Steel Machine,* the book on which he and Thad were going to collaborate. He helped Liz with the kids—always keeping one hand free and close enough to the gun tucked into his belt to keep her convinced—while she unlocked the summer house and let them in. She had been hoping for cars parked in at least some of the driveways leading off Lake Lane, or to hear the sounds of voices or chainsaws, but there had been only the sleepy hum of the insects and the powerful rumble of the Toronado's engine. It seemed that the son of a bitch had the luck of the devil himself.

All the time they were unloading and bringing things in, Stark went on talking. He didn't even stop while he was using his straight-razor to amputate all but one of the telephone jacks. And the book sounded good. That was the really dreadful thing. The book sounded very good indeed. It sounded as if it might be as big as *Machine's Way*—maybe even bigger.

"I have to go to the bathroom," she said when the luggage was inside, interrupting him in mid-spate.

"That's fine," he said mildly, turning to look at her. He had taken off the sunglasses once they arrived, and now she had to turn her head aside from him. That glaring, mouldering gaze was more than she could deal with. "I'll just come along."

"I like a little privacy when I relieve myself. Don't you?"

"It doesn't much matter to me, one way or

another," Stark said with serene cheeriness. It was a mood he had been in ever since they left the turnpike at Gates Falls—he had the unmistakable air of a man who now knows things are going to come out all right.

"But it does to *me*," she said, as if speaking to a particularly obtuse child. She felt her fingers curling into claws. In her mind she was suddenly ripping those staring eyeballs out of their slack sockets . . . and when she risked a glance up at him and saw his amused face, she knew *he* knew what she was thinking and feeling.

"I'll just stay in the doorway," he said with mock humility. "I'll be a good boy. I won't peek."

The babies were crawling busily around the living-room rug. They were cheerful, vocal, full of beans. They seemed to be delighted to be here, where they had been only once before, for a long winter weekend.

"They can't be left alone," Liz said. "The bathroom is off the master bedroom. If they're left here, they'll get into trouble."

"No problem, Beth," Stark said, and scooped them up effortlessly, one under each arm. She would have believed just this morning that if anyone but herself or Thad tried something like that, William and Wendy would have screamed their heads off. But when Stark did it, they giggled merrily, as if this were the most amusing thing under the sun. "I'll bring them into the bedroom, and I'll be watching *them* instead of you." He turned and regarded her with an instant's coldness. "I'll keep a good eye on them, too. I wouldn't want them to come to any harm, Beth. I like them. If anything happens to them, it won't be *my* fault."

She went into the bathroom and he stood in the doorway, his back to her as he had promised, watching the twins. As she raised her skirt and lowered her panties and sat down, she hoped he was a man of his word. She wouldn't die if he turned around and saw her squatting on the john . . . but if he saw the sewing scissors inside her underwear, she might.

And, as usual, when she was in a hurry to go, her bladder hung on obstinately. *Come on, come on,* she thought with a mixture of fear and irritation. *What's the matter, do you think you're going to collect interest on that stuff?*

At last. Relief.

"But when they try to come out of the barn," Stark was saying, "Machine lights the gasoline they've poured into the trench around it in the night. Won't that be great? There's a movie in it, too, Beth—the assholes who make movies *love* fires."

She used the toilet paper and pulled her panties up very carefully. She kept her eyes glued to Stark's back as she adjusted her clothes, praying that he would not turn around. He didn't. He was deeply absorbed in his own story.

"Westerman and Jack Rangely duck back inside, planning to use the car to drive right through the fire. But Ellington panics, and—"

He broke off suddenly, his head cocked to one side. Then he turned to her, just as she was straightening her skirt.

"Out," he said abruptly, and all the good humor had left his voice. "Get the fuck out of there right now."

"What—"

He grabbed her arm with rough force and yanked her into the bedroom. He went into the bathroom and opened the medicine cabinet. "We've got company, and it's too early for Thad."

"I don't—"

"Car engine," he said briefly. "Powerful motor. Could be a police interceptor. Hear it?"

Stark slammed the medicine cabinet shut and jerked open the drawer to the right of the washstand. He found a roll of Red Cross adhesive tape and popped the tin ring off the doughnut.

She heard nothing and said so.

"That's okay," he said. "I can hear it for both of us. Hands behind you."

"What are you going to—"

"Shut up and put your hands behind you!"

She did, and immediately her wrists were bound. He criss-crossed the tape, back and forth, back and forth, in tight figure-eights.

"Engine just quit," he said. "Maybe a quarter of a mile up the road. Someone trying to be cute."

She thought she might have heard an engine in the last moment, but it could have been nothing but suggestion. She knew she would have heard nothing at all if she had not been listening with all of her concentration. Dear God, how sharp were his ears.

"Gotta cut this tape," he said. "Pardon me gettin personal for a second or so, Beth. Time's a little short for politeness."

And before she even knew he was doing it, he had reached down the front of her skirt. A moment later, he pulled the sewing scissors free. He didn't even prick her skin with the pins.

He glanced in her eyes for just a moment as he

reached behind her and used the scissors to cut the tape. He seemed amused again.

"You saw them," she said dully. "You saw the bulge after all."

"The scissors?" He laughed. "I saw them, but not the bulge. I saw them in your *eyes,* darlin Bethie. I saw them back in Ludlow. I knew they were there the minute you came downstairs."

He knelt in front of her with the tape, absurdly—and ominously—like a suitor proposing marriage. Then he looked up at her. "Don't you get ideas about kicking me or anything, Beth. I don't know for sure, but I think that's a cop. And I don't have time to play fiddlyfuck with you, much as I'd like to. So be still."

"The babies—"

"I'm gonna close the doors," Stark said. "They're not tall enough to reach the knobs even when they get up on their feet. They may eat a few dust-kitties under the bed, but I think that's the worst trouble they can get into. I'll be back very shortly."

Now the tape was winding figure-eights around her ankles. He cut it and stood up again.

"You be good, Beth," he said. "Don't go losing your happy thoughts. I'd make you pay for a thing like that . . . but I'd make you watch *them* pay, first."

Then he closed the bathroom door, the bedroom door, and was gone. He absented himself with the speed of a good magician doing a trick.

She thought of the .22 locked in the equipment shed. Were there bullets in there, too? She was pretty sure there were. Half a box of Winchester .22 Long Rifles on a high shelf.

Liz began to twist her wrists back and forth. He had interwoven the tape very cunningly, and for awhile she wasn't sure she was going to be able to even loosen it, let alone work her hands free of it.

Then she started to feel a little give, and began to work her wrists back and forth faster, panting.

William crawled over, placed his hands on her leg, and looked questioningly into her face.

"Everything's going to be fine," she said, and smiled at him.

Will smiled back and crawled away in search of his sister. Liz tossed a sweaty lock of hair out of her eyes with a brisk shake of her head and returned to rotating her wrists back and forth, back and forth, back and forth.

3

So far as Alan Pangborn could tell, Lake Lane was entirely deserted . . . at least, it was entirely deserted as far as he dared to drive in. That was the sixth driveway along the road. He believed he could have driven at least a little farther in safety—there was no way the sound of his car's engine could be heard at the Beaumont place from this distance, not with two hills in between—but it was better to be safe. He drove down to the A-frame cottage which belonged to the Williams family, summer residents from Lynn, Massachusetts, parked on a carpet of needles under a hoary old pine, killed the engine, and got out.

He looked up and saw the sparrows.

They were sitting on the roofpeak of the Williams house. They were sitting on the high branches of the trees that surrounded it. They perched on rocks down by the lakeshore; they jostled for place on the Williamses' dock—so many of them he couldn't see the wood. There were hundreds and hundreds of them.

And they were utterly silent, only looking at him with their tiny black eyes.

"Jesus," he whispered.

There were crickets singing in the high grass which grew along the foundations of the Williams house, and the soft lap of the lake against the permanent part of their dock, and a plane droning its way west, toward New Hampshire. Otherwise, everything was silent. There was not even the harsh buzz of a single outboard motor on the lake.

Only those birds.

All those birds.

Alan felt a deep, glassy fright creeping along his bones. He had seen sparrows flock together in the spring or the fall, sometimes a hundred or two hundred at once, but he had never in his life seen anything like *this*.

Have they come for Thad . . . or for Stark?

He looked back at the radio mike again, wondering if he shouldn't call in after all. This was just too weird, too out of control.

What if they all fly at once? If he's down there, and if he's as sharp as Thad says, he'll hear that, all right. He'll hear that just fine.

He began to walk. The sparrows did not move . . . but a fresh flock appeared and settled into the trees. They were all around him now, staring down at him like a hard-hearted jury staring at a murderer in the dock. Except back by the road. The woods bordering Lake Lane were still clear.

He decided to go back that way.

A dismal thought, just shy of being a premonition, came to him—that this might be the biggest mistake of his professional life.

I'm just going to recon the place, he thought. *If the birds don't fly—and they don't seem to want to—I should be okay. I can go up this driveway, cross the Lane, and work my way down to the Beaumont house through the woods. If the Toronado's there, I'll see it. If I see it, I may see him. And if I do, at least I'll know what I'm up against. I'll know if it's Thad, or . . . someone else.*

There was another thought, as well. One Alan hardly dared think, because thinking it might queer his luck. If he *did* see the owner of the black Toronado, he might get a clear shot. He might be able to take the bastard down and end it right here. If that was the way things worked out, he would take a heavy roasting from the State Police for going against their specific orders . . . but Liz and the kids would be safe, and right now that was all he cared about.

More sparrows fluttered soundlessly down. They were carpeting the asphalt surface of the Williamses' driveway from the bottom up. One landed less than five feet from Alan's boots. He made a kicking gesture at it and instantly regretted it, half-expecting to send the bird—and the whole monster flock with it—into the sky at once.

The sparrow hopped a little. That was all.

Another sparrow landed on Alan's shoulder. He couldn't believe it, but it was there. He brushed at it, and it hopped onto his hand. Its beak dipped, as if it meant to peck his palm . . . and then it stopped. Heart beating hard, Alan lowered his hand. The bird hopped off, fluttered its wings once, and landed on the driveway with its fellows. It stared up at him with its bright, senseless eyes.

Alan swallowed. There was an audible click in his throat. "What *are* you?" he muttered. "What the fuck *are* you?"

The sparrows only stared at him. And now every pine and maple he could see on this side of Castle Lake appeared to be full. He heard a branch crack somewhere under their accumulated weight.

Their bones are hollow, he thought. *They weigh next to nothing. How many of them must it take to crack a branch like that?*

He didn't know. Didn't want to know.

Alan unsnapped the strap across the butt of his .38 and walked back up the steep slant of the Williamses' driveway, away from the sparrows. By the time he reached Lake Lane, which was only a dirt track with a ribbon of grass growing up between the wheel-ruts, his face was oiled with sweat and his shirt was stuck damply to his back. He looked around. He could see the sparrows back the way he had come—they were all over the top of his car now, roosting on the hood and the trunk and the roof-flashers—but there were none up here.

It's as if, he thought, *they don't want to get too close . . . at least not yet. It's as if this were their staging area.*

He looked both ways along the Lane from what he hoped was a place of concealment behind a tall sumac bush. Not a soul in sight—only the sparrows, and they were all back on the slope where the Williamses' A-frame stood. Not a sound except for the crickets and a couple of mosquitoes whining around his face.

Good.

Alan trotted across the road like a soldier in enemy territory, head low between his hunched shoulders, jumped the weed- and rock-choked ditch on the far side, and disappeared into the woods. Once he was in concealment, he concentrated on working his way down to the Beaumont summer house as quickly and silently as he could.

4

The eastern side of Castle Lake lay at the bottom of a long, steep hill. Lake Lane was halfway down this slope, and most of the houses were so far below Lake Lane that Alan could see only their roofpeaks from his position, which was about twenty yards up the hill from the road. In some cases they were hidden from his view entirely. But he could see the road, and the driveways which branched off from it, and as long as he didn't lose count, he would be okay.

When he reached the fifth turn-off beyond the Williamses', he stopped. He looked behind him to see if the sparrows were following him. The idea was bizarre but somehow inescapable. He could see no sign of them at all, and it occurred to him that perhaps his overloaded mind had imagined the whole thing.

Forget it, he thought. *You didn't imagine it. They were back there . . . and they're still back there.*

He looked down at the Beaumonts' driveway, but could see nothing from his current position. He began to work his way down, moving slowly, crouched over. He moved quietly and was just congratulating himself on this fact when George Stark put a gun into his left ear and said, "If you move, good buddy, most of your brains are going to land on your right shoulder."

5

He turned his head slowly, slowly, slowly.

What he saw almost made him wish he had been born blind.

"I guess they'll never want me on the cover of *GQ,* huh?" Stark asked. He was grinning. The grin showed more of his teeth and gums (and the empty holes where other teeth had been) than even the widest grin should have done. His face was covered with sores and the skin seemed to be sloughing off the underlying tissue. But that wasn't the whole trouble—that wasn't what made Alan's belly crawl with horror and revulsion. Something seemed to be wrong with the underlying structure of the man's face. It was as if he were not simply decaying, but *mutating* in some horrible way.

He knew who the man with the gun was, all the same.

The hair, lifeless as an old wig glued to the straw head of a scarecrow, was blonde. The shoulders were almost as broad as those of a football player with his pads on. He stood with a kind of arrogant, light-footed grace even though he was not moving, and he looked at Alan with good humor.

It was the man who couldn't exist, who never *had* existed.

It was Mr. George Stark, that high-toned son of a bitch from Oxford, Mississippi.

It was all true.

"Welcome to the carnival, old hoss," Stark said mildly. "You move pretty good for such a big man. I almost missed you at first, and I been lookin for you. Let's go on down to the house. I want to introduce you to the little woman. And if you make a single wrong move, you'll be dead, and so will she, and so will those cute little kids. I have nothing whatever in the wide world to lose. Do you believe that?"

Stark grinned at him out of his decaying, horribly wrong face. The crickets went on singing in the grass. Out on the lake, a loon lifted its sweet, piercing cry into the air. Alan wished with all his heart that he was that bird, because when he looked into Stark's staring eyeballs he saw only one thing in them other than death . . . and that one thing was nothing at all.

He realized with sudden, perfect clarity that he was never going to see his wife and sons again.

"I believe it," he said.

"Then drop your gun in the puckies and let's go."

Alan did as he was told. Stark followed behind him, and they descended to the road. They crossed it and then walked down the slope of the Beaumonts' driveway toward the house. It jutted out of the hillside on heavy wooden pilings, almost like a beach house in Malibu. So far as Alan could see, there were no sparrows around it. None at all.

The Toronado was parked by the door, a black and gleaming tarantula in the late afternoon sun. It looked like a bullet. Alan read the bumper sticker with a mild sense of wonder. All of his emotions felt oddly muted, oddly mild, as if this were a dream from which he would soon wake up.

You don't want to think like that, he warned himself. *Thinking like that will get you killed.*

That was almost funny, because he was a dead man already, wasn't he? There he had been, creeping up on the Beaumont driveway, meaning to sneak across the road like Tonto, take-um good look round, get-um idea how things are, Kemo Sabe . . . and Stark had simply put a pistol in his ear and told him to drop his gun and there went the ballgame.

I didn't hear him; I didn't even intuit him. People think I'm quiet, but this guy made me look like I had two left feet.

"You like my wheels?" Stark asked.

"Right now I think every police officer in Maine must like your wheels," Alan said, "because they're all looking for them."

Stark gave voice to a jolly laugh. "Now why don't I believe that?" The barrel of his gun prodded Alan in the small of the back. "Get on inside, my good old buddy. We're just waiting for Thad. When Thad gets here, I think we'll be ready ready Teddy to rock and roll."

Alan looked around at Stark's free hand and saw an extremely odd thing: there appeared to be no lines on the palm of that hand. No lines at all.

6

"Alan!" Liz cried. "Are you all right?"

"Well," Alan said, "if it's possible for a man to feel like an utter horse's ass and still be all right, I guess I am."

"You couldn't have been expected to believe," Stark said mildly. He pointed to the scissors he had removed from her panties. He had put them on one of the night-tables which flanked the big double bed, out of the twins' reach. "Cut her legs free, Officer Alan. No need to bother with her wrists; looks like she's almost got those already. Or are you Chief Alan?"

"Sheriff Alan," he said, and thought: *He knows that. He knows* ME—*Sheriff Alan Pangborn of Castle County—because Thad knows me. But even when he's got the upper hand he doesn't give away everything he knows. He's as sly as a weasel who's made a career out of henhouses.*

And for the second time a bleak certainty of his own approaching death filled him. He tried to think of the sparrows, because the sparrows were the one element of this nightmare with which he did not believe George Stark was familiar. Then he thought better of it. The man was too sharp. If he allowed himself hope, Stark would see it in his eyes . . . and wonder what it meant.

Alan got the scissors and cut Liz Beaumont's legs free of the tape even as she freed one hand and began to unwrap the tape from her wrists.

"Are you going to hurt me?" she asked Stark apprehensively. She held her hands up, as if the red marks the tape had left on her wrists would somehow dissuade him from doing that.

"No," he said, smiling a little. "Can't blame you for doin what comes naturally, can I, darlin Beth?"

She gave him a revolted, frightened look at that and then corralled the twins. She asked Stark if she could take them out in the kitchen and give them something to eat. They had slept until Stark had parked the Clarks' stolen Volvo at the rest area, and were now lively and full of fun.

"You bet," Stark said. He seemed to be in a cheerful, upbeat mood . . . but he was holding the gun in one hand and his eyes moved ceaselessly back and forth between Liz and Alan. "Why don't we all go out? I want to talk to the Sheriff, here."

They trooped out to the kitchen, and Liz began to put together a meal for the twins. Alan watched the twins while she did it. They were cute kids—as cute as a pair of bunnies, and looking at them reminded him of a time when he and Annie had been much younger, a time when Toby, now a senior in high school, had been in diapers and Todd had still been years away.

They crawled happily hither and yon, and every now and then he had to redirect one of them before he or she could pull a chair over or bump his/her head on the underside of the Formica table in the kitchen galley.

Stark talked to him while he babysat.

"You think I'm going to kill you," he said. "No need to deny it, Sheriff; I can see it in your eyes, and it is a look I'm familiar with. I could lie and say it's not true, but I think you'd doubt me. You have a certain amount of experience in these matters yourself, isn't that right?"

"I suppose," Alan said. "But something like this is a little bit . . . well, outside the normal run of police business."

Stark threw back his head and laughed. The twins looked toward the sound, and laughed along with him. Alan glanced at Liz and saw terror and hate on her face. And there was something else there as well, wasn't there? Yes. Alan thought it was jealousy. He wondered idly if there was something else George Stark didn't know. He wondered if Stark had any idea of how dangerous this woman could be to him.

"You got *that* right!" Stark said, still chuckling.

Then he grew serious. He leaned toward Alan, and Alan could smell the cheesy odor of his decomposing flesh. "But it doesn't *have* to go that way, Sheriff. The odds are against you walking out of this affair alive, I will freely grant you that, but the possibility exists. I have something to do here. A bit of writing. Thad is going to help me—he's going to prime the pump, you might say. I think we'll probably work through the night, he and I, but by the time the sun comes up tomorrow morning, I should pretty much have my house in order."

"He wants Thad to teach him how to write on his own," Liz said from the galley. "He says they're going to collaborate on a book."

"That's not quite right," Stark said. He glanced at her for a moment, a ripple of annoyance passing over the previously unbroken surface of his good temper. "And he owes me, you know. Maybe he knew how to write before I showed up, but *I* was the one who taught *him* how to write stuff people would want to read. And what good is it, writing a thing, if no one wants to read it?"

"No—you wouldn't understand that, would you?" Liz asked.

"What I want from him," Stark told Alan, "is a kind of transfusion. I seem to have some sort of . . . of gland that's quit on me. *Temporarily* quit. I think Thad knows how to make that gland work. He ought to, because he sort of cloned mine from his own, if you see what I mean. I guess you could say he built most of my equipment."

Oh no, my friend, Alan thought. *That's not right. You might not know it, but it's not. You did it together, you two, because you were there all along. And you have been terribly persistent. Thad tried to put an end to you before he was born and couldn't quite do it. Then, eleven years later, Dr. Pritchard tried his hand, and that worked, but only for awhile. Finally, Thad invited you back. He did it, but he didn't know what he was doing . . . because he didn't know about* YOU. *Pritchard never told him. And you came, didn't you? You are the ghost of his dead brother . . . but you're both much more and much less than that.*

Alan caught Wendy, who was by the fireplace, before she could topple over backward into the woodbox.

Stark looked at William and Wendy, then back at Alan. "Thad and I come from a long history of twins, you know. And, of course, I came into being following the deaths of the twins who would have been these two kids' older brothers or sisters. Call it some sort of transcendental balancing act, if you like."

"I call it crazy," Alan said.

Stark laughed. "Actually, so do I. But it happened. The word became flesh, you might say. How it happened doesn't much matter—what matters is that I'm here."

You're wrong, Alan, thought. *How it happened may be all that* DOES *matter now. To us, if not to you . . . because it may be all that can save us.*

"Once things got to a certain point, I created *myself*," Stark went on. "And it really isn't so surprising that I've been havin problems with my writing, is it? Creating one's own self . . . that takes a lot of energy. You don't think this sort of thing happens every day, do you?"

"God forbid," Liz said.

That was either a direct hit or close to it. Stark's head whipped toward her with the speed of a striking snake, and this time the annoyance was more than just a ripple. "I think maybe you better just shut your pie-hole, Beth," he said softly, "before you cause trouble for someone who can't speak for himself. Or herself."

Liz looked down at the pot on the stove. Alan thought she had paled.

"Bring them over, Alan, would you?" she asked quietly. "This is ready."

She took Wendy on her lap to feed, and Alan took William. It was amazing how fast the technique came back, he thought as he fed the chubby little boy. Pop the spoon in, tilt it, then give it that quick but gentle flick up the chin to the lower lip when you take it out again, preventing as many drips and drools as possible. Will kept reaching for the spoon, apparently feeling he was quite old enough and experienced enough to drive it himself, thank you. Alan discouraged him gently, and the boy settled down to serious eating soon enough.

"The fact is I can use you," Stark told him. He was leaning against the kitchen counter and running the gunsight of his pistol idly up and down the front of his quilted vest. It made a harsh whispering sound. "Did the State Police call you, tell you to come down and check this place out? That why you're here?"

Alan debated the pros and cons of lying and decided it would be safer to tell the truth, mostly because he did not doubt that this man—if he *was* a man—had a very efficient built-in lie detector.

"Not exactly," he said, and told Stark about Fuzzy Martin's call.

Stark was nodding before he had finished. "I *thought* I saw a glint in the window of that farmhouse," he said, and chuckled. His good humor seemed quite restored. "Well, well! Country folks can't help bein a little nosy, can they, Sheriff Alan? They got so little to do it'd be a wonder if they weren't! So what did *you* do when you hung up?"

Alan told him that, too, and now he did not lie because he believed Stark knew what he had done—the simple fact that he was here alone answered most questions. Alan thought that what Stark really wanted to know was if he was stupid enough to try an untruth.

When he had finished, Stark said: "Okay, that's good. That improves your chances of livin to fight another day all to hell, Sheriff Alan. Now you listen to me, and I'll tell you exactly what we're goin to do once these babies are fed up."

7

"You sure you know what to say?" Stark asked again. They were standing by the telephone in the front hall, the only working telephone left in the house.

"Yes."

"And you're not going to try leaving any little secret messages for your dispatcher to pick up?"

"No."

"That's good," Stark said. "That's good because this would be just an *awful* time to forget you're a grown-up and start playing Pirates' Cave or Robbers' Roost. Someone would surely get hurt."

"I wish you'd stop with the threats for a little while."

Stark's grin widened, became a thing of pestiferous splendor. He had taken William along to assure himself of Liz's continued good behavior, and he now tickled the baby under one arm. "I can't very well do that," he said. "A man who goes against his nature gets constipated, Sheriff Alan."

The phone stood on a table by a large window. As Alan picked it up, he checked the slope of the woods beyond the driveway for sparrows. There were none in sight. Not yet, anyway.

"What are you lookin for, old hoss?"

"Huh?" He glanced at Stark. Stark's eyes stared at him flatly from their decomposing sockets.

"You heard me." Stark gestured toward the driveway and the Toronado. "You ain't lookin out that window the way a man does just because there's a window to look out of. You're wearin the face of a man who expects to see something. I want to know what it is."

Alan felt a cold thread of terror slip down the center of his back.

"Thad," he heard himself say calmly. "I'm keeping my eye out for Thad, the same as you are. He should be getting here soon."

"That better be all of the truth, don't you think?" Stark asked him, and lifted William a little higher. He began to run the barrel of his gun slowly up and down William's pleasantly pudgy midriff, tickling him. William giggled and patted Stark's decaying cheek gently, as if to say Stop it, you tease . . . but not just yet, because this is sort of fun.

"I understand," Alan said, and swallowed dryly.

Stark slid the pistol's muzzle up to William's chin and wiggled the little dewlap there with it. The baby laughed.

If Liz comes around the corner and sees him doing that, she'll go mad, Alan thought calmly.

"You *sure* you told me everything, Sheriff Alan? Not holdin out on me, or anything?"

"No," Alan said. *Just about the sparrows in the woods around the Williams place.* "I'm not holding out."

"Okay. I believe you. For the time being, at least. Now go on and do your business."

Alan dialed the Castle County Sheriff's Office. Stark leaned close—so close that his ripe aroma made Alan feel like gagging—and listened in.

Sheila Brigham answered on the first ring.

"Hi, Sheila—it's Alan. I'm down by Castle Lake. I tried to get through on the radio, but you know what transmission's like down here."

"Nonexistent," she said, and laughed.

Stark smiled.

8

When they were out of sight around the corner, Liz opened the drawer under the kitchen counter and took out the biggest butcher-knife in there. She glanced toward the corner, knowing Stark could poke his head around it at any moment to check on her. But so far she was okay. She could hear them talking. Stark was saying something about the way Alan had been looking through the window.

I have to do this, she thought, *and I have to do it all by myself. He's watching Alan like a cat, and even if I could say something to Thad, that would only make things worse . . . because he has access to Thad's mind.*

Holding Wendy in the crook of her arm, she slipped off her shoes and walked quickly into the living room on her bare feet. There was a sofa there, arranged so one could sit on it and look out over the lake. She slid the butcher-knife under the flounce . . . but not too far under. If she sat down, it would be within reach.

And if they sat down together, she and foxy George Stark, *he* would be within reach, too.

I might be able to get him to do that, she thought, hurrying back toward the kitchen again. *Yes, I just might. He's attracted to me. And that's horrible . . . but it's not too horrible to use.*

She came into the kitchen, expecting to see Stark standing there, flashing his remaining teeth at her in that terrible, mouldering grin of his. But the kitchen was empty, and she could still hear Alan on the telephone in the hall. She could picture Stark standing right next to him, listening in. So *that* was all right. She thought: *With any luck, George Stark will be dead when Thad gets here.*

She didn't want them to meet. She didn't understand all the reasons why she so badly wanted to keep that from happening, but she understood at least one of them: she was afraid that the collaboration might actually work, and she was even more afraid that she knew what the fruits of success would be.

In the end, only one person could lay claim to the dual natures of Thad Beaumont and George Stark. Only one physical being could survive such a primal split. If Thad *could* provide the jump-start Stark needed, if Stark began to write on his own, would his wounds and sores begin to heal?

Liz thought they would. She thought Stark might even begin to take over her husband's face and form.

And afterward, how long would it be (presuming Stark left them all alive here and made good his escape) before the first sores showed up on *Thad's* face?

She didn't think it would be long. And she doubted very much if Stark would be interested in keeping Thad from first decaying and ultimately rotting away to nothing, all his happy thoughts gone forever.

Liz slipped her shoes back on and began to clean up the remains of the twins' early supper. *You bastard,* she thought, first wiping the counter and then beginning to fill the sink with hot water. YOU'RE *the pen name,* YOU'RE *the interloper, not my husband.* She squirted Joy into the sink and then went to the living-room door to check on Wendy. She was crawling across the living-room floor, probably looking for her brother. Beyond the sliding glass doors, the late afternoon sun was beating a bright gold track across the blue water of Castle Lake.

You don't belong here. You're an abomination, an offence to the eye and the mind.

She looked at the sofa with the long, sharp knife lying beneath it, within easy reach.

But I can fix that. And if God lets me have my way, I WILL *fix it.*

9

Stark's smell was really getting to him—making him feel as if he were going to gag at any moment—but Alan tried not to let it show in his voice. "Is Norris Ridgewick back yet, Sheila?"

Beside him, Stark had begun tickling William with the .45 again.

"Not yet, Alan. Sorry."

"If he comes in, tell him to take the desk. Until then, Clut's got it."

"His shift—"

"Yeah, his shift's over, I know. The town'll have to pay some overtime and Keeton will ride me about it, but what can I do? I'm stuck out here with a bad radio and a cruiser that vapor-locks every time you cross your eyes at it. I'm calling from the Beaumont place. The State Police wanted me to check it out, but it's a bust."

"That's too bad. Do you want me to pass the word to anyone? The State Police?"

Alan looked at Stark, who seemed wholly absorbed in tickling the wriggling, cheerful little boy in his arms. Stark nodded absently at Alan's look.

"Yes. Call the Oxford Barracks for me. I thought I'd catch a bite at that take-out chicken place and then come back here and double-check. That's if I can get my car to start. If not, maybe I'll see what the Beaumonts have got in their pantry. Will you make a note for me, Sheila?"

He felt rather than saw Stark tighten up slightly beside him. The muzzle of the gun paused, pointing at William's navel. Alan felt slow, cold trickles of sweat running down his ribcage.

"Sure, Alan."

"This is supposed to be a creative guy. I think he can find a better place to stash his spare key than under the doormat."

Sheila Brigham laughed. "I've got it."

Beside him, the muzzle of the .45 began to move again and William began to grin again. Alan relaxed a little.

"Would it be Henry Payton I should talk to, Alan?"

"Uh-huh. Or Danny Eamons if Henry's not there."

"Okay."

"Thanks, Sheila. More b.s. from the State, that's all. Take care of yourself."

"You too, Alan."

He hung up the telephone gently and turned to Stark. "Okay?"

"Very much okay," Stark said. "I particularly liked the part about the key under the doormat. It added that extra touch that means so much."

"What a dink you are," Alan said. Under the circumstances it wasn't a very wise thing to say, but his own anger surprised him.

Stark surprised him, too. He laughed. "Nobody likes me very much, do they, Sheriff Alan?"

"No," Alan said.

"Well, that's okay—I like myself enough for everybody. I'm a real New Age sort of fella that way. The important thing is that I think we're in pretty good shape here. I think all that will fly just fine." He wrapped one hand around the telephone wire and ripped it out of the telephone jack.

"I guess it will," Alan said, but he wondered. It was thin—a lot thinner than Stark, who perhaps believed all the cops north of Portland were a bunch of sleepy Deputy Dawg types, seemed to realize. Dan Eamons in Oxford would probably let it pass, unless someone from Orono or Augusta lit a fire under him. But Henry Payton? He was a lot less sure Henry would buy the idea that Alan had taken a single quick, casual look for Homer Gamache's murderer before going off for a chicken basket at Cluck-Cluck Tonite. Henry might smell a rat.

Watching Stark tickle the baby with the muzzle of the .45, Alan wondered if he wanted that to happen or not, and discovered he didn't know.

"Now what?" he asked Stark.

Stark drew a deep breath and looked outside at the sunlit woods with evident enjoyment. "Let's ask Bethie if she can rustle us up a spot of grub. I'm hungry. Country living's great, isn't it, Sheriff Alan? Goddam!"

"All right," Alan said. He started back toward the kitchen and Stark grabbed him with one hand.

"That crack about vapor-lock," he said. "That didn't mean anything special, did it?"

"No," Alan said. "It was just another case of . . . what did you call it? The extra touch that means so much. Several of our units have had carburetor troubles this last year."

"That better be the truth," Stark said, looking at Alan with his dead eyes. Thick pus was running down from their inner corners and down the sides of his peeling nose like gummy crocodile tears. "It'd be a shame to have to hurt one of these kids because you had to go and get clever. Thad won't work half so good if he finds out I had to blow one of his twins away in order to keep you in line." He grinned and pressed the muzzle of the .45 into William's armpit. William giggled and wriggled. "He's just as cute as a warm kitten, ain't he?"

Alan swallowed around what felt like a large dry fuzz-ball in his throat. "You doing that makes me nervous as hell, fellow."

"You go ahead and stay nervous," Stark said, smiling at him. "I'm just the sort of guy a man wants to stay nervous around. Let's eat, Sheriff Alan. I believe this one's gettin lonesome for his sister."

Liz heated Stark a bowl of soup in the microwave. She offered him a frozen dinner first, but he shook his head, smiling, then reached into his mouth and plucked a tooth. It came out of the gum with rotten ease.

She turned her head aside as he dropped it into the wastebasket, her lips pressed tightly together, her face a tense mask of revulsion.

"Don't worry," he said serenely. "They'll be better before long. *Everything's* going to be better before long. Poppa's going to be here soon."

He was still drinking the soup when Thad pulled in behind the wheel of Rawlie's VW ten minutes later.

Twenty-five

STEEL MACHINE

1

The Beaumont summer house was a mile up Lake Lane from Route 5, but Thad stopped less than a tenth of a mile in, goggling unbelievingly.

There were sparrows everywhere.

Every branch of every tree, every rock, every patch of open ground was covered with roosting sparrows. The world he saw was grotesque, hallucinatory: it was as if this piece of Maine had sprouted feathers. The road ahead of him was gone. Totally gone. Where it had been was a path of silent, jostling sparrows between the overburdened trees.

Somewhere a branch snapped. The only other sound was Rawlie's VW. The muffler had been in bad shape when Thad began his run west; now it seemed to be performing no function at all. The engine farted and roared, backfiring occasionally, and its sound should have sent that monster flock aloft at once, but the birds did not move.

The flock began less than twelve feet in front of the place where he had stopped the VW and thrown its balky transmission into neutral. There was a line of demarcation so clean it might have been drawn with a ruler.

No one has seen a flock of birds like this in years, he thought. *Not since the extermination of the passenger*

pigeons at the end of the last century . . . if then. It's like
something out of that Daphne du Maurier story.

A sparrow fluttered down on the hood of the
VW and seemed to peer in at him. Thad sensed a
frightening, dispassionate curiosity in the small
bird's black eyes.

How far do they go? he wondered. *All the way to*
the house? If so, George has seen them . . . and there will
be hell to pay, if hell hasn't been paid already. And even
if they don't go that far, how am I supposed to get there?
They're not just in the road; they ARE *the road.*

But of course he knew the answer to that. If he
meant to get to the house, he would have to drive
over them.

No, his mind almost moaned. *No, you can't.*
His imagination conjured up terrible images: the
crunching, breaking sounds of small bodies in their
thousands, the jets of blood squirting out from
beneath the wheels, the soggy dots of stuck feathers
revolving as the tires turned.

"But I'm going to," he muttered. "I'm going to
because I have to." A shaky grin began to stitch his
face into a grimace of fierce, half-mad concentration. In that moment he looked eerily like George
Stark. He shoved the stick-shift back into first gear
and began to hum "John Wesley Harding" under
his breath. Rawlie's VW chugged, almost stalled,
then blatted three loud backfires and began to roll
forward.

The sparrow on the hood flew off and Thad's
breath caught as he waited for all of them to take
wing, as they did in his trance-visions: a great rising dark cloud accompanied by a sound like a hurricane in a bottle.

Instead, the surface of the road ahead of the

VW's nose began to writhe and move. The sparrows—some of them, at least—were pulling back, revealing two bare strips . . . strips which exactly matched the path of the VW's wheels.

"Jesus," Thad whispered.

Then he was among them. Suddenly he passed from the world he had always known to an alien one which was populated only by these sentinels which guarded the border between the land of the living and that of the dead.

That's where I am now, he thought as he drove slowly along the twin tracks the birds were affording him. *I am in the land of the living dead, and God help me.*

The path continued to open ahead of him. He always had about twelve feet of clear travel, and as he covered that distance, another twelve feet opened before him. The VW's undercarriage was passing over sparrows which were massed between the wheel-tracks, but he did not seem to be killing them; he didn't see any dead birds behind him in the rearview mirror, at least. But it was hard to tell for sure, because the sparrows were closing the way behind him, recreating that flat, feathery carpet.

He could *smell* them—a light, crumbly smell that seemed to lie on the chest like a fall of bone-dust. Once, as a boy, he had put his face into a bag of rabbit pellets and inhaled deeply. This smell was like that. It was not dirty, but it was overpowering. And it was *alien.* He began to be troubled by the idea that this great mass of birds was stealing all the oxygen from the air, that he would suffocate before he got where he was going.

Now he began to hear light *tak-tak-tak* sounds from overhead, and imagined the sparrows roost-

ing up there on the VW's roof, somehow commu-
nicating with their fellows, guiding them, telling
them when to move away and create the wheel-
tracks, telling them when it was safe to move back.

He crested the first hill on Lake Lane and looked
down into a valley of sparrows—sparrows everywhere, sparrows covering every object and filling
every tree, changing the landscape to a nightmarish bird world that was more than beyond his abil-
ity to imagine; it was beyond his greatest powers of
comprehension.

Thad felt himself slipping toward a faint and
slapped his cheek viciously. It was a small sound—
spat!—compared to the rough roar of the VW's
engine, but he saw a great ripple go through the
sweep of the massed birds . . . a ripple like a shudder.

I can't go down there. I can't.

*You must. You are the knower. You are the bringer.
You are the owner.*

And besides—where else was there to go? He
thought of Rawlie saying, *Be very careful, Thaddeus.
No man controls the agents of the afterlife. Not for long.*
Suppose he tried to reverse back out to Route 5?
The birds had opened a way before him . . . but he
did not think they would open one behind him. He
believed that the consequences of trying to change
his mind now would be unthinkable.

Thad began to creep down the hill . . . and the
sparrows opened the path before him.

He never precisely remembered the rest of that
trip; his mind drew a merciful curtain over it as
soon as it was over. He remembered thinking over
and over again, *They're only SPARROWS, for Christ's
sake . . . they're not tigers or alligators or piranha fish . . .
they're only SPARROWS!*

And that was true, but seeing so many of them at once, seeing them *everywhere,* crammed onto every branch and jostling for place on every fallen log . . . that did something to your mind. It hurt your *mind.*

As he came around the sharp curve in Lake Lane about half a mile in, Schoolhouse Meadow was revealed on the left . . . except it wasn't. Schoolhouse Meadow was gone. Schoolhouse Meadow was black with sparrows.

It hurt your *mind.*

How many? How many millions? Or is it billions?

Another branch cracked and gave way in the woods with a sound like distant thunder. He passed the Williamses', but the A-frame was only a fuzzy hump under the weight of the sparrows. He had no idea that Alan Pangborn's cruiser was parked in the Williamses' driveway; he saw only a feathery hill.

He passed the Saddlers'. The Massenburgs'. The Paynes'. Others he didn't know or couldn't remember. And then, still four hundred yards from his own house, the birds just stopped. There was a place where the whole world was sparrows; six inches farther along there were none at all. Once again it seemed that someone had drawn a ruler-straight line across the road. The birds hopped and fluttered aside, revealing wheel-paths that now opened onto the bare packed dirt of Lake Lane.

Thad drove back into the clear, stopped suddenly, opened the door, and threw up on the ground. He moaned and armed sick sweat from his forehead. Ahead he could see woods on both sides and bright blue winks of light from the lake on his left.

He looked behind and saw a black, silent, waiting world.

The psychopomps, he thought. *God help me if this goes wrong, if he gains control of those birds somehow. God help us all.*

He slammed the door and closed his eyes.

You get hold of yourself now, Thad. You didn't go through that just to blow it now. You get hold of yourself. Forget the sparrows.

I can't forget them! a part of his mind wailed. It was horrified, offended, teetering on the brink of madness. *I can't. I CAN'T!*

But he could. He *would.*

The sparrows were waiting. He would wait, too. He would wait until the right time came. He would trust himself to know that time when he arrived. If he could not do it for himself, he would do it for Liz and the twins.

Pretend it's a story. Just a story you're writing. A story with no birds in it.

"Okay," he muttered. "Okay, I'll try."

He began to drive again. At the same time, he began to sing "John Wesley Harding" under his breath.

2

Thad killed the VW—it died with one final triumphant backfire—and got out of the little car slowly. He stretched. George Stark came out the door, now holding Wendy, and stepped onto the porch, facing Thad.

Stark also stretched.

Liz, standing beside Alan, felt a scream building not in her throat but behind her forehead. She wanted more than anything else to pull her eyes away from the two men, and found she couldn't do it.

Watching them was like watching a man do stretching exercises in a mirror.

They looked nothing whatever alike—even subtracting Stark's accelerating decay from the picture. Thad was slim and darkish, Stark broad-shouldered and fair in spite of his tan (what little remained of it). Yet they were mirror images, just the same. The similarity was eerie precisely because there was no one thing the protesting horrified eye could pin it on. It was *sub rosa*, deeply buried between the lines, but so real it shrieked: that trick of crossing the feet during the stretch, of splaying the fingers stiffly beside either thigh, the tight little crinkle of the eyes.

They relaxed at exactly the same time.

"Hello, Thad." Stark sounded almost shy.

"Hello, George," Thad said flatly. "The family?"

"Just fine, thanks. You mean to do it? Are you ready?"

"Yes."

Behind them, back toward Route 5, a branch cracked. Stark's eyes jumped in that direction.

"What was that?"

"A tree-branch," Thad said. "There was a tornado down here about four years ago, George. The deadwood is still falling. You know that."

Stark nodded. "How are you, old hoss?"

"I'm all right."

"You look a little peaky." Stark's eyes darted over Thad's face; he could feel them trying to pry into the thoughts behind it.

"You don't look so hot yourself."

Stark laughed at this, but there was no humor in the laugh. "I guess I don't."

"You'll let them alone?" Thad asked. "If I do what you want, you'll really let them alone?"

"Yes."

"Give me your word."

"All right," Stark said. "You have it. The word of a Southern man, which is not a thing given lightly." His bogus, almost burlesque, cracker accent had disappeared entirely. He spoke with a simple and horrifying dignity. The two men faced each other in the late afternoon sunlight, so bright and golden it seemed surreal.

"Okay," Thad said after a long moment, and thought: *He doesn't know. He really doesn't. The sparrows . . . they are still hidden from him. That secret is mine.* "Okay, we'll go for it."

3

As the two men stood by the door, Liz realized she had just had the perfect opportunity to tell Alan about the knife under the couch . . . and had let it slip by.

Or had she?

She turned to him, and at that moment Thad called, "Liz?"

His voice was sharp. It held a commanding note he rarely used, and it seemed almost as if he knew what she was up to . . . and didn't want her to do it. That was impossible, of course. Wasn't it? She didn't know. She didn't know anything anymore.

She looked at him, and saw Stark hand Thad the baby. Thad held Wendy close. Wendy put her arms around her father's neck as chummily as she had put them around Stark's.

Now! Liz's mind screamed at her. *Tell him now! Tell him to run! Now, while we've got the twins!*

But of course Stark had a gun, and she didn't think any of them were fast enough to outrun a bullet. And she knew Thad very well; she would never say it out loud, but it suddenly occurred to her that he might very well trip over his own feet.

And now Thad was very close to her, and she couldn't even kid herself that she didn't understand the message in his eyes.

Leave it alone, Liz, they said. *It's my play.*

Then he put his free arm around her and the whole family stood in a clumsy but fervent four-way embrace.

"Liz," he said, kissing her cool lips. "Liz, Liz, I'm sorry, I'm so sorry for this. I didn't mean for anything like this to happen. I didn't know. I thought it was . . . harmless. A joke."

She held him tightly, kissed him, let his lips warm hers.

"It's okay," she said. "It *will* be okay, won't it, Thad?"

"Yes," he said. He drew away so he could look in her eyes. "It's going to be okay."

He kissed her again, then looked at Alan.

"Hello, Alan," he said, and smiled a little. "Changed your mind about anything?"

"Yes. Quite a few things. I talked to an old acquaintance of yours today." He looked at Stark. "Yours, too."

Stark raised what remained of his eyebrows. "I didn't think Thad and I had any friends in common, Sheriff Alan."

"Oh, you had a very close relationship with this guy," Alan said. "In fact, he killed you once."

"What are you talking about?" Thad asked sharply.

"It was Dr. Pritchard I talked to. He remembers both of you very well. You see, it was a pretty unusual sort of operation. What he took out of your head was *him*." He nodded toward Stark.

"What are you talking about?" Liz asked, and her voice cracked on the last word.

So Alan told them what Pritchard had told him . . . but at the last moment he omitted the part about the sparrows dive-bombing the hospital. He did it because Thad hadn't said anything about the sparrows . . . and Thad had to have driven past the Williams place to get here. That suggested two possibilities: either the sparrows had been gone by the time Thad arrived, or Thad didn't want Stark to know they were there.

Alan looked very closely at Thad. *Something going on in there. Some idea. Pray to God it's a good one.*

When Alan finished, Liz looked stunned. Thad was nodding. Stark—from whom Alan would have expected the strongest reaction of all—did not seem much affected one way or the other. The only expression Alan could read on that ruined face was amusement.

"It explains a lot," Thad said. "Thank you, Alan."

"It doesn't explain a goddam thing to me!" Liz cried so shrilly that the twins began to whimper.

Thad looked at George Stark. "You're a ghost," he said. "A weird kind of ghost. We're all standing here and looking at a ghost. Isn't that amazing? This isn't just a psychic incident; it's a goddam *epic!*"

"I don't think it matters," Stark said easily. "Tell

em the William Burroughs story, Thad. I remember it well. I was inside, of course . . . but I was listening."

Liz and Alan looked at Thad questioningly.

"Do you know what he's talking about?" Liz asked.

"Of course I do," Thad said. "Ike and Mike, they think alike."

Stark threw back his head and laughed. The twins stopped whimpering and laughed along with him. "That's good, old hoss! That is *gooood!*"

"I was—or perhaps I should say we were—on a panel with Burroughs in 1981. At the New School, in New York. During the Q-and-A, some kid asked Burroughs if he believed in life after death. Burroughs said he did—he thought we were all living it."

"And that man's *smart,*" Stark said, smiling. "Couldn't shoot a pistol worth shit, but *smart.* Now—you see? You see how little it matters?"

But it does, Alan thought, studying Thad carefully. *It matters a lot. Thad's face says so . . . and the sparrows you don't know about say so, too.*

Thad's knowledge was more dangerous than even *he* knew, Alan suspected. But it might be all they had. He decided he had been right to keep the end of Pritchard's story to himself . . . but he still felt like a man standing on the edge of a cliff and trying to juggle too many flaming torches.

"Enough chit-chat, Thad," Stark said.

He nodded. "Yes. Quite enough." He looked at Liz and Alan. "I don't want either of you trying anything . . . well . . . out of line. I'm going to do what he wants."

"Thad! No! You can't do that!"

"Shhh." He put a finger across her lips. "I can, and I will. No tricks, no special effects. Words on paper made him, and words on paper are the only things that will get rid of him." He cocked his head at Stark. "Do you think *he* knows this will work? He doesn't. He's just hoping."

"That's right," Stark said. "Hope springs eternal in the human tits." He laughed. It was a crazy, lunatic sound, and Alan understood that Stark was also juggling flaming torches on the edge of a cliff.

Sudden movement twitched in the corner of his eye. Alan turned his head slightly and saw a sparrow land on the deck railing outside the sweep of glass that formed the living room's western wall. It was joined by a second and a third. Alan looked back at Thad and saw the writer's eyes move slightly. Had he also seen? Alan thought he had. He had been right, then. Thad knew . . . but he didn't want *Stark* to know.

"The two of us are just going to do a little writing and then say goodbye," Thad said. His eyes shifted to Stark's ruined face. "That *is* what we're going to do, isn't it, George?"

"You got it, guy."

"So you tell me," Thad said to Liz. "Are you holding back? Got something in your head? Some plan?"

She stood looking desperately into her husband's eyes, unaware that between them, William and Wendy were holding hands and looking at each other delightedly, like long-lost relatives at a surprise reunion.

You don't mean it, do you, Thad? her eyes asked him. *It's a trick, isn't it? A trick to lull him, put his suspicions to sleep?*

No, Thad's gray gaze answered. *Right down the line. This is what I want.*

And wasn't there something else, as well? Something so deep and hidden that perhaps she was the only one who could see it?

I'm going to take care of him, babe. I know how. I can.

Oh Thad, I hope you're right.

"There's a knife under the couch," she said slowly, looking into his face. "I got it out of the kitchen while Alan and . . . and him . . . were in the front hall, using the telephone."

"Liz, *Christ!*" Alan nearly screamed, making the babies jump. He was not, in fact, as upset as he hoped he sounded. He had come to understand that if this business was to end in some way that did not mean total horror for all of them, Thad would have to be the one to bring it about. He had made Stark; he would have to unmake him.

She looked around at Stark and saw that hateful grin surfacing on the remains of his face.

"I know what I'm doing," Thad said. "Trust me, Alan. Liz, get the knife and throw it off the deck."

I have a part to play here, Alan thought. *It's a bit part, but remember what the guy used to say in our college drama class—there are no small parts, only small actors.* "You think he's going to just let us *go?*" Alan asked incredulously. "That he's going to trot off over the hill with his tail bobbing behind him like Mary's little lamb? Man, you're crazy."

"Sure, I'm crazy," Thad said, and laughed. It was eerily like the sound Stark had made—the laughter of a man who was dancing on the edge of oblivion. *"He* is, and he came from me, didn't he? Like some cheap demon from the brow of a third-rate Zeus. But I know how it has to be." He turned and looked at Alan fully and gravely for this first time. *"I know how it has to be,"* he repeated slowly and with great emphasis. "Go ahead, Liz."

Alan made a rude, disgusted sound and turned his back, as if to disassociate himself from all of them.

Feeling like a woman in a dream, Liz crossed the living room, knelt down, and fished the knife out from under the couch.

"Be careful of that thing," Stark said. He sounded very alert, very serious. "Your kids would tell you the same thing if they could talk."

She looked around, brushed her hair out of her face, and saw he was pointing his gun at Thad and William.

"I *am* being careful!" she said in a shaky, scolding voice that was close to tears. She slid the door in the window-wall back on its track and stepped out onto the deck. There were now half a dozen sparrows perched on the rail. They moved aside in two groups of three as she approached the rail and the steep drop beyond it, but they did not fly.

Alan saw her pause for a moment, considering them, the handle of the knife pinched between her fingers and the tip of the blade pointing down at the deck like a plumb-bob. He glanced at Thad and saw Thad watching her tensely. Last of all, he glanced at Stark.

He was watching Liz carefully, but there was no look of surprise or suspicion on his face, and a sudden wild thought streaked across Alan Pangborn's mind: *He doesn't see them! He doesn't remember what he wrote on the apartment walls, and he doesn't see them now! He doesn't know they're there!*

Then he suddenly realized Stark was looking

back at *him,* appraising him with that flat, mouldy stare.

"Why are you looking at me?" Stark asked.

"I want to make sure I remember what real ugly is," Alan said. "I might want to tell my grandchildren someday."

"If you don't watch your fucking mouth, you won't have to worry about grandchildren," Stark said. "Not a bit. You want to quit doin that starin thing, Sheriff Alan. It's just not wise."

Liz threw the butcher-knife over the deck rail. When she heard it land in the bushes twenty-five feet below, she *did* begin to cry.

4

"Let's all go upstairs," Stark said. "That's where Thad's office is. I reckon you'll want your type-writer, won't you, old hoss?"

"Not for this one," Thad said. "You know better."

A smile touched Stark's cracked lips. "Do I?"

Thad pointed to the pencils which lined his breast pocket. "These are what I use when I want to get back in touch with Alexis Machine and Jack Rangely."

Stark looked absurdly pleased. "Yeah, that's right, isn't it? I guess I thought this time you'd want to do it different."

"No different, George."

"I brought my own," he said. "Three boxes of them. Sheriff Alan, why don't you be a good boy and trot on out to my car and get em? They're in the glove-compartment. The rest of us will babysit."

He looked at Thad, laughed his loony laugh, and shook his head. "You *dog,* you!"

"That's right, George," Thad said. He smiled a little. "I'm a dog. So are you. And you can't teach old dogs new tricks."

"You're kind of up for it, ain't you, hoss? No matter what you say, part of you is just *raaarin* to go. I see it in your eyes. You *want* it."

"Yes," Thad said simply, and Alan didn't think he was lying.

"Alexis Machine," Stark said. His yellow eyes were gleaming.

"That's right," Thad said, and now his own eyes were gleaming. " 'Cut him while I stand here and watch.' "

"You got it!" Stark cried, and began to laugh. " 'I want to see the blood flow. Don't make me tell you twice.' "

Now they both began to laugh.

Liz looked from Thad to Stark and then back at her husband again and the blood fell from her cheeks because she could not tell the difference.

All at once the edge of the cliff felt closer than ever.

5

Alan went out to get the pencils. His head was only in the car for a moment, but it seemed much longer and he was very glad to get it out again. The car had a dark and unpleasant smell that left him feeling slightly woozy. Rooting around in Stark's Toronado was like sticking his head into an attic room where someone had spilled a bottle of chloroform.

If that's the odor of dreams, Alan thought, *I never want to have another one.*

He stood for a moment beside the black car, the boxes of Berol pencils in his hands, and looked up the driveway.

The sparrows had arrived.

The driveway was disappearing beneath a carpet of them. As he watched, more of them landed. And the woods were full of them. They only landed and sat staring at him, ghastly-silent, a massed living conundrum.

They are coming for you, George, he thought, and started back toward the house. Halfway there he stopped suddenly as a nasty idea struck him.

Or are they coming for us?

He looked back at the birds for a long moment, but they told no secrets, and he went inside.

6

"Upstairs," Stark said. "You go first, Sheriff Alan. Go to the rear of the guest bedroom. There's a glass case filled with pictures and glass paperweights and little souvenirs against the wall there. When you push against the left-hand side of the case, it rotates inward on a central spindle. Thad's study is beyond it."

Alan looked at Thad, who nodded.

"You know a hell of a lot about this place," Alan said, "for a man who's never been here."

"But I *have* been here," Stark said gravely. "I have been here often, in my dreams."

7

Two minutes later, all of them were gathered outside the unique door of Thad's small study. The glass case was turned inward, creating two entrances to the room separated by the thickness of the case. There were no windows in here; give me a window down here by the lake, Thad had told Liz once, and what I'll do is write two words and then stare out of the damned thing for two hours, watching the boats go by.

A lamp with a flexible goose-neck and a brilliant quartz-halogen bulb cast a circle of white light on the desk. An office chair and a folding camp chair stood behind the desk, side by side, facing the two blank notebooks which had been placed side by side in the circle of light. Resting on top of each notebook were two sharpened Berol Black Beauty pencils. The IBM electric Thad sometimes used down here had been unplugged and stuck in a corner.

Thad himself had brought in the folding chair from the hall closet, and the room now expressed a duality Liz found both startling and extremely unpleasant. It was, in a way, another version of the mirror-creature she fancied she had seen when Thad finally arrived. Here were two chairs where there had always been one; here were two little writing stations, also side by side, where there should have been only one. The writing implement which she associated with Thad's

(better)

normal self had been shunted aside, and when they sat down, Stark in Thad's office chair and Thad in the folding chair, the disorientation was complete. She felt almost sea-sick.

Each of them had a twin on his lap.

"How long do we have before someone gets suspicious and decides to check on this place?" Thad asked Alan, who was standing in the doorway with Liz. "Be honest, and be as accurate as you can. You have to believe me when I tell you this is the only chance we have."

"Thad, *look* at him!" Liz burst out wildly. "Can't you see what's happening to him? He doesn't just want help writing a book! He wants to steal your *life!* Don't you *see* that?"

"Shhh," he said. "I know what he wants. I think I have since the start. This is the only way. I know what I'm doing. How long, Alan?"

Alan thought about it carefully. He had told Sheila he was going to get take-out, and he had already called in, so it would be awhile before she got nervous. Things might have happened quicker if Norris Ridgewick had been around.

"Maybe until my wife calls to ask where I am," he said. "Maybe longer. She's been a cop's wife for a long time. She expects long hours and weird nights." He didn't like hearing himself say this. This was not the way the game was supposed to be played; it was the exact opposite of the way the game was supposed to be played.

Thad's eyes compelled him. Stark did not seem to be listening at all; he had picked up the slate paperweight which sat atop an untidy stack of old manuscript in the corner of the desk and was playing with it.

"I think it will be at least four hours." And then, reluctantly, he added: "Maybe all night. I left Andy

Clutterbuck on the desk, and Clut isn't exactly Quiz Kids material. If someone gets his wind up, it will probably be that guy Harrison—the one you ditched—or someone I know at the State Police Barracks in Oxford. A guy named Henry Payton."

Thad looked at Stark. "Will it be enough?"

Stark's eyes, brilliant jewels in the ruined setting of his face, were distant, hazed. His bandaged hand toyed absently with the paperweight. He put it back and smiled at Thad. "What do *you* think? You know as much about this as I do."

Thad considered it. *Both of us know what we're talking about, but I don't think either of us could express it in words. Writing is not what we're doing here, not really. Writing is just the ritual. We're talking about passing some sort of baton. An exchange of power. Or, more properly put, a trade: Liz's and the twins' lives in exchange for . . . what? What, exactly?*

But he knew, of course. It would have been strange if he had not, for he had been meditating on this very subject not so many days ago. It was his *eye* that Stark wanted—no, demanded. That odd third eye that, being buried in his brain, could only look inward.

He felt that crawling sensation again, and fought it off. *No fair peeking, George. You've got the firepower; all I've got is a bunch of scraggy birds. So no fair peeking.*

"I think it probably will be," he said. "We'll know it when it happens, won't we?"

"Yes."

"Like a teeter-totter, when one end of the board goes up . . . and the other end goes down."

"Thad, what are you hiding? What are you hiding from me?"

There was a moment of electrical silence in the

room, a room which suddenly seemed far too small for the emotions careening around inside it.

"I might ask you the same question," Thad said at last.

"No," Stark replied slowly. "All *my* cards are on the table. Tell me, Thad." His cold, rotting hand slipped around Thad's wrist with the inexorable force of a steel manacle. *"What are you hiding?"*

Thad forced himself to turn and look into Stark's eyes. That crawling sensation was everywhere now, but it was centered in the hole in his hand.

"Do you want to do this book or not?" he asked.

For the first time, Liz saw the underlying expression in Stark's face—not on it but *in* it—change. Suddenly there was uncertainty there. And fear? Maybe. Maybe not. But even if not, it was somewhere near, waiting to happen.

"I didn't come here to eat cereal with you, Thad."

"Then *you* figure it out," Thad said. Liz heard a gasp and realized she had made the sound herself.

Stark glanced up at her briefly, then looked back at Thad. "Don't jive me, Thad," he said softly. "You don't want to jive me, hoss."

Thad laughed. It was a cold and desperate sound . . . but not entirely without humor. That was the worst part. It was not entirely without humor, and Liz heard George Stark in that laugh, just as she had seen Thad Beaumont in Stark's eyes when he was playing with the babies.

"Why not, George? I know what *I* have to lose. That's all on the table, too. Now do you want to write or do you want to talk?"

Stark considered him for a long moment, his flat and baleful gaze painting Thad's face. Then he said, "Ah, fuck it. Let's go."

Thad smiled. "Why not?"

"You and the cop leave," Stark said to Liz. "This is just the boys now. We're down to that."

"I'll take the babies," Liz heard herself say, and Stark laughed.

"That's pretty funny, Beth. Uh-uh. The babies are insurance. Like write-protect on a floppy disk, isn't that so, Thad?"

"But—" Liz began.

"It's okay," Thad said. "They'll be fine. George can mind them while I get us started. They like him. Haven't you noticed?"

"Of *course* I've noticed," she said in a low, hate-filled voice.

"Just remember that they're in here with us," Stark said to Alan. "Keep it in mind, Sheriff Alan. Don't be inventive. If you try pulling something cute, it'll be just like Jonestown. They'll bring all of us out feet first. You got that?"

"Got it," Alan said.

"And shut the door on the way out." Stark turned to Thad. "It's time."

"That's right," Thad said, and picked up a pencil. He turned to Liz and Alan, and George Stark's eyes looked out at them from Thad Beaumont's face. "Go on. Get out."

8

Liz stopped halfway downstairs. Alan almost ran into her. She was staring across the living room and out through the window-wall.

The world was birds. The deck was buried beneath them; the slope down to the lake was black with them in the failing light; above the lake the sky was dark with them as more swarmed toward the Beaumont lake house from the west.

"Oh my God," Liz said.

Alan grabbed her arm. "Be quiet," he said. "Don't let him hear you."

"But what—"

He guided her the rest of the way downstairs, still holding firmly to her arm. When they were in the kitchen, Alan told her the rest of what Dr. Pritchard had told him earlier this afternoon, a thousand years ago.

"What does it mean?" she whispered. Her face was gray with pallor. "Alan, I'm so frightened."

He put his arms around her and was aware, even though he was also deeply afraid, that this was quite a lot of woman.

"I don't know," he said, "but I know they're here because either Thad or Stark called to them. I'm pretty sure it was Thad. Because he must have seen them when he came in. He saw them, but he didn't mention them."

"Alan, he's not the same."

"I know."

"Part of him loves Stark. Part of him loves Stark's . . . his blackness."

"I know."

They went to the window by the telephone table in the hall and looked out. The driveway was full of sparrows, and the woods, and the small area-way around the shed where the .22 was still locked away. Rawlie's VW had disappeared beneath them.

There were no sparrows on George Stark's Toronado, however. And there was a neat circle of empty driveway around it, as if it had been quarantined.

A bird flew into the window with a soft thump. Liz uttered a tiny cry. The other birds shifted restlessly—a great wavelike movement that rolled up the hill—and then they were still again.

"Even if they *are* Thad's," she said, "he may not use them on Stark. Part of Thad is crazy, Alan. Part of him has *always* been crazy. He . . . he likes it."

Alan said nothing, but he knew that, too. He had sensed it.

"All of this is like a terrible dream," she said. "I wish I could wake up. I wish I could wake up and things would be the way they were. Not the way they were before Clawson; the way they were before *Stark*."

Alan nodded.

She looked up at him. "So what do we do now?"

"We do the hard thing," he said. "We wait."

9

The evening seemed to go on forever, the light bleeding slowly out of the sky as the sun made its exit beyond the mountains on the western side of the lake, the mountains that marched off to join the Presidential Range of New Hampshire's chimney.

Outside, the last flocks of sparrows arrived and joined the main flock. Alan and Liz could sense them on the roof overhead, a burial mound of sparrows, but they were silent. They were waiting.

When they moved about the room their heads turned as they walked, turned like radar dishes locked in on a signal. It was the study they were listening to, and the most maddening thing was that there was no sound at all from behind the trick door which led into it. She could not even hear the babies babbling and cooing to each other. She hoped they had gone to sleep, but it was not possible to silence the voice which insisted that Stark had killed them both, and Thad, too.

Silently.

With the razor he carried.

She told herself that if something like that happened the sparrows would know, they would do something, and it helped, but only a little. The sparrows were a great mind-bitching unknown surrounding the house. God knew what they would do . . . or when.

Twilight was slowly surrendering to full dark when Alan said harshly, "They'll change places if it goes on long enough, won't they? Thad will start to get sick . . . and Stark will start to get well."

She was so startled she almost dropped the bitter cup of coffee she was holding.

"Yes. I think so."

A loon called on the lake—an isolated, aching, lonely sound. Alan thought of them upstairs, the two sets of twins, one set at rest, the other engaged in some terrible struggle in the merged twilight of their single imagination.

Outside, the birds watched and waited as twilight drew down.

That teeter-totter is in motion, Alan thought. *Thad's end is going up, Stark's end is going down.* Up there, behind that door which made two entrances when it was open, the change had begun.

It's almost the end, Liz thought. *One way or the other.*

And as if this thought had caused it to happen, she heard a wind begin to blow—a strange, whirring wind. Only, the lake was as flat as a dish.

She stood up, eyes wide, hands going to her throat. She stared out through the window-wall. *Alan,* she tried to say, but her voice failed her. It didn't matter.

Upstairs there was a strange, weird whistling sound, like a note blown from a crooked flute. Stark cried out suddenly, sharply: "Thad? What are you doing? *What are you doing?*" There was a short banging sound, like the report of a cap pistol. A moment later Wendy began to cry.

And outside in the deepening gloom, a million sparrows went on fluttering their wings, preparing to fly.

Twenty-six

THE SPARROWS ARE FLYING

1

When Liz closed the door and left the two men alone, Thad opened his notebook and looked at the blank page for a moment. Then he picked up one of the sharpened Berol pencils.

"I am going to start with the cake," he said to Stark.

"Yes," Stark said. A kind of longing eagerness filled his face. "That's right."

Thad poised the pencil over the blank page. This was the moment that was always the best—just before the first stroke. This was surgery of a kind, and in the end the patient almost always died, but you did it anyway. You had to, because it was what you were made for. Only that.

Just remember, he thought. *Remember what you're doing.*

But a part of him—the part that really wanted to write *Steel Machine*—protested.

Thad bent forward and began to fill up the empty space.

STEEL MACHINE
by George Stark

Chapter 1: The Wedding

Alexis Machine was rarely whimsical, and for him to have a whimsical thought in such a situation as this was something which had never happened before. Yet it occurred to him: Of all the people on earth—what? five billion of them?—I'm the only one who is currently standing inside a moving wedding cake with a Heckler & Koch .223 semiautomatic weapon in my hands.

He had never been so shut up in a place. The air had gotten bad almost at once, but he could not have drawn a deep breath in any case. The Trojan Cake's frosting was real, but beneath it was nothing but a thin layer of a gypsum product called Nartex—a kind of high-class cardboard. If he filled his chest, the bride and groom standing on top of the cake's top tier would probably topple. Surely the icing would crack and . . .

He wrote for nearly forty minutes, picking up speed as he went along, his mind gradually filling up with the sights and sounds of the wedding party which would end with such a bang.

Finally he put the pencil down. He had written it blunt.

"Give me a cigarette," he said.

Stark raised his eyebrows.

"Yes," Thad said.

There was a pack of Pall Malls lying on the desk. Stark shook one out and Thad took it. The cigarette felt strange between his lips after so many years . . . too big, somehow. But it felt good. It felt *right*.

Stark scratched a match and held it out to Thad, who inhaled deeply. The smoke bit his lungs in its old merciless, necessary way. He felt immediately woozy, but he didn't mind the feeling at all.

Now I need a drink, he thought. *And if this ends with me still alive and standing up, that's the first thing I'm going to have.*

"I thought you quit," Stark said.

Thad nodded. "Me too. What can I say, George? I was wrong." He took another deep drag and feathered smoke out through his nostrils. He turned his notebook toward Stark. "Your turn," he said.

Stark leaned over the notebook and read the last paragraph Thad had written; there was really no need to read more. They both knew how this story went.

> Back in the house, Jack Rangely and Tony Westerman were in the kitchen, and Rollick should be upstairs now. All three of them were armed with Steyr-Aug semi-automatics, the only good machine-gun made in America, and even if some of the bodyguards masquerading as guests were very fast, the three of them should be able to lay down a fire-storm more than adequate to cover their retreat. Just let me out of this cake, Machine thought. That's all I ask.

Stark lit a Pall Mall himself, picked up one of his Berols, opened his own notebook . . . and then paused. He looked at Thad with naked honesty.

"I'm scared, hoss," he said.

And Thad felt a great wave of sympathy for

Stark—in spite of everything he knew. *Scared. Yes, of course you are,* he thought. *Only the ones just starting out—the kids—aren't scared. The years go by and the words on the page don't get any darker . . . but the white space sure does get whiter. Scared? You'd be crazier than you are if you weren't.*

"I know," he said. "And you know what it comes down to—the only way to do it is to do it."

Stark nodded and bent over his notebook. Twice more he checked back at the last paragraph Thad had written . . . and then he began to write.

The words formed themselves with agonized slowness in Thad's mind.

Machine . . . had . . . never wondered . . .

A long pause, then, all in a burst:

. . . what it would be like to have asthma, but if anyone ever asked him after this . . .

A shorter pause.

. . . he would remember the Scoretti job.

He read over what he had written, then looked at Thad unbelievingly.

Thad nodded. "It makes sense, George." He fingered the corner of his mouth, which suddenly stung, and felt a fresh sore breaking there. He looked at Stark and saw that a similar sore had disappeared from the corner of Stark's mouth.

It's happening. It's really happening.

"Go for it, George," he said. "Knock the hell out of it."

But Stark had already bent over his notebook again, and now he was writing faster.

2

Stark wrote for almost half an hour, and at last he put the pencil down with a little gasp of satisfaction.

"It's good," he said in a low, gloating voice. "It's just as good as can be."

Thad picked up the notebook and began to read—and, unlike Stark, he read the whole thing. What he was looking for began to show up on the third page of the nine Stark had written.

> Machine heard scraping sounds and stiffened, hands tightening on the Heckler & Sparrow, and then understood what they were doing. The guests—some two hundred of them—gathered at the long tables under the huge blue and yellow striped marquee were pushing their folding sparrows back along the boards which had been laid to protect the lawn from the punctuation of the women's high-heeled sparrows. The guests were giving the sparrow cake a fucking standing ovation.

He doesn't know, Thad thought. *He's writing the word* sparrows *over and over again and he doesn't have the slightest . . . fucking . . . idea.*

Overhead he heard them moving restlessly back and forth, and the twins had looked up several times before falling asleep, so he knew they had noticed it, too.

Not George, though.

For George, the sparrows did not exist.

Thad went back to the manuscript. The word began to creep in more and more frequently, and by the last paragraph, the whole phrase had begun to show up.

> Machine found out later that the sparrows were flying and the only people on his hand-picked string that really were his sparrows were Jack Rangely and Lester Rollick. All the others, sparrows he had flown with for ten years, were all in on it. Sparrows. And they started flying even before Machine shouted into his sparrow-talkie.

"Well?" Stark asked when Thad put his manuscript down. "What do you think?"

"I think it's fine," Thad said. "But you knew that, didn't you?"

"Yes . . . but I wanted to hear you say it, hoss."

"I also think you're looking much better."

Which was true. While George had been lost in the fuming, violent world of Alexis Machine, he had begun to heal.

The sores were disappearing. The broken, decaying skin was growing pink again; the edges of this fresh skin were reaching across the healing sores toward each other, in some cases already knitting together. Eyebrows which had disappeared into a soup of rotting flesh were reappearing. The trickles of pus which had turned the collar of Stark's shirt an ugly sodden yellow were drying.

Thad reached up with his left hand and touched the sore which was beginning to erupt on his own left temple, and held the pads of his fingers in front of his eyes for a moment. They were wet. He reached up again and touched his forehead. The skin was smooth. The small white scar, souvenir of the operation which had been performed on him in the year when his real life began, was gone.

One end of the teeter-totter goes up, the other end has to come down. Just another law of nature, baby. Just another law of nature.

Was it dark outside yet? Thad supposed it must be—dark or damned near. He looked at his watch, but there was no help there. It had stopped at quarter of five. The time didn't matter. He would have to do it soon.

Stark smashed a cigarette out in the overflowing ashtray. "You want to go on or take a break?"

"Why don't *you* go on?" Thad said. "I think you can."

"Yeah," Stark said. He was not looking at Thad. He had eyes only for the words, the words, the words. He ran a hand through his blonde hair, which was becoming lustrous again. "I think I can, too. In fact, I *know* I can."

He began to scribble again. He looked up briefly when Thad got out of his chair and went to the pencil-sharpener, then looked back down. Thad sharpened one of the Berols to a razor point. And as he turned back, he took the bird-call Rawlie had given him out of his pocket. He closed it in his hand and sat down again, looking at the notebook in front of him.

This was it; this was the time. He knew it as well and as truly as he knew the shape of his own face under his hand. The only question left was whether or not he had the guts to try it.

Part of him did not want to; a part of him still lusted after the book. But he was surprised to find that feeling was not as strong as it had been when Liz and Alan left the study, and he supposed he knew why. A separation was taking place. A kind of obscene birth. It wasn't his book anymore. Alexis Machine was with the person who had owned him from the start.

Still holding the bird-call cupped tightly in his left hand, Thad bent over his own notebook.

I am the bringer, he wrote.

Overhead, the restless shifting of the birds stopped.

I am the knower, he wrote.

The whole world seemed to still, to listen.

I am the owner.

He stopped and glanced at his sleeping children. *Five more words,* he thought. *Just five more.*

And he discovered he wanted to write them more than any words he had ever written in his life.

He wanted to write stories . . . but more than that, more than he wanted the lovely visions that third eye sometimes presented, he wanted to be free.

Five more words.

He raised his left hand to his mouth and gripped the bird-call in his lips like a cigar.

Don't look up now, George. Don't look up, don't look out of the world you're making. Not now. Please dear God, don't let him look out into the world of real things now.

On the blank sheet in front of him he wrote the word PSYCHOPOMPS in cold capital letters. He circled it. He drew an arrow below it, and below the arrow he wrote: THE SPARROWS ARE FLYING.

Outside, a wind began to blow—only it was no wind; it was the ruffling of millions of feathers. And it was inside Thad's head. Suddenly that third eye opened in his mind, opened wider than it ever had before, and he saw Bergenfield, New Jersey—the empty houses, the empty streets, the mild spring sky. He saw the sparrows everywhere, more than there had ever been before. The world he had grown up in had become a vast aviary.

Only it wasn't Bergenfield.

It was Endsville.

Stark quit writing. His eyes widened with sudden, belated alarm.

Thad drew in a deep breath and blew. The bird-call Rawlie DeLesseps had given him uttered a strange, squealing note.

"Thad? What are you doing? *What are you doing?*"

Stark snatched for the bird-call. Before he could touch it, there was a bang and it split open in Thad's mouth, cutting his lips. The sound woke the twins. Wendy began to cry.

Outside, the rustle of the sparrows rose to a roar.

They were flying.

3

Liz had started for the stairs when she heard Wendy begin to cry. Alan stood where he was for a moment, transfixed by what he saw outside. The land, the trees, the lake, the sky—they were all blotted out. The sparrows rose in a great wavering curtain, darkening the window from top to bottom and side to side.

As the first small bodies began to thud into the reinforced glass, Alan's paralysis broke.

"Liz!" he screamed. *"Liz, down!"*

But she wasn't going to get down; her baby was crying, and that was all she could think about.

Alan sprinted across the room toward her, employing that almost eerie speed which was his own secret, and tackled her just as the entire window-wall blew inward under the weight of twenty thousand sparrows. Twenty thousand more followed them, and twenty thousand more, and twenty thousand more. In a moment the living room was filled with them. They were everywhere.

Alan threw himself on top of Liz and pulled her under the couch. The world was filled with the shrill cheeping of sparrows. Now they could hear the other windows breaking, all the windows. The house rattled with the thuds of tiny suicide bombers. Alan looked out and saw a world that was nothing but brown-black movement.

Smoke-detectors began to go off as birds crashed into them. Somewhere there was a monstrous crash as the TV screen exploded. Clatters as pictures on the walls fell. A series of metallic xylophone bonks as sparrows struck the pots hanging on the wall by the stove and knocked them to the floor.

And still he could hear the babies crying and Liz screaming.

"Let me go! My babies! Let me go! I HAVE TO GET MY BABIES!"

She squirmed halfway out from beneath him and her upper body was immediately covered with sparrows. They caught in her hair and fluttered madly there. She beat at them wildly. Alan grabbed her and pulled her back. Through the eddying air of the living room he could see a vast black cord of sparrows flowing up the stairs—up toward the office.

4

Stark reached for Thad as the first birds began to thump into the secret door. Beyond the wall, Thad could hear the muffled thud of falling paperweights and the tinkle of breaking glass. Both twins were wailing now. Their cries rose, blended with the maddening cheeping of the sparrows, and the two of them together made a kind of hell's harmony.

"Stop it!" Stark yelled. *"Stop it, Thad! Whatever the hell you're doing, just stop it!"*

He snatched for the gun, and Thad buried the pencil he had been holding in Stark's throat.

Blood poured out in a rush. Stark turned toward him, gagging, clawing at the pencil. It bobbed up and down as he tried to swallow. He got one hand around it and pulled it out "What are you doing?" he croaked. "What is it?" He heard the birds now; he did not understand them, but he heard them. His eyes rolled toward the closed door and Thad saw real terror in those eyes for the first time.

"I'm writing the end, George," Thad said in a low voice neither Liz nor Alan heard downstairs. "I'm writing the end in the real world."

"All right," Stark said. "Let's write it for all of us, then."

He turned toward the twins with the bloody pencil in one hand and the .45 in the other.

5

There was a folded afghan on the end of the sofa. Alan reached up for it, and what felt like a dozen hot sewing needles jabbed at his hand.

"Damn!" he yelled, and pulled the hand back.

Liz was still trying to squirm out from under him. The monstrous whirring sound seemed to fill the whole universe now, and Alan could no longer hear the babies . . . but Liz Beaumont could. She wriggled and twisted and pulled. Alan fastened his left hand in her collar and felt the fabric rip.

"Wait a minute!" he bellowed at her, but it was useless. There was nothing he could say to stop her while her children were screaming. Annie would have been the same. Alan reached up with his right hand again, ignoring the stabbing beaks this time, and snagged the afghan. It opened in tangled folds as it fell from the couch. From the master bedroom there was a tremendous crash as some piece of furniture—the bureau, perhaps—fell over. Alan's distracted, overburdened mind tried to imagine how many sparrows it would take to tip over a bureau and could not.

How many sparrows does it take to screw in a lightbulb? his mind asked crazily. *Three to hold the bulb and three billion to turn the house!* He yodeled crazy laughter and then the big hanging globe in the center of the living room exploded like a bomb. Liz screamed and cringed back for a moment, and Alan was able to throw the afghan over her head. He got under it himself. They weren't alone even beneath it; half a dozen sparrows were in there with them. He felt feathery wings flutter against his cheek, felt bright pain tattoo his left temple, and socked himself through the afghan. The sparrow tumbled to his shoulder and fell from beneath the blanket onto the floor.

He yanked Liz against him and shouted into her ear. "We're going to *walk! Walk,* Liz! Under this blanket! If you try to run, I'll knock you out! Nod your head if you understand!"

She tried to pull away. The afghan stretched. Sparrows landed briefly, bounced on it as if it were a trampoline, then flew again. Alan pulled her back against him and shook her by the shoulder. Shook her hard.

"Nod if you understand, goddammit!"

He felt her hair tickle his cheek as she nodded. They crawled out from beneath the sofa. Alan kept his arm tightly around her shoulders, afraid she would bolt. And slowly they began to move across the swarming room, through the light, maddening clouds of crying birds. They looked like a joke animal in a county fair—a dancing donkey with Mike as the head and Ike as the hindquarters.

The living room of the Beaumont house was spacious, with a high cathedral ceiling, but now there seemed to be no air left. They walked through a yielding, shifting, gluey atmosphere of birds.

Furniture crashed. Birds thudded off walls, ceilings, and appliances. The whole world had become bird-stink and strange percussion.

At last they reached the stairs and began to sway slowly up them beneath the afghan, which was already coated with feathers and birdshit. And as they started to climb, a pistol-shot crashed in the study upstairs.

Now Alan could hear the twins again. They were shrieking.

6

Thad groped on the desk as Stark aimed the gun at William, and came up with the paperweight Stark had been playing with. It was a heavy chunk of gray-black slate, flat on one side He brought it down on Stark's wrist an instant before the big blonde man fired, breaking the bone and driving the barrel of the gun downward. The crash was deafening in the small room. The bullet ploughed into the floor an inch from William's left foot, kicking splinters onto the legs of his fuzzy blue sleep-suit. The twins began to shriek, and as Thad closed with Stark, he saw them put their arms around each other in a gesture of spontaneous mutual protection.

Hansel and Gretel, he thought, and then Stark drove the pencil into his shoulder.

Thad yelled with pain and shoved Stark away. Stark tripped over the typewriter which had been placed in the corner and fell backward against the wall. He tried to switch the pistol over to his right hand . . . and dropped it.

Now the sound of the birds against the door was a steady thunder . . . and it began to slip slowly open on its central pivot. A sparrow with a crushed wing oozed in and fell, twitching, on the floor.

Stark felt in his back pocket . . . and brought out the straight-razor. He pulled the blade open with his teeth. His eyes sparkled crazily above the steel.

"You want it, hoss?" he asked, and Thad saw the decay falling into his face again, coming all at once like a dropped load of bricks. "You really do? Okay. You got it."

7

Halfway up the stairs, Liz and Alan were stopped. They ran into a yielding, suspended wall of birds and simply could make no progress against it. The air fluttered and hummed with sparrows. Liz shrieked in terror and fury.

The birds did not turn on them, did not attack them; they just thwarted them. All the sparrows in the world, it seemed, had been drawn here, to the second story of the Beaumont house in Castle Rock.

"Down!" Alan shouted at her. *"Maybe we can crawl under them!"*

They dropped to their knees. Progress was possible at first, although not pleasant; they found themselves crawling over a crunching, bleeding carpet of sparrows at least eighteen inches deep. Then they ran into that wall again. Looking under the hem of the afghan, Alan could see a crowded, confused mass that beggared description. The sparrows on the stair-risers were being crushed. Layers and layers of the living—but soon to be dead—stood on top of them. Farther up—perhaps three feet off the stairs—sparrows flew in a kind of suicide traffic zone, colliding and falling, some rising and flying again, others squirming in the masses of their fallen mates with broken legs or wings. Sparrows, Alan remembered, could not hover.

From somewhere above them, on the other side of this grotesque living barrier, a man screamed.

Liz seized him, pulled him close. *"What can we do?"* she screamed. *"What can we do, Alan?"*

He didn't answer her. Because the answer was nothing. There was nothing they *could* do.

8

Stark came toward Thad with the razor in his right hand. Thad backed toward the slowly moving study door with his eyes on the blade. He snatched up another pencil from the desk.

"That ain't gonna do you no good, hoss," Stark said. "Not now." Then his eyes shifted to the door. It had opened wide enough, and the sparrows flowed in, a river of them . . . and they flowed at George Stark.

In an instant his expression became one of horror . . . and understanding.

"*No!*" he screamed, and began to slash at them with Alexis Machine's straight-razor. "*No, I won't! I won't go back! You can't make me!*"

He cut one of the sparrows cleanly in half; it fell out of the air in two fluttering pieces. Stark ripped and flailed at the air around him.

And Thad suddenly understood

(*I won't go back*)

what was happening here.

The psychopomps, of course, had come to serve as George Stark's escort. George Stark's escort back to Endsville; back to the land of the dead.

Thad dropped the pencil and retreated toward his children. The air was filled with sparrows. The door had opened almost all the way now; the river had become a flood.

Sparrows settled on Stark's broad shoulders. They settled on his arms, on his head. Sparrows struck his chest, dozens of them at first, then hundreds. He twisted this way and that in a cloud of falling feathers and flashing, slashing beaks, trying to give back what he was getting.

They covered the straight-razor; its evil silver gleam was gone; buried beneath the feathers that were stuck to it.

Thad looked at his children. They had stopped weeping. They were looking up into the stuffed, boiling air with identical expressions of wonder and delight. Their hands were raised, as if to check for rain. Their tiny fingers were outstretched. Sparrows stood on them . . . and did not peck.

But they were pecking Stark.

Blood burst from his face in a hundred places. One of his blue eyes winked out. A sparrow landed on the collar of his shirt and sent his beak diving into the hole Thad had made with the pencil in Stark's throat—the bird did it three times, fast, *rat-tat-tat*, like a machine-gun, before Stark's groping hand seized it and crushed it like a piece of living origami.

Thad crouched by the twins and now the birds lit on him as well. Not pecking; just standing.

And watching.

Stark had disappeared. He had become a living, squirming bird-sculpture. Blood oozed through the jostling wings and feathers. From somewhere below, Thad heard a shrieking, splintering sound—wood giving way.

They have broken their way into the kitchen, he thought. He thought briefly of the gas-lines that fed the stove, but the thought was distant, unimportant.

And now he began to hear the loose, wet plop and smack of the living flesh being torn off George Stark's bones.

"They've come for you, George," he heard himself whisper. "They've come for you. God help you now."

9

Alan sensed space above him again, and looked up through the diamond-shaped holes in the afghan. Birdshit dripped onto his cheek and he wiped it away. The stairwell was still full of birds, but their numbers had thinned. Most of those still alive had apparently gotten where they were going.

"Come on," he said to Liz, and they began to move up over the ghastly carpet of dead birds again. They had managed to gain the second-floor landing when they heard Thad shriek: *"Take him, then! Take him! TAKE HIM BACK TO HELL WHERE HE BELONGS!"*

And the whirring of the birds became a hurricane.

10

Stark made one last galvanic effort to get away from them. There was nowhere to go, nowhere to run, but he tried, anyway. It was his style.

The column of birds which had covered him moved forward with him; gigantic, puffy arms covered with feathers and heads and wings rose, beat themselves across his torso, rose again, and crossed themselves at the chest. Birds, some wounded, some dead, fell to the floor, and for one moment Thad was afforded a vision which would haunt him for the rest of his life.

The sparrows were eating George Stark alive.

His eyes were gone; where they had been only vast dark sockets remained. His nose had been reduced to a bleeding flap. His forehead and most of his hair had been struck away, revealing the mucus-bleared surface of his skull. The collar of his shirt still ringed his neck, but the rest was gone. Ribs poked out of his skin in white lumps. The birds had opened his belly. A drove of sparrows sat on his feet and looked up with bright attention and squabbled for his guts as they fell out in dripping, shredded chunks.

And he saw something else.

The sparrows were trying to lift him up. They were trying . . . and very soon, when they had reduced his body-weight enough, they would do just that.

"Take him, then!" he screamed. *"Take him!* TAKE HIM BACK TO HELL WHERE HE BELONGS!"

Stark's screams stopped as his throat disintegrated beneath a hundred hammering, dipping beaks. Sparrows clustered under his armpits and for a second his feet rose from the bloody carpet.

He brought his arms—what remained of them—down into his sides in a savage gesture, crushing dozens . . . but dozens upon dozens more came to take their places.

The sound of pecking and splintering wood to Thad's right suddenly grew louder, hollower. He looked in that direction and saw the wood of the study's east wall disintegrating like tissue-paper. For an instant he saw a thousand yellow beaks burst through at once, and then he grabbed the twins and rolled over them, arching his body to protect them, moving with real grace for perhaps the only time in his life.

The wall crashed inward in a dusty cloud of splinters and sawdust. Thad closed his eyes and hugged his children close to him.

He saw no more.

11

But Alan Pangborn did, and Liz did, too.

They had pulled the afghan down to their shoulders as the cloud of birds over them and around them shredded apart. Liz began to stumble into the guest bedroom, toward the open study door, and Alan followed her.

For a moment he couldn't see into the study; it was only a cloudy brown-black blur. And then he made out a shape—a horrible padded shape. It was Stark. He was covered with birds, eaten alive, and yet he still lived.

More birds came; more still. Alan thought their horrid shrill cheeping would drive him mad. And then he saw what they were doing.

"Alan!" Liz screamed. "Alan, they're lifting him!"

The thing which had been George Stark, a thing which was now only vaguely human, rose into the air on a cushion of sparrows. It moved across the office, almost fell, then rose unsteadily once more. It approached the huge, splinter-ringed hole in the east wall.

More birds flew in through this hole; those which still remained in the guest-room rushed into the study.

Flesh fell from Stark's twitching skeleton in a grisly rain.

The body floated through the hole with sparrows flying around it and tearing out the last of its hair.

Alan and Liz struggled over the rug of dead birds and into the study. Thad was rising slowly to his feet, a weeping twin in each arm. Liz ran to them and took them from him. Her hands flew over them, looking for wounds.

"Okay," Thad said. "I think they're okay."

Alan went to the ragged hole in the study wall. He looked out and saw a scene from some malign fairy-tale. The sky was black with birds, and yet in one place it was *ebony,* as if a hole had been torn in the fabric of reality.

This black hole bore the unmistakable shape of a struggling man.

The birds lifted it higher, higher, higher. It reached the tops of the trees and seemed to pause there. Alan thought he heard a high-pitched, inhuman scream from the center of that cloud. Then the sparrows began to move again. In a way, watching them was like watching a film run backward. Black streams of sparrows boiled from all the shattered windows in the house; they funnelled upward from the driveway, the trees, and the curved roof of Rawlie's Volkswagen.

They all moved toward that central darkness.

That man-shaped patch began to move again . . . over the trees . . . into the dark sky . . . and there it was lost to view.

Liz was sitting in the corner, the twins in her lap, rocking them, comforting them—but neither of them seemed particularly upset any longer. They were looking cheerily up into her haggard, tear-stained face. Wendy patted it, as if to comfort her mother. William reached up, plucked a feather from her hair, and examined it closely.

"He's gone," Thad said hoarsely. He had joined Alan at the hole in the study wall.

"Yes," Alan said. He suddenly burst into tears. He had no idea that was coming; it just happened.

Thad tried to put his arms around him and Alan stepped away, his boots crunching dryly in drifts of dead sparrows.

"No," he said. "I'll be all right."

Thad was looking out through the ragged hole again, into the night. A sparrow came out of that dark and landed on his shoulder.

"Thank you," Thad said to it. "Th—"

The sparrow pecked him, suddenly and viciously, bringing blood just below his eye.

Then it flew away to join its mates.

"Why?" Liz asked. She was looking at Thad in shocked wonder. "Why did it do that?"

Thad did not respond, but he thought he knew the answer. He thought Rawlie DeLesseps would have known, too. What had just happened was magical enough . . . but it had been no fairy-tale. Perhaps the last sparrow had been moved by some force which felt Thad needed to be reminded of that. Forcibly reminded.

Be careful, Thaddeus. No man controls the agents of the afterlife. Not for long—and there is always a price.

What price will I have to pay? he wondered coldly. Then: *And the bill . . . when does it come due?*

But that was a question for another time, another day. And there was this—perhaps the bill *had* been paid.

Perhaps he was finally even.

"Is he dead?" Liz was asking . . . almost begging.

"Yes," Thad said. "He's dead, Liz. Third time's the charm. The book is closed on George Stark. Come on, you guys—let's get out of here."

And that was what they did.

EPILOGUE

Henry did not kiss Mary Lou that day, but he did not leave her without a word, either, as he could have done. He saw her, he endured her anger, and waited for it to subside into that blockaded silence he knew so well. He had come to recognize that most of these sorrows were hers, and not to be shared or even discussed. Mary Lou had always danced best when she danced alone.

At last they walked through the field and looked once more at the play-house where Evelyn had died three years ago. It was not much of a goodbye, but it was the best they could do. Henry felt it was good enough.

He put Evelyn's little paper ballerinas in the high grass by the ruined stoop, knowing the wind would carry them off soon enough. Then he and Mary Lou left the old place together for the last time. It wasn't good, but it was all right. Right enough. He was not a man who believed in happy endings. What little serenity he knew came chiefly from that.

—The Sudden Dancers
by Thaddeus Beaumont

People's dreams—their real dreams, as opposed to those hallucinations of sleep which come or not, just as they will—end at different times. Thad Beaumont's dream of George Stark ended at quarter past nine on the night the psychopomps carried his dark half away to whatever place it was that had been appointed to him. It ended with the black Toronado, that tarantula in which he and George had always arrived at this house in his recurrent nightmare.

Liz and the twins were at the top of the driveway, where it merged with Lake Lane. Thad and Alan stood by George Stark's black car, which was no longer black. Now it was gray with bird droppings.

Alan didn't want to look at the house, but he could not take his eyes from it. It was a splintered ruin. The east side—the study side—had taken the brunt of the punishment, but the entire house was a wreck. Huge holes gaped everywhere. The railing hung from the deck on the lake side like a jointed wooden ladder. There were huge drifts of dead birds in a circle around the building. They were caught in the folds of the roof; they stuffed the gutters. The moon had come up and it sent back silverish tinkles of light from sprays of broken glass. Sparks of that same elf-light dwelt deep in the glazing eyes of the dead sparrows.

"You're sure this is okay with you?" Thad asked. Alan nodded.

"I ask, because it's destroying evidence."

Alan laughed harshly. "Would anyone believe what it's evidence *of?*"

"I suppose not." He paused and then said, "You know, there was a time when I felt that you sort of liked me. I don't feel that anymore. Not at all. I don't understand it. Do you hold me responsible for . . . all this?"

"I don't give a fuck," Alan said. "It's over. That's all I give a fuck about, Mr. Beaumont. Right now that's the only thing in the whole *world* I give a fuck about."

He saw the hurt on Thad's tired, harrowed face and made a great effort.

"Look, Thad. It's too much. Too much all at once. I just saw a man carried off into the sky by a bunch of sparrows. Give me a break, okay?"

Thad nodded. "I understand."

No you don't, Alan thought. *You don't understand what you are, and I doubt that you ever will. Your wife might . . . although I wonder if things will ever be right between the two of you after this, if she'll ever want to understand, or dare to love you again. Your kids, maybe, someday . . . but not you, Thad. Standing next to you is like standing next to a cave some nightmarish creature came out of. The monster is gone now, but you still don't like to be too close to where it came from. Because there might be another. Probably not; your mind knows that, but your emotions—they play a different tune, don't they? Oh boy. And even if the cave is empty forever, there are the dreams. And the memories. There's Homer Gamache, for instance, beaten to death with his own prosthetic arm. Because of you, Thad. All because of you.*

That wasn't fair, and part of Alan knew it. Thad hadn't asked to be a twin; he hadn't destroyed his twin brother in the womb out of malice (*We're not talking about Cain rising up and slaying Abel with a rock,* Dr. Pritchard had said); he had not known what sort of monster was waiting when he began writing as George Stark.

Still, they had been twins.

And he could not forget the way Stark and Thad had laughed together.

That crazy, loony laughter and the look in their eyes.

He wondered if Liz would be able to forget.

A little breeze gusted and blew the nasty smell of LP gas toward him.

"Let's burn it," he said abruptly. "Let's burn it all. I don't care who thinks what later on. There's hardly any wind; the fire trucks will get here before it spreads much in any direction. If it takes some of the woods around this place, so much the better."

"I'll do it," Thad said. "You go on up with Liz. Help with the twi—"

"We'll do it together," Alan said. "Give me your socks."

"What?"

"You heard me—I want your socks."

Alan opened the door of the Toronado and looked inside. Yes—a standard shift, as he'd thought. A macho man like George Stark would never be satisfied with an automatic; that was for married Walter Mitty types like Thad Beaumont.

Leaving the door open, he stood on one foot and took off his right shoe and sock. Thad watched him and began to do the same. Alan put his shoe back on and repeated the process with his left foot. He had no intention of putting his bare feet down in that mass of dead birds, even for a moment.

When he was done, he knotted the two cotton socks together. Then he took Thad's and added them to his own. He walked around to the passenger-side rear, dead sparrows crunching under his shoes like newspaper, and opened the Toronado's fuel port. He spun off the gas cap and stuck the makeshift fuse into the throat of the tank. When he pulled it out again, it was soaked. He reversed it, sticking in the dry end, leaving the wet end hanging against the guano-splattered flank of the car. Then he turned to Thad, who had followed him. Alan fumbled in the pocket of his uniform shirt and brought out a book of paper matches. It was the sort of matchbook they give you at newsstands with your cigarettes. He didn't know where he had gotten this one, but there was a stamp-collecting ad on the cover.

The stamp shown was a picture of a bird.

"Light the socks when the car starts to roll," Alan said. "Not a moment before, do you understand?"

"Yes."

"It'll go with a bang. The house will catch. Then the LP tanks around back. When the fire inspectors get here, it's going to look like your friend lost control and hit the house and the car exploded. At least that's what I hope."

"Okay."

Alan walked back around the car.

"What's going on down there?" Liz called nervously. "The babies are getting cold!"

"Just another minute!" Thad called back.

Alan reached into the Toronado's unpleasantly

smelly interior and popped the emergency brake. "Wait until it's rolling," he called back over his shoulder.

"Yes."

Alan depressed the clutch with his foot and put the Hurst shifter into neutral.

The Toronado began to roll at once.

He drew back and for a moment he thought Thad hadn't managed his end . . and then the fuse blazed alight against the rear of the car in a bright line of flame.

The Toronado rolled slowly down the last fifteen feet of driveway, bumped over the little asphalt curb there, and coasted tiredly onto the small back porch. It thumped into the side of the house and stopped. Alan could read the bumper sticker clearly in the orange light of the fuse: HIGH-TONED SON OF A BITCH.

"Not anymore," he muttered.

"What?"

"Never mind. Get back. The car's going to blow."

They had retreated ten paces when the Toronado turned into a fireball. Flames shot up the pecked and splintered east side of the house, turning the hole in the study wall into a staring black eyeball.

"Come on," Alan said. "Let's get to my cruiser. Now that we've done it, we've got to turn in the alarm. No need for everybody on the lake to lose their places over this."

But Thad lingered a moment longer and Alan lingered with him. The house was dry wood beneath cedar shingles, and it was catching fast. The flames boiled into the hole where Thad's study was, and as they watched, sheets of paper were caught in the draft the fire had created and were pulled outward and upward. In the brightness, Alan could see that they were covered with words written in longhand. The sheets of paper crinkled, caught fire, charred, and turned black. They flew upward into the night above the flames like a swirling squadron of dark birds.

Once they were above the draft, Alan thought that more normal breezes would catch them. Catch them and carry them away, perhaps even to the ends of the earth.

Good, he thought, and began to walk up the driveway toward Liz and the babies with his head down.

Behind him, Thad Beaumont slowly raised his hands and placed them over his face.

He stood there like that for a long time.

November 3, 1987—March 16, 1989

AFTERWORD

The name Alexis Machine is not original to me. Readers of *Dead City,* by Shane Stevens, will recognize it as the name of the fictional hoodlum boss in that novel. The name so perfectly summed up the character of George Stark and his own fictional crime boss that I adopted it for the work you have just read . . . but I also did it as an *hommage* to Mr. Stevens, whose other novels include *Rat Pack, By Reason of Insanity,* and *The Anvil Chorus.* These works, where the so-called "criminal mind" and a condition of irredeemable psychosis interweave to create their own closed system of perfect evil, are three of the finest novels ever written about the dark side of the American dream. They are, in their own way, as striking as Frank Norris's *McTeague* or Theodore Dreiser's *Sister Carrie.* I recommend them unreservedly . . . but only readers with strong stomachs and stronger nerves need apply.

S.K.